To Rich

Thanks to your excellent proofreading skills I was finally able to get the book out.

Shivana

MIRACLES
and
CLOUDBERRIES

A young East German Girl's Courage of Survival and Escape

Shívana Alexís

BALBOA
PRESS
A DIVISION OF HAY HOUSE

Balboa Press books may be ordered through booksellers or by contacting:

Balboa Press
A Division of Hay House
1663 Liberty Drive
Bloomington, IN 47403
www.balboapress.com
1-(877) 407-4847

ISBN: 978-1-4525-3433-6 (sc)
ISBN: 978-1-4525-3435-0 (hc)
ISBN: 978-1-4525-3434-3 (e)

Library of Congress Control Number: 2011906033

Printed in the United States of America

Balboa Press rev. date: 5/25/2011

For

My children Richard and Terrance
and Katherine

My Thanks and Appreciation
to

Harriet and Gordon, Sandra, Wayne, Rich H., and Joanne
Your friendship and support means everything

Prologue

My name is Ariane. It is neither an uncommon nor peculiar name. What *is* peculiar is that I already had a name before a stranger made a mistake and issued me a new one. Moreover, the circumstances under which I received it were even more than peculiar. Perhaps the severe times or frail and fallible human nature that was responsible for my name change were an indication of how extraordinarily unpredictable my own life would be.

But I must start from the beginning.

When I was born, our country was at war. German troops had already advanced deep into the Soviet Union, and the *Führer* had declared war on the United States. Still, life in the little, quaint town in which I was born continued as it did. It was a beautiful place. The surrounding large pine forest and the Havel river, which wraps its arms around it, gave it a special beauty and character. But soon peace was shattered even here. Before the madness of war came to an end, most of our town was totally destroyed.

Without warning, we came under heavy attack. B-17 and B-24 bombers were circling over our heads day and night. Artillery shells exploded and planes unloaded their deadly cargo. When the nightly drone of the bomber's engines, the tattoo of the anti-aircraft defense, and the frenzy of war finally ended, ninety percent of our town's center, and nearly eighty percent of the rest of town lay in rubble. Hundreds of people died, and the survivors were faced with having to put their fractured lives together again. Perhaps it was a small price Germany had to pay for the actions of the *Führer* and for the millions of people who had been persecuted or had suffered a horrible death.

When the war was over and the sirens in our town had stopped screaming, the inner and outer worlds of surviving citizens seemed like a barren and rocky moonscape. Fear, loss, hunger, and stress had taken a toll on their spirits and bodies. Husbands, sons and brothers were either missing or dead. Homes lay in ruins, while food and everything else needed for survival was scarce.

Few people were willing to discuss the cause of the Second World War. Most wanted to forget the past and bore their new circumstances in silence. Shame hung over them like a dense cloud. People made the best of the wretched squalor that they now found themselves in. Their country had been defeated and lay destroyed. The women in our town had no strength left to tear down the ghostlike ruins that stared back at them at every turn of the way or rid the streets of rubble. The task seemed daunting, overwhelming. Few men had returned from the war to assist in the clean-up effort. Everything had to be cleared by hand because tools and machines were nowhere to be found. Citizens lived their lives minute by minute and hour by hour. The future lay dimly on the horizon. No one knew what would come next. Moreover, everyone found it difficult to believe that our little town had been assaulted by such fury of war. In fact, our little town had been one of the hardest hit places in all of Germany.

I remember having asked my Uncle Emil when I was much younger, "Why did other countries hate us so and want to kill us. Did we do something bad?"

"Yes, *meine Kleine*, my little one," he answered. "We did. You might not fully understand what I will tell you now. But here is a simple explanation of what happened: The cause for World War Two can be found not only in politics but in ordinary people who willingly bestowed power onto one man. They allowed him to use it as he saw fit. You see, after World War I, when Germany's economy collapsed and our country felt the effect of hyperinflation, the *Führer* promised to give all citizens a better life. Communist agitation was ever present, and unemployment was high. Most everyone trusted Hitler to restore traditional values and save our country from forces that threatened to destroy it. People looked on him as a savior. They believed that he would cure the ills of our nation. His charisma simply hypnotized the masses. It made them blind to the price they would have to pay before the spell was broken. When his quest to make us a great nation finally went beyond the limits of sanity, and when he entered into the dark side of his ideology of Nationalism, he had already taken us on a course that was irreversible. By then, people felt powerless. They simply responded by pulling shades over their eyes in shame and helplessness.

"It should be a lesson to all of us, little one," my uncle said. "But, look at us now. The conditions of our side of the country have not improved after the war. Only the names of the leaders have changed. I fear that we are, once again, doomed to endure new hardships. People's spirits are low. But in order to survive these new times and remember what happened in the past, we must keep our hearts and thoughts pure, *meine Kleine*. We must rise above the new ideologies of hate and the lies that are thrown at us once again. We must remember that there is goodness in us and discover who we are in our soul. We must place our faith in something higher and infallible and follow its calling."

I was very young, then, when my uncle told me this. Yet, his words made an impact on me. I wanted to believe that there was something better and permanent in all of us than what I had seen of life so far. I needed to know who I was, needed to discover that inner part of myself of which my uncle spoke. I needed something to hold on to in all the confusion and all the uncertainty that surrounded us. Was there a purpose in living a life of chaos? Moreover, why had I been born into such a life?

My mother never agreed with my uncle and called him an idealist. She believed in nothing that she could not see or touch. And what she saw was nothing but devastation all around us. Perhaps that was the reason why she was always so miserable. If life had been worth living before, it had no meaning for her any longer. She doubted that anything would ever be easy again. She claimed that there was nothing good left in people, especially not in those who were sitting in power over us in our the German Republic of East Germany, the GDR. She said that we had jumped from the frying pan into the fire where we were left to roast over the coals of false promises. We, once again, had become victims and had fallen into the hands of the wrong side, the wrong regime.

She was weary and tired of it all. She mostly hated her life and often wanted to give up. To make herself feel better, she often pretended that life was a party. She wanted to throw off anything that tied her down. However, she had a child. She had me. and she resented that. She said that she had given up too much already to be bound by responsibility and that caring for a child limited her freedom. She said that our government had done a good job of that already, namely taking away people's freedom, her freedom. What's more, the war had taken away more than that. She not only had lost her possessions and a man she had loved but had also lost her birth name. I could understand her reasoning. But when it came to names, she had not been the only one who had lost hers. I, too, had been stripped of the name that had been given to me at birth. I had to give it up because our birth records had become lost and buried under a mountain of rubble that once had been our house. What made things worse was that our original documents, which had been recorded and kept in the governmental hall of birth records in town, had been consumed by fire.

Several blocks from our home stood city hall. An incendiary bomb had landed on it shortly before the end of the war, causing the wing that contained our birth records to go up in smoke. My mother joined the lines of tired and emaciated looking survivors who showed up with the required petitions in hand to be reissued replacement identification papers.

Oma, my grandmother, had joined us to vouch for our identities and declare that we were, indeed, the persons listed on the petitions. I remember clinging to my grandmother's hand, feeling happy to see her again. We had lost all contact with one another the previous year after she had joined a group of people who fled before the advancing Russian army captured our town. She had come looking for us but had been unable to make contact with my mother. When the war was over, she took the first running train from West Berlin, where her escape had taken her, and located us in town with the help of friends.

That day at city hall, the faces of the people in line reflected hardship and trauma. Many showed resignation, accepting their new circumstances until they were strong enough to rise above the present conditions. Everyone knew that living in a Russian occupied zone would not be easy. However, most had nowhere else to go.

The elderly clerk at city hall, who presided over the waiting mob of applicants, struggled to process everyone's petition. She, too, was tired and carried her own particular burden. She had become half deaf when a bomb exploded close to her. The concussion had torn one eardrums to shreds and had damaged the other. Perhaps that day at city hall she became overwhelmed by the onslaught of people or, perhaps, believed herself capable of reading lips. Oma noticed that the woman stopped examining the petitions.

The clerk asked my mother, "What is the child's name?"

"Adrianna," my mother replied.

"Middle name?" The clerk continued.

My mother waved her off. "No middle name. The child needs only one. Another one is too many. *Zu viel.*

"Too many" translates into *zu viel.*

When a few days later my birth certificate arrived, my first name had been changed from Adrianna to Ariane. Furthermore, I had received the middle name of Sophie. The clerk had apparently misheard.

My mother's birth name of Johanne had encountered a similar fate. Her name was changed to Annie. In her case, the mistake could, perhaps, be justified. A close friend of my grandmother, who had known my mother all of her life, verified that she was present at "Annie's" birth. Annie was her nickname for my mother. That error later cost my mother her happiness and deprived me of a father.

Subsequent requests to restore our original names were ignored. We were told that the fate of our new identities became sealed the moment our new names were entered into the New Official Book of Birth Records.

Oma said that the cover of the New Book bore the coat of arms of a red eagle and that of two swans in flight. The former seal of the Swastika had quickly been replaced with the red eagle, the emblem of the city of Brandenburg and the greater administrative area to which our town belonged. The swans in flight depict the seal of the area of Havelland.

The confusion over my name did not originate at city hall, however, but began before I was born. My absent father, who was fighting in the trenches of Russia at the time of my birth, wished me to carry the name of a little girl in France whose life he saved two years before he married my mother. Both he and his friend, Karl, had visited there. They were taking a leisurely stroll alongside the many canals in the region of Alsace-Lorraine when they heard the frightened scream of a young woman. Her small child had torn away from her hand and fallen into the canal. By the time my father and Karl ran to her side, the girl had sunk below the surface of the water. My father quickly threw off his shoes and jumped into the canal. He made several diving attempts before he retrieved the two-year-old girl from the deep. Her name was Ariana.

Concerns that the little girl might have suffered brain damage were quickly laid to rest. Her mother wrote a letter to my father, informing him that her daughter was recovering well. A second letter told that little Ariana was growing up perfectly normal and healthy and still showed no ill effect from her terrible ordeal. From that time forward, my father came to believe in miracles.

After my father married my mother, and I later was born healthy and alert as well, he believed that I was his second miracle. Oma told me that my mother had attempted to interfere with my birth but had lost. She said that her Good Lord in Heaven had wanted me to be born over the protests of my mother.

"Inquiring about the name my father had wanted me to have, I asked my Uncle Emil, "Do you think that Mutti intentionally ignored Vati's wish to name me Ariana? What's more, do you think that a stranger should have been allowed to change my name from my original one?"

"Don't fret about it, little one," Uncle Emil replied. "Nothing happens without a reason. It is no coincidence that your new name is very close to the one that your father wanted you to have. It is a good name and differs only by one letter. You see, every name hides a secret within it. It supports who you are. Ariane Sophie is a name of strength and faith. Perhaps God knows that you need those qualities to make it through much adversity in life. Your soul knows it as well. Listen to it and trust it. It will never steer you wrong."

My uncle always knew how to comfort me. He was my mentor. He knew of my mother's unbalanced nature and her temper. He knew that she carried much anger against my father for having left her to raise me by herself. My grandmother knew it too.

"Your mother, as so many others, has become a sacrifice to the horror and the aftermath of the war," she told me on one of her visits to our home. "Her nerves and heart are weakened from the stress. Promise me that you will look after her since I cannot be with you."

I promised that I would. Even though young, I understood that Mutti had more than her share of problems. I wanted to make things easy for her., and promised Oma to look after my mother.

One day, after having endured an especially bad day at home, I ran to my Uncle Emil. I cried. "Why is Mutti always so angry with me? How can I make her love me?"

Uncle Emil gazed at me with his penetrating eagle-like eyes before he rose from his chair. He limped over to the shelves that held his many precious books. He reached for a journal that was bound in black leather.

"Here, little one." He handed it to me.

I opened it and saw that the pages were blank.

"This is yours to keep. Write in it. Fill the pages with everything that troubles you. Write about your pain and confusion. And when you feel joy, write about that too. Later, when you are older, you might understand your life better than you do now. You also might also discover a secret and find that you always have been surrounded by protection. Miracles have kept you safe."

Perhaps my beloved uncle knew that he would not always be able to be my mentor or tend to my physical and emotional bruises. If he believed in miracles, they were absent when he, himself, needed them. They failed him when the STASI, the Secret State Police of East Germany, came to take him away and put him into a dark dungeon of a prison. When I learned of his disappearance, I instinctively knew that I would never see him again. I lost him, just as I had lost my father, who had been reported as "missing in action."

Mutti was convinced that this information was incorrect. "He's not missing," she told me in a sour tone of voice. "I also do not believe that he is dead. I am convinced that he has simply left me to take care of you."

She never seemed to grieve his absence much. Instead, she said that she would not mind if he never returned home. It was Karl whom she wanted to come back to her. Karl had been her great love. When neither he nor my father returned, she became hard and declared that she was through with men. But that particular promise did not last long. Neither did her lovers who frequently came to our door and who changed with the seasons. Then she finally met Fritz Neumann.

I heard my uncle warn her. "Sister, that Communist will be your downfall one of these days."

But my mother ignored him. Perhaps my uncle knew the secret that would be her undoing. I, on the other hand, was convinced that it would be me who would be her downfall. Few days went by without her telling me that she would end her life because she felt burdened by having to care for a stubborn child.

And now it had happened. She had done it. She had done that unspeakable thing, which she had vowed to do for so long. She had ended her life. I blamed myself because I had failed to keep the promise that I had given my grandmother before her Good Lord in Heaven took her away, too. Aside from the promise, I might have done other things to my mother that I could not remember. Perhaps the trouble I had caused her had been too great. It had overwhelmed her until she no longer wanted to live.

I was tortured by guilt. I yearned for redemption. How could I go on when I knew that I could have prevented her death? Telling anyone of my sin of neglect toward my mother would be exposing myself. What was I to do? I not only felt guilty but utterly alone and abandoned. I wanted to die, too.

My uncle often said that living takes courage but that we don't have to feel alone. We should not be afraid because there is a part in all of us that will never abandon us. Our soul will be our guide. And, if we will listen, we could hear it speak. It will be there for us and give us peace in troubling times.

"Little one," he reminded me, "Whatever trouble you may find yourself in, whatever confusion you may feel, listen to your soul. Trust what it is telling you. Let it be your guide. If you feel that there is too much noise in your head that prevents you from hearing it speak, write your troubles into the journal that I gave you. Ask for help and guidance from up high. The answers will come. And if you ever find that you have lost your direction in life, ask for a miracle to bring you to the place where you need to be."

I was in trouble now. Could he be correct? Could it be that writing would let me discover the secrets that lay within my soul? Would it give me guidance and relief from my pain? Would writing truly help me uncover miracles? Would it reveal the mystery of my life? Would it help me sort out the memories of the past, which haunted me without ceasing? Would writing help me find peace and help me to glue the shattered pieces of my young life together again?

I felt as though I was drowning in despair. I was lost, felt confused and abandoned. My father had believed in miracles, and my uncle had suggested that they were all around us. I knew that I needed to experience one more miracle in my life. I needed it right now. I knew that without it, I would not survive.

Chapter One

1953
New Year's Eve

I slouched on Tante Helga's old three-legged kitchen chair with the feeling that I was sitting in the middle of a raging current. I had struggled for a week now, had braced against the tide of despair that wanted to pull me under and drown me. Memories spun around in my head and kept me on a downward spiral. I could not believe that my mother had left me the way she did. She had often talked about leaving, had given into depression or raged about her fate. But of late, she had been calmer, less volatile or depressed. She had even seemed happy. I was confused, could not understand what had driven her to finally do it. Was it my fault?

I yearned to return to the upstairs bedroom, which I was sharing with Dagmar, Tante Helga's teenaged daughter. I wanted to crawl back onto the lumpy straw filled mattress and cover myself with the huge down cover, which Wolfgang, Tante Helga's son had retrieved a week earlier from my old home. I wanted to stuff my big, square feather pillow over my head and pretend that all was well. But Tante Helga had asked me to stay downstairs. She wanted me close by. I knew that she feared my mental break-down.

To make things worse, guests had arrived a while earlier. Their dissonant chatter was difficult to bear. Each laugh and shrill word attached themselves like leeches to my brain. The high notes of their voices tore at my last measure of resistance and desire to keep myself together. I knew that I was doomed to suffer the guests and the noise that had invaded the house. How could I object to visitors in a home in which I felt a guest?

Tante Helga had taken me into her home only a few days ago. She had given me shelter when I had nowhere else to go. I knew that she had a difficult time with me. I had removed myself from her and her children, had refused to accept their sympathy and kind words. I had built a wall, which none of them could climb. But if they could climb it, I was certain that they could not understand my pain. Neither would they know how to ward off the memories, which paraded through my head like uninvited ghosts. The images I saw haunted me by day and tortured me by night.

How could any of them understand the shock that I felt when I found my mother lying dead in the dim light of our old bedroom? It took me a while to grasp what she had done. I stood immobile, numbed by the hard blow that tore open my heart. Time seemed suspended, hanging like a barren void over me. The alarm clock on the nightstand of my mother's bed, which earlier had loudly ticked away the minutes, seemed to have stopped moving. Even the wind, which moments earlier whipped around the window panes with fury, leaving an eerie howling sound in its path, laid low. When a sudden tremor in my body made me shift my feet, the old floor boards gave off their usual squeal. It was then that I, once again, became aware of where I was. My senses sharpened for a mere split second. I heard as the storm outside the house picked up in force and knew without a doubt that it would continue to pounce with fury on each soft and delicate sky-flower that drifted from the cold, darkening sky to the ground. I knew that the strength of the wind would leave them in a tangled dance, when all they wanted to do was nothing more than to rest on the ground and cover the world in peaceful innocence. How could I share my shock, my pain, with Tante Helga or her children? No one could possibly understand or eradicate the memory of her in life and death. The pictures kept marching past my inner eye like uninvited ghosts and in no particular order.

Why did my mother cause such pain on Christmas Eve? Was it not a special night of the year that once had brought salvation? Oma said it was. She believed in a savior. and had wanted Mutti to do the same. But my mother's ears were like the Star of Bethlehem flowers, which closed before nightfall arrived.

"I know that life is difficult, Annie," Oma told her. "But, trusting in the Good Lord will help you fight your battles and win."

Mutti scoffed at her words. She angrily countered with, "If He, in truth and as you say, exists, He has been negligent of His duties to all of us. Did you forget what He made us endure, Mother?" She yelled. "Look at the destruction that is all around us and the conditions that we are living in. You claim that He will take care of us. Yet, we have neither a decent place to live nor nourishing food to eat. You claim that He has come to save us, to make things new. I see none of that. Show me anything that your imagined Lord has done for us!" My mother laughed with derision. "Listening to you regurgitating old tales from an old book will not change our conditions or fate!"

Oma's eyes tore wide open. She was horrified and called her daughter blasphemous.

My mother tauntingly picked up one of the plain, sugared *Pfannkuchen* from the batch that my grandmother had brought as a treat from West Berlin. She held it up and said with a smirk on her face, "See how soft and airy this is? That is what I think of your old wives' tales. It's nothing but fluff. In no time at all, this doughnut will turn stale. And tomorrow, it will be harder yet and difficult to digest."

My quick-witted grandmother responded with a smile, "Well, then, Annie. Choose one of the other doughnuts from the bag. Choose the ones with the filling in the center. Even if the outside appears dry to the eye or to the touch, there's a soft and sweet surprise waiting in the center. Just think of that as being the sweetness of life, which the Good Lord has waiting for you if you dare to bite into what you call staleness."

Oma believed that my mother's emotional pain and lifestyle were responsible for her mood changes.

A few weeks ago, however, my mother's had mood brightened. I suspected that Fritz Neumann had something to do with that. She had become enamored with him, even though both their morals and ideology were as distant as the earth is from the moon. Fritz is a Communist, a Party functionary of high standing, while my mother was not. In fact, as long as I can remember, she despised the Communist Party and its doctrines. To my surprise, and even in the face of such disparity, she was pleased for having landed such a desirable catch.

"He is an intellectual who was educated at a fine old German university," she told me with pride. "You should be proud that he has taken an interest in me."

Mutti admired him, even though his *Weltanschauung,* his world view, was in line with that of Walter Ulbricht, the leader of our East German state. My mother was opposed to Communism, which led her to quarrel about politics with Fritz. "You are just as gullible as my mother is," I once overheard her tell him. "Communism, and your belief that it will stabilize our country, will leave us as bankrupt as my mother's belief that there is a God. Neither will bring us salvation."

Because our home life had improved a bit lately, and Mutti had managed to control her violent outbursts, I believed that she had become well. I forgot the promise I had made to my grandmother and neglected my mother at a time when she most needed me.

The festive mood, which had descended onto Tante Helga's house, jarred me back to the present. I glanced through the open door of the kitchen. From where I sat, I could observe the guests in the hallway. They had brought along musical instruments. Their animated chatter and loud laughter promised me a long evening of torture. All had arrived in good spirits, prepared to celebrate New Year's Eve.

My guardian had displayed a gracious smile before encouraging everyone to clean off the layers of snow that clung to everyone's shoes. The musicians hung up their coats and gathered around tall Herr Donner. "*Nun dann!*" He said. His voice rolled like sonorous thunder through the hallway. He rubbed his cold hands and blew into them. "Let's get on with it." He bent down and began to dig through his shiny pigskin briefcase. When he located several sheets of musical scores, he waved them in the air and waited until silence descended onto the noisy group.

He ceremoniously handed them to Tante Helga and said, "This is in appreciation for your hospitality all year and for putting up with us. Hermann and I composed this bagatelle in your honor. We would have given it to you for Christmas, but Hermann's brother in the Golden West was not able to mail us the paper in time. You know that it is impossible to find any kind of paper here. In any case, when it arrived, we went to work on it. Everyone present offered suggestions."

Herr Donner grinned when he noticed the satisfaction on the face of his musical colleagues for having included them in his mention. He could not help but add, "Of course, Frau Helga, you can imagine what *that* was like. I mean, all of us having to agree on something was an accomplishment in itself."

Tante Helga smiled as the man called Hermann added, "We decided to call the piece *Ode to Friendship*. It's our thanks for your tolerance. We know that we can be an unnerving bunch at times. Nonetheless, Helga, you always were a gracious hostess and true friend."

Tante Helga was visibly moved.

Quickly, the balding Herr Sommer presented Tante Helga with two bottles of champagne. "Here's more to enjoy," he announced. "After all, tonight is a special night. We have heard that our economy will soon recover. Walter Ulbricht assures us that this coming year will turn out better for all of us in the GDR."

He passed the bottles around. From the murmur of appreciation, it was clear that the champagne was purchased on the black market. Herr Sommer grinned with satisfaction. Only Herr Fink made a sour face and glared at him with furrowed brows. The famous label of the champagne came as a surprise to him. It left him wondering whether Herr Sommer had fallen in with the likes of his Communist brother-in-law, who had been able to obtain goods from sources other than were for sale at the *Konsums,* the government run stores in our GDR. Soon, Herr Fink decided that it did not matter how the champagne came into the hands of Herr

Sommer. He would simply enjoy the opportunity of a good glass of the bubbly beverage.

A moment later, Frau Heinrich, who was displaying a frizzy, permanent-infused hairdo because quality products were not available, attempted to catch the eye of her husband. "Helmut!" she whispered urgently.

Herr Heinrich took no note of her but continued his conversation with Wolfgang, who was nodding politely.

"Thank you for the compliment, Herr Heinrich," Wolfgang said. "I took your advice and changed the tempo of the piece that we planned to include in the concert."

The friendly slap on his back and the praise of those who overheard the conversation was evidence that young Wolfgang was a cherished member of the chamber music group.

"Helmut," Frau Heinrich called a bit louder now. "Hell-moot! Don't forget to give the plant to Frau von Waldheim. And, please, take off your wet galoshes before I will be required to fetch a rag and get on my knees to clean the floor!"

"*Jawohl*, Helmut!" The others cried. "Listen to your wife!"

Helmut looked up. "*Ach so, ja*," he answered and turned to Tante Helga with an embarrassed smile. He offered his apology as he unwrapped the potted plant of four leaf clover that he brought. "Wait!" He pulled back his gift. It needs one more thing!" He dug into his coat pocket and retrieved a small ornamental black chimney sweep, which he stuck into the soil of the plant.

Chimney sweeps and four leaf clover were favorite New Year's tokens of luck and prosperity. He offered Tante Helga a handshake. "May happiness, health and prosperity fill your home in the coming year, dear friend."

"*Danke, danke*, everyone." Their hostess looked around the circle and beamed. "But it is I who must thank you for your continued participation in our little orchestra and for taking my children under your wing. Even though they are doing well with Frau Römer, their teacher, the added guidance and critique from the group helps them hone their skills."

"*Ach,* we are only too happy to promote their talent, Helga," assured strawberry blond Frau Fröhlich. Her words tumbled from her mouth in the melodic way of a bird's chirp. "I am convinced that they will be able to bring joy to many classical music lovers in the future."

She glanced around the circle to catch the nods of her companions. "The children are both such gifted artists. You are truly blessed Helga! I believe that Wolfgang and Dagmar have inherited the best qualities of you and your dear departed husband."

Tante Helga gave a sad smile. "Thank you, Else. If only that dreadful war would have kept him alive."

Frau Fröhlich saw the shadow that swept over her friend's face and quickly chirped anew, "But wait, we've got something else for you. What would New Year's Eve be without the traditional *Berliner Pfannkuchen?* From the delicious aroma that is drifting from the kitchen, I can tell that you have baked some doughnuts, as well. The more the better. It will make the evil spirits happy, appease them and keep them at bay."

She laughed when she noticed the expression on the face of Frau Geist. "*Jawohl,* Gerda," she affirmed, turning to the woman standing next to her. "Trust me. It's the only bribe that the ghouls will accept this evening."

She let her gaze sweep over the group. "Don't you all agree that we need to do everything to keep evil at bay during these hard times?"

Frau Fröhlich handed Tante Helga the doughnuts. "They are fresh. I had placed an order with the baker days ahead of time, as I always do." The petite and buxom Frau Fröhlich gave a poetic sweep with her arm and bowed deeply as the others watched her with amusement.

"That's our Else, always making sure to keep us sweet and happy," Herr Donner boomed with pride. He let his eyes linger on her.

The guests smiled at each other. "*Na endlich,*" someone remarked. "Finally! We're all breathing a sigh of great relief. The...err...tension between the two of you has finally broken. What has taken you so long to come together, Franz?"

Herr Donner laughed but ignored the question. Instead he said, "She is a true gem, our Else. What would we do without her as our jolly flautist?"

I had already heard stories about Else Fröhlich. A few days earlier, as our family sat at the dinner table, Tante Helga commented that Else had decided to liven up her social interactions and display a few old fashioned curtsies and bows. She had announced, "I am tired of seeing so many sour faces around me. We need some humor to keep us going."

Tante Helga further related that she and Else had gone to the *Konsum* on that very day but found only bare shelves. Upon leaving the store, Else bade everyone in line a goodbye, telling them to find nourishment in loving everyone. She bowed and recited a few lines from a funny poem. People were shocked at seeing her so lively and unconcerned in these hard times. When Tante Helga took her arm and pulled her along, she noticed how everyone stared after them. Some remarked that the woman was touched in the head. "It's the war," someone whispered. "The poor dear is still suffering from it. How can love keep us alive?"

Frau Fröhlich heard the remark and burst out in laughter. She knew that frivolous, public displays of nonconformity were not easily understood or tolerated by an old crop of stout and proper German citizens. Most were taught to obey the rules, harden their hearts, and tolerate their fate until it nearly broke them.

It was clear that friends and acquaintances of Frau Fröhlich adored her. She now turned to Tante Helga and chirped. "May the delicious aroma of the *Pfannkuchen* drift into the abode of the benevolent spirits above." She spread out her arms and raised them upward. "May they hold you in good stead in the new year, Helga von Waldheim."

"What nonsense are you speaking!" Herr Fink immediately exclaimed.

Frau Fröhlich ignored him and turned to the rest of the females. "We women understand these things, don't we? We know that the mythical and magical creatures in the unseen world are ready to aid us if we ask for help, don't we? They listen better than most men do and are not as dense as some in our midst."

"Ha!" Herr Fink snorted in protest. "Whom are you referring to, Else?"

Frau Fröhlich winked at her friends, clearly finding pleasure in teasing him. "Hmm, let me think, Hans."

He took the bait. His voice sounded as though it was laced with deadly nightshade when he continued. "All this talk about spirits and magic is absurd. If you continue with such nonsense, Else, it will give all of us here a bad reputation. Furthermore, it is time that you women hand the reins back to us men. You need *us* to guide you. You, for one, are a woman that is never rational or logical."

He glared at Frau Fröhlich, who had a habit of projecting her chest outward when she wanted to make a point. Her upright posture gave her additional presence. She obviously prepared herself for a lengthy argument but thought better of it. She simply responded with a short, melodic laugh. "Oh, is that so!"

"Your head needs to be reworked, Else!" Herr Fink continued. "You are as irrational as Gerda Geist. She, too, believes in fairy tales. Only she prays to some old man in the sky instead of little elves that you claim are all around us. Both of you are deluding yourselves. Be careful whom you share your beliefs with. I agree with our government leaders, who warned us against people like you and Gerda. There is no room in our new socialistic state for your beliefs or practices. Put your trust in our government instead of some invisible creatures. It's the only source of truth. Moreover, anyone who is against our new government doctrines should be re-educated or even silenced."

The rest of the group had heard and remained painfully quiet. No one wanted to pick a fight with Herr Fink about the various government practices that left our economy in a slump. Feeling encouraged, he addressed Frau Geist. "I know of your prayer meetings, Gerda. I will do you a favor and give you a warning. Pay attention to what I am telling you now. Sooner or later, you will experience the scorn of our government when they find out that you are attending your hallelujah church meetings. You should heed the words of our leader and not those of your minister. Our leader has made us firm promises and has shown his willingness to guide us in a new direction. Pay homage to Ulbricht instead of to something that you cannot prove. He and the others will be the ones who will be protecting us from evil and from the infiltration of Fascists who are eager to start a new war. Walter Ulbricht is working to keep us safe. He wants to make things right for us. We should support him in his efforts. Listen to him and stop depending on some imaginary spirits in the unseen ether."

Herr Donner could not help himself but laugh. "Which Fascists are you speaking of, Hans? *You* are the Fascist among us! You are constantly at war with each one of us. You are totally closed minded to anything that does not fit your own beliefs. You need to allow people the freedom to explore what works for them and gives them comfort. Whatever happened to tolerance? You are out to win your battles with us, even though we don't want to fight with you. However, you are forcing us into constant quarrels. As far as Ulbricht is concerned, he doesn't know what he is doing. He is a fanatic, an admirer of Joseph Stalin. You are becoming a fanatic, yourself. What has happened to you, Hans? How can you support the elite or show them respect when they insult our intelligence? They take away our freedom of speech and freedom of travel. They confiscate our individual property. Moreover, they promise equality for everyone when they, themselves, are living high and mighty, while the working class is starving."

He turned to his friends in the room. "May I point out to everyone that Hans' brother-in-law, the STASI officer, is one of the privileged members of our society! Just take a look at the home he is living in."

Herr Donner addressed Herr Fink once more. "By the way, Hans, have you joined the Party since the last time we met here?"

"That is my secret." Herr Fink's voice became splintered and rough.

"Speaking of honor, Hans," Frau Geist needed to have her say. "You should reconsider your belief. Every bit of honor and gratitude should go to God and His son and not to the Communists. The Party is doing us no favors, and Ulbricht has left us without bread and butter. But no matter. It is God to whom we must turn for comfort and nourishment instead of depending on men whose minds are twisted and whose hands are covered with blood." Frau Geist took a deep breath before continuing. "And, by the way, Hans, since you are so opposed to the practice of Christianity, why are you celebrating Christmas along with the rest of us?"

Herr Fink glared at her, while the others exchanged uncomfortable glances again. It was too late to salvage the error that Frau Geist had committed. Herr Fink did not have to guess her position any longer. She had confessed her Christian beliefs clearly. They feared for her. Herr Fink was on the verge of entering the Communist Party or was perhaps a member already. He would surely report her confession to his brother-in-law. If any of them were to defend her, they, too, would find themselves in jeopardy. One wrong word had brought the hated STASI to the doors of others and had put them away for years.

Tante Helga finally interceded and steered the group down the hall. "Enough of this nonsense!" She commanded. "This is New Year's Eve. Let us not end the old year with a quarrel. I would like to keep my house a place of peace. Off you go now, all of you, into the parlor."

There was no person alive in our German Democratic Republic who did not know what it meant to be marked as a traitor to our government. Many people had already been dragged out of their homes by the secret police, who always came after dark. The neighbors of the accused could do nothing but watch silently from behind curtained windows. Surely, Frau Geist knew that Herr Fink was a dangerous man. He might even belong to the ranks of informers that the STASI had recruited. The informers exchanged information for goods that only the STASI could obtain. A person needed to be careful to express an opinion to anyone. Informants were betraying friends and family without remorse. Some even avenged themselves on innocent neighbors for having lost an argument with them. Their self-serving deeds had helped put guilty and innocent people away.

As the group passed the kitchen door, I noticed that Frau Geist was walking with assurance, carrying herself upright. I marveled at her courage to stand up for her belief and wondered whether she really expected God to rescue her if Herr Fink dared to report her.

Chapter Two

Politics in the GDR

Frau Geist was correct in her remark about Christmas and questioning Herr Fink about his participation. It was obvious that professed atheists, such as he, gladly participated in celebrating the holy days of the year. Although the leader of our government did not openly forbid people to renounce the birth of Christ, he forbade ministers or priests to preach the message of salvation from the pulpit. Church leaders needed to follow prescribed rules of how to minister to their flock of believers. The church was seen as a hindrance to the cause of Communism. Perhaps the Secretary General of the Central Committee of the Socialist Unity Party, Walter Ulbricht, who ruled us all with an iron hand, was aware that he would not be able to make people forget the old time-honored traditions. Therefore, he allowed people to celebrate Christmas, Easter, or Pentecost. Even those who were not deeply committed to their Christian faith looked forward to a few days of good old German *Gemütlichkeit*. Celebrations let everyone forget their problems and the long food lines, which at the end offered nothing to buy. When people were happy, they forgot that they were the stepchild of the other part of our Germany, the West, which lay across the border from us.

Following our country's defeat in the Second World War, we became a divided nation. The West fared better than the East. Allies allowed the people in West Germany to take back their own government and vote. Our

Russian occupied zone was not as fortunate. We were given no free elections, and the GDR remained under the control of the Politburo in Moscow.

The conflict between our two German governments continued to escalate because of severe differences in political views and ambitions. Berlin became divided by the four powers of America, Britain, France, and Russia. There were no demarcation lines between the western sections, but moments before entering the Russian zone, signs announced, "You are Leaving the American Sector."

In the GDR, Walter Ulbricht was hated by many. In spite of his ambitious promise to pull us out of the economic slump it had fallen in, he was unable to do so. Conditions continued to worsen. The new "improved" 2-Year-Plan that followed the previous 5-Year-Plan to reconstruct the East met with failure. The new plan included a stipulation for "voluntary contribution of work hours." That meant that each worker was required to work overtime past their regular 48-hour work week without the benefits of additional pay. Anyone who failed to comply faced reduction in food ration stamps or was demoted in rank or seniority at work.

Banners, which denounced Capitalism and Fascism, were visible all over town. So were posters, which lauded the continued friendship and unity with our Russian comrades. Pictures of Soviet farmers, who happily maneuvered their tractors through golden wheat fields, smiled down on passing citizens. The posters meant to entice the population into believing that joyful participation in the cause of Socialism-Communism, and heeding the examples of their Russian comrades, would allow the East to surpass the West in their standard of living. Other messages proclaimed, "Long Live the Proletariat" or "Long Live the Working Class."

Ulbricht promised to rot out the class of the Bourgeoisie, who once owned land or private businesses. The upper and middle class was ordered to hand over their property to the Volk. To bring East Germany in line with Russia, SED, the Socialist Unity Party, which was lumped together with the Communist Party, pushed for the *Sovietization* of the GDR. The leaders envisioned a system based on Russian laws, Russian customs and ways of life. Ulbricht announced the *"Planmässiger Aufbau des*

Socialismus," the Systematic Implementation of Socialism. Anyone who opposed the plan was persecuted as a class enemy. And if a person could not hold his tongue, he faced internment into a re-education camp.

People were told to help rebuild the nation. Even children were called on to do their duty. My classmates and I were bussed to cooperative farms to help plant potatoes, pick potato bugs off the leaves, and dig up potatoes at harvest time. Other schools participated in the threshing of wheat, and such. Being in the company of farmers who lost their private land or were forced to join a collective opened my eyes to their plight. I listened to their unhappy tales of sacrifices for the sake of Socialism-Communism and felt sorry for their loss.

We were flooded with propaganda. We were told to join the "*Junge Pioniere*," the organization of boys and girls in their white shirts and blue neckties who were groomed as future Communists. They, as well as their adult leaders, threatened to report us non-conformers to the Committee if we would not pay obeisance to the Party. Luckily, only a few of my schoolmates complied.

Our principal gave passionate speeches that began with citations of Karl Marx and Friedrich Engels and ended in threats. Without fail, his closing lines held the promise that he would promote none of us if we refused to step in line with the goals of Walter Ulbricht. We knew he meant it. In larger cities, students, who were in their twelfth and final year of school, and who belonged to the forbidden Evangelical Youth Group, the *Junge Evangelische Gemeinde*, were denied graduation. This prohibited them from entering a university. Since most students in our town were not interested in obtaining a higher education, they remained unimpressed by such threats.

On occasion, when a student found himself a thorn in the political posterior of the principal, or was being punished for the political sins of his parents, a teacher needed to follow the administration's request and demote even the smartest or most beloved student.

Much to our displeasure, all of us were required to assemble daily and sing the national anthem of the GDR. Its words are, "*Auferstanden aus Ruinen und der Zukunft zugewandt.*" I intensely disliked singing, "Risen from the ruins, our eyes are now turned to the future." I had realized long ago that the words belied what they said. The truth was that our town still lay in the same shambles to which it was reduced by the war. Nowhere was it apparent that we had risen from the ashes of destruction. Entire blocks of town continued to lie in ruins even five years after the war. Mountains of rubble were everywhere. We saw no progress, even though residents repeatedly assisted in clean up efforts.

"Clean up" was a misnomer. Salvage operation was a better description, because our State needed the iron scraps and other useful material that lay beneath the rubble. Teachers ushered us kids to the work sites and gave us a list of needed items to dig for. We scrambled up ruins, stepped into fallen structures, and scraped away the debris with bare hands to pull out whatever the government asked us to salvage. The more squeamish girls in my class agonized over the eventuality of finding dead bodies. The rest of fearless scavengers enjoyed teasing the timid ones by pretending that they discovered skeletons and other gruesome remains. Although it was a mean thing to do, the pouting faces of those who found themselves the butt of the jokes resulted in great laughter among the rest of the students. A bit of humor made the salvage operation more pleasurable for all of us.

At first, we eagerly participated because we thought that our efforts would help re-build our own town. But we were wrong. The iron scraps and mountains of materials, which we uncovered, went to the melting pots in other cities. Soon, some of my classmates complained about the injustice and refused to participate any longer. They simply feigned illness, and no threat from the principal could make them show up and take part in another salvage operation.

Then there was travel. Riding the train to the border and getting on another train that took us into East Berlin, which then allowed us to continue on to West Berlin, was difficult but not yet impossible. Listening to Western radio broadcasts, however, was prohibited by threat of imprisonment. When citizens ignored the threat, the GDR blocked the radio waves coming from the West. More often than not, the squeals and whines that the interference produced made the voices of the broadcasters almost unrecognizable. Nevertheless, many people sat with their ear to the speaker to glean some news from the West or hear the latest broadcast of the Voice of America.

It was not long before many recognized that if they were to remain in the GDR, they would suffer more hardships in the years to come. They decided to leave. The result was that the government began to tighten security along the border between East and West. The ones who did not leave displayed optimism. "Unification will come soon," they remarked with hope reflected in their voices. "We are certain that the GDR and the West will find a peaceful solution."

Once again, and just as after the Second World War, people longed for the Americans to come and claim them like a herd of lost sheep. They wanted to be brought into the fold of Capitalism. There wish was left unanswered. They endured shortages of food and availed themselves of shoddily manufactured supplies, if available. Some complained that Party members adhered to double standards and lived in the style and manner of the Bourgeoisie. The Party hated the middle class; yet, functionaries made sure that they enjoyed the very things, which all knew were the fruits of Capitalism. High Party members enjoyed a healthy lifestyle and partook in quality foods, which were inaccessible to the rest of the population. Members of the upper political crust were given large and beautiful homes that had been confiscated from their legal owners. Party members lived a life of dichotomy, betraying the ideology to which they had sworn allegiance.

Yet, many ordinary people, in spite of their meager existence, steadfastly supported the visions of our leaders and aligned themselves with their ambitions. They supported the development of a State of Workers. My uncle once said that our people were vulnerable to being led by the noses once again because they felt guilty for the atrocities that the Nazi government had committed. Their self-respect had been damaged. He added that if people were not careful, they would find themselves in quicksand again.

My grandmother had repeatedly urged my mother to join her in West Berlin when it had still been possible to easily get across. Despite our depressed situation, Mutti declined each time. Consequently, Oma made several trips to visit us until the train rides became an exhausting ordeal for her. Each visit left her feeling worn. The search and seizure of the Secret State Police who harassed citizens and often confiscated gifts that visitors brought with them from the West disturbed her greatly. A nervous laugh, a fearful look, unusual looking luggage or packages were eyed with suspicion. People were singled out and pulled off the train and interrogated. Even an unassuming old person, such as my grandmother, was suspect of wanting to do harm to the GDR.

Soon, barbed wire was strung between the borders of East and West Germany. West German citizens needed permits to visit the GDR. While access from East Berlin to West Berlin remained open, checkpoints between East Germany and East Berlin were erected. People who wanted to board the train to East Berlin, or those who wanted to cross from East Berlin into West Berlin were often forced to endure body searches. Oma took issue with being treated roughly and needing to endure the intrusive questions of the Secret Police. She resented having to obey the orders of the young men who were the age of grandsons. Consequently, her trips became less frequent.

Because people began to escape, the dangers of doing so increased. Mines were placed around the perimeters of the border. Even though several escapees managed to reach the promised safe zone of the No Man's Land, the neutral strip between East and West, GDR border guards did not hesitate to fire at them. Everyone became aware that the strip had become a death trap, even though the guards tried to hide their murderous intent from the public. However, radio broadcasts from RIAS Berlin, the forbidden radio in the American Sector, kept us informed. It harshly condemned such actions. Nonetheless, our leaders simply ignored the outcry against inhumanity and claimed that the atrocities committed by the border guards were justified. They declared, "To leave the GDR is an act of treason, and anyone fleeing will be shot."

Chapter Three

My New Home

Not a day passed without people having some kind of political discussions with trusted friends. This evening was no different. The guests fell into a debate. Tante Helga left them to it and came into the kitchen. I did not hear her enter and jumped when she put her hand on my arm. She wanted to know, "How are you holding up, Ariane?"

I shrugged my shoulders without answering. What was there to say? Had she not asked me the same question a dozen times over the course of the past week?

"My friends are an unruly bunch, aren't they?" It was more a statement than a question. "One would never know that they come from fine old, educated German stock." She tucked a loose strand of her blond hair back into a hairpin that had escaped the coiled braid at her nape. Then she gently lifted my chin. "You might not believe me, but all will be well with you in the end."

I held her glance for a moment but quickly turned away. What would I do if she succeeded to penetrate my wall of silence? Would I crumble and totally fall apart? What would happen to me if I broke? Would I scream? Go mad? Would they haul me away to that insane asylum in the next town, which everyone made fun of? I could not take the chance. I looked up once more and stared back at her. I knew that she would not punish me if I remained silent and withdrawn. Her temperament was different from that of my mother, who would often bring out the belt. Tante Helga, however, stood over me and stroked my hair in silence.

When sudden animated laughter echoed from across the hallway. I flinched. Tante Helga seated herself across from me. She reached for my hand. "Truly, Ariane-chen, I wished you would open up to me. It will lighten your load ever so much. I know that laughter is not what either of us wants to hear at this time." She paused and peered closely at me. "Would you like me to ask the guests to leave? I am sure that they have heard the news and will understand. I am certain that they would have stayed away had they known that you are living with us now"

"No. It's okay," I mumbled. "Let them stay and celebrate."

Who was I to decide who could visit this home into which I came as an orphan? Driving her friends away would change nothing. It would not bring my mother back or reverse events in time. Why should anyone else suffer for my own misfortune? It was my fault that I did not prevent her death.

"Well then, perhaps if we play some music later, it might lighten your heart. Meanwhile, please stay close to Dagmar and keep her company."

Tante Helga let her eyes rest quietly on me for another moment before she let out a long sigh. "I am so sorry that I could not do more for your mother. I've tried to save her from herself and cheer her up whenever I saw her. But you know how resistant and headstrong she could be."

I nodded my head slightly and responded in a toneless voice. "I know. It is certainly is not *your* fault that she did that terrible thing!"

I knew that I was to blame. Without warning, the dreadful scene of that night arose once again before my inner eye. The same thought that had tortured me for the last week, returned once more. If only I had come home that very afternoon she would still be alive. The often turbulent times at home would have continued, but that would have been better than letting her die. I feared that my grandmother was displeased with me. God, too, would be angry. I was sure that He had overheard the promise that I had given her.

Dagmar, who was frying doughnuts in a heavy iron kettle, had politely refrained from interrupting her mother and me. She now put the slotted spoon down and turned to me. "Ariane, if you want to take over and fry some of the Berliners, I will let you do that. It might take your mind off things and cheer you up."

"No." I shook my head, "I don't feel like it. I'm tired."

Tante Helga nodded. "Well, then. Just relax, Ariane-chen. Take your time. But Dagmar is correct. Occupying your mind with mundane things might do you good."

She turned to her daughter. "There's someone else whom I worry about. It's Herr Fink. He has become increasingly aggressive over the last few weeks. I fear that his brother-in-law has managed to convince him to join the Party."

"I'm afraid that you might be correct, Mama," Dagmar replied. "Just don't let him get angry at you, Mama."

Wolfgang's dark head peeked through the kitchen door. "Mama, did I hear you mention our most unpopular chamber music member? I am here to report that he has put an order in for coffee. He wants me to bring him a cup quickly. He claims that some of the raspberry seeds from the jam of the *Pfannkuchen* are are stuck in his throat. And, Mama, listen to this." Wolfgang let out an amused laugh. "Fink told me to tell you that if you don't have any *real* coffee beans in the house, he will not hold it against you and settle for *Ersatzkaffee*."

"That piggish man!" Dagmar remarked with a scowl. "He knows all too well that real coffee is nowhere to be found in the East! Except on the Black Market, of course, but..."

"Well, perhaps he's just bragging. He wants to let us know that his brother-in-law has connections." Wolfgang interrupted his sister. "Apparently, that man is able to get genuine South American coffee from *somewhere*. I think that it annoys Fink that Herr Sommer has brought French champagne. What he doesn't know is that Herr Sommer saved it for a special occasion. His relatives in the West gave the bottles to him as a birthday present a couple of years ago. Herr Sommer told me that when I asked him about it."

"Mama, don't let Fink abuse your hospitality." Dagmar picked up a tin of *Ersatzkaffee* and poured the mixture of acorns and beechnuts, which were laced with a hint of barley, rye, or chicory, into a coffee grinder. She began to turn the crank. The coffee mill let out a dull grumble, resisting the kernels which fought against being crushed by the jagged blades of the mill. She stopped pushing the handle and frowned.

"Fink is a good viola player. But he scares me. Why did you ever agree to let him participate in our chamber music evenings, Mama? You must ask him to leave before he alienates the entire group. Why don't you confront him about his bad behavior? You've tolerated it far too long. If you are worried that you will lose another string instrument, we can ask around and find someone else to take his place."

"I had a reason for allowing him to join," her mother responded. "Unfortunately, your dear father was indebted to his family. But since Papa is no longer with us, I've decided to balance the account myself. Of course, Herr Fink might be unaware of the history between his own father and your Papa."

Dagmar and Wolfgang were immediately intrigued. They barely remembered their father and wanted to hear about him. "What kind of obligation is it? Tell us Mama!"

Tante Helga shook her head and walked over to the battered white kitchen *Schrank* that held her set of fine Meissen china, which she had found abandoned in an alley after the end of the war. She counted off ten dessert plates before reaching for cups and saucers. Then she placed them with care onto a wooden tray.

"Now is not the time to discuss it, children," she finally said. "We'll talk about it later when we are alone."

The teenagers showed disappointment. "I hope we don't owe the family any money?"

"Not at all." Tante Helga shook her head. "Furthermore, children, I must insist that you address Hans Fink properly. Please do not call him "Fink" to his face. No matter how rude he is, he is still Herr Fink to you. I do not want him to assume that I am raising disrespectful children. And for now, let's finish frying the doughnuts."

She turned to her son. "Perhaps you can help your sister, Wolfie. I've noticed that Herr Fink was devouring some of the *Berliners* while all of us were still standing out in the hallway. He could not restrain himself to wait until everyone else had their pick, too. The doughnuts that Frau Fröhlich has brought us are almost gone."

"I, too, have noticed him doing that," Wolfgang laughed. "Fink stuffed one into his mouth and tried to get hold of another before he even chewed and swallowed the first one. His throat was bulging out like that of a boa constrictor that caught a fat mouse. Frau Fröhlich gave him a searing look when he tried to pull the box out of her hands to make another selection. He actually left a telltale sugar trail behind himself. It leads all the way into the parlor."

I had never met Herr Fink before but had heard about the past misdeeds of the man. True enough, he was as awful as Dagmar had described him to be. His complexion was gray. Deep furrows lined his forehead. His complexion looked like a dried up sea sponge. In spite of the humidity, which the Havel river spread over our town, his face was uncommonly shriveled. His sparsely seeded head, which politely allowed him to keep a few strands of longish hair combed over his forehead, was held up by a narrow stick of a neck. His affect was troubling to me, even in my own guilt and sorrow.

"Perhaps Herr Fink wanted to claim as many *Pfannkuchen* as he could before anyone else could get to them. Perhaps he needs to calm his guilty conscience." I had involuntarily spoken. My voice cracked like a fine piece of Meissen china, dropped on a table. "Perhaps he lied when he said that he didn't believe in spirits and became scared when he heard Frau Fröhlich make mention of them. Perhaps he is helping himself to as many doughnuts as he can to make sure that the ghouls won't harm him. Perhaps he believes in them after all but won't admit to it."

The family turned to me in surprise because I had spoken. Wolfgang grinned. "You're making a good point, Ariane. He's hiding something. I don't think that he is a very honest man. I've caught him earlier in another lie when he claimed to have given solo performances in Papa's orchestra in Leipzig. He said that everyone loved him. The truth is that Fink merely gave an audition. Herr Heinrich, who was Papa's good friend, said that Papa did not hire Fink because he lacked skill and experience. Fink's father was not too happy that Papa refused to give his son an opportunity to play with a fine orchestra, such as Papa's. Herr Heinrich said that Fink's father was chivalrous enough to acknowledge later that his son did not have the training or the discipline that was required to hold down such a position."

Dagmar's labored efforts rose above the saw-like noise of the coffee mill. "Really Mama. I'm afraid that Fink might do something awful to all of us. He might even report every word that our friends are saying. Our own family even might be in danger."

"I, too, have considered it," her mother responded. "If that is the case, or if he has stepped over to the other side, it might be more dangerous for us if we dismissed him. He has heard too much already. Everyone here is too trusting and open with their comments. We'll just have to watch ourselves from now on and pay attention to what we say around him."

Wolfgang began busying himself with squirting home made jam into the fat bellies of the golden pastry. He dropped one on the floor. "These things are pretty greasy," he commented.

I looked over at the plate of glistened doughnuts. He was correct. However, there was nothing anyone could do about it. We sometimes were able to purchase brown paper. But that had not been available for a long time now. If it had been available, we could have blotted off the pig's fat. In any case, I knew that I would not be able to eat any of them. In the past, the fat from the hog, the only fat available for cooking or for using as sandwich spread, had upset my stomach.

"Look on the bright side, Wolfie," his mother remarked. "The sugar coating will stick better if the outside is a bit greasy. But, tell me son. When did you ever complain about food? I'm sure that by tomorrow morning, not a crumb of these will be left over for breakfast."

She reached for an ornate decanter and poured milk into it. She would serve milk with the *Ersatz* coffee to make it more palatable. She handed a tray with the dishes to Wolfgang. "Please be a dear, Wolfie, and take this to the guests," she said.

I was once again overcome by the desire to leave the warm and cozy kitchen. I wanted to go upstairs. I wanted to crawl back under my feather covers where I had spent most of the day until Dagmar had pulled me out of bed and had insisted that I dress and follow her downstairs. I had done it to please her. I felt that I had been downstairs long enough and could bear it no longer. The activities in the kitchen and the arrival of the guests was too much for me. I craved to shut out the noise. If I had silence around me, perhaps I would finally fall into a dreamless sleep. Perhaps I would even remain asleep forever. Because, if I were dead, I would not have to face another day. I announced my intended departure.

Tante Helga quickly took my arm. "You should not be alone right now, *Kindchen*. Stay downstairs with us for a while longer. Dagmar will go up with you later, *nicht wahr*? Why not follow me into the parlor, Ariane-chen where I can keep an eye on you. Dagmar will join us when she is finished with the doughnuts."

Her invitation surprised me, remembering that I had never been allowed to remain in the apartment when my mother received guests. She had always sent me outside, where I mostly explored the alleys and vacant structures in our neighborhood whenever my friends needed to be at home with their families for dinner or such things.

Alright then. I would please Tante Helga. I would stay downstairs. I would sit alone and endure them all until the night was over. I blinked hard. My eyes were dry and achy from having held back my tears. My throat was constricted and felt wrung out. A mass resembling a *Knödel,* a potato dumpling, seemed to have lodged itself permanently in the back of my throat. Would I always feel like this? Would I find the strength to live one more day? Why did God not prevent *it* from happening? My stomach felt as though a roll of steel wire had unraveled inside of it. I felt cut, felt drained of all life. I had no idea what was expected of me in this house. My mother and I had never been like a *real* family. She had been happy to be away from home and to leave me on my own. Living here was different. Everyone seemed to care about each other.

I rose listlessly from the chair. "Well, I'll go and sit on the steps in the hallway where you can check on me if you'd like."

I needed to show my guardian that I was not a bad girl. I did not want her to send me away. My mother had once remarked that Helga von Waldheim was a gracious and generous woman. Mutti had admired her even though she had not wanted to emulate her character.

Chapter Four

The Revolt
June 17, 1953

I seated myself on the steps in the hall, which led up to the upper floor. I could see Herr Fink glaring at Herr Donner. Both were still arguing about politics.

The raspy voice of Herr Fink sounded like a high pitched foghorn when he yelled, "Why rehash the revolt again, Franz. It's over and done with! We won. You might as well face it. I hope your particular version of the account is not included in your history lesson in class. My brother-in-law has told me that teachers are not allowed to address anti-government activities in class."

I knew that Herr Donner was a teacher in Dagmar's school. He responded, "Never mind that. What do mean by, 'we won?' Were you helping to put down the demonstration? Were you present at the market place that day, collecting the names of everyone whom you recognized? Did you later hand your list over to the STASI? Your brother-in-law was one of the men in charge of security. It is still incomprehensible to think that he arrested innocent people and dragged them to slaughter."

Herr Fink became heated. "The revolt was a Fascist plot to topple our government! It is time that you understand that. Our leaders are doing their best to keep anyone from sabotaging their continued efforts to turn us into a utopian society. We are not like the West, where the rich get richer and the poor remain as they are! Capitalism, I tell you, can do nothing that Socialism and Communism can't do better."

Herr Donner exploded in derisive laughter. "Really, Hans. You are brainwashed. What devilish ray has blinded you to what's going on in our State?"

Herr Fink snorted. "Well then, Franz. If you cannot tolerate it here any longer, why not leave the GDR. Do you think that you can find a better life across the border? Just one warning, though. If you are thinking about fleeing, don't let yourself be caught by the Vopos or the STASI. You *do* know that there is a 4.8 kilometer wide forbidden zone established along the whole border? No one is allowed to go near it. My brother-in-law has told me that in confidence! I don't mind divulging that secret to you because you are a musical comrade."

Satisfied with himself for having tried to warn Herr Donner, he reached across Frau Stein help himself to another *Pfannkuchen.*

"What you are telling me is old news. I'm aware of the security at the border, Hans. What you are referring to is the so-called anti-Fascist protection barrier." Herr Donner informed him. "It's not only supposed to keep us in but to keep out the West. Ulbricht is afraid that the powers over there will come and topple him from his throne."

Someone whistled through his teeth at that remark. Perhaps he wanted to remind Herr Donner that he was entering a minefield. "Careful Franz," someone said.

"Yes, Franz," another person remarked. "Don't get carried away. Leave it alone."

Herr Sommer tried to smooth things out. "Alright you two. Enough of politics. I only have one comment, Hans. As far as I remember, Communism encourages equality and sharing. Does it not? I just want to remind you that you have eaten your quota of *Berliner Pfannkuchen* already. Leave some for me and the others."

The guests laughed, breaking the tension in the room.

But Herr Fink would not let the subject rest. "I have one more thing to add, Franz. I think that you bring up the revolt to drum up supporters for a new anti-government rebellion."

"You are crazy, Hans," Herr Donner thundered. "If I wanted to do that I would not bring up the subject in the presence of you!"

The women in the group had enough of it now. They nudged Tante Helga, asking her to silence both men. They knew that she endorsed neither of their behaviors. While she barely tolerated Herr Fink's, Herr Donner, too, caused her a few headaches. He was able to stir up the emotions of his fellow chamber members. Tante Helga wanted no more disturbance in her house tonight. She suggested that, even though the day of June 17 was a horrid day for all of us, it was time to change the subject.

"Thank you Helga," Frau Heinrich remarked. "I cannot bear to think about it any longer. My sister and her husband are still missing. We don't know what has happened to them or whether they are even alive."

Frau Heinrich's sister had been a member of the chamber orchestra before she disappeared.

I, too, could remember that fateful day of June 17, 1953 when many people in the neighborhood were arrested and imprisoned. Some simply disappeared. No one knows what became of them. It was a day that began as any other but ended with violence and bloodshed.

The revolt actually began on June 16, when construction workers in East Berlin, banded together and demanded that Walter Ulbricht pay attention to their needs. They wanted him to promise a higher standard of living and better conditions at work. News of the demands traveled quickly to other cities in the GDR. Workers united and demonstrated. The next day saw a full fledged revolt, which spread through all of East Germany. No one anticipated that it would end in disaster and would leave people wounded or even dead. A great many citizens were arrested and taken to prison.

For us in our town, it all began as a peaceful march to the town square. I was in school that morning. The day was sunny, and the windows of the classroom stood open. A warm breeze gently wafted into the room, carrying with it a slight fragrance of jasmine and lilacs that grew in the garden out back. I was daydreaming until I was torn out of my reverie. My classmates were giggling. I wondered whether our teacher, Frau Wohlmeister, was finished explaining the grammatical rules of prepositions, which required the appropriate use of German case articles. I knew them already, and her reiteration of them bored me. Apparently, someone made a joke.

I heard her tell the class, "Children, the correct way to say it is, *Ich gebe dem Hund den Knochen.* I give the dog the bone. The reason for using *dem Hund,* and not as some of you incorrectly wrote in your papers, *den Hund,* is because *Hund* is an indirect object and requires the use of *dem.*"

Ulli, our class clown, made another joke, which caused the students to laugh again. "Frau Wohlmeister," he said. "I need to raise one objection. I would give my dog the bone if we had one. My mother said that there isn't one single piece of meat or soup bone available at the butcher shop. She said that the Party members are helping themselves to everything they can lay their hands on. But since you mentioned food, it's almost lunchtime. I am dying of hunger and would not object to a nice bowl of beef stew or even to a morsel of meat left on the bone."

Frau Wohlmeister kept her composure and smiled. "Well, then, Ulli. Your observation is duly noted. I, too, would like a bowl of beef stew. I would even share it with you if I had one. But remember, should you come across a soup bone in the future, remember to give it to *dem Hund,* not *den Hund.*"

I loved my teacher for her sense of humor. She remained unflappable whenever students wanted to try her patience or when the boys became rowdy.

Frau Wohlmeister continued with her instruction but was interrupted by loud and animated shouts from outside. A few of my classmates rushed to the street to see what was taking place there. They returned quickly but ignored Frau Wohlmeister's command to take their seats.

They yelled, "Come on, everyone. Hurry up. You need to take a look outside! Hundreds of factory workers are marching down the street. They want us to join them!"

I was skeptical. What did a group of adults want with children? Nevertheless, I was as curious as the rest of my classmates. Something important seemed to have happened. We begged our teacher to release us from class. She excused us, and we almost fell over each other to bolt out the door. We enjoyed any unexpected vacation from school. Once on the street, we stared in awe at the men and women who passed us in their blue or gray work smocks. As far as we could see, people streamed together from all directions until they formed one long marching column right in front of our building.

The workers shouted slogans, such as "Down with Communism," and "Down with Ulbricht." Others yelled, "Kick out the Russkies."

Everyone seemed to be of one mind, marching for a common goal. The ripples of excitement were infectious and spread to us children. "Freedom from Tyranny," a voice shouted. "*Jawohl*," the crowd answered.

I remained standing close to my school building and watched the scene in amazement until my classmate Susie pulled me by the hand. "Come on, Ariane," she called over the roar. "Let's march with them."

I hesitated. What would my mother say if I got caught up in a demonstration? It never took much for me to be in trouble with her. Susie did not wait for me but snaked her way into the column of workers.

When a woman of my mother's age beckoned me to join, I jumped in. "Come on, *Mädchen*," she called. "We are not only demonstrating for ourselves but also for the future of all children." She took me by the hand. "We are marching so that everyone of us will become free from suppression."

"That's right!" A person walking next to her confirmed. "It is time that young and old shake off the chains of bondage that Walter Ulbricht has put around us. We deserve a better life! We want higher wages and shorter work hours. We need more food for our families. Moreover, we want the one thing, which every person in the Golden West enjoys. That is Freedom! Freedom from Tyranny!"

The people around us applauded. Their patience with Walter Ulbricht had finally reached the breaking point.

It was not so long ago that our East German radio stations had re-broadcast the promises of our leader. His assurances were meant to keep the people calm. Too many fled the GDR. The Russian government was disturbed by the exodus because the reduction in workforce caused a disastrous impact on our economy. It depleted the ranks of trained professionals in the fields of medicine, education, and engineering, and such. Their departure had already undermined the government's ability to provide needed services to the general public. Russia wanted to put a stop to the exodus. Ulbricht, along with Grotewohl, were ordered to appear in Moscow. Ulbricht was asked to explain why the GDR was experiencing what the western world called a "brain drain." Everyone expected the Goatee to be chastised for his hard line Communist approach and his Stalinist methods of governing. But people's hope that Russia would topple Ulbricht from power went unfulfilled. As far as people knew, he was simply told to change his methods of ruling if he wanted to create a flourishing nation that would outshine the West.

Ulbricht returned from Moscow, announcing his new plan. East Germany would embark on a "New Course." One of the items on his list of changes was that he would give the Bourgeoisie a financial break. They, too, would now be allowed to purchase groceries and other goods in the *Konsums*, the government subsidized stores. In the past, they had been required to pay higher prices elsewhere because Ulbricht had refused to issue them ration coupons available to the rest of the citizens. Another item on Ulbricht's list was to allow the clergy to conduct their traditional church services and programs from now on.

In spite of his concession to the Bourgeoisie and to the clergy, Ulbricht had ignored the needs of the workers. He now demanded that they increase their production quotas. This meant longer work hours without additional pay. He promised to punish those who would not meet production quotas. Everyone knew that longer hours, coupled with poor nourishment, would lead to even greater physical and emotional exhaustion. But there was more to come. There also would be an increase in prices and taxes. The date Ulbricht's "New Course" was to go in effect was June 30th. That was the day of his 60th birthday.

The workers simply revolted.

I marched with the crowd and wondered whether my mother was marching with us. I quickly unhooked the arm of the woman who pulled me along and left my row to run up and down the lines to see if I could catch a glimpse of her. Soon I gave up. There was no end to the line of people. I rejoined another column, which, just as the previous one, walked shoulder to shoulder.

When we arrived in the market place, people squeezed together to make room for the new arrivals. I was somewhere in the middle of the plaza but pushed my way to the front, where a platform was erected.

A man stood on it, shouting demands for an end of totalitarianism and for the demise of the Communist Party. "We are fighting for human rights. We are fighting not for a limited few but for everyone in the East Zone. The Communist pigs get fat and rich while we, the working people, are left with nothing! Dear people, we are gathered here as one Volk. We are demanding the same treatment, which our brothers and sisters in the West are receiving. We deserve the same standard of living!"

The crowd became jubilant and roared in agreement. I, too, yelled. The thought of being able to buy bananas and oranges, spreading butter on my bread, and walking around in smooth, fine clothes, was a pleasant thought.

"*Ja, Jawohl!*" The crowd shouted again. "We will stand together as one people! We want more liberties and free elections!"

Other speakers followed the first one. They called for the end of the Kremlin's interference in GDR politics. Each speaker concluded with a call for Freedom! Freedom above everything! The call was echoed by several hundred people in the market place.

The high energy of hope, which was mixed with anger against the Party, escalated to a frightening crescendo. Even though I became uneasy, I wanted to see and hear everything. Soon, I could no longer remain in the front. My slight body felt the hard squeeze from those around me. I struggled to breathe and decided to make my way to the very back. I took my place next to a row of bollards that were connected to one another by low hanging chains. Behind me flowed the Havel. Because I could not see the speakers, I climbed on top of one of the bollards.

Soon, I saw a handful of men in suits jump onto the platform. They punched the speaker to the ground, stomping him with their feet. A harsh murmur rippled through the crowd. "SED pig! Communist pig! STASI pig!" Apparently the speaker belonged to the other side of the camp.

Suddenly, a dull roar was heard. Soon, the earth began to shake. The squeal of tank tracks sounded. The grind of metal against metal was heard. Something heavy and ominous moved closer. The chains of the bollard that connected one with the other began to vibrate.

"Russian Tanks!" A high alarm went through the crowd. People froze. Some were undecided whether to stay or to leave. A handful of brave citizens climbed up on the podium and tried to calm the crowd. But before they could speak, they were subdued by government agents and dragged to the ground.

More factory workers jumped onto the platform and shouted, "Listen up everyone! Let us not be frightened by these Communist pigs or by the threat of tanks, which are manned by an unwelcome occupier! This is our country! Our land! The Russians have no lawful right to be here. They should not be allowed to exert control over us. Remember to stand strong. Let us not retreat until our demands are heard. Let us not be subdued by force!"

The crowd gathered faith. They ignored the roar of the tanks, which by now surrounded the market place in a half shaped circle. A few seconds later, truckloads of soldiers arrived. They pointed their machine guns, on which the ever present bayonets were mounted, into the crowd. Every exit from the square became blocked, except one. The only escape would be the path that led alongside of the river. The path led to a bridge in the distance.

I crouched low on the column. A Party member, who was flanked by a person in military uniform with a revolver in hand, climbed onto the stage and ordered the people to disperse. The crowd responded with a menacing growl. "Hold your ground, everyone."

I was hypnotized by what I saw and held my breath. Instead of leaving the square as ordered, people became angrier and jeered at the soldiers. They shouted obscenities and raised their fists against the tanks. Within moments, there were shots. Then screams. More gunfire followed. I could not tell whether bullets were fired into the air or at the people because the scene in front of me became one of pandemonium. Terrified demonstrators were fleeing in all directions. They pushed against one another, scrambling to find a way out of the market place. Some stumbled over the chains by me and plunged into the river. When I turned to look, I saw that the water was red.

The market place was half empty now. The only people left were those lying on the ground. I could not tell whether they were dead or injured. I was unable to move.

A stranger came and grabbed me by the arm. He pulled me down. "Run, *Mädchen*, run!" He shouted.

I came out of my daze. I was on the ground now and pressed my body tightly against the pillar. It was just wide enough to shield me from being seen by the soldiers. My heart began to race. Would I be shot if I ran? I stood shaking, listening for more shots to come. When I thought it safe enough, I ran as fast as my feet would carry me along the river's edge. I only stopped when I reached he bridge. It would take me to the other side of the river, to Old Town. After a moment of rest, I continued running until I was home.

Upstairs in the apartment, I sank exhausted into a chair. My heart was beating high into my throat. My body was overheated. My face was flushed. I was close to collapsing. I called for my mother. She was not there. A new fear came over me. Did she participate in the demonstration? Was she hurt? I turned on the radio and, and with my ear to the speaker, listened to the forbidden radio station of RIAS Berlin. Announcements about the uprising came every few minutes. It swept throughout all of East Germany before it was suppressed by sixteen Soviet divisions. Twenty thousand soldiers and and eight thousand Vopos had been mobilized to subdue the demonstrators.

I knew then that our fate was sealed. Future life would continue to be as harsh as it was before. In addition, thousands were injured, put in prison, or were marked for execution. Others died. A very dark cloud, one that was more noxious than the previous one, was hanging over East Germany.

Finally, at the onset of dusk, I heard footsteps coming up the staircase. My mother was home! She looked tired. I immediately assaulted her with questions. Was she in the market place? Was she hurt?

She, however, was in no mood to talk and waved me off. "Go to bed," she ordered. That was all she said.

The next day, the SED sponsored newspaper *"Das Neue Deutschland,"* The New Germany, ran headlines. They blamed the Americans for attempting to create a Fascist coup. Our town was placed under marshal law. People needed to be off the streets by 7 p.m. To enforce the curfew, truckloads of Russians stopped in each neighborhood. They marched down each street in squads of four with machine guns slung over their shoulders. Citizens, who were standing in front of their homes were motioned at gunpoint to go inside. Others who did not make it home in time, were arrested. Fear settled over the town, while Walter Ulbricht and Moscow were celebrating their victory.

Then, after what seemed a long and unsettling time, the curfew was lifted. The atmosphere in town and in school was oppressive. My own classroom was half-empty. Some of my friends were missing. Frau Wohlmeister did not have to give an explanation for the vacant seats. We all knew what had happened to our classmates. They had been placed into the town's orphanage after their parents had been arrested. I never saw them again.

I was heartbroken and felt powerless. It suddenly dawned on me that the price of freedom was high. Many people were willing to pay for it with their blood. For us in the GDR, the word "freedom" simply remained a word written in a dictionary.

The day immediately after the revolt, people were convinced that American soldiers would come to rescue everyone. An invasion of Western Allies would bring us unification. But that did not happen. Instead, we were told that West Germany had stepped forward to offer us nutritional assistance. People rejoiced. They were happy that the West paid attention to our plight.

At first, our government refused to give permission for people to travel across the border. Finally, when the cry for food became louder, it relented. A specific checkpoint was set up and became guarded by East German police and reinforced by the Russian military, which was on alert. It was clear that Russian troops would be mobilized if there would be another revolt. Each person's border crossing was documented, each name and address noted. The list became known as a list of traitors. It was collected by the SED, the *Soziale Einheitspartei Deutschlands* and dropped from planes over towns and boroughs throughout all of East Germany. A heavy campaign followed, enlisting informers into the services of the STASI. The job of the informers was to keep watch on their neighbors, associates, and even friends and families.

When citizens continued to clamor for food packages, the government used psychological warfare to instill fear. "Go ahead. Get your food packages if you must," it was announced. "No harm will come to you." But as soon as people were on their way to claim them, permission was withdrawn. Even train stations were forbidden to sell tickets to towns, which were located near the border.

When finally the government announced that Vopos would arrest anyone asking for handouts, the atmosphere in the GDR turned volatile once more. Because Ulbricht feared new riots, security was increased. Pro-Communist activists and STASI informers were planted in factories to report the slightest signs of anti-government activities. In addition, disinformation was spread. The public was told that the Fascist West was distributing tainted food to produce an epidemic. In the end, no one knew any longer what to believe. The result was that few dared to go and ask for food packages.

When the bottom seemed to fall out of our State, the Soviet Union came to the rescue. It offered the GDR economic support and food relief. In a gesture of servility and gratitude, Ulbricht ordered banners to be strung on public buildings that praised the USSR for its kindness and for being our savior. With food in their bellies, the mood of the people changed. Everyone began to settle down. The anger, which had exploded so violently during the revolution, subsided. If frustration and discontent continued to smolder in some circles, it was closely monitored and squelched before another revolt could break out.

Chapter Five

Wolfgang's Revenge

Frau Heinrich could not help herself but reminded everyone once again that her sister and brother-in-law were missing. She feared that they had been arrested and taken to prison. She had inquired at the STASI headquarters but had not been able to obtain information about them. She now turned to Herr Fink and asked whether he could help. He merely shrugged his shoulders and replied, "No."

Frau Fröhlich quipped, "What kind of a friend are you, Hans? You could get in contact with your connections. Trudi and her husband were our dear friends. You might want to ask your brother-in-law whether he has any information about them. After all, Trudi was a member of our group. You owe it to her and us."

Hans Fink, glared at her stoically before telling her about security measures that were in place and that information was given only on a need-to-know basis. He would not get his brother-in-law involved in trivial matters.

"Trivial?" Everyone exclaimed at once.

Frau Fröhlich was fed up with him. She announced that she was not in the mood to see the rest of the evening totally destroyed. She reached for her lover's arm. "Franz, my dear little Sugar Mouse, let's forget the trouble of the world for one evening. Let's not end the old year downcast and unhappy."

I screwed up my face. My dear little Sugar Mouse? Had I heard correctly? Frau Fröhlich managed to make me smile. I found her expression of endearment a hilarious one. My eyes searched for Dagmar. I wanted to see her reaction. But she had gone to the kitchen to fetch another plate of fresh doughnuts.

Tante Helga cleared her throat. "Listen everyone. I don't want to spoil the mood again, but I need to tell you something about friendship. I, too, lost someone on Christmas Eve. A friend." She glanced around the room over which a sudden hush fell. "Annie Berger passed away. She was a friend. I have taken her daughter into my house. The child has no relatives left to care for her. Let me introduce her to you all, because she will be part of our family from now on."

Tante Helga came out to the hallway and took me by the hand. "Come on, Ariane-chen." Let me introduce you to them."

Not eager in the least for attention, I resisted her. "No. I'd rather that you didn't."

But Frau Stein, who said next to nothing all evening, got up and stood before me. "*Ach Gott, oh Gott,* dear child. It is your mother, then, about whom people are talking. I was wondering who you were when I caught a glimpse of you earlier. I assumed that you were a friend of Dagmar's. Please accept my condolences, my dear child."

"Is the girl alright, Helga?" Frau Geist asked Tante Helga, who pushed me into the room. "I can see that the poor girl has not recovered from the shock yet. It is understandable, of course."

She rose and held out her hand. I was embarrassed but walked over to her and extended my hand in return. I felt too old to curtsy; but out of respect for her age, I bent my knees a few degrees to acknowledge her condolences. I was aware that everyone was watching me, inspecting me.

Frau Stein gave me a gentle smile and continued, "Fate is not always kind to us, is it, child? But I am sure that you will be very happy here in your new home." She turned her eyes to her musical companions. They nodded in agreement. Frau Stein added, "You must try to be grateful to Frau von Waldheim for her hospitality to you, my dear child."

"Nonsense, Charlotte," Tante Helga quickly interceded. "I am happy to welcome Ariane into my family."

The other women in the room reached out to me, as well, and the men followed. Herr Fink was the exception. He ignored me. No one mentioned the manner in which my mother left this world. But I knew that all of them had heard the gossip.

Tante Helga put her hand around my shoulder and drew me closer. "I would like to take the opportunity to tell you about the generosity of her mother.

"Annie and I met each other at the end of the war when both of us were looking for a place to live. We sought shelter in a bombed out apartment. The floor was badly damaged. There were gaping holes everywhere. I was afraid that my children would fall through. The floor was held up by an iron beam but looked as though it would crash to the ground at any moment. We slept on one mattress, which I found under a pile of rubble. Annie knew that the owner of this house lived alone. He lost his wife in one of the air raids. Annie helped plead my case. The man agreed to let me and the children move into the upper floor. As you know, not long after we settled in, he packed a suitcase and left for the Golden West, where he has a brother. Annie could have claimed the rooms for herself but graciously allowed me to take them. She said that we needed them more than she since I had a girl and a boy. She moved with her daughter into a single room by the river, an unacceptable place, I might add. It took her a long while to clean it up.

"So, my dear friends, if it were not for her good will toward me and my little family, we would have slept among rubble. Even though the two of us did not always agree on many issues, Annie and I remained friends. I owe it to her to look after her daughter."

The guests nodded in appreciation of my mother's kindness. Tante Helga gave me one last squeeze and turned me loose. I offered a curtsy to the group and went back to sit on the stairs. The compassion that I felt in the room added to my misery. I hated that Tante Helga presented me to them as an orphan. I knew that people looked with pity on children without parents. Moreover, I was afraid that if the group would find out that I neglected my mother on the afternoon of her death, they might not feel so sympathetic toward me.

"I hope that the girl manages to recover from the trauma. Perhaps she is still in shock, just as Gerda said," Frau Heinrich stated.

"I've tried to support her the best that I can, but she turns away from any kind of comfort." Tante Helga's voice betrayed the same concern that she showed for me all week. "I know that Ariane is managing the best she can. What worries me is that she has not cried once since her mother...well, you know, since it happened. I asked myself what I can possibly do to help her. I've consulted with a physician. He assured me that time would take care of it. You know that there's no one left in this town who specializes in childhood trauma. We have lost most of our medical staff to the West. I think that Ariane believes that she must hold it all together and conceal her grief. How can I make her understand that it is alright to cry?" Tante Helga let out an audible sigh. "I am convinced that if she does not spill tears soon, the trauma from finding her mother dead might break her."

I cringed. How could Tante Helga share my personal business with strangers? How could I show my face to anyone ever again? My mother had repeatedly reminded me that it was important to keep our private affairs to ourselves. She had often made me repeat my pledge of secrecy to her.

The members of the group turned to each other, each of them expressing their observation and opinion about whether a person had the right to choose death by his or her own hand. It appeared that some of them were Existentialists while others expressed a Christian view. Two or three simply expressed compassion for me.

The discussion almost reached a crescendo when the raspy voice of Herr Fink rose above everyone else's. No one paid attention to him until he stook up and repeated his words, "I dare say, Helga, this is what I think. The woman simply checked out and left her daughter behind. I think that it would be very difficult to look after other people's snotty-nosed kids, especially those that are emotionally damaged, as this girl must certainly be." As if to confirm his diagnoses, his eyes found me through the open doorway. I quickly looked away to avoid his glance.

"Helga," he continued, "In spite of the fuss we make amongst ourselves, and the arguments we have, I know that everyone here cares for your well-being. I, for one, think that you do not need to take on that extra responsibility. Why do you care for someone who might suffer from a mental or emotional disorder? The reputation of the girl's mother alone should be a warning to you. The child might be just as unstable and confused as the woman was. It will be better if you handed her over to the orphanage. You should have taken her there in the first place."

I listened with beating heart, wanted to run away from such unkind words. But I could not move. I remained seated where I was.

Instantly, Herr Donner's voice came flying through the room. "Hans, *ich bitte Dich*! I beg you! Just this once, keep your obnoxious words to yourself, even though it may be difficult. I think everyone of us here has enough of the poison that you continue to spew."

Frau Sommer nodded her head vigorously. She commented in her colorful Saxon dialect, "Shame on you, Hans! Whatever has caused you to be such an intolerant tyrant!"

The others, too, confronted Herr Fink. They began talking over each other. But Frau Geist topped them all with a high and shrill voice. "Pray, tell. Where are your sentiments, Hans! Your behavior is inexcusable. How can you even think of expressing such an opinion while the child is right there in the hall, listening to all of it? I, for one, am proud of Helga for having a big, charitable heart. She is doing just what God expects us to do. His commandment to us is to be merciful to each other! If you are not careful, you will succumb to the venom which you spit into everyone's eye!" Frau Geist became so upset that she choked on her saliva. She coughed.

"Easy now, Gerda." Frau Stein placed a comforting hand on the arm of her friend. "Don't mind him."

Herr Fink seemed more surprised than hurt by the verbal assault on him. He could not grasp the violent response his words had caused. Had his hostess not asked for advice? Well, he had given it to her!

My guardian, who momentarily was left speechless and stared at him in disbelief, gave him a piece of her mind. "Hans Fink! Please *do* behave more like a gentleman and human being. If you cannot find it in your heart to be kind, or if you cannot speak pleasantly about anyone, please keep your advice and comments to yourself. It should not concern you that I have made a commitment to the girl. I will not listen to any more foolish talk from you. The poor girl has already suffered enough. If you have anything else of a disparaging nature to say, please leave us!"

The group applauded. Herr Fink, however, revealed a stubborn nature. He neither rose nor offered apologies. He remained firmly seated on the sofa. He stuck out his jaw to show that he was prepared to lock horns with anyone who would pick another fight with him. "Ha!" He finally called out and turned to his musical colleagues. "Ha! You cannot shut me up so easily. You'll see."

The guests glanced at one another with perplexed expressions, unsure what to make of the comment. They considered hoisting him out of the house. But something prevented them from taking action.

Within moments, Frau Geist was at my side. "Don't worry child," she said in a comforting voice. "God will see to it that no harm will come to you."

I looked up at her. Even though I wanted to believe her, doubts nagged at me. Things around me seemed to be in perpetual chaos. "How can you be sure?" My voice trembled.

"Just have faith. You'll see." She smiled warmly.

She seemed to know as much about God as my grandmother knew. I gathered courage and continued. "Do you think that my mother will go to hell for what she has done?"

I considered confessing my own sin to her but was afraid that if I would tell, she might judge me before God would be able to review my case. As it was, I was almost certain that He would throw me into a fiery pit for having neglected my mother.

"I cannot answer what the Good Lord has in store for your mother, child. But I do know that He has forbidden us to do what she has done. But fear not. If *you* remain a good girl, He will continue to look after you."

She turned and walked back into the room. I was glad that I refrained from disclosing what was bothering me ever since my mother's death. I put my head on my knees. I wanted her to say that my mother would be forgiven. The memory of her restless soul, which I saw after her passing, continued to haunt me. Would she be lost for all eternity? I had no idea as to how long eternity would last. Whenever I attempted to picture it, an impenetrable blackness descended over my mind. I could not fathom it.

I suddenly felt someone touching my hair. Wolfgang was standing before me. "Are you alright?" He hesitantly took my hand and held it for a moment. I swallowed hard and nodded.

"Don't worry," he said, looking down at me with his dark eyes. "I promise you that I will make Fink pay for hurting you. In fact, I already have an idea how to go about it."

"It doesn't matter," I mumbled.

"Yes, it does. We all care about you." He seated himself next to me and began stroking my arm. "I'm so sorry that you heard all the things he said."

Dagmar, too, came to comfort me. "I'm angry at that mean old Fink. Don't listen to him, Ariane. He's an old oaf. Mama told us a while ago that it is people like Fink, who with their inflexible mindset, give all Germans a bad name. I wished I knew why she is so tolerant of him. But you know how Mama is. She wants to be kind to everyone and not judge a person too harshly."

Dagmar's and Wolfgang's sympathy made matters worse. The question was, would they continue to be pleasant to me if they found out that I could have prevented the death of my mother?

Wolfgang left us to go back into the room, while Dagmar and I sat for a while in silence. Suddenly, we heard a loud commotion coming from the room. I heard a chair being pushed over. Hearty laughter followed. Herr Donner's baritone boomed above everyone.

"Hans, I dare say, you sure have a perverse way of paying homage to the spirits, which you've been trying to seduce all evening in an attempt to seek their favor. You are meant to consume the *Pfannkuchen*, not exhume them."

"You…You….You! I'll get you for this…all of you…" Herr Fink became so unhinged that words to express his anger failed him. His voice ended in a shrieking vibrato.

"*Haha, hoho,* Hans." Herr Sommer and Herr Heinrich slapped themselves on their thighs with great delight. Their laughter was infectious and invited everyone else to join in.

"We think you've outdone yourself this time. Else's horrified expression shows that she is absolutely certain that you have infuriated the genies of the underworld by abasing the very offering that she brought for them. We can only imagine the punishment that will be yours for your vulgar disrespect of them."

Before we knew it, Herr Fink came running toward us. He did not stop but made a straight line for the washroom. We caught sight of his backside, on which a greasy *Berliner Pfannkuchen* hung like the tuft of a rabbit's tail. What's more, gooey raspberry jam jetted through the center of the doughnut and formed a ring around his seat. The seeds of the jam resembled the droppings of a little mouse.

As soon as Herr Fink closed the bathroom door behind him, we heard the stifled sound of a snort. We turned our heads. Wolfgang stood grinning by the door of the room. He displayed a look of smug satisfaction. Dagmar laughed but quickly put her hand over her mouth when her mother hurried past us with a towel to assist the victim of her son's revenge.

"Isn't my brother the naughtiest ever?"

"I did not know that he is capable of doing such a thing," I answered. "Wolfgang is always so nice."

"He probably laid the doughnut on Fink's seat when he rose up to reach for another pastry."

Soon a disgruntled Hans Fink reappeared with a checkered apron wrapped around his wet behind. That vision prompted his musical colleagues to offer one more round of witty taunts. But Herr Fink sat down and merely sneered at them all.

Tante Helga, who rarely became unraveled, called the group to order. "Alright, my friends! I won't ask the guilty person to step forward. But please let's not forget that we are all adults. In any case, midnight is approaching fast. I dare say that our instruments must feel neglected. Let's make some music. I suggest that we play the second movement from *Jupiter.*"

"What is Jupiter?" I pulled on Dagmar's sleeve before she could escape and fetch her violin. "I've never heard it being played on the radio."

"I'm sure that you have," Dagmar replied. "The stations play it often. It is a name that some classical musicians gave Mozart's *Symphony No. 41*. They say that the composition is so complex and majestic that it is fit for the ears of a god."

"Isn't Jupiter a planet?" I asked. "I think my teacher told us that."

"I suppose it is that, too. But in the old days, he also was known as the Roman god of light and sky. In addition, he protected people when they went to war against each other. I think Mama suggested that we play that piece because she wants everyone to stop quarreling."

"If Jupiter is supposed to protect people when they are fighting against each other, whose side will he take?" I asked flatly.

"I don't know. When Wolfie asked that same question, Mama said that she was almost certain that a god is always on the side of people who show faith in him."

Chapter Six

1945
A Sign of Providence

Tranquility finally descended onto the room. The second movement of Jupiter began in soft tones. I stretched out over the steps and listened while I thought about what Dagmar had said. Her mother had spoken of faith and that God would protect anyone who honored Him with showing it. I believed that she was correct. I thought of my own grandmother, who had behaved as though she had a special telephone line to God. Her trust and belief in His goodness had been unshakeable. She used to say her prayers of protection for all of us so convincingly and assuredly as if she knew that God and Jesus would hear her right then and there. I was convinced that she had been responsible for that extra cushion of protection that had surrounded my mother and me.

My mother, in contrast, had faith in no one. She neither trusted in God nor in people. I think that she did not even trust herself. She believed that doom would always have the last word. "Trust in the Providence of God," my grandmother told her. But my mother simply brushed that off. "The notion that Providence exists is nonsense," she said.

There were times when death could have easily claimed us but walked away. And then, there came that special day that could have put an end to us all but did not. Even though I was very young at the time, I remember that day very clearly. I also remember the perilous days and nights that followed.

The air raid siren had wailed almost every night for two weeks. My grandmother, who lived not far from us, visited us regularly. She came at dusk to sit with my mother and a few friends to wait out the night. If each day slid past in relative quiet, the nights were long and torturous. They left everyone wishing for the light of dawn to arrive. When morning came, the noise would stop. People relaxed. They knew that they had been given another day to live. What came after that, lay in the hands of either God or fate.

Each evening, as soon as darkness descended onto our town, the air was torn apart by the roar of airplanes. Soon, bombs came whistling down. Their high pitch was followed by the boom of the Flak, the anti aircraft defense guns. My grandmother always insisted on taking me to the basement, where she thought me to be safer. She seated herself next to my little make-shift bed and told me stories of cherubim and other heavenly creatures, which she said were hovering over my bed to protect me. She spoke with such certainty that I believed her and fell asleep without fear.

Proof of protection came when I awoke one morning and saw that a bomb had crashed through the roof of our house. It had not exploded but had become stuck in the floor tiles of the hallway, right next to where I had slept. Even though barely out of diapers, I believed that the power of my grandmother's prayers and faith had been at work.

But one day, the sirens began to wail at noon instead at night. No one had expected that, and their alarm came too late. Before people could take shelter, planes were already droning above their heads and unloading their bombs. My mother decided to run out of the house. She grabbed my hand and pulled me outside. Seconds later, every structure around us exploded and tumbled. I was convinced that my life, too, would be snuffed out at any moment.

My mother ran, dragging me behind her. She ran so fast that my own feet barely touched the ground. My arm kept twisting around, but she yelled at me to keep up with her.

We were met by a few scared horses. "The Baron's horses are loose," my mother shouted over the explosions. "I wonder who let them out."

The Baron's estate was located a few blocks from our own house. She ran to it. To our surprise, it was still was standing, while the other houses around it had caved in. To her dismay, the doors were chained and the windows boarded up. She decided to run for the stables. When we reached them, hands of strangers pulled us inside. When our eyes adjusted to the murky dimness in the room, we noticed that it was packed with unfamiliar people of all ages.

If everyone was convinced that our confinement would last mere hours, they were mistaken. The night and the following day stretched into fourteen additional days and nights. When the bombs were not falling from the sky, the tanks were firing their deadly cargo. No one in the shelter knew who was fighting whom. Finally, the fighting reached the streets of our neighborhood.

The endless days and nights in the shelter remained a blur in my memory. We lay piled up like sardines, waiting for the deafening noise to end and for the building to stop shaking. Spring had not arrived yet, or so it seemed, and the cement floor, on which everyone huddled together for warmth, was miserably cold. Then, after days and nights of booms and echoes of machine guns, the clear signal of a siren sounded. The nightmare, which stretched everyone's nerves to breaking, appeared to be finally over.

It was an eerie silence. People peeked through the door but were afraid to go outside. The stables lay in the back of the property, away from the street. I suddenly felt the urge to pee and tugged on my mother's arm. She, at first, refused to take me outside to do my business. I was toilet trained early and knew a pair of wet pants would bring a scolding. Finally, when I felt that I could not wait one minute longer, she relented and took me to the street. I could do my business, and she would have a chance to see how much damage the fighting left behind. The moment we walked out on the street, we came face to face with four Russian soldiers that were standing guard at each corner of the intersection. They quickly raised their weapons and pointed them at us.

My mother let out a sharp breath. She had, along with everyone else, expected the Americans to arrive. Believing that the soldier would not harm a woman with a child, she pushed me ahead and told me to squat by the curbside. I stared at the barrels of the soldiers' rifles. Long, menacing metal rods were protruding from them. I was convinced that at any moment, the soldiers would walk over and pierce my body with their bayonets.

With their fingers on the trigger and a motion of their weapons, the soldiers shouted something in their language. It needed no translation. We were ordered to turn back. I looked up at my mother and began to whimper. The pressure on my bladder increased even more. Would Mutti permit them to execute me before I was able to relieve myself? My mother became defiant and ignored the command of the soldiers. She pushed me down but I refused to pee while being watched by the young men. I wanted her to shield me.

I stood up, holding my crotch with my hands. I crossed my legs to keep my bladder from exploding and began to cry. "Mutti! Please don't make me do it here!"

My mother began to yell. "Behave yourself and show them that we are human beings. Stop your whining!"

She pulled at my panties. When I felt the cold air hit my bare behind, I let go. To my surprise, the soldiers lowered their weapons. They stood as if hypnotized. Their expressionless eyes followed the stream of water that spilled down the curb.

When I was finally finished, my mother ceremoniously pulled up my panties and said, "Let's go!"

I tensed up again and could not move. "Now they will kill us, Mutti," I whispered.

I stared at the soldiers. Neither spoke or moved. When my mother began pulling me by the arm to leave, their trance broke. With a sweep of their weapons, they motioned us back into the stables.

I had stopped crying but began to sob again as soon as we were back in the stables. I cried not only for having escaped death but for having to squat down in front of the soldiers. Why did my mother make me do it? Could she not understand that, although I was a small child, I felt violated?

The news of the invasion spread quickly. The appearance of the Russians instead of the Americans brought tears to the eyes of many. Knowing that they were doomed, people began to wail.

"Nothing good will come to us from Russia," they told each other. The older ones in the crowd remembered that our troops had pushed through Russia's own country. They knew how much the Russian's hated us because of the destruction our army brought to their own land. They huddled together for a while longer, but when the siren remained quiet and no new alarms came, people left the shelter to find a place they could call home.

We found out that people, who tried to escape the town during the fighting, were apprehended by advancing enemy troops. Each person was interrogated. Many were tortured. The women were raped. Even at a young age, I knew what that action meant.

Suspected Nazi supporters were executed on the spot. The rest of the survivors were found walking like zombies in the woods. They appeared disconnected from reality. Their eyes and expression were glazed over.

Oma had been convinced that her Good Lord sent his angels to save and protect my mother and me. My mother, however, denied it and refused to speak of that time ever again.

Long after leaving the shelter, I could remember the smell of it. It was a smell of fear, of human bodies, and of waste. Those days remain etched in my memory forever.

After days of searching for a place to live, my mother finally found a small damp room in a house that was situated several feet from the banks of the Havel river. Our windows faced an abandoned loading dock where big, yellow rats kept scurrying about. Our living quarters were similarly vermin infested. They gnawed on whatever little food my mother managed to steal from the fields in the countryside. Looting and stealing grain was punishable with imprisonment. Nonetheless, Mutti would rise before dawn to join a group of other women who trekked to the surrounding wheat fields. As the sun came up, they plucked whatever kernels they could find on the stalks. One day, when my mother remained home, all of the women were caught and taken to prison. My mother never ventured back into the fields after that. She began placing all of her energy into our small room to clear it of the infestation of bedbugs and flees. She also declared war on the lice that began to rear entire families in our hair. She dragged our landlady's mattress out into the yard by the river and found a new one. She scrubbed our hair, our bodies, and everything in the room, with disinfectant. Her efforts paid off. Not long after, our room was restored to more sanitary living conditions. So was our hair. My mother could finally put away the special lice comb with its double row of teeth and the germicidal liquid, which she kept on hand.

A month before Christmas my mother's endurance weakened. Her nerves took a turn for the worse. Nevertheless, she promised that we would celebrate Christmas. She gathered branches of fir, which she bound into the traditional *Adventskranz*. It would hold four candles and be hung from the ceiling. The first of the candles was lit on the fourth Sunday before Christmas. Each consecutive Sunday, another one was lit, until all four of them would burn on Christmas day.

I felt excited as I looked forward to the arrival of Santa Claus, our *Weihnachtsmann*. One Sunday afternoon, my mother prepared to light the third candle and went looking for matches. She momentarily left the room. I discovered matches lying nearby. Eager to help, I crawled up on the table over which the wreath dangled from the ceiling. But before I was able to strike a match, my mother returned. Soon, I felt the leather belt on me.

"I wanted to help," I sobbed, choking on my breath. Her anger became so violent that it made me vomit. Soiling the only dress I owned sealed my fate. My mother totally lost control of herself. She dragged me into the backyard where the Havel river lazily flow past the property.

The winter was mild that year, and the water was not frozen over. Its surface was dark green and murky from the large oil spills, which the ship traffic left in its wake. I did respect the water but was not afraid of it. Instead, I was afraid of my mother. I knew that she was going to drown me. I screamed like a banshee.

But it was of no use. Soon, she was up to her knees in the river. She held me under. I fought to free myself. I gasped for air and sputtered. I choked on the foul tasting, dirty water. But she would not let go. Just before I lost consciousness, I was torn from her grip.

Frau Müller, who lived in a house next to us and shared the same backyard, heard my screams. She grabbed the back of my dress and pulled me out of the water. She said not a word to my mother but took me into her house, where she offered me a cup of warm milk. She was an old, stooped over woman but had a nice way with a young child.

After I calmed down, she introduced me to her goat, Zickie. As I petted the goat, Frau Müller told me the story of Zickie's own survival.

Zickie lived in a cellar beneath Frau Müller's kitchen floor, which could only be accessed by a trapdoor over which a rug was placed. There were cracks in the bricks of the cellar below, so that the goat could breathe and was able to see the river. She even was able to catch a few sun rays if she moved close to the wall.

Zickie hated to be alone and would bleat all day long. But one fateful day, when Russian soldiers came to the house, the goat sensed trouble. For the first time that Frau Müller could remember, Zickie made no sound. She kept very still. She lay among the patches of straw and held her breath as the uninvited invaders ripped out the sink and toilet bowl, and anything else that was of use to them in Russia. Then they harassed and hurt Frau Müller. But only when the soldiers left the house and were a safe distance away, Zickie let loose and bleated her heart out. Frau Müller told me that by being quiet and using her intelligence, the goat saved herself from being slaughtered. If she would have bleated, she would have been roasted over an open spit in the backyard.

I quickly made the goat my confessor. I told her my troubles and how I had made my mother so angry. Zickie answered me with a bleat. I knew, then, that she had understood everything that I had told her. Somehow,

I felt a common bond with the goat because both of us had been able to escape death.

Frau Müller kept me in her house for two days and showed me much care. She washed my dress and ironed it. Before she took me back to our house, she instructed me to be as smart as her goat. "Be a good little girl and don't upset your mother. The war has damaged her nerves. You must give her time to be well again."

I was afraid to go back home but relaxed when my mother received me coldly, without saying a word. She did not mention what happened then, but I saw that she had taken down the wreath from the ceiling.

When Christmas day came and went without celebration, I knew that she was still angry with me. And when my fourth birthday came around, it, too, was like any other day. There was no celebration. The only present I received from my mother was a promise that she would not let me forget the upset that I had caused at Christmas time.

Chapter Seven

1953
The Day Before Christmas Eve

An oppressive gloom hung over our apartment the week before Christmas. My mother sat motionlessly by the window of our living room and stared into the drabness of the sky. Ever so often, she rolled herself a cigarette and stuck it into a long porcelain holder. She once told me that it refined the aroma of the tobacco. I tiptoed around her as if walking on jagged fragments of glass. Anything I said incited her. I had previously asked for permission to join my friend, Andra, to celebrate her thirteenth birthday. My mother denied my request. I sulked for a while and settled next to our warm little tile stove to read a book. I enjoyed reading. My Uncle Emil had taught me how to read before I became enrolled in school. I remembered the very moment that books took on a special meaning for me. Frau Wohlmeister was teaching us our ABC's. She brought a book of her own to class. I was curious what was written in it. I wondered whether she would read us a story from it. I loved stories and wanted to have a peek inside of it. When recess came, and she left the classroom with the rest of the children, I cautiously strolled over to the desk and picked up the book. I put my nose to it. The cover smelled of leather, and the pages had yellowed a bit. Before I could turn the pages, and to my horror, my teacher returned. I looked at her with guilt ridden eyes, stammering an apology. She smiled and merely asked, "Well, Ariane. Are you interested in books? Can you read already?"

I nodded. "Yes."

"Well, then. Read me this." She opened her book and pointed to a short paragraph.

I began to read and faltered only over one or two foreign words. Frau Wohlmeister praised me. I could feel my cheeks flush with pleasure. I was happy that someone other than my uncle and grandmother noticed that I could do something well. From that moment on, I wanted to please my teacher even more. I began to pore over the dictionary in our library. I studied words and filled my head with their meaning. I was grateful when Frau Wohlmeister never singled me out to show my skill to the other children. Only when she became frustrated with a student who failed to decipher one of the long German compound words, did she ask me to read. I practiced deciphering long words on my own. Soon, I was able to read common words, such as *Kirschenblütenduft* (the fragrance of cherry blossoms) *Marienkäferpünktchen* (the little spots on a lady bug,) or *Apothekenangestellter*, (a male pharmacy clerk,) and many more. While other students were convinced that our written language was a conspiracy devised by great thinkers who wanted to challenge our minds, I welcomed the opportunity to sound out difficult words and approached compound words like a detective. I practiced reading them anywhere I saw them written. I loved the challenge.

As my reading skills advanced, I began to delve into French and Russian classical literature, whose subject matter was unquestionably above my maturity level. Fictional protagonists, who were involved in sordid affairs and who suffered because of them, held me spellbound. I admired the brave heroes and charming heroines who were courageous enough to sidestep the cultural expectations of their day. It always surprised me when some were brave enough to ignore them altogether and follow their hearts at great cost. My favorite books were those of love, rejection, or sacrifice. I think that they reminded me of my mother, whose own complex relationships brought her many heartaches, as well. My mother liked it when I read. She said that it kept me quiet and invisible.

On afternoon, in the midst of her gloom, she decided to leave the apartment and find a public phone booth to call Fritz Neumann, with whom she had quarreled a few days earlier. She pulled on her dark woolen trousers that my grandmother had given her a couple of years earlier and put on her coat. I looked up from my book and marveled at her courage to wear pants in public. No other woman in our neighborhood owned a pair of them. They were considered avant-garde by some and unfeminine by others. My mother's view of them was different. She claimed that they were fashionable. Our local *Kino*, the cinema around the corner from us in Old Town had presented films in which movie stars wore trousers like hers. Mutti said that she did not wear them as a fashion statement but that they kept her legs warm.

When she later returned from having made her phone call, she actually looked cheerful. The dark cloud that had hung over her seemed to have lifted. "Fritz will come later to the house and pick me up," she announced. "The little problem we had is solved. He told me that he has a surprise waiting for me. I am convinced that he will finally propose to me. In fact, I am certain of it. We will go out and celebrate our engagement. I don't expect to be home before morning. You might as well go to your friend's birthday party."

"Really?" I was happy but surprised. My mother did not easily share her secret life with me. I would hurry to Andra's house. She would be surprised to see me, because I had previously told her that I was not allowed to join her. I did not tell her that my mother was constantly afraid that strangers would quiz me about my home life.

"Be back at a decent hour and go to bed right away," my mother warned. "Don't roam the streets after dark. You know that the neighbors are forever nosey and have watchful eyes. I do not want to be reported again to the welfare agency for neglecting you. We need to be careful about our reputation, now that I will marry Fritz."

I understood and nodded. "*Danke,* Mutti," I said. "No one will know that you're gone. I promise."

I then thought about her impending engagement and wondered what would become of me after she had married Fritz Neumann. Would he send me away so that both of them could be free of me?

I tried to put that out of my mind and quickly made my way to Andra Fischer's house. She lived at the edge of the other side of town. Andra was a year older than I, and I was proud that she had accepted me as her friend. When I arrived at her house, I joined the other girls, who were already playing games. We had a good time. And when later everyone made their farewells, Andra held me back. "Don't go yet, Ariane," she pleaded. "Stay a while longer. I don't want my party to end just yet."

Knowing that my my mother would be out all night, I quickly agreed. I figured that I would be home by bedtime. But if darkness were to fall before I got home, the glow of the gas lamps on the street would light my way. As always, the lamplighters would have made their rounds through their assigned areas in precise stopwatch fashion to light the burners. I loved the gas lamps because they often had been a source of comfort to me.

Frau Fischer had locked the window shutters of her apartment after the girls had left. She had closed the door behind them, commenting that a few dark clouds were gathering in the sky. "The weather is turning," she announced. "But if we get a storm, it won't be here until early morning."

The shutters prevented any sight or sound from entering the house. For that reason, we did not notice that a storm had descended over town quicker than Frau Fischer had expected. When it was time for me to leave and we opened the door, a strong gust of wind flung itself at us and blew big swirls of white flakes into the hallway.

"Oh my!" Frau Fischer exclaimed. "Look at all that snow! There will be a white Christmas after all. *Der Weihnachtsmann,* Santa Claus, will have a difficult time finding you in this thick white mess of soft snow, Ariane."

We stood admiring the sight. But when the wind picked up in speed and bellowed a discordant tune as it whipped around the trees in the street, a thick branch suddenly snapped and fell to the ground. Frau Fischer turned to me. "I cannot let you go home in this weather. I won't have one minute of peace but will worry about you. I will be wondering whether you will make it home alright. Moreover, even if it weren't snowing now, it would be too dark for you to leave now. No female should walk alone after sundown, especially not so close to the woods. One never knows whether another one of those predators from the barracks will escape again."

I knew that Frau Fischer was referring to the Russian soldiers who were stationed in a nearby military compound. Every woman was scared of them, because a few soldiers had previously made their way into German neighborhoods. They had waited in the shadows of houses or in a line of trees for female prey. It did not matter how old their victims had been. Several young and old women had been attacked and raped. Two of them had even been murdered. The Russian commandant of the compound had offered effusive apologies to the mayor of our town. He even had ordered the criminals to be executed. Yet, the harsh punishment had not been able to deter some of the soldiers from breaking curfew once again. Citizens in our town had complained violently, demanding that the Russian forces be withdrawn from our town. They wanted all to be returned to their homeland.

Frau Fischer, therefore, insisted that I stay overnight. "How can we get word to your mother?" She asked. She looked worried.

I assured her that I would not be missed. "My mother is not at home," I said. "She won't be back until morning."

Frau Fischer's face registered concern. "Where did she go to? Does she often leave you alone?"

"Yes," I nodded. "But don't worry. I'm used to it. She left me alone since I was very young."

"*Ach, Mädchen, Mädchen.* That is not right. Who cares for you when your mother is gone?"

I shrugged my shoulders and remained silent.

"Dear me!" Frau Fischer said. "I'm sorry to put you on the spot. But a young child needs to be cared for and not left alone."

I had not wanted to acknowledge that I often had been afraid to be left alone. Our apartment always felt spooky to me, especially at night.

Frau Fischer took my arm because she saw the expression on my face. "I did not mean to pry. Perhaps someone should have a talk with your mother. I am worried about your welfare, Ariane, even though you might be old enough now to be left alone. But, let's close the door and go inside to where it's warm."

She said nothing more about it; and when bedtime arrived, Andra and I cuddled up under the heavy feather covers that kept us snug and warm. We told each other jokes and giggled for a while. When morning arrived, neither of us could remember who had been the first one to fall into the arms of the sandman.

I could not remember the time when I had slept so comfortably. Only after waking did I notice the whine of the harsh wind that tried to bore its way under the wooden shutters. Andra and I dressed quickly and entered the kitchen where steaming cups of milk were waiting for us. I appreciated that Frau Fischer was kind enough to share her family's milk ration with me.

There had been occasions when I had stood in line at the milk store in town and had listened to the men, who had come to fetch their family's allotment of milk. They had shouted at the milkman and had pounded their fist on the counter. "We don't like to drink fat free milk. Where is the cream? Who gets it?"

The milkman trembled but continued ladling the milk into their pails with downcast eyes. I could tell that he was nervous. The bullies were larger and taller than he.

"Go ahead spill the information!" The men shouted again. "Who else would know but you!"

The milkman remained silent.

"You won't say because you are afraid of what *they* will do to you if you squeal on them. You know very well that the cream is skimmed off and given to the elite, the Communist pigs. People like you help them cheat us out of it."

The milkman finally spoke up softly. He assured the men and all the other customers in line that he, like the rest of us, had not laid eyes on cream or butter since the days of the war. He could barely recall what it tasted like. The people in line nodded their heads in support of him. They, too, missed the delicious sweet taste of butter on their bread instead of the pig's fat that everyone used for sandwich spread.

I felt sorry for him. He seemed to be an honest man. Not only that, but he had always been pleasant to me when I had come to fetch our ration of a quart of milk. On the days when the milk supply ran, he offered me *Molke* to take home. *Molke* is the liquid that is left after milk is made into cheese. He knew that I liked it, even though other kids refused to drink it. They hated the sour taste and shuddered at the sight of the deep yellow color that reminded them of horse pee.

After a breakfast of black bread and strawberry jam, Frau Fischer went to fetch the previously purchased pine tree from the backyard and dragged it into the living room.

"Come on girls," she cheerfully called. "You may help me decorate it."

I was more than happy to oblige. I knew that there would be no tree waiting for me in our house. As usual, my mother would keep her promise that she had made me eight years earlier. I had once asked her, "Mutti, how long will you be angry at me for having upset you when we lived in that house by the Havel?"

My mother had simply shrugged her shoulders and had replied. "As long as it takes. You almost gave me a heart attack when I saw you with the matches. You upset me so much that you almost killed me. Each time I look at you, I am reminded what you did to me. I will not reward you for misbehaving. Hopefully, you will remember that. Let that be a lesson to you."

I could never understand why my mother could hold a grudge this long. Nevertheless and for a while, I anticipated each subsequent Christmas to be different for us. But it was not. I finally gave up thinking about it. However, once again, and even though I did not expect much to change, I carried the tiniest hope in my heart that everything would be different. She seemed to be in love with Fritz. Did love not have the ability to soften a person's heart? I believed it. And, because of it, she would finally forgive me. And if she did, perhaps she would want to celebrate Christmas once again, even though she and Fritz Neumann were declared atheists.

Chapter Eight

Christmas Eve

After a warm lunch of flavorless cabbage soup, I left the warmth of Andra's home and walked along the edge of the river until I came to a steep embankment. Above was the drawbridge that I needed to cross. I crawled up to the road, digging my fingers into the snow in the hope that I would find something firm to keep me from sliding down. After several tries, I finally made it to the top. I stopped for a second to catch my breath. The bridge was the dividing line between New and Old Town. The Siberian-like air cut across my cheeks like forged, cold steel. I was shivering badly and could barely feel my toes and fingers. An especially forceful blast tore apart the flaps of my threadbare coat. I grabbed them, trying to close them again. It was useless, and I finally gave up. I intensely disliked this coat. It was a hand-me-down from Tanya Koslowski, a neighbor girl who lived across the street from us. Ever since we had moved into the neighborhood, her mother had sought to make me the object of her charity and dress me with her daughter's outgrown garments. My mother, who rarely accepted gifts from anyone, allowed Frau Koslowski such liberties. When I objected, she remarked, "These people get their clothes from the Golden West. The material is of good quality. You should be grateful, even if Tanya has worn some of the clothes down to bare threads."

I had known Tanya all my life. In contrast to her warmhearted mother, she was an uppity and proud girl. She carried her nose high in the air to signal her superiority over every other girl in the neighborhood. Her family had more money than any of us. The Koslowskis occupied an entire second floor of a house. They had more rooms than they could occupy. Tanya's father was a trader in furs and received daily truckloads of pelts. He took them and hung them to dry in several rooms of their home. His daughter lacked for nothing that his money could buy or trade for on the Black Market. She owned more clothes than any other girl in the neighborhood. What annoyed everyone was that she craved to be noticed. She strutted around like a colorful peacock, flaunting a new sweater one day or a dress and pair of leather shoes the next. As a result, not one of the girls wanted to be her friend. Each despised her for her obnoxious display of pride. I swore to myself that I would rather go without a stitch of clothing than to accept anything else from her. But then the winter arrived once more, and I began to freeze. I swallowed my pride and reluctantly accepted another one of her coats.

I hoped that she would give me a pair of her leather shoes one day. I looked down at my aching feet. The unbending pigskin of my own shoes had hardened in the frost. The back of them had ripped holes in the heels of my knee highs. Even though my feet were numb, I could feel large blisters rising up.

I had often dreamed of owning a pair of new leather shoes from the Golden West. I imagined them to feel like soft butter on my feet. They would be magical shoes, which would let me float over the uneven cobblestones in our neighborhood and past the envious eyes of Tanya. They would be vibrantly red, just like the color of fire hydrants. My grandmother had promised to search for such a pair; however, before she was able to find them and bring them to me, her Good Lord in Heaven took her to Him. I remembered how her departure had left me sad. She had loved me but was gone now. After she died, I never gave my dream shoes another thought.

I stepped close to the railing of the draw bridge and looked down at the frozen river. The ship traffic would not resume before the spring thaw.

After that, it would wake up from its wintry slumber and rid itself of its thick coat of ice. When it was flowing again, it would carry barges up and down its arms and on to the Elbe River and beyond.

Even though my life almost ended in the Havel, I continued to love it. After all, it was the very river on which my father had made his living many years before I was born. My grandfather owned a shipping business, which he inherited from my great-grandfather long before the Second World War. My father was my grandfather's apprentice. He taught him everything he needed to know about tug boats and navigation. He also instructed him in how to operate a business. My father's older brother was also an apprentice, but he died before my parents met. When my father went to war, my grandfather was left to run the business by himself.

When after the war the GDR became a Socialist-Communist State, our leaders decided to confiscate privately owned companies. Party functionaries arrived at my grandfather's doors and demanded the keys to his shipping operation. He was forced to hand them over without being given any kind of compensation. My grandfather was furious. He called everyone in high government a thief and a criminal. It did not take long before men in trench coats appeared at his doorstep once more. They warned him to let the matter rest. But my grandfather could not hold his tongue. Then, one day, he vanished from the face of the earth. My mother believed that her father-in-law was forcibly silenced. She did not say whether she mourned him, but confided that she would miss out on the occasional business profits, which my grandfather had promised to share with her. Soon, I came to understand that before the war, we had belonged to the class of the Bourgeoisie but that now we were poorer than most people.

I never worried about our lack of money but thought that it would be nice if we could live in a warmer and more comfortable place than the two-room apartment we occupied now. My consolation was that our landlord and our old neighbor were friendly. Unfortunately, neither of them were home tonight. Their presence would make the house feel less spooky. The owners, Herr and Frau Ritter, who lived in the apartment on the first floor, and Frau Meyer, who lived next door to us upstairs in a one-room efficiency place, had gone to celebrate Christmas with their own family members.

I liked Frau Meyer very much. Her room faced the back of the house. From her window, she could see oak trees and wild shrubs, which thrived in the moist and fertile soil below. In the summer, a carpet of wildflowers covered the ground beneath the trees around which bees swarmed and gathered their nectar. Birds of every kind made their nests in the trees. At night, owls hooted nonstop. Their cry penetrated the walls of our apartment. My mother claimed that they called for people, whose time had come to die, to follow them.

Sometimes Frau Meyer would open her door and catch me before I made my way downstairs. "Come and visit with me for a while, *Kindchen*," she would call in a hushed voice. "Let's sit by the window and watch the storks build their nests. They soon will have babies."

Frau Meyer knew about my mother's rule, which prohibited me from entering anyone's home. But, she paid no attention to it and gave me a conspiratorial smile. "It'll be our secret," she whispered.

I always went willingly into her room because her window gave a nice view over the roofs of the 15th Century section of Old Town. One could see portions of the thick wall, which once surrounded the settlement and shielded it from outsiders. Most of it had crumbled. The whole section of Old Town encircled a smaller inner core of houses that were established in the 11th Century. Everything in that inner core smelled of must and mold. No one living in the houses there seemed to mind the odor but was grateful to have a home to live in. Both the inner core and Old Town had survived the Thirty Year War and the Seven Year War. When later, bridges were built across the Havel river to make access easier, newer sections of town were added. They received the ingenious name of New Town. It was that part, which was destroyed in World War Two., and still lies in ruins.

I crossed the bridge into Old Town and imagined my mother being back from her date with Fritz Neumann. She would be angry with me for not having come home sooner. I knew that none of my explanation would be enough to keep her calm. I knew from experience that the more

I was trying to explain myself, the angrier she would get. I knew that punishment was awaiting me. On the positive side, the apartment would be warm. I would be able to sit near the tile oven and thaw out my frozen bones. The more I thought about it, the more I convinced myself that she might not be angry after all. If Fritz Neumann proposed marriage to her, she would be less inclined to yell at me. She might even be in good cheer, sitting in her favorite chair, sipping tea from the delicate Rosenthal china cup that she loved so much. The cup belonged to a fine bone colored tea service, which was given to her by an acquaintance who had escaped to the Golden West.

The woman had arrived one evening at the door of our apartment. "I know that you love beautiful things, Annie," she had announced, trying to catch her breath from having climbed the steep stairs. She had handed my mother a big box. "I know that you lost your china in the war. Here. I want you to have this. It's my gift to you."

Mutti had looked at her with a perplexed expression but accepted the gift. We hadn't known it then, but found out later that the woman fled the GDR that very night. She had committed *Republiksflucht*.

"Will you take us to the Golden West, too, Mutti?" I had asked. "We can live with Oma."

"Don't talk nonsense," she had replied. "Neither your grandmother nor I would survive each other if we were to live together in close quarters. And, going to live in a refugee camp is out of the question. It could be years before the West German government will find a place for us to live and give me a job."

So, we had stayed. My mother loved the tea service and made good use of it by brewing many pots of green tea. "We have our government's relations with China to thank for being able to buy this tea," she told me. "At least Walter Ulbricht has done something right amidst his many other failures." It was the only compliment that she ever gave the Goatee.

I always cherished the moments of my mother's tea ceremony because for a little while, peace would descend on our home. She would pour the pale, delicately fragrant liquid of China tea from the low belly of the Rosenthal pot into her cup and lean back in her chair. When it was cool enough, she would take the cup between her hands and take slow sips of tea. Then, she would reach for the small box of cigarette papers that lay on the small cocktail table next to her. She would slide a thin sheet of paper from it, make a crease in the paper, and begin to arrange several pinches of tobacco leafs into its fold and distribute them evenly. She would roll the paper into an oblong shape, lightly squeezing it into a perfectly rounded cigarette. She would lightly moisten the edges of the paper with her tongue and seal them. After reviewing her artwork, she would place it into her long porcelain cigarette holder, take her cigarette lighter, and flick it. She would place the holder between her lips and pull the smoke through it. Satisfied, she would tilt her head back, purse her lips into a shape of an "O" and blow blue circles of smoke into the air. She would sit without speaking, following the ringlets of smoke as they curled away from her. They soon dissolved into nothingness.

Finally, she would take the last few sips from her tea and spin the dregs in the cup. For me, this would be a sign of her next ritual, which I knew by heart. I was always mesmerized by it. My mother would bend her head and stare at the pattern of the tea leaves that would emerge at the bottom of her cup.

"The array of the leaves is auspicious and foretell my future," she said.

I remember how I became excited. "Will you read me my fortune, too?"

She answered laconically. "I don't need to do that. Your future is intertwined with mine."

I remember how her answer unsettled me. I stared at her, was afraid that I would find myself as unhappy as she was. I knew that I wanted things to be different for myself. But I also knew that I needed to grow up before I could make it so. Until then, I looked forward to the calm moments of tea ceremony. They brought peace to our apartment. And for a little while, everything was alright with the world.

I was thinking that perhaps after tonight everything would be alright forever. I pushed against the wind as I hurried through Old Town.

When I finally reached our street, I was pleasantly surprised to find our neighborhood lying in tranquility. The glow of candles shown through the windows of the crooked houses. For once, the neighbors had left their living room windows uncovered by curtains or shutters. It had been a gesture of good will and Christmas spirit. The snow, which had piled up in front of the windows, reflected the golden, mellow glow of the candles. The entire street appeared bathed in radiant splendor.

I was overcome by the wish to be part of that brightness inside of one of the homes. I wanted to share the comfort and peace, which I imagined was residing there, with others. But I knew that it could not be. I averted my eyes and continued walking until I reached the house where I lived. I climbed the stone steps and pushed hard on the heavy oak door to open it. The ground floor was unlit, as always. I peered up to the second floor. It, too, was dark. I stiffly reached for the banister and pulled myself up step by step. The worn steps groaned in resistance to being walked on. Frau Meyer once told me that the staircase objected to our feet because it was tired from having been trampled on for the past two centuries.

Upstairs, I fumbled for our door handle and pushed down on it. The door, too, resisted to being opened. I pushed harder. It finally gave way, squealing in its rusty hinges.

"Mutti, I am home!" I called out.

My heart beat loudly in my chest. Would she be angry? There was no answer.

"I am sorry, Mutti!" I called again through the closed door. "The storm was really bad last night. Frau Fischer thought that it would be best if I slept at her house."

Again, I heard no sound, no scolding. I breathed a sigh of relief. I would be safe. I knew from experience that whenever she was not answering me immediately, she would not be eager to argue much. I walked across the kitchen and carefully opened the door to the living room. To my surprise, the room was empty. I knew that she could not be far. The door to the apartment was unlocked when I came home. Perhaps she was fetching coal briquettes from the basement to heat the stove. She would be annoyed if I went looking for her.

I shivered as I placed my wet coat over the unsteady chair that stood next to the table. The kitchen was wrapped in the usual wintry bleak early evening murkiness. Only the gas lamp under our windows below, which the lamplighter tended to earlier, was casting a faint bluish glow through the window. I searched for matches to light a few candles. My fingers refused to cooperate; but finally, after a few strikes, the match lit. I reached for the empty copper kettle on the gas stove and walked over to the faucet. Relieved that the pipes had not frozen, I filled the kettle with water and heated it to a lukewarm temperature before I poured it into a white enamel wash bowl. Then I crouched low to soak both my hands and feet at once.

The stillness around me was eerie and palpable. The longer I sat waiting for life to return into my hands and feet the more disturbing the emptiness of the room became. A deep melancholy hung over the place. Where *was* my mother? She should have returned from her date with Fritz Neumann. Hadn't she told me that she would be back by noon this day? What took her so long down there in the cellar? But, if she was not downstairs, why had she left the door unlocked?

Soon I convinced myself that I knew the reason for her absence. An involuntary smile spread across my face. Mutti had found herself happy and carefree after Fritz had asked for her hand in marriage. The joy she had felt had left her unusually scatterbrained and careless. Surely, things would be easier for us from now on. Our lives would improve because Fritz was able to obtain supplies that we could not get. Perhaps Mutti was still celebrating the joyous event.

As quickly as my smile had come, it left. I felt betrayed. I would, once again be alone. I would have to make it through another cheerless holiday by myself. There would be no Christmas celebration, no festive trimmings or presents. The fantasy that I had entertained in my head for mere seconds, the wish to spend a happy holiday with her, quickly vanished. She once again had chosen to spend an important evening with someone else. I began to pity myself. Did she not realize that I needed her too? The nurturing that I had received from both my uncle and grandmother had helped to quell my lonely feelings in the past. But both of them were gone now. There was no one else left to comfort me.

I got up, dried my feet, and limped into the living room to check on the stove. The tiles were icy cold. I did not need to open the little iron door below and look inside to know that the embers, which were brightly glowing a day earlier, died down a long time ago. If I wanted to be warm, I needed to fetch coal briquettes from the cellar below. It would take more than an hour before the stove would be warm enough to heat the room. I felt tired and depressed. I decided to forgo that pleasure. Instead, I would crawl under my bed covers and shiver until I generated enough heat to be warm. I would pull the covers over my head and shut out the room with its loneliness. I would refuse to allow any other thoughts of sadness make me more miserable than I already was. I would suffocate them before they could overwhelm me.

I would think of my grandmother and the care she had given me on one particular Christmas Eve when I had been very young. "Christ was born on this very night," she had said. "He came to set things right."

That thought suddenly screeched to a halt. If that was true, if Christ came to set things right, then why did I feel so empty inside? I would cry myself to sleep. I would sob as loud as I could. I would make noise. I would scream and fling my hurt against the walls. I would share it with the apartment, as I had done so often before.

But moments later, I changed my mind. I was too tired, too depressed, to have a crying fit. Instead, I lit two more candles and stuck them into pewter holders. I would go to bed, roll myself up into a ball and pretend that all was well. Instead of screaming, I would hum a Christmas song. Oma had said that singing lifted the spirit. I would sing and imagine myself being in a better place. I would sing until the hurt went away.

Chapter Nine

My Shocking Discovery

The door to the bedroom opened with the rusty creak of dry hinges. I placed the candles on a shelf above my bed to undress. I casually glanced over at my mother's bed. For a moment I stood stupefied. She was at home! I stepped closer. She seemed to be fast asleep. It disturbed me that she was lying uncovered in the frostbitten room. The flickering candles cast a long, spooky shadow across her face. It made her look unwell. I thought that she must be exhausted from her engagement party. I stepped closer and carefully attempted to pull the comforter from under her and cover her with it. I could not get it to move. I reached for her shoulder to shake her awake.

Why was she not waking up? A fearful thought gripped me. But no! It was nonsense. I pushed the thought aside. She was happy when I left the apartment yesterday. If my mother felt frozen to the touch, it was because she has lain uncovered for a long while now, I imagined her being exhausted from having partied all night. That was it! That had to be it! No need to give in to panic. She was finally resting from the years of struggle. She would marry Fritz Neumann. He was not a bad man, even though he was a Communist. A marriage to him would make us a family. She would no longer have to struggle on alone. She would be able to pay the bills instead of having to depend on other boyfriends for gifts.

I stepped back and felt something under my foot. It was her pill bottle with the heart medication. It was empty. Stark terror rose in me. But, no! I fought against the racing thoughts that attempted to invade my head. It was Christmas Eve! No one left like this on Christmas Eve! She was merely taunting me, just as she used to when when she described the fiery oven, which would burn her body after she was dead. She found joy in watching my face. She smiled when I begged her to stop.

No! This was a trick. She was only *pretending* to be dead. She wanted to teach me a lesson in obedience. She wanted to punish me for having stayed away overnight because she wanted me home in bed after dark. Yes, that was it! I knew that I needed to apologize to her.

My voice trembled. "Mutti, I am sorry. Please don't play with me like this! *Bitte, bitte*, yell at me. Be angry. But please say something! I need you to say something! Please, tell me that I am making life difficult for you. But, please, speak to me!"

Hard as I begged, she made no sound. She did not move. I bent down to listen to a flutter of breath. There was none. I stared at her waxen face and body. She must be dead, really dead! Was this what death looked like? I had never seen dead people up close. But wait, I *had* seen them. They had littered the street during the bomb raid. But that was different. We had been at war then. People were killed by others. Everyone said that it was a greater sin to kill themselves. How could my mother take her own life when neither I, nor anyone else I knew, wanted her to die? How could she leave me without a sign, without telling me just once in my life that she loved me? I had always craved to receive just one tender look from her, one sweet word! I begged for it now, but it did not come. I heard a cry before my thoughts became disjointed and dizziness overtook me. I heard the cry ever so faintly. It sounded like the cry of a wounded animal. After that, my head stopped spinning and everything went dark.

How long I had lain on the floor, I did not know. I picked myself up and stared at the sight before me. It was true! She was gone. I could feel no emotions now. The place where my heart should have been felt hard and frozen. Zombie-like, I turned and walked into the living room where

I lowered myself into her favorite chair. After a while I became aware that I needed to do something. My brain was fuzzy, and I could not make out what it was that I needed to do.. So I let it slide.

On the little round cocktail table next to the chair lay a rolled cigarette, which she had left. I reached for it with shaky hands and placed it between my lips. I struck a match, and when the cigarette lit, I pulled on it. Instantly, the smoke closed up my lungs, and my eyeballs felt as though they wanted to pop out of my head. I choked and gasped for air as I flung the cigarette into the ashtray. Moments later, I remembered what I needed to do. I had to go for help, needed to fetch Herr Ritter, our landlord! I walked to the door before I remembered that I was alone in the house. He was gone. If he was not there, I must find someone else to tell. I must run to the neighbors across the street perhaps. But no, I could not do that. Mutti would be angry. I needed to keep her secrets. Did she not always insist that I keep quiet about what took place in our home?

"Swear to me that you will not tell anyone what is taking place in our apartment," she said. "I trust you to do that. You are old enough to keep secrets."

I had been so proud that she had trusted me to do something for her. I finally had become valuable to her. I thought that if she could not love me, then I had to show her that she could like me for something I could do well. I swore to her to stay silent. I knew how she loathed gossip, knew that every other woman in the neighborhood had talked about her for years. If I were to go to any of them now, she would never forgive me. No. I would wait for Herr Ritter to come home. He knew my mother, knew of her depression. He and Frau Meyer had saved her once before. Herr Ritter would know what to do.

My mother had often told me that she wanted to be cremated. She did not want to be buried in the ground because she was afraid to be eaten by bugs. My young mind, however, was convinced that the reason for wanting to be cremated was that she wanted her soul to burn up with her body. She wanted to make sure that God would not get to it in case she had a soul. My grandmother had often suggested that my mother's soul would burn in hell if she would not hurry up and repent her heathen way of life. Mutti said that she did not believe that she had a soul. I think that she really didn't know that for sure. And, just in case she found herself to be wrong, she wanted her soul to burn before God could lay his hands on it.

I stared at her frozen body and wondered whether her soul had become frozen as well. If that was the case, it would be stuck, unable to escape before Herr Gerhard, the body collector, would arrive with his wagon and old and tired horses. Perhaps her soul would remain inside of her body even after he nailed the casket shut. It would make my mother happy if it were to burn up, along with her body, in the hot fire of the crematory.

I knew Herr Gerhard. I had often tested his patience when I had tortured him with questions about death and the afterlife. Finally, when his patience snapped, he became so angry that he did not want to speak to me at all. I came to know him from his many visits to our neighborhood. I was six or seven years old when I engaged him in a conversation. "Why do your horses wear these awful shades?" I asked. "How can they find their way to the cemetery if they only can look straight ahead and don't know at which corner to turn?

Herr Gerhard laughed. "They are called blinders," he answered. "The horses are old and sensitive to everything they see and hear. They don't like cars and get disturbed by them. It's important that they keep their hoofs steadily on the ground when I am hauling a boxes of corpses in the cart. It would be a disaster if the boxes were to slide into the gutter and break open. The blinders keep them calm."

"Yes, but how do the horses know where to make a turn if they can't see?" I insisted.

"When I pull on the left or the right side of the reins, my horses know where I want them to go. I make sure that they don't stumble up onto the pedestrian walk and turn the cart over. The caskets would break and scatter dead bodies all over the street. God knows, I already picked up too many limbs and body parts in my lifetime."

"Eek…" I let out a shriek and stared at him in disbelief. "You've collected arms and legs, and such things? When did you do that?"

"That was my job on the battlefield during the war." He observed me quizzically. "By the way, what is your name? I see you hanging around my wagon each time I come to do a job in this neighborhood."

"My name is Ariane," I answered. "I live on this street. But, please tell me about the war. Was it bad in Russia? My father was there as well."

Herr Gerhard rested one foot on the wheel of his cart and told me awful things that happened in Russia. He was a field medic and survived battles and the freezing cold, which most of his comrades did not.

After he finished speaking, he began to stare pensively into space. Then he commented with a nonchalant look in his eyes, "You ask too many questions for someone your age. Why don't you run along and play now."

Our conversation came to an end. The next time he came around, he was not as nice. I wondered, then, whether he was as moody as my mother was. Nevertheless, whenever Herr Gerhard and his companion showed up in our neighborhood, I took a stand next to the cart and waited for them to appear from whichever house they had entered to box up the dead. Then I watched them load up the pine box. When Herr Gerhard saw me, he would glare at me with annoyance. On occasion, he would shout, "Thunderbolts and Lightening, *Mädchen*! It is you again! This is not a circus show! How do you know where to find us?"

"Well, it's easy," I responded. "I recognize your old horses. You always park them in front of a house where someone died. I just wanted to see whom the owls called to go away with them last night."

"The owls?" He seemed confused. I could see that he did not know about the meaning of their hooting and such but could tell that he was annoyed. I quickly added, "I kept your horses company. I shooed the big and ugly iridescent looking flies away, too. They kept picking at the eye lids of the poor animals."

I probed his weather-beaten face for signs of danger. If he would become very angry, I would turn and run away. The undertaker held my stare with watery gray eyes before deciding to give me a crooked half smile. "*Ach so. Ach so.* You are concerned about the horses. There's nothing I can do about the flies."

Since he was done speaking and did not yell at me, I interpreted his response as permission to let me stand by the animals whenever he came into the neighborhood.

One particular hot and sultry August afternoon, Herr Gerhard's appearance on our street left me very sad. Dark, heavy thunderclouds formed on the horizon. I knew that soon there would be a downpour, a cloud break, as we so often experienced in the summer. I heard the rumble of thunder in the distance, and the air began to smell of sulfur. I was returning from doing an errand for my mother. When I approached the house of Herr and Frau Schulz, I stopped in my tracks. The windows of their upstairs apartment stood open. I could hear Herr Gerhard's booming voice but could not tell whether he was here on business or whether he was paying a social visit to Herr and Frau Schulz.

Old Frau Schulz was my friend. I knew her to be a gentle woman who always had a kind word for me. We made each others' unconventional acquaintance when she looked out of her window one day and called down to me.

"*Hallo, Mädchen*," she waved and called in a brittle voice. "What is your name?"

"It's Ariane," I replied, interrupting a lone game of hopscotch.

"*Kindchen*, would you be so kind as to go to the store for me? I need some food for me and my husband. Our old bones are not cooperating very well today. The staircase has become too steep for us."

My usual playmates were nowhere in sight, and there was nothing else to occupy myself with. Therefore, I happily agreed to do the errand for her. Frau Schulz went to fetch her ration stamps and money, stuffed them into a little pouch and threw them down together with a shopping bag.

"Don't worry, Frau Schulz." I called up to her. "I will be back in a flash with your groceries. That is, if the line is not too long. If it is, it will take a little while longer. And if the store does not have what you want, I will run across town and see if I can find what you want."

"That's a good girl." She smiled gratefully and waved. "Just get me what is available, child. But be careful. Don't fall before you get to the store. You seem to run more than you walk. I know, because I've often watched you from my window."

On that day, she and I became friends. Whenever I passed her house thereafter and looked up, she opened the window and waved at me.

On that particularly oppressive and hot day, Herr Gerhard seemed to take his time with whatever he was doing upstairs. I felt impatient, needed to know if something had happened to my dear Frau Schulz. I opened the front door of the house and peeked inside. When my eyes adjusted to the dimness, I saw that the door to the upstairs apartment stood open. I called up with an anxious voice. "Herr Gerhard, has something happened to Herr or Frau Schulz?"

"Who is it that wants to know? We're busy right now!"

"It's Ariane! Please tell me what has happened."

Herr Gerhard stuck his head around the door frame and looked down. "*Donnerwetter nochmal*! Thunderbolts and Lightning, girl. It's you again!"

"Is it Herr Schulz whom you have come for?"

"No, girl. I'm here for both of them. And now, off with you! This is not a place for you to be right now!"

"But, Herr Gerhard, it cannot be possible," I cried. "It cannot be both of them. Were they sick? Did they eat some bad fish or die from a vaccination?"

My mind could not wrap itself around the thought that two people could die in the same room at the same time. I had heard that the local market had recently sold spoiled fish and that some people had died from food poisoning. In addition, we heard that some people, who were vaccinated against influenza, died from a batch of bad serum. Following that, people refused the serum. The government took action and sent health workers into every neighborhood, where they set up tables at which the head of each household was asked to register the names of every member in his family. The workers received orders not to hand over food ration cards unless each person showed proof of having received his vaccination. My mother heard about the tainted vaccine. She refused to let us both be vaccinated. Instead, she went to find someone who would help her circumvent government orders. I believed that it was Fritz Neumann who came to our rescue. Mutti, later, walked away with ration cards in hand that allowed us to buy food.

"I guess the old couple wanted to leave this world together when their time came," Herr Gerhard growled at me that day. "Go home, girl! Leave the dead to me!"

I did not wait until the boxes with the corpses were loaded onto the cart but turned and ran home. Tears were streaming down my face. How could it be that such lovely people were taken from this world at the same time? Perhaps they took their own lives. But why would they do that? They had always smiled and had never complained. I would miss them. I would especially miss Frau Schulz. She brought rays of sunshine into my young life.

I arrived distraught and out of breath at my home. "Mutti, Frau and Herr Schulz are dead," I sobbed.

My mother became irritated. "What's wrong with you? Everyone has to die sooner or later. The couple was old. What's more, you didn't even know them."

"I *did* know them," I whined. "They were nice. How can they just leave without saying goodbye to me? Didn't they know that I would miss them?"

"Should they have asked your permission to die? You were nothing to them. Why should they care about the feelings of a child?"

My mother did not know that the old woman's dependable presence at her window gave me comfort. Even though she and I often just waved to each other in passing, and without saying a word, I was able to count on her being there. I looked up, and when I saw her wrinkled face transformed into a radiant smile, I felt cared for. Knowing that made my day brighter.

"She *did* care about me!" I stubbornly called to my mother as I stomped back downstairs to sit on the steps in front of our house to grieve the loss of a familiar face.

The next time I saw Herr Gerhard, he refused to talk to me. But, I was persistent. "Please tell me why they died," I begged in a shaky voice. "Do you believe that Frau Schulz went to heaven to be with the angels? They must have come to fetch her because she was such a nice person."

Herr Gerhard squinted at me with bloodshot eyes and responded grumpily that he was getting tired of answering my questions about life and death. "Why are you so interested in the dead and whether angels come to fetch them? You are too young to concern yourself with that subject. Questions about winged creatures or whatever happens to us in the afterlife are best answered by a philosopher or a priest. I am neither one. My job is to haul away the bodies. That's all. If you want to know more, go home and ask your parents. Perhaps they can enlighten you."

His foul mood disturbed me. Why could he not understand that I needed to know what would happen to people after they died? Whom could I ask if not him? He, of all people, would know more about the subject than anyone else. I needed to know because my mother talked about dying so often, especially after nightfall arrived. She would sit me down at the table, pull up a chair across from me, and describe to me her own demise. Her tale would fill me with such fear and trepidation that I began to shake. I would stick my fingers into my ears to shut her out. I begged her to stop. It was useless. She demanded that I listen to her description of her cremation. The pictures, which she painted, were horrid. She seemed to find pleasure in seeing me so shaken. "The fire is very hot, and everything will go very quickly," she assured me. "Before you know it, nothing but ashes will be left of me."

After such frightful evening, a rash would appear on my arms and chest. It would remain there for several weeks.

"It's nothing contagious," the doctor simply said. "But if you are concerned, keep the child quiet and in bed for a day if you are worried that she'll infect others."

Because I was forever worried that my mother would die and be burned in a hot fire, how then, could I tell Herr Gerhard that it was imperative for me to know the truth about death? I needed to know whether everyone had a soul and whether it escaped before the body was cold. I wanted to know whether he had seen a soul and whether the angels came to take away the bad ones along with the good. I needed to know whether my grandmother was correct. She had said that the wings of the angels were not strong enough to fly away with bad people's souls because their sins weighed them down.

Now, that my mother had done the unthinkable, I was worried more than ever about her future in the afterlife. I blamed myself for not having come come home the day before. If I had, she might have lived many more years. And, had she lived, she might have let go of a few of her sins. She might, then, have been light enough for the angels to carry her to God.

Chapter Ten

Mutti's Search for Heaven

I remained sitting in near stupor when a rustling sound made me lift my head. To my left appeared a glowing form of pale amber. It seemed to have come right through the wall. Colors of blue and pink sparked from its edges as it moved around the room with a crackling sound. I remembered hearing such noise before when after a summer storm I saw two downed electric wires lying in the street. They slowly snaked toward each other. When they touched, bluish-white sparks burst in all directions. The noise they made sounded like tiny exploding firecrackers.

I felt no fear but knew that the bulb-like shape held the signature of my mother's essence. It was beautiful to look at; yet, it appeared very tortured. The form seemed to speak to me. What it communicated filled me with a hollow sadness. Its first communication was one of regret, the second one spoke of despair. I watched the form circle the room once, then twice. I longed for it to tell me, "I love you my daughter." Instead, it let me know that it was in great turmoil. It appeared that my mother's essence was searching for that certain place of peace, which it knew existed. Only, her soul was unable to find its way to it.

I watched her form circle one more time before it disappeared in the opposite direction from which it came. I asked myself whether I had gone mad or whether I had imagined it all. No, I decided. I knew that I had seen it clearly. I also knew without a doubt that it had spoken to me.

I became sadder yet and made myself a bed by pulling two chairs together before I drew the feather covers tightly around me. I was colder than I had ever been before. My body was shaking violently. The frost in the room was almost unbearable. So was my worry about my mother. Where would she spend her eternity if she would not find the door to heaven? She had appeared as broken on the other side as she had been alive. She had seemed so desperately alone.

But so was I. I was alone. I felt abandoned and sacrificed. Sudden nausea cramped my body. I ran to the kitchen sink and threw up.

The winter air had painted delicate patterns of ice flowers on the windows. They blocked out the light from the gas lamp below. I could hear the wind pick up in renewed strength. It whistled and hooted and left an unearthly sound in its trail. I lay curled up, shaking. Every nerve in my body felt raw. My chest shuddered with each breath that I drew in and breathed out. I began to pray. I did not know how I would be able to make it through the night. My first thought was that I did not want to live either. Yet, I could not leave the earth as Mutti had done. Not now, anyhow. I was afraid to go to hell for my neglect of my mother. I was afraid to be punished for having broken my promise to my grandmother. I began to pray for forgiveness for that and for every sin that I had ever committed in my young life. I prayed, just as my grandmother had taught me to do. I called on her, wanting her to present my case to God.

Suddenly, I heard a hum close to my ears. Then a voice was speaking. "Don't despair, *Liebchen,* my love. Trust Him."

I shot up straight like an arrow from my make-shift bed. "Oma?" I called. But as quick as the voice came, it was gone. Was I going mad? In the candlelight, I could see the vapors of my breath rising in the air. A moment later, the words of the 23rd Psalm from the Bible came to me. They spilled out of my mouth, just as Oma had taught them to me. *The Lord is my Shepherd.* Pictures of a green meadow and a running stream appeared before my inner vision; and, there, peacefully stretched out next to me, lay a lion. He crept closer and kept me warm. I stopped wondering whether I had gone over the edge of sanity. But it was alright with me if I had. I kept holding on to the serene picture in my mind and continued to recite the words. *He maketh me lie down in green pastures...He restoreth my soul... Surely goodness and mercy shall follow me all the days of my life...*

The psalm became my lifeline, my survival in my dark night. It kept me from drowning in a pool of despair and insanity. I kept repeating it until sleep came to take me away. It came and offered me a respite from the wounds of life and fear of damnation.

A loud knock at the door woke me. Sleep dazed, I rubbed my eyes and promptly fell through the crack of the chairs. I landed on the floor. The jolt woke up my body, but my brain was slow to follow. Was it morning already? The ice layers on the windows had grown in thickness. They obscured the light of the new day. It took a minute before I remembered the events of the previous evening. I wondered how I was able to sleep at all.

The knock on the door turned into a near pounding sound. I stumbled to it with my feather covers trailing behind me. Frau Meyer stood before me with a cheerful face. "*Guten Morgen,* Ariane, *Kindchen,*" she announced brightly. Still asleep, are you?" She pressed a colorful, star shaped Christmas plate into my hands. I saw that it held an assortment of holiday sweets.

"*Frohe Weihnachten!* Merry Christmas!" She gave me a penetrating look. "Gracious me. You *were* asleep! *Entschuldigung.* I am sorry, child, for waking you. I just returned from my daughter's house. She sends her good wishes and hopes that Santa Claus was good to you this year."

I avoided old Frau Meyer's eyes and pulled the covers tighter around my shoulders. She reached out and touched my face. "*Ach, Mädchen,* you are cold. The fire in your oven must have gone out. Well, I suppose that your mother will soon get up and make it cozy and warm in the apartment."

My neighbor's gaiety totally overwhelmed me. I remained mute.

"Well, then, I will leave you to your sweets. Don't eat too many of them before you get some breakfast into your stomach."

When I still said nothing, she responded by wrinkling her forehead. She leaned closer and peered into my eyes. "Perhaps you have another case of laryngitis, which seems to trouble you so often? Has the doctor found no cure for it yet?"

I shook my head. "No."

"Well, then. If your throat is not hurting too much, just snack on a few little marzipan potatoes and some cookies that my daughter has sent along. That will keep you busy until your mother gets up, *ja?*"

I put my head down, wondering whether I should give up my secret to her instead of waiting for Herr Ritter to come home. She spoke again before I could make up my mind as to what to say.

"What is the matter, my girl? You look frightfully pale. Why don't you go back to bed for a while."

A big sigh heaved my body and escaped in short, labored spurts. "Huh-huh-huh." My breath made a wheezing sound. I tried to silence it but she noticed my breathing. She had known me long enough to know that something was amiss. There were times when she found me sitting on the uppermost step of our staircase with my hands covering my face when she opened her door. Each time, I was unable to hide my tears.

"What is wrong this time, child? What has upset you so? Did Santa Claus not bring you the gifts that you wanted?"

With a resolute gesture she squeezed past me into our living room. "Oh, I see. You poor girl." Her voice took on a soothing quality. "I see what is troubling you so. There's no Christmas tree. And perhaps there were no presents either?" She patted me on the head. "Never mind that now. I'll tell you what we'll do. You come over to my apartment after I have made a nice fire. I will let you light the candles on my little tree. Then you and I we will sit and keep each other company. Would you like that? I am sure your mother won't object to it today. If she does, I will tell her that all children are entitled to experience *some* Christmas cheer. That is why the Christmas child came to earth, was it not? He came to bring happiness into this world. Don't you agree?"

I did not know that Frau Meyer believed in God or Jesus but found comfort in hearing her speak just like my grandmother. How could

I tell her without feeling ashamed what my mother had done on His birthday?

"Has your mother gone out already or is she recovering in bed from a late night out?" I was aware that Frau Meyer's patience with me was leaving her. "Speak, child!" She demanded.

"No. She... she's in there." I pointed to the bedroom.

"*Na ja, na ja*. Well, then. *Gut dann*. If she is still sleeping, we will leave her to it. Why don't you heat some water, wash your face, and come over to my room in a few minutes?" She smiled softly and turned to leave our apartment.

I could not bear the pressure in my chest any longer and took heart. I began to sputter, "Wait! Please wait, Frau Meyer! *Bitte*, do not leave! Please help me! I don't know what to do!"

"I knew there was something troubling you. What is the matter, child?"

I pointed to the bedroom. "Mutti is in there. Please go and look."

Frau Meyer resolutely walked over to the bedroom door and knocked. When no response came, she opened it. At the sight of my mother, who appeared to be even deader in the gloom of the wintry morning light than she looked last night, a long gasp escaped her. She turned around and stared at me. All blood drained from her face when she called, "*Oh Gott, Oh Gott, Oh Gott*," in quick succession and threw up her hands. "Oh, no, dear lord! What has she done to herself! Oh my dear child, my dear child! *Mädchen*! What has your mother done to you! Oh, God! Oh God! She has finally done it!"

Frau Meyer became frenzied. "I must call Herr Ritter to help. I must go downstairs." She took a few steps forward. I saw that she was as confused as I was last night. "*Ach*, but, no, he is not at home. It's Christmas day. A telephone, then. I must find a telephone. There is one close to the river, by the *Kino*. Wait here, my girl. I hope that the phone there is in working order. Sometimes the boys in the neighborhood break it when they play with it. I must hurry. I must call the undertaker."

She climbed down the stairs with her short crooked legs but quickly turned and climbed back up again. "A coat, I need to get my coat. And a scarf."

Frau Meyer was in a tizzy. She ran to her room next door and grabbed her coat and shawl from a hook and made her way down again. Before she opened the main door, she turned to me and called, "You wait here, Ariane. Don't do anything foolish."

She pulled the door open and was assaulted by a strong gust of wind that left swirls of thick, heavy snowflakes on the floor. I seated myself on the top step of the landing, feeling lighter, relieved that help was on its way.

Three quarters of an hour passed before Frau Meyer returned. I had dozed off with my head leaning against the wall but jerked up when I heard her panting breath on the staircase. Dim light shown through the half moon shaped glass window above the front door below and I saw as she grasped the banister with her arthritic fingers to pull herself upwards in slow motion. Once in her room, she took off her coat and shawl. The icy air and wind had taken a toll on her appearance. Snowflakes had made their nest in her disheveled gray hair. Her cheeks and nose were frost bitten, and her hands looked discolored.

"The phone at the *Kino* was out of order. When I found another, I could not reach the undertaker." Frau Meyer was out of breath. "It took a long while before someone answered the phone at the police station. Even though it is still early in the day, the Vopos seemed to have helped themselves to a bit of holiday cheer already. God only knows how long it will take before they will send someone to pick up your mother's body."

She reached for my hand. "*Kindchen*, come. Sit down. You must not go back into your apartment. We will wait together in my place. It is not right that a child should carry out a deathwatch over her mother's body. I will make us a good fire in the stove. You can help me with it."

She went to her *Schrank* and found another shawl to wrap around me. "*Ach Kindchen,* you feel as frozen as I am. I do not know how your nerves could withstand the horror of it all. Surely, you must be in shock, not really comprehending what has taken place. God help you through this awful tragedy."

The old woman busied herself with the fire that refused to burn. The wood belched and fumed. She grabbed the iron poker and continued to stoke it, pulling the pieces apart and rearranging them into a different order. The low flame began to spit black spirals of soot laden clouds through the little iron door and out into the room. Frau Meyer continued to coax and prod the wood to feed it air. Not long after, the wood hissed. It made small crackling noises before it allowed the flames to rise.

"Soon it will be warm in here," she comforted us both. "Meanwhile, I will heat up some *Ersatz* coffee for us."

She put an enameled pot on her little one-eyed gas burner and heated the two or three day old substitute coffee that she prepared for herself before leaving for her daughter's house. "I hope someone will come soon," she mumbled as she worked.

I could tell that she was badly shaken and that she did not know what words of comfort to give me. I knew that she, too, was trying to come to terms with the final deed of my mother.

Frau Meyer was no stranger to my mother's depressive moods. She had even rescued her once from killing herself on a nice summery day. I was playing with my friends somewhere in the neighborhood that day. My mother came home early from work. The house was quiet. Frau Ritter was doing whatever she occupied herself with while her husband was on duty at the fire station. Frau Meyer spent her time watching the birds outside her window. My mother had turned on the radio. After a while, the signals from RIAS Berlin became scrambled and squealed loudly, making unearthly and cacophonous sounds. The irritating, high pitched noise spilled through our walls into Frau Meyer's room. It jarred her ears. She went to knock on our door, wanting my mother to change the station. When there was no answer, she let herself into the apartment. To her alarm, she found Mutti lying on the sofa with an empty bottle of pills beside her. She ran downstairs and found Herr Ritter, who just arrived home from work. He took my unconscious mother to the hospital.

When my mother returned to the apartment a few days later, I anxiously begged her to tell me why she wanted to do die. "Did I do something bad?" I asked fearfully.

She seemed surprised at first, then became annoyed. "Don't bother me with any of your questions."

"But I want to know." My voice trembled. "Did I do something wrong to make you feel tired and sad again?"

Her first inclination was to brush me off once more, but she changed her mind. "Well, since you insist, I will tell you what the problem is," she stated. "Life is not easy. I barely can find my way through it. It is even more difficult for me since I have to care for you. I wished I hadn't let your father talk me into keeping you before you were born. But how could I know that he would simply abandon me and leave me to raise you alone? I am tired of life, but everyone keeps reminding me of my responsibilities to you."

I stared at her wide eyed, shocked. "I am sorry that I cause you so much trouble, Mutti. But Vati, he *had* to go to war and leave me with *someone*. He didn't abandon you on purpose. It isn't his fault that he was told to go to war and was killed." Secretly I hoped that he wasn't dead. But, if he wasn't, why did he not come home?

"There you go again, believing that you know the answer to everything when you are a mere child who knows nothing! You're just like your father. He, too, had his own special brand of logic. You just stay out of my affairs."

I knew that I needed to be on my best behavior around her and promised myself that I would be a good daughter. I wanted to make her happy so that she would want to live. I did not mind that she compared me to my father, but I minded that she despised us both. Why did it make her so angry that I looked or behaved as he had? I was convinced that she liked him once. After all, she married him.

After my mother's previous attempt of suicide, a social worker paid us a visit. She directed my mother to a specialist. He prescribed rest and sent her to a health resort to soothes her nervous condition. I, in turn, became the ward of the State and was sent on a long vacation to the island of Rügen. That was a happy time in my life, and I often wished to be back there again.

I moved closer to the tile oven, which had warmed up. Frau Meyer put her arm around me and rocked me from side to side. "*Kindchen*," she asked, "when did you find your mother in the apartment?"

"Late yesterday afternoon." I responded.

"In God's name, why did you not go for help right away?"

"I didn't know whom to go to, Frau Meyer. You and Mr. Ritter weren't at home, and everyone else in the neighborhood was celebrating Christmas Eve. Besides…"

I paused, recalling the scene that met me as I entered our street. It would have torn apart the serenity that lay over it. Telling anyone that my mother was dead would have started tongues wagging.

"It's alright, child. I know that you did your best. You don't need to say more." Frau Meyer reached for me and put her arm around my shoulder. "It is a good thing that I came home early from my daughter's house. You might have frozen to death had I not knocked on your door. Whatever made you stay with her all through the night?"

I shrugged my shoulders. "I don't know. I just did."

The old woman became pensive and stared ahead of herself, then shook her head. "Ariane, God only knows what it is that has made you so resilient." She sighed once more and muttered under her breath, "I think that the event has not sunk in entirely or has reached your understanding. Perhaps the full shock of it is yet to come. I must confess that I worried about you often. The walls between our places are thin, you know. As much as I was tempted to say something to your mother about the fuss she used to make with you, I kept quiet. She would have told me to stay out of her business, saying that I have no right to interfere with the raising of her child. I must admit that I was relieved when the social department sent you away occasionally. At least it gave you a break from it all."

Frau Meyer gave me a resigned look and added, "For what it's worth, I hope that God will forgive me for having spoken ill of the dead."

"Will I be taken to that terrible orphanage now?" I inquired in a shaky voice.

I remembered the orphanage in town that was filled to the brim with children. One of my girlfriends had been placed there earlier this year. I knew because I had knocked on her door one day, wanting her to come out and play.

"I can't come outside," she said.

"Why not?" I wanted to know. "Are you in trouble with your mother?"

She quickly pulled me into her apartment. "The STASI has arrested my parents. Swear that you won't tell anyone."

She said that the men took her parents but left her and her four young siblings behind. The neighbors finally called the welfare agency to come and take all of them away. I never saw any of them again, neither in town nor in school.

I looked at Frau Meyer and said with as much conviction as I could muster, "I will not let them take me there, Frau Meyer. I will run away if they come for me. I might even run to the Golden West."

The old woman responded with a worried sigh. "Who would take you in, my girl? There are no relatives left to care for you." She paused before she exclaimed, "But, wait. Don't you have an uncle who lives in town?"

"The STASI took him away a while ago. Mutti thinks that they made false allegations against him. He was not an activist but was a peace loving man. He is in prison; that is, if they did not kill him already. I, too, will die in a place like the orphanage, Frau Meyer."

Regret spread over the old woman's face. "Child, I would keep you here with me if I could. Unfortunately, that is not possible. Only relatives could take you now and keep you. But, don't worry about anything. Herr Ritter will be home soon and will know what to do. He will sort things out. Until then, you will be safe here with me." She looked at me to seek my approval. "Meanwhile, I will make you a nice little bed from blankets over there on the floor, right next to my own bed. I'll keep my little tile stove fed with briquettes so that it will keep us cozy and warm. No one will come to take you away during the Christmas and New Years holidays because all of the government offices are closed."

Frau Meyer appeared relieved that she found a temporary solution for my dilemma. She put her trust in our landlord. He always helped anyone who needed his assistance. .

I adored Herr Ritter and often imagined him being my father. He had the nicest smile of anyone I knew, and he was good to people. I remember how pleased he had been when he saw me looking so tanned and well after I had returned from my trip to Rügen on the Baltic Sea.

"You look very healthy, and your mother's condition has improved, as well," he had assured me. "Perhaps everything will be easier for the two of you from now on."

Even though I had wanted everything to be alright, it was not.

Chapter Eleven

1949
On the Island of Rügen

Iwas seven, going on eight, when a social worker came to our home and took me to the train station. On the way I learned that I would go to a home for children in Sellin, a small town that was located on a beautiful island in the Baltic. She said that it was a special and magical place, which was endowed with great earth energies.

"Albert Einstein visited it once and liked it very much," the social worker added. "You, too, will love it there. You will meet other children, just like you. They too, are getting a break from their chaotic homes."

I wore my best dress of dark blue velvet and white collar that was one of Tanya's hand-me-downs. For once, the dress suited my taste. The velvet was as soft as a kitten's fur. I felt as elegant as a princess when I put it on. On the train, I quickly formed friendships with all the girls who rode with me to the same destination. Silly as it may seem, I at first was convinced that they, as well as some of the boys, liked me because of my pretty dress. However, when after arriving on the island I changed into my old and worn clothes and my newly found friends still liked me, I knew that they liked me for myself. I was happy. I found that I was one of the youngest children in the home.

Our whole group of about a dozen kids spent glorious hours on the beach each day. We tumbled in the water or build sandcastles. I had forgotten my near drowning ordeal in the Havel river several years earlier and became known as the group's little sea nymph. I learned to swim under water and hold my breath. To my surprise, my friends wanted me to teach them how to swim. My favorite chaperone, Fräulein Hilde, gave permission, and I agreed. She watched with laughter as my students flopped their arms and legs in the air as I held them, or when we struggled to brace ourselves against an especially large wave that crashed over us. When two or three kids learned to swim, I became the mirror image of Tanya back home. I strutted around like a proud peacock. But more than that, I found that others valued me as person of ability.

When our caregivers grew tired of the sea, they took us on long walks through the meadows and hills that make up the terrain of the island. We rested in the green grass of some embankment and lay among the wild flowers. At other times, we gathered under a massive old oak tree where we watched the many squirrels fight for provision or chase each other through the branches.

I loved the beauty and tranquility of Sellin and the area surrounding it. Life there was uncomplicated and enjoyable. The healthy atmosphere and excellent attention we received from our caregivers raised us up from being downcast and neglected children to understanding that we, even though young, were worthy human beings.

One bright and sunny day was especially memorable. A field trip took us to the top of an old tower from which we had a magnificent view of the Baltic coastline. Above it, the deep blue sky was dotted with little fluffy clouds. I kept close to my adorable Fräulein Hilde, who pointed to the direction of northeast.

"Sweden lies just beyond where the water meets the sky. It's one of the countries that belongs to Scandinavia. Did you know that Rügen was once conquered by Sweden? But that was in 1645 AD, a long time ago. The Swedes gave it back to Germany one hundred and seventy years later."

"Really?" I was impressed. I remembered seeing Scandinavia's funny dog-shaped outline on a map in school.

"Yes," Fräulein Hilde continued. "Sweden is a neutral country, but still is considered to be part of the Capitalistic West."

"You mean that it is not ruled by Communists?"

"That's correct."

Aside from my Uncle Emil, I was convinced that Fräulein Hilde was the smartest young woman in all of East Germany. She knew so many things. I decided that I wanted to be smart and pretty like her one day. I asked, "Do the people there speak a different language? Do they look like us?"

"Yes, they speak Swedish. And they are a handsome people, too. The women, especially, are very beautiful. Not only that, but everyone is rich and prosperous there."

"Does that mean that they have enough money to buy anything they want?"

"Yes, that's correct."

"I don't see any land. Is Sweden far from here, Fräulein? All I can see is water."

"Well, it is many hours by boat from here. You can sometimes see the smoke of a ferry as it travels to Trelleborg. That is a harbor town in Sweden."

I remained silent for a while, trying to image what this big dog-shaped peninsula would be like to live on. I could not comprehend what a free and neutral country was like, but I was convinced that it would be a place where people lived a happy and carefree life.

"I would like to go there some day and see it."

Fräulein Hilde looked at my eager face and laughed. "Perhaps you will. By the time you are old enough, any one of us might be able to travel without restrictions to any place we want to go. Let's not give up hope that it will happen one day."

I nodded in response. "*Ja*. Perhaps I will be able to visit Sweden one day."

My stay on the island of Rügen was an amazing and healing time for me. I almost forgot my life back home; and when time came to leave, I was sad. Most of us children cried. We were a family now and did not want to be separated.

After I returned home, the visits of a social worker continued for a while. But when my mother began to show signs of being healthy and stable, the visits stopped. Several months later, and against all hope that everything would be well for us both, her nervous condition returned.

Chapter Twelve

The Undertaker Arrives

Dusk had settled when Frau Meyer and I heard the main door open. Heavy footsteps made their way upward. Herr Gerhard and his companion had finally arrived with the death cart and the horses. Moments later, we heard an outcry that was followed by a few choice cuss words. One of the men hit his shin on the stairs. Frau Meyer quickly went to light the way with a candle.

"You picked a most inconvenient time to get us away from our holiday evening meal, woman!" Herr Gerhard remarked after the two men made it to the top with the empty pine box between them.

"You are lucky we've made it here at all in this awful weather. The horses almost ran us into a ditch just as we came down Cemetery Hill. The cart was slipping and sliding all over the road. Don't you know that everyone's place is at home tonight, old woman? It's Christmas, for God's sake. But since we've made it here without having an accident, let us make this quick. Just show us where the body is. And bring more light! I need to have a closer look to make sure that the woman is, indeed, as dead as you say she is before we box her up."

Herr Gerhard sounded grumpier than ever. I slowly followed them into the apartment but remained shielded from view by the half open door of our kitchen from where I could see their activities.

Frau Meyer pointed to the bedroom where my mother lay and hurried to light the way with more candles. Herr Gerhard entered the bedroom, and I now felt safe to step farther into the living room. I saw him bend down to pick up the empty pill bottle that I left lying on the floor before he took a look at my mother's body.

"She's deader than a doornail," he commented dryly, touching her skin. "From the looks of it, she's been dead for at least two days. Lucky for you and the corpse, the frost has kept it from deteriorating."

He called to his companion. "Klaus, you can make out the death certificate and list it as 'Suicide.' I will sign it later. What's this woman's name?" He shot a side-glance at Frau Meyer.

"Annie Berger," she answered.

I felt myself trembling. Somehow, hearing my mother's name spoken made it all final. Timidly I stepped closer to observe what else the men would do with my mother. Klaus, Herr Gerhard's companion, looked up and saw me. He did not speak but continued to write.

Herr Gerhard cleared his throat. "She was pretty. Too young to die, if you ask me. She must have been mighty desperate to cut her life short on Christmas Eve. It's not that unusual, though. People do it all the time."

At his comment, a small whimper escaped my throat. Frau Meyer turned her head in my direction. Herr Gerhard's eyes followed her. He recognized me immediately and let out a long groan. Then he took a few steps toward me. The light in the room was dim, but I could see that a deep red color was spreading over his face. He was angry. The veins on his temples were protruding as he began to yell at me.

"Good God! *Donnerwetter nochmal.* Thunderbolts and lightning, *Mädchen*! What are you doing here. Is nothing sacred to you? Do you have some kind of radio receiver built into your head that lets you know where to find us? Get out of here! Now! Don't let me come over there and drag you out by your hair."

Frau Meyer gasped. "*Oh Gott! Mein Herr!* What has gotten into you? Do not speak to the child in this tone of voice!"

"Be quiet, old woman!" He commanded. "Let me say my piece. I am the undertaker here and decide who will be present at the scene of death.

Certainly, no children are allowed, especially not those who are street urchins. What you do not know, old woman, is that I am all too familiar with this girl. She is a hearse chaser and shows up wherever there is a death in the home. She is itching to catch a glimpse of a corpse."

He turned back to me and ranted on. "Your obsession with dead bodies has to end right here, young lady. Someone needs to teach you good manners and respect. You cannot simply walk into someone's home to satisfy your curiosity, hoping to see angels flying away with the corpse. Can you not let your morbid fascination rest even on Christmas Day!"

He turned back to Frau Meyer. "I swear that there is something very wrong with this girl!" Sparks of anger flew from his eyes.

I recoiled from his verbal onslaught and began to tremble. I hated him at that very moment but was unable to bring one word over my lips. Frau Meyer, too, stood speechless.

His voice thundered even louder when he continued, "Go home to where you belong and play with your new Christmas toys." He added a few unsavory cuss words.

Frau Meyer found her voice and grabbed his arm. She was breathing hard. "Watch what you are saying, *mein Herr*," she yelled. "I'm not begging you but are ordering to do so! Stop shouting at the poor girl. Don't destroy what's left of her sanity!"

Herr Gerhard simply cut her off, did not let her continue. "Save the rest of her sanity? That explains it." He let out a chuckle. "So then, the girl is a bit touched in her head, is she? I thought so. Nevertheless, no matter her condition, she is not permitted in here." He pointed to the door with his thick forefinger and yelled at me. "Get out! I told you to go home and play with your dolls like a girl your age should."

Frau Meyer became so upset that I saw a purple color rise in her face. She gathered every ounce of strength that she could muster. She stomped her foot on the floor and shouted so loud that her voice topped Herr Gerhard's own. "Stop this nonsense right this minute! Have you lost your senses? You do not know what you are saying. This woman here is her mother. Show her some kindness. She has suffered enough. She spent the night alone. There was no one available to comfort her. She kept vigil over her mother's dead body. Show some humanity and compassion! If you keep shouting at her, you will manage to drive her over the edge yet! And, one more thing. Watch your mouth. There is no need to shout obscenities at her or to anyone, for that matter. And, above all, mind your manners in the presence of a corpse."

Frau Meyer was done shouting, but her distress caused her to burst into tears. Her anguish troubled me. I walked up to her and shyly touched her arm. I wanted to cry with her, but the knot in my throat and the cramp in my heart had built a dam and prevented tears from flowing.

"Frau Meyer," I croaked. My voice was breaking. "Herr Gerhard thinks that I am obsessed with dead people. But I'm not. I just thought that he could help me understand what would happen afterward."

"*Ist schon gut, Mädchen.* It's all right," she said as she pulled herself together. She reached for her apron to wipe her tears away. "Never mind me. I just need a moment to compose myself."

Herr Gerhard, too, looked as if he needed a moment of his own. I saw how his body had jumped as if his butt had been stung by a big, ugly horse fly when Frau Meyer told him that I was the daughter of the woman he came to pick up. He took a step backward. I had never seen him at loss for words before. But his mouth dropped open and he became mute.

His companion, Klaus, broke the silence and said in a low voice, "Calm down, Walter. Show some compassion. Leave the girl alone and let us get to work. The old woman is right. If this girl were my daughter, I'd knock some sense into you, too. You should clean up your language around womenfolk. It is not the first time that your big mouth got you into trouble."

Herr Gerhard feigned deafness to his colleague's remark but turned to Frau Meyer. He mumbled under his breath, "*Na ja dann.* All right then, don't get excited, old woman. It's not good for your heart. We only brought a box for one corpse. Two won't fit inside of it."

Herr Gerhard was not a master at offering apologies but tried to lighten up the awkward situation. He wanted to smooth things over.

But Frau Meyer was not appeased and angrily retorted, "Whatever is it that comes over boorish men like you? It would not hurt a bit if you showed more respect and civility toward anyone. It behooves you to be civil in your profession. An apology would be in order to let the child see that you have *some* compassion in you and a heart to go along with it." She continued breathing hard but stood her ground.

Herr Gerhard turned to me with a sheepish look on his face. "Sorry, girl," he grumbled. "My sympathy for your loss. I believed that you belonged to one of the families at the other end of the street, you know, the couple who has the many kids that are forever roaming the streets unsupervised. I saw you with them, even though I noticed that you always looked cleaner and neater than the rest of them. I thought to myself that, well, at least one of the kids in the family won't turn out to be a hooligan. But I dare say that I sometimes doubted that you were in your right mind when you posed the many questions of the hereafter. I know not one other child who is interested in wanting to know about death. But then again, I don't have children of my own, and am glad of it."

He turned to Frau Meyer and snorted through his nose, still attempting to regain his dignity. "How could I know that the girl's interest in the dead was more than a perverse curiosity?"

"Walter!" The man called Klaus quickly interrupted. "Now that you offered your shameful and appalling version of an apology, let's just get to work before you develop a worse case of hoof and mouth disease."

"My condolences, *Mädchen*," Klaus turned to me and gave me an apologetic smile. He raised his shoulders to show regret for his comrade's display of rudeness.

Frau Meyer showed no patience for more nonsense. "Ariane, I think it is best if you go back to my room and wait there until the men are finished." She took me by the arm.

But I was unwilling to leave my mother alone with Herr Gerhard and his companion.

"Well, alright then. If you must absolutely watch to make sure that your mother is properly placed into the box, let's both of us stand in the kitchen until the men are done."

We stood and watched the men lift Mutti's stiff body into a wooden pine box. Then they hammered a few nails into the lid. When they were ready to take it to the cart outside, Frau Meyer quickly pulled me out of the kitchen and pushed me over the threshold of her apartment. Then she climbed down the stairs, ahead of the men, holding up candles to illuminate the way. The men labored down the narrow steps, which moaned and creaked with every step they took.

I followed a few paces behind and watched as they loaded the box into the back of the wooden cart. Then Herr Gerhard and Klaus climbed into their seats and wrapped fleece ponchos around themselves. Klaus took over the reigns and called a command to the horses. "*Hü!*" He said. The horses snorted and struggled forward. But the wheels of the wagon were frozen to the cobblestones and refused to turn. "*Hü!*" Klaus called again, more forcefully this time. The animals pulled again. The cart made of planks began to groan under the weight of its load.

I remained standing and watched the wagon carry my mother's lifeless body away. When it reached the end of the street, the unvarnished wooden box, in which she lay, was covered by a blanket of pure, white snow.

I awoke the next morning to the sound of muffled voices coming from downstairs. It took me a moment to orient myself before I remembered that the Second Day of Christmas had arrived and my mother was dead. It was another holiday in Germany, and I would be safe for one more day before the welfare agency would arrive and decide on my fate. I hoped that God and Herr Ritter were on my side and that each one of them would be merciful. I rose from my pallet on the floor and walked out to the top of the staircase. Directly below me our landlords were engaged in a conversation with Frau Meyer.

"Please, Herr Ritter," I heard her say in an imploring tone of voice, "if there is anything at all that you can do. I beg you. I am not asking for the sake of the girl alone but also for myself. I need to set things right. Perhaps I should have spoken up more to protect the girl while Frau Berger was still alive. But, you know yourselves that she was a difficult woman to approach." Frau Meyer let out a heavy sigh. "You must have *some* influence with someone at city hall, Herr Ritter. I believe it would be best for Ariane to be placed with a private family, a caring home, where she can recover from the tragedy. She told me last night that her uncle had been arrested. There's no other family member left to take her in."

Frau Ritter shook her head and interrupted, "I'm against interfering with government regulation. The girl needs to be placed in the orphanage. We must report the case to the welfare agency tomorrow. Moreover, I do not want my husband to be brought into the middle of this. The child needs a structured life and a good political education. The State can give her that."

"Just calm yourself, *meine Liebe*," Herr Ritter interrupted his wife, "My dear, I know that you tried to have Ariane taken away from her mother before. I am glad that your interference has not succeeded. I am aware of the conditions at the orphanage. Placing her there would be unforgivable. We don't need to add one more person to the group of neglected and troubled children in that place."

He turned to Frau Meyer. "I think you are correct in suggesting that we should find a private home for Ariane. The State should be glad if it has one less little person to care for. If we could find a family, who would be willing to take her, perhaps we can convince city hall to overlook regulations."

No sooner did he speak when Frau Meyer's face lit up with excitement. "Ah, I just remembered something and might see a solution! There's Frau von Waldheim. She might take Ariane into her home. She is ...I mean... was Frau Berger's friend. Her husband's family comes from aristocratic blue blood."

Frau Meyer's voice turned to almost a whisper when she mentioned the family's heritage. Everyone knew that the little word of "von" in a last name identified a family as being of noble heritage.

Frau Ritter glared at our neighbor and admonished her with a hint of disgust in her voice, "You need not make a point of it, Frau Meyer. Are you not aware that we do not tolerate class differences any longer?"

"She's a pianist," Frau Meyer responded without paying attention to the landlady's comment. "Frau von Waldheim is a lovely person. She would take care of Ariane in the way a mother should."

Herr Ritter nodded. "I think you are correct. I don't know her very well, but Gisela and I attended one of her performances. I, too, was impressed with her. She carried herself regally, yet without the slightest hint of arrogance. Gisela, of course," he turned to his wife as if to ascertain whether she still held the same opinion, "was not satisfied with the selection of classical works that were offered that evening."

From where I stood, I could see Frau Ritter giving her husband the evil eye. She was annoyed that he paid no heed to her desire to have me put away. She challenged him once again, but he merely waved her off. "Let's drop it, Gisela" he said. "Let's do something that is humane for a change, something our conscience can live with."

At that very moment I knew that Herr Ritter would do everything he could to help me. Finding a home with Frau von Waldheim, whom I had been told to call Tante Helga, would suit me just fine.

I tried to tiptoe back up the steps but stubbed my toe on a step. Herr Ritter looked up "Ah, there you are, little Mademoiselle." He always called me Mademoiselle because I had told him how my name change happened and that my father initially had wanted me to be named after a French girl.

"Please come down here for a moment."

I walked downstairs and looked up at him.

"I'm awfully sorry about your mother," he said with sadness in his voice.

His wife glared at him, turned, and walked back into their apartment. To my astonishment, Herr Ritter paid her no heed.

"Frau Meyer just told me that the STASI came to pick up your uncle. Is that true?"

"Yes."

"I am shocked to hear it. I was not aware that he was a threat to the Party. Are you sure that he was arrested?"

I nodded my head once again. "Yes. I went to his place to look for him. The cottage is empty and his garden looks totally neglected. I'm afraid that I don't know what happened to the dog."

"Could it be that he has left for the West?"

"No. He would not be able to take his dog along, and he would never leave him behind. In any case, he told me that he would not leave my mother and me here alone in the GDR."

I suddenly missed not only the comfort and advice of my uncle, but I missed his face. I was fascinated with faces and tried to read them. My uncle's face, in particular, mesmerized me. I studied it whenever we quietly sat across from each other in his little garden among the many flowers. His face has the contours of the terrain map that hung in our classroom. I determined that the hollows in his cheeks and the cleft in his chin were the valleys, while his cheekbones were the hills. When he smiled, the area around his eyes would crinkle into narrow stream beds. I knew that his features were carved by the hardships of the Second World War and the years he spent in a prisoner of war camp. He returned home haggard and tired and found peace once again in his little cottage.

My uncle was an interesting conversationalist. In contrast to so many other men who refused to speak of their experiences, he willingly shared some of them with me. When one day he expressed his views on our government and its politics, I asked anxiously, "Will you escape like so many other people?"

"Don't worry, *meine Kleine*," he said in a soothing tone of voice. "I will stay and keep an eye on your mother and you. Even though she does not permit me to interfere in your upbringing, I will be close enough if you ever need me."

He looked at me for a moment, and I saw a sad expression in his eyes. "But if something should happen to me, you must promise me to keep up your courage and faith."

"Yes. I'm sure my Uncle Emil is gone," I told Herr Ritter. "I knew that he always worried about my mother and me. He wouldn't leave me."

A shadow fell over my landlord's face. "I'm sorry," he said and placed a hand on my shoulder. "Your uncle was a good man. But say," he quickly changed the subject. "How well do you know Frau von Waldheim and her

children? Would you want me to inquire whether she would allow you to
live with her?"

"Yes."

"Are you certain?" Herr Ritter asked once again.

I nodded a bit confused. Did he not want me to go there? He asked
me that very question already.

"Just making sure." He gave me a penetrating look. "Frau Meyer told
me that you would run away from the orphanage if you were placed there.
I don't want you to be unhappy and run away from the Waldheims if we
receive permission for you to stay with them."

"I won't run away. I like them!" I protested.

"All right then. It is settled." He turned to Frau Meyer. "If you would
be so good and accompany us later. We'll walk over to their home to
discuss the situation. Meanwhile, I must make peace with my wife, as
usual. I think a bee has crawled up her behind a few moments ago, as it
so often does."

I was stunned, as was Frau Meyer, to hear Herr Ritter speak of his
wife in this manner. We stared at him. He noticed our perplexed faces and
winked at us before disappearing into his apartment.

"That woman is too surly and harsh for my liking," Frau Meyer
murmured. "But don't worry about anything at all, *Kindchen*." She took
me by the hand and pulled me upstairs. "Frau von Waldheim, she is not
like *that* one. I am convinced that her character is spun from a finer yarn.
She's made of cashmere rather than burlap."

I could remember when I met Tante Helga's children, Dagmar and
Wolfgang, for the first time. It was only four months ago on a Sunday
in August. The humidity and oppressive heat became broken by a cloud
burst. It left the roads flooded and the gullies overloaded. Mutti needed
some sodium bicarbonate to cure her upset stomach and sent me to Tante
Helga's house to fetch it. It was still drizzling, and I waded as quickly as
I could through the knee-deep water that flowed in the streets. When I
arrived at the Waldheim home, a violin solo drifted past the open window
with the sheer, white-curtains that fluttered in the fresh breeze. I was

transfixed by the sweet sounds and seated myself on the door step to listen. When one melody ended, another one followed. Finally, I remembered my errand and knocked on the door. There was no answer. I knocked again, louder this time. After a few moments, a tall, lanky teenaged boy opened the door. He surveyed me with a curious look before his face melted into a pleasant grin.

"Oh, I was right. There *is* someone at the door. I'm sorry. Did you wait here long? It's difficult to hear anyone knock when we play music. How can I help you?"

As he spoke, I took a quick inventory of him. I was struck by his polite manners and handsome features. His brown eyes glistened like soft and shiny licorice. I sensed that he was just as surprised to find a strange girl standing before him, as I was to see him. I wondered why Tante Helga never mentioned having a son. But then, we never spoke much. My mother always sent me away when she came to visit.

The handsome boy left me tongue tied. I tried to think of something intelligent to say so that he would not mistake me for a street urchin. I knew of the family's reputation. Mutti said that every one of them was smart and talented.

Wolfgang looked down at my muddy feet and grinned. I shrank back in embarrassment and began to wind my fingers nervously through my wet curls that, as usual, fell in wild disarray around my face. I knew that I was a frightful sight. I had skidded through mud holes, had tripped over obstacles that had been hidden by the scummy whirlpool of water, and had fallen down. I was convinced that he thought me to be a member of the band of gypsies that recently set up camp in the meadow at the edge of town. The gypsies came through each summer and stayed for a few months. In contrast to me, Wolfgang looked exceedingly well groomed.

He brushed a strand of dark hair from his forehead and repeated, "*Ja, bitte*? How can I help you? Are you lost and need directions to the outskirts of town? It is quite far from here."

I squirmed. I knew it! He thought of me as the daughter of a nomad. His eyes took on a teasing expression. "You *do* speak German, don't you? I don't speak Romani or such, but perhaps I could try out my school Russian on you. Unfortunately, I am absolutely terrible at it." He grinned.

I read him correctly. "I speak Russian," I said. "I like learning it. But it's alright. I speak German better. I mean, I *am* German just like you."

"Alright then." He grinned again. "I just thought you might be..."

"*Entschuldigung.* I am Ariane Berger." I took hold of myself. "My mother is your mother's friend."

His face lit up. "Oh yes. I'm sorry for making you uncomfortable, but you looked so...so... Well, never mind. It must have rained more than I realized. Come in please. Perhaps you want to dry off." He stepped aside and offered me entrance to the house. "I know who you are, even though we've never met."

"Really? How so?" I was relieved to find that my shyness disappeared. I wiped my feet at the doormat.

"Mama has spoken of you before."

If Tante Helga had repeated anything that Mutti might have told her about me, it might not be anything to be proud of. My expression registered concern.

"Don't worry," he laughed. "It was all good, even though it was very interesting. I heard that you sometimes come home with your pockets full of frogs, which you collect at the pond. They horrify your mother. She believes that they will give you warts. Do you have warts? If you do, can you let me see them?"

"No!" I called out. "Don't be silly. I don't have warts."

"Well. In any case, Mama said that she considers you to be Nature's Child. I don't know exactly what she meant by that, but I think that she meant that you like the outdoors. I, too, like to be outside."

My eyes widened. "You do? That's great. I rather be out in the open than anywhere else."

"I would like to be outside more than I am. But unfortunately I must spend most of my time inside the house. I must practice my cello."

"Sorry," I said. "There's nothing for me to do at home, and so I'd rather be outside in the sunshine. Except, of course, when I read. Then I'm inside. But I do that in the evenings before I go to bed."

"Well...I like the outdoors, as I said. But I don't mind staying at home either. I know that I need to be disciplined an practice my instrument if I want to be a famous musician one day," the boy answered.

I instantly was in awe of him again. "Really? Do you think you will be famous?"

"Perhaps. But, wait. I did not introduce myself. I'm Wolfgang von Waldheim. My sister, Dagmar, was the one who was playing the violin. She needed to practice since she will give a performance to our little musical group later this week."

"It sounded wonderful," I responded with enthusiasm. "The melody was very sad in the beginning but became very uplifting. She played so well!"

"Ah, so you know something about music, too?" Wolfgang inquired with interest.

"No. But I like to listen to classical music on the radio. I can remember some of the titles."

A beautiful blond girl, who appeared to be a year older than I, walked up to me and held out her hand. "I am Dagmar. Did you come to see Mama? Please have a seat. Do you want to dry your hair? It looks awfully wet."

She turned to her brother, asking him to fetch a towel. Then she invited me to sit on the wide dark maroon velvet sofa that displayed an ornately carved wooden backing. It gave a slight squeal when I lowered myself onto it. I immediately jumped back up when I felt something poking my behind.

Dagmar laughed. "The springs in this piece of furniture are older than Beethoven himself. They probably rusted through the years and need oiling or something like that. We are used to the squeal. It probably sat out in the rain at some time or another. Mama rescued it from some burned out house shortly after the war. She cleaned it up very nicely. If you don't want to sit on it, you may sit on the overstuffed chair over there instead, if you'd like."

I shook my head. "*Nein, nein.* This is alright. It's nice and soft if I scoot over to the side."

Dagmar seated herself next to me before turning to her brother, to whom I handed back the towel after rubbing it through my hair. He now stood leaning against the door frame observing us.

"Wolfie, please be a dear and fetch Mama. Tell her that we received an unexpected guest."

I marveled at Dagmar's poise. As I waited for their mother to appear from the kitchen, I took a shy look around the living room. It was much larger than our own. Several old wooden chairs were placed around a piano in a half circle. In front of them stood metal stands with sheets of music. Two string instrument cases leaned against the wall.

"We host a chamber musical group once a week," Dagmar informed me.

I nodded. Then, my eye caught a framed photograph that featured an elegantly dressed, dark haired man in some kind of suit with two tails. He stood poised before an orchestra, holding a baton. A few strands of hair had fallen over his forehead, just as Wolfgang's hair did earlier. Dagmar followed my gaze.

"That's my father. The picture was taken either in Dresden or Leipzig before the war. Mama and Papa were not married then. She was a pianist in his orchestra."

"Oh." I was thoroughly impressed again. "He looks so elegant and important."

"Yes, but I don't have any memories of my father. I was very small when he died."

"Mine died too," I offered and hesitated, considering whether I should reveal more and tell her that I could remember my father just a little bit. Dagmar seemed nice enough, and so I continued. "Well, actually, I don't know whether my father is really dead. He didn't come home from the war."

"Then, where is he now?"

"I don't know. My mother thinks that he has gone off to somewhere else instead of coming home to us. But I believe that he is dead. Really. I don't think that he would simply abandon me. Everyone said that my father loved me. In any case, no one knows for sure whether he's dead or alive because no one has found his body. The authorities told us that he is missing in action. I think that my mother is confused about the whole thing. Sometimes she believes what they told her, while at other times she doesn't."

"That must be difficult for your mother, not knowing what has happened to him. It must be difficult for you as well."

"I don't know what the truth is about all of that." I looked uncertainly at her. "My mother is very secretive about everything surrounding my father. I think I know what it is because my grandmother and uncle told me their version of what they believe is true. But one thing is for sure. My mother doesn't seem to like my father very much any more."

Dagmar looked at me with sympathy. We remained silent for a moment, smiling shyly at each other. I was shocked at myself for having revealed my family situation so easily. Somehow, I liked and trusted this girl. I quickly searched for another subject to talk about. "You have inherited your musical gift from your parents, then. I listened to you play before I knocked on the door. I liked it very much. I heard that piece over the radio before. I don't think you made any mistakes at all."

Dagmar's face blushed with pleasure. "*Danke schön.* I try to do my best. I took lessons since I was very small. Mama has made sure that Wolfie and I practice daily. Perhaps I will be able to enter a music school one day. Unfortunately, there is no such school in our town. All the famous schools are located in Berlin, Leipzig, or Dresden. I might have been accepted in one of them already when I began school, but I didn't want to leave Mama and Wolfie then."

I sat and looked at her in wonderment, wishing that my mother would have allowed me to meet the Waldheim children sooner. They were so different from my own friends. They fascinated me.

Soon Tante Helga entered the room. When she saw me, her eyes lit up. "Ariane-chen, my dear. What brings you here? Did your mother finally concede to letting you come for visit? God knows, I asked her often enough to send you over here to meet my children. But, my goodness.

What has happened to you? You look wet all over. Did you fall? Are the gutters overloaded again?"

I nodded and, remembering my manners, I quickly scooted off the sofa to give her the customary curtsey.

"It's been a while since I laid eyes on you. Where are you hiding whenever I stop by to see your mother?"

I shrugged my shoulders and quickly told her the reason for my visit. Time with the Waldheims flew fast; and before long, I left with the Sodium Bicarbonate and a homemade jar of blueberry jam.

"A gift for your mother," Tante Helga explained. "I made it myself. Perhaps it will sweeten her up a bit and keep her calm when she sees how wet you are. I know how she is. A neat and clean appearance is important to her."

I thanked Tante Helga and her children for their hospitality and trudged back home, avoiding the large puddles that remained from the rain. In the months following my visit, I often remembered the gracious hospitality of the Waldheims and wished that I were born into such a lovely family.

Chapter Thirteen

1950
The Old Reinhardts

People in our area did not give compliments easily. Therefore, Frau Meyer's comments about Tante Helga's character reinforced my belief that I would be safe in her care. There had been two other people in my life, strangers, who had earned my love and trust. They were an elderly couple by the names of Herr and Frau Reinhardt. I once spent a summer with them after my mother fell ill once again. Another social worker had come to the house and had taken me to the train station without any explanation.

"Where is my mother?" I anxiously asked. I feared that she had died while I was at school.

"She needs a rest. You'll soon see her again before long. But until then, we've found a temporary home for you in the countryside. You need to take the journey alone. I have other obligations to attend to. So, listen carefully and do as I tell you." The woman looked sternly at me as she gave me instructions. "It will take an hour and a half before you reach your destination. The train will make two stops. Be sure to get off at the third one. I cannot vouch for what will happen to you if you miss it."

The woman managed to frighten me into paying attention. I was eight years old and had never taken a train by myself. Soon, the long train stopped, and the social worker handed me my little suitcase.

"Go find a compartment and stay seated in it," she said. "And don't strike up conversations with strangers or run along the corridor of the car."

I nodded and climbed the metal steps to find a seat. Shortly after I found an empty compartment, the train began to roll in labored slow motion. I pulled down the window to wave goodbye to the woman. But she had already disappeared from the platform. I sat back on the upholstery. It smelled of stale cigarette smoke and sweat. I stared at the ceiling, was bored, and wished for company. The social worker, however, was adamant that I keep to myself.

I once took a trip with my mother to a different town. On the ride back home, we shared a compartment with a Russian major who sat across from us. He was traveling in fully decorated uniform. His medals were impressive and covered his whole chest. He smiled when I walked over to him and looked at each and every one of them.

"Where did you get this one, and that one?" I asked shyly.

My mother immediately chastised me, telling me to sit down. But the major waved her off and began a conversation with her. His fluent German added to my respect for him. He missed his little girls back in Russia, he told us, and offered me a piece of candy.

"He was nice, Mutti, wasn't he?" I said when we got off the train. I was amazed that a declared enemy was so gracious.

"He's different from the others because he is well educated," my mother responded.

I knew that she liked smart people. Seeing that the major made an impression on her, I immediately promised myself to learn well in school and become smart. Because if I were smart, she would be proud of me and love me. The trip left me with the conviction that it was safe and pleasurable to ride the train.

Now, with nothing else to do, I listened to the labored "choo-choo, choo-choo" sounds of the train but soon became bored once more. I leaned out the window to locate the locomotive car up front but could not see it through the cloud of black smoke that streaked past me from the smokestack, which chucked up clouds of black coal soot. I quickly left the window and occupied myself with a game of hopscotch in the narrow gangway outside my compartment. But each time the wheels screeched around the many curves in the track, I was forcefully thrown through the open door of my compartment and fell back into one of the overstuffed seats. Soon, we crossed a country road heard the signals at the barrier. "Ding, ding, ding, ding." The call of the bell was high and came in quick succession. It was followed by the throaty, deep sound of the locomotive horn. Awe-*hooo*-awe, Awe-*hooo*-awe. It gave off a long moaning squall.

After the train made its first stop, and then the second, I peered through the window and felt increasingly nervous. The next stop would be mine. I began to chew on my lower lip until I tasted blood.

The train arrived at my destination and stopped with a jolt. I quickly gathered up my things and reminded myself to be on my best behavior at the house of the unknown couple. I wanted them to like me. If they would not and would return me home on the very next train, I would have no place to go. I dragged my suitcase down the iron steps of the train and looked around.

"Ah, there you are, *Mädchen*," a female voice called. *"Hallo, Hallo. Willkommen*! Are you alone? Where is the social worker?" A short round woman with graying hair walked up to me.

In faltering words I explained that the social worker had left me to pursue some other important matter. Frau Reinhardt wrinkled her forehead in displeasure. Her less rotund husband saw it and quickly motioned to his wife to say no more. He turned to me. *"Ach, ja. Nun dann, Mädchen.* Well, then, girl. Since you are the only passenger getting off in our sleepy town, you must be the guest that we are expecting. You are the little Ariane, then?"

I nodded, "Yes" and smiled. I immediately noticed that each of them had their own funny idiosyncrasy which they wove into their sentences. Perhaps they were as nervous as I was.

"Well, then. We did not wait long at the station. The train is right on time, as it always is. Good old German engineering time, that's what it is. I can set my watch by it." His face showed a satisfied expression.

I curtsied an uncertain, *"Guten Tag"* and stuck out my hand to greet them.

"Nun dann," Herr Reinhardt repeated redundantly. "Well, then, I hope that you will like it here with us old folks."

His eyes rested on my face in the manner that grown ups do when they are trying to look right into your very soul. I, in turn, behaved as I always did when shyness descended on me. I looked down at my feet and pulled up my knee-highs. They, of course, needed no attention because I inspected my dress and stockings before I stepped off the train. I wanted to make sure that both were in perfect order.

His wife surveyed me with a smile and added her own peculiar rhetorical words. *"Aber doch,* Ariane. For sure, you *do* look like a sweet girl, but you are so thin. Well, it is to be expected, for sure. You must be hungry then? Come on, we have a little bit of a walk ahead of us, but it will not be too far. Dinner is waiting for us at the house. I prepared a nice welcome meal for you. It's simmering on the stove right as I speak. We'll have Sauerkraut and *Ribchen.* I'm sure you love little pork ribs, don't you?"

A smile spread over my own face. "You have meat for dinner?" I exclaimed with delight. I knew that I would enjoy my stay with them. Things were beginning to look up nicely. Who would be dissatisfied with a plate full of delicious food?

Herr Reinhardt laughed, "Certainly, *Mädchen.* I promise that we will let you eat as much as your little heart desires. Well, then. Now that the most important thing is settled, let's head for home."

Frau Reinhardt clutched my hand as we walked down the county road whose sides were lined with apple trees. We passed long fields of yellow wheat and pale oats and barley. I could see their stalks rippling in the light breeze. Everything smelled of warm sun and earth. Next to the fields were green meadows, which boasted a sea of blue cornflowers and red poppies. It was a glorious sight. I knew that I could feel at home here.

After a twenty minute walk, we arrived at the Reinhardt home. I stopped in surprise and shouted, "It looks like a gingerbread house!"

It was a lovely and comfortable place, indeed. And when we entered it, I could smell the fragrance of sweet berries and spices. I learned that Frau

Reinhardt had just finished preserving the first batch of fruit this year; and if I felt so inclined, I could assist her the next day when she would prepare her secret recipe of plum butter, which was much in demand by both her husband and her neighbors.

"Well, then," Herr Reinhardt winked at me, "I can already tell that you will feel comfortable with us. I think that we all will get along just splendidly."

"*Aber doch.* For sure." Frau Reinhardt agreed and beamed. Her wide smile created little fleshy mounds on her cheeks that made them look like shiny red apples. I nodded my head with enthusiasm before I turned my gaze to the kitchen window. It gave a view on a spectacular garden. There were vegetable beds with red tomatoes and green cucumbers. I recognized pea pods with little round bulges inside of them. Farther to the right, string beans climbed up a wooden pole. I pressed my nose against the glass and let my gaze drift into the distance where the Elbe River snaked its way through the green landscape. I knew that I was stepping into a fairy tale. Nothing here was like my own home. But all was more than well. The longer I stayed with the Reinhardts, the more pleased I was to be with them instead of any other place on earth.

Next to my grandmother, the old couple were the sweetest people I had ever met. It did not take me long before I began to wish that I never needed to leave again. They became my family, even if just for a little while. I told them about my uncle and my grandmother, who was living in the Golden West. Frau Reinhardt confessed that they, too, had relatives there but that they would not leave their country home. Their little garden produced fruits and vegetables. They had a pig and had just begun to raise a few chickens, which supplied them with eggs that they used as barter for other things their household needed.

"We have it better than most, my Gretchen and I," my host told me.

"For sure," His wife agreed. "We miss our sisters and brothers, but we are too old to start up a new life somewhere else. Why would we leave this treasured plot of earth behind and exchange it for a relocation camp over there?"

"*Over there*," of course, meant the Golden West. "*Da drüben*," everyone said, and people knew what that meant.

When not helping his wife with chores, Herr Reinhardt and I meandered through the fields and orchards. One particular day, not long after I arrived at their house, we came upon a meadow filled with colorful wildflowers.

"Oh how lovely they are!" I cried and rushed down the hill to pick a mixed bouquet before I ran back to him. "These are for your wife. Smell them, Herr Reinhardt," I begged. "I am sure she will love these. I will pick some for you, too, if you would like."

"No, no, *Mädchen*." He laughed. "*Nein, doch*. That is not necessary."

"But I want to give you a present for always being so kind to me. You never yell at me for anything. And you are very nice to your wife, too. You even smile at her when she mislays her reading glasses and cannot find them. And you don't get upset either when she stays at a neighbor's house too long or fixes dinner late because she likes to talk so much and forgets what time it is."

Herr Reinhardt began to chuckle. "Well, then, my girl. You think that we should be angry at each other for such little things, eh? *Nein, doch*. No, no. Such matters are unimportant. I am happy with her just the way she is, my Gretchen. No one is as warm and cheerful as she. I wouldn't know what I would do without her. She is a true angel. We are married for forty years, and I wouldn't want her to be any other way."

He saw that I was impressed. He added, "Sure enough, *Kindchen* we've had our share of troubles. Just as everyone else has theirs. Life is not without struggle. There were the hardships of the war and the times thereafter. We were nervous and worried how we would manage. But after Gretchen's brother passed away, he left us his house. And so we moved here after our own house was destroyed. When later my kindhearted Gretchen suggested that we take in a young child who would otherwise be deprived of care and love, I agreed. And here you are, my dear girl."

"Thank you." I mumbled shyly. "I like being with you very much."

"You don't need to thank us, child. Just seeing how happy you are with us makes us think that we made the right decision. It harms no one to be kind to others. Gretchen and I learned that every good deed, which you show to someone else, is returned in kind."

I thought for a moment before I responded. "I know that people were kind to me even though I haven't done anything for them. But my mother says that there is no kindness in the world."

"Oh? Well, then, perhaps she has not paid enough attention to the small things, which surely came her way. No one ever goes without receiving *some* kindness from others. Even a smile can warm a person's heart and make a day look brighter. Perhaps your mother has experienced too many heartaches, which made her close her mind and heart to the goodness of others. Some people find it difficult to overcome the hardships that life bestows on them. Perhaps the conditions during and after the war took away your mother's faith in humanity. Perhaps she needs more time to adjust. After all, only a handful of years have passed since the turmoil has ended." He paused and smiled down at me before continuing.

"I know the town in which you live. Both of you found yourselves in the midst of a great battle that was waged there in 1944. You are perhaps too young to remember it, but B-17 and B-24 airplanes dropped more than one hundred bombs in just one night. Then, in 1945, when you were around three years old, the whole town and surrounding area was chosen to be a stronghold for the German army."

"I remember the fighting," I interrupted him, surprised that he knew our history.

He surveyed me with a curious expression. "Hmm. Is that right?"

"Yes," I answered. "I remember the noise of the guns and the day the Russians came. I was very scared. But, anyway, Herr Reinhardt, what's a stronghold?"

"A stronghold is a place where hundreds of soldiers are sent to keep the enemy from passing a certain point or cross a line that would allow them to advance farther into a territory. You see, the army forms a big defensive wall with guns and tanks, and such, to keep the enemy from getting through. Big, important battles are fought in places that are strongholds.

Your town was chosen to be such a place. The Americans had advanced to the Elbe, the very river that you see flowing in the distance there, while the Russian troops were approaching from the other direction. Both armies were fighting against our German troops. Unfortunately for all of us, the Red Army conquered your town before the Americans could get there. When the Russians arrived, they fought our army for twelve days and nights without ceasing. At the end of the battle, your town lay in ashes. I've seen the destruction and was horrified."

"It still looks very bad." I informed him. "There are ruins everywhere, and some people even sleep in them because they have no other place to live."

"Yes, I know. Everyone has suffered much. The battle killed an incredible number of people. I remember that one of our German generals, who inspected the destruction later, said that it would take a whole generation before the area would be cleared of rubble. The streets were littered with disabled tanks and empty cartridge cases. Chaos reigned everywhere. Refugees with nothing but the clothes on their back were fleeing the area. No one knew where it was safe to run to. People who were Nazi sympathizers were pursued and executed on the spot."

"I've heard some women in the neighborhood speak of it." I offered.

"Well then, child, taking all of that into account, your mother suffered along with all the other survivors. Only, her experiences affected her more severely."

Herr Reinhardt and I walked quietly for a few minutes before he announced, "So, then. Let's forget the war, shall we? The fight is over now, and we must create a better future for us all from hereon out. We must be kinder to our own kind and to the people who are different from us."

As we walked, a question began to nag at me. I needed to ask him. Taking a deep breath, I said, "Herr Reinhardt. What would you do if you tried to be nice to someone but that person is not always nice in return? And, what would you do if you tried to be good, but that person tells you that no matter how hard you try, you will never be good enough? She says that you will turn your back on her, just as everyone else has." I took a deep breath and continued. "But Herr Reinhardt, that isn't really true. I mean, not everyone will turn her back on someone she loves. Don't you agree? I told her so. But she only yells and says that what I am saying is nonsense. And then…Well, anyway, Herr Reinhardt, what would you do if that happened to you?"

I had talked myself into a frenzied dead end and paused abruptly. I looked anxiously at him. Would he laugh at me? Mutti always told me not to jabber senselessly or speak of things that were insignificant and unimportant to others.

The old man stopped walking and looked down at me for a long moment before he responded. "Could it be that you are asking about someone who is very close to you?"

I nodded, "Uh huh."

"Well, then. One should never give up hope that a person might change one day. Sometimes it takes a while before a closed heart opens up again and will accept love from others."

"How long do you think it will take?"

"Well, it depends what kind of soil the person's heart is made of and the quality of seed that is sown into it. If a seed is planted with love into fertile soil, it will grow fast. But even then one must tend to it with care, just as my Gretchen tends to her plants. At times, the soil is too hard to receive a seed and must be loosened up. Sometimes, rocks need to be removed before a crop can be planted. It takes much patience and commitment to do the work.

"The soil in a heart that has suffered is often hard or filled with rocks. Those must be removed before a person will be totally free and happy again.

"Perhaps the person that you are asking about has a heart just like that. As I said, we should never give up hope that the heart can heal. Does that make sense to you?"

I nodded hesitantly but remained silent. I needed time to think about what he had told me.

Later that evening, I made my decision. I needed to be patient with *her,* give her more time to heal. I needed to wait a while longer, just as Herr Reinhardt had suggested. Then, when she finally removed all the rocks in her heart, she might be able to accept me as her daughter. After that, she would be nice to me and even love me.

I remembered the words of the old man and patiently waited for my mother's heart to heal. But that did not happen. Instead, she decided to leave me. I wondered whether she cared about what would happen to me after she was gone.

Chapter Fourteen

1954
A River of Tears

If Herr Ritter had thought it easy to obtain permission to place me into Tante Helga's care, he found that he had been mistaken. He used all of his skills of persuasion but found that the men at city hall, whom he thought to be his friends, let him down. Just when he wanted to give up, he encountered a miracle.

A few days after the new year, he came knocking on our door. He waved a document in the air. "Good news, everyone! Just when I became convinced that my request would be ignored, I received a surprise. Look here. I bring you the governmental stamp of the eagle, which affirms that our little Mademoiselle is now the legal ward of Frau Helga von Waldheim until her eighteenth birthday."

He related how he called on the humanity and compassion of his friends and begged them to process the petition. But all refused to help. To each and every one of the men I was like any other faceless child that became abandoned. I was a statistic to them and was given a number in their files.

"Ah, you are talking about Orphan Number One Hundred Eighty Nine," they commented after reading the police report they received. Someone had already entered my name into their official books and had assigned me the next number in line.

"We've just received this case. It has yet to be processed. But we can assure you that the girl will be taken to the orphanage."

But, as luck would have it, a young man, who quietly stood by and listened to the conversation, asked Herr Ritter to follow him into the hallway.

"My grandfather holds the seat of a judgeship in Havelland," the young man told him. "I will bring the matter to his attention and get the petition approved."

My case touched his heart because he had a little girl of his own waiting for him at home.

The news that I was allowed to stay with Tante Helga affected me in a curious way. Up till then, I tried to be courageous, depending on my strong will to see me through. The courage, which my Uncle Emil wanted me to display, suddenly left me. I began to sink into total apathy and drifted into a twilight zone where nothing mattered at all. A pit opened before me. I was convinced that I would fall into it at any moment.

"Ariane-chen! What is happening to you?" Tante Helga lightly shook my shoulder one day. "I waited long enough and gave you time enough to talk. I thought that if I let you grieve in your own way, you would finally open up. I fear that you will slip away from us."

I blinked hard, not wanting to acknowledge her. Why did she fuss over me so? My mother never gave me the attention Tante Helga placed on me. Her compassion made things worse.

"Everyone in this house cares about you, Ariane-chen. How can I help you if you do not let us know what is going through your mind?"

I looked to the floor, kept quiet. I wondered whether I should let my guard down. But what would happen if I, subsequently, broke into tiny little pieces that could not be fitted back together again? That surely would be the end of me. I tried to keep company with my journal and make my confessions in it. But it was difficult. I put it back down and stared at blank pages.

Wolfgang observed us and announced that I needed a cup of hot *Melissentee*, a tea of lemon balm. "Drink it, he encouraged me when he returned with it. Mama always gives it to my sister and me before a recital in town. It will soothe you and calm your nerves."

His mother nodded and smiled at him as I obeyed and took a sip. The tea was fragrant and pleasing. Wolfgang sweetened it with real honey. I recognized the flavor immediately. Oma had occasionally brought us some honey from the Golden West. It tasted far better than the artificial honey, the only one available in the *Konsum*. It cannot compare to the real stuff and is made from starch and glucose. Herr Donner was kind enough to share a jar of genuine bee honey with us, which he had brought back from the countryside.

"Well, then, if you cannot talk just yet, I insist that you go outside and catch some fresh air, Ariane-chen," Tante Helga spoke emphatically. "The weather has cleared." She turned to her children. "Why don't you all go? It will refresh you and bring color into your cheeks as well."

"Let's go ice skating in Meadow Park. The Bullfrog Pond is frozen solid." Wolfgang immediately suggested.

"No, I'd rather not." I shook my head. "Perhaps I'll come with you some other time."

I read disappointment in his eyes. Dagmar, too, gave me a resigned glance. Why did everyone think that I could simply go ice skating when I wanted nothing more than to die! How could they even suggest it? Moreover, I was never on skates before. Had they forgotten that we needed to fasten them to the rim of sturdy shoe soles and that I possessed no such shoes?

As though Dagmar could read my mind, she suggested, "If you change your mind, I have a pair of shoes that might fit you. And Wolfie will teach you if you don't know how to skate, Ariane. You don't need to be afraid of falling. He is strong enough to hold you up. Aren't you Wolfie?"

Her brother agreed and clasped his right hand over his heart in a theatrical gesture. "I will be the obedient servant to my ladies and worthy of rescuing a gypsy princess should she find herself in distress."

Dagmar gave her brother a nudge on the head. "Silly, you. You remind me of Frau Fröhlich. Have you taken lessons from her?"

"Ariane-chen, dear," Tante Helga ignored her children and encouraged me once more, "I insist that you go with them. The fresh air will lift your spirits. You need to take a break from all the ruminations in your head. Wolfie will be the perfect gentleman and escort you home if you find that being in a large crowd will prove too much for you. But remember, I will let you out of my sight only because I know that you'll be in good hands. When you return, we will sit down and talk. Agreed?"

I looked doubtfully at her but nodded my head. I was bound by duty because of her kindness. I needed to show my appreciation. I was afraid that if I would not comply with her request, she might send me to the orphanage after all.

Meadow Park with its many walking trails and wonderful trees was one of my favorite spots. I spent many happy hours there in the company of my friends. We lay on the carpet of lush, green grass and among yellow buttercups and talked about anything that dropped into our heads. Then, when we found nothing else to talk about, we listened to the serenade of bullfrogs in the pond or stared into the sky, following the ever changing patterns of cloud formations. I loved the peace of the place and the fragrance of nature all around us. At such times, my happiness was complete.

Today, the Bullfrog Pond was crowded with children of all ages who were trying out their newly acquired Christmas skates. The air was crisp and biting and colored everyone's cheeks a dark red. The snow-laden branches of the two willow trees, which stood at the edge of the pond, bent deep and almost touched the ground. The meadow and the area surrounding the pond looked like a majestic winter wonderland.

We sat down and fastened our skates onto the soles of our shoes and climbed onto the ice. No sooner did I step on it when my backside hit the ground. My companions laughed. I did not expect to be this clumsy and was embarrassed. After a few more unsteady wobbles and crashes, Wolfgang proposed to give me a skating lesson. "Hang on to me, Ariane. Steady now. Push and glide. Easy now. See, like this!"

I felt safe on Wolfgang's arm, proud to hold his hand. The patience he showed touched me. Soon, my confidence rose. I forgot the woes of my inner world and hung on to him until I was able to let go of his arm and glide over the ice without assistance.

Earlier than we expected, the shadows of late afternoon began to lengthen. The sun hung low and announced its departure. Bullfrog Pond began to clear of skaters. We hobbled onto a grassy knoll where Wolfgang knelt down to assist me in loosening the clamps of my skates. He looked up and smiled.

"I believe that you enjoyed yourself after all. I hope that you will feel better from now on."

His head came to the height of my own; and, for the first time I noticed golden flecks in his brown eyes. The flecks were similar to the color of *Bernstein,* the amber stones that washed ashore on the island of Rügen. Fräulein Hilde told me that the amber from the Baltic was of the highest quality. I felt their gentle energy as I held them in my hands and took a few pieces home with me. I kept them under my pillow.

Wolfgang's eyes were just like the stones that were precious to me. I suddenly became shy because of his closeness. I stammered, "*Tut mir leid.* I'm sorry. It's just that... that I..." The words remained stuck in my throat.

"No, no. It's alright," he quickly assured me. "No need to apologize. I don't know how I would behave if I were to lose Mama. Your mother's passing came as such a shock to all of us."

"Yes. I saw Mama cry. She is really sad that she was not able to help your mother more than she was able to." Dagmar agreed. "I cannot imagine how you must feel. I think it is inexcusable, though, that your mother hadn't considered what would happen to you after she... you know...did *that.* I mean, I am glad that you came to live with us. Truly I am. But I just cannot imagine what she was thinking of. How could she just abandon you like that!"

"Dagmar!" Her brother warned.

He turned to me. "It's alright, Ariane. Don't ever be offended by what one of us may say at times. Mama said that we offer our opinions too quickly, even though she has tried to teach us to think before we open our mouths. But, you must agree that we are not as bad as that awful Fink." He grinned at me in an attempt to lighten the situation. Then his face turned thoughtful.

"I don't want to sound as harsh as my sister. However, I must admit that…Well, it was Christmas, after all, and you were left all alone with your mother after she…hum… well… But she would have known that you would be the one who would find her. I know that I, too, should not say it. But I think that it was a cruel thing for her to do. I'm sorry."

I stared at him. He was sorry, but he was correct. Why did she want *me* to find her? It *was* cruel. Bad things always happened to me at Christmas time.

I swallowed hard. Suddenly, I knew not what came over me. Perhaps it was the fresh air or the exercise that unwound my insides. I felt unexpected tears in my eyes. I had not been able to cry since my mother's death and did not want anyone see me spill them now. Especially not Wolfgang. But it was too late. He saw them and offered me the sleeve of his coat to wipe them away.

I tried to collect myself and stammered, "I… I really wished that I could have spoken to my mother one last time to find out why she did this…this thing and whether she wanted to punish me one final time. I don't know what I did to her to make her so angry at me. I thought that it would be best if I died too."

"But surely you won't do an awful thing like that, Ariane!" Dagmar exclaimed and anxiously reached for my hand.

"I don't know. I feel so lost now." My voice was thick with tears. "I thought about it but I'm afraid to do it. Now, I'm nothing but a burden to all of you." I began to sob.

"*Unsinn*, Ariane! Nonsense!" Dagmar called. "You are no burden. We liked you from the very minute we first met you. Didn't we, Wolfie!"

Her brother nodded. "Yes, my sister is right. We are happy that you came to live with us." He took my hand.

"You are part of our family now." Dagmar continued. "You must always remember that." She gently shook my shoulder. "And, listen,

I'm awfully sorry about what I said just now. I didn't mean to speak disrespectfully of your mother, even though I hate what she has done to you."

I avoided looking at either of them as my tears continued streaking down my face.

They watched me in momentary silence until Dagmar said. "Don't cry any more. I have an idea. Let's pretend that I am your *real* sister and Wolfie is your *real* brother."

She turned to him. "What do you think, Wolfie. It would be alright, wouldn't it be? All three of us will be siblings from now on. Ariane will stay with us until she is grown."

Dagmar spoke with such conviction that the wall that I had built around me, and which had kept my emotions hidden from them these past days, totally crumbled. The knot in my throat that had thickened daily since Christmas Eve began to unravel. All my pent up sadness and feelings of abandonment began to spill like a waterfall. I could not believe that either of them wanted me as their sister. They were blessed with the special genes of blue blood, while I was not. In my opinion, they were better than I was. But I discovered that it did not matter to them.

I sat on the bank of the icy pond as my body continued to shudder in great sobs. Dagmar seated herself next to me and cradled me close as I imagined a mother would have done to her child. She wiped my tears with her mittens. "Don't cry, Ariane. Everything will be alright from now on. You are not alone. You have a family now."

It took me some time to calm down. Wolfgang knelt before me and rubbed my sock covered feet with his hands. After they warmed up, he struggled to put my shoes on my feet. Before he tied the shoelaces, he asked, "Feeling better now?"

A wide grin spread over his face. "Look here, my new little sister, Prince Wolfgang has found the perfect slippers for your feet. Now all of us will live happily ever after."

"Since when do you believe in fairy tales, Wolfie?" Dagmar teased her brother. "But, if you must insist on playing the part, Your Witty Royal

Highness, why not command your footman to bring the carriage with the white horses so that it can carry us back to our palace."

"My Lady-in-Waiting. As you please." Wolfgang bowed in jest. "Unfortunately, I must offer my regrets. The coachman found that his behind became too chilled. He simply left us here."

Dagmar quickly turned to me. "It is unfortunate, indeed, my little sister. Now we need to hurry and walk home like commoners before we will turn into frozen icicles."

For the first time in a long while, I smiled. We rose and interlaced arms to keep ourselves steady on the slippery path that took us home. Minutes later, Wolfgang pointed to the sky. "Look, how beautiful. Heaven is aglow."

We lifted our eyes and saw as the last rays of the sunlight disappeared in the west. The sky was streaked with red, and a large, golden moon rose amidst white, feathery clouds. I held on tighter to them and knew that their compassion and kindness would help me soften my pain.

Chapter Fifteen

Guilt vs. Forgiveness

Exquisite sounds of music greeted us when we entered the house. We quietly pulled off our shoes and hung our coats on the coat tree in the hall. I felt myself becoming emotional once more.

"What is your mother playing?" I whispered.

"It's called Claire de Lune by Claude Debussy," Wolfgang responded as he took his thumb to wipe away another tear that ran down my cheek.

The music was haunting. It created a longing in me. I yearned for soft arms, wich would wrap around me and hold me close until eternity. I noticed with embarrassment that Wolfgang stared at me with a curious expression that I could not place. I looked for a handkerchief.

"Don't worry about it," he finally said in a low voice. "It's alright. Music sometimes makes me want to cry, too."

If I had felt drawn to him before, I was more so now. He seemed to understand me and knew how to put me at ease. We entered the room and waited until Tante Helga finished playing and rose from the piano.

"Ariane," she looked at me in astonishment. "How flushed you are. The exercise and cold air have done wonders for you."

She turned to her children. "Why don't the two of you play us a bit of your own favorite pieces after you have warmed up. I think I will take

Ariane into the kitchen where we can talk." She took me by the arm and pulled me along.

"Your eyes are puffy. Was it windy outside or is it what I think it is?"

I nodded. "I became sad because Mutti made sure that it would be I who would find her."

"I am so sorry, Ariane-chen, but I don't think that your mother in her desperation was capable of thinking her actions through."

"It is my fault that she died that night."

"What nonsense are you speaking, child!"Tante Helga gasped. "Who has put such dreadful thoughts into your head?"

"Well, she often said that it would be I who would send her to the grave. I could never please her. And, had I come home that evening..." I paused and sighed.

Tante Helga took my hand into hers. "Oh dear! My dear girl. Did you believe all this time that you were responsible? No wonder that you tried to keep it to yourself. But please, you must get that idea out of your head! Listen to me carefully. No mother would kill herself because of her own child. Regardless of what she might have told you, I am convinced that deep inside her heart she felt love for you, even though she did not show it. Moreover, I want you to remember something equally important. No child is ever responsible for the actions of a parent."

"Yes, but she knew that it would be I who would find her dead. She knew that I would come home that evening. It just happened that a storm kept me away."

"I don't know what went on in her despondent mind before she took those pills. I only know that your mother was looking forward to her date with Fritz. In fact, I went to speak to her for a few minutes before she was to leave. She seemed well enough then and did not complain about anything."

"Then, if it isn't my fault that she died, whose fault is it? Did Fritz Neumann have something to do with it? Wasn't he the last person who saw her?" I swallowed hard. A small version of that familiar lump was making its way back into my throat.

Tante Helga's eyes lingered on my face for a moment before she responded. "I did not want to discuss it with you, Ariane-chen, but since you are convinced that you are responsible, let me tell you what I found out. She and Fritz quarreled after he arrived at the apartment. I spoke to him a few days ago. Your mother must have simply lost her head after he left her."

"What happened?" I stared at Tante Helga.

"Well, I ran into Fritz unexpectedly in town a few days ago and asked him whether he had heard that your mother passed away. He glared stoically at me and responded that she was no longer his concern because their relationship ended on Christmas Eve. When I saw that I was upset, he assured that she had seemed well enough before he left her. When I pressed him to tell what had happened, he was most reluctant to tell me the reason for his break-up with her. He finally mumbled that your mother knew what consequences her actions would have." Tante Helga paused a moment before continuing. "What actions?" I wanted to know. I pressured him to tell me. He finally said that she betrayed not only him but the government."

"What did Mutti do to make him think that she was a traitor?"

"Well, he told me that he planned to propose marriage to her on Christmas Eve. But just as he was leaving his own house to go to her, a STASI member, who also is his friend, came to warn him. He said that Fritz had come under suspicion for fraternizing with a woman who was engaged in seditious activities. That woman, supposedly, was your mother. His friend told him that she associated with a group of colleagues at work who were arrested only a few days earlier. The group is accused of helping to organize the revolt on June 17. Their activity was only recently discovered.

"I reminded Fritz that your mother liked to socialize and that being seen in the company of others does not make her a traitor. But you know that any association with someone who has fallen under suspicion is cause for interrogation or even arrest. It does not matter whether that person is guilty or not."

I nodded. I knew that.

"Fritz maintained that it did not matter how much, or if at all, your mother was involved with such a group. What mattered to him was that a file on him had landed on the desk of a STASI agent with whom he once had severe disagreements. Fritz believed that the man would do anything to soil his reputation. He would look at the file and find him guilty. Fritz needed to distance himself from your mother. He needed to save himself."

Tante Helga paused and looked at me with sad eyes. Both of us knew how serious such an accusation was.

"That is not all, Ariane-chen," Tante Helga continued. "Fritz was furious that your mother had hidden from him that your Uncle Emil was taken away by the STASI. She knew that her name had been added to the Black List, but she kept it from him. Fritz claimed that she wanted to use him and destroy his reputation and career."

I stared dumbfounded at my guardian. "Is that really true what he said about her?"

"Well, unfortunately, he believed the report of his STASI friend. Instead of taking your mother out that night, as he had initially planned, he came to confront her. He was angry. It would not surprise me at all if he had told her that he, too, would report her. He needs to save his backside and proof his loyalty to the Party.

I was stunned. Tante Helga, too, fell silent. Finally she offered, "I find it unbelievable that Fritz accuses your mother of having made him the victim instead of acknowledging that it was she who was victimized."

My guardian and I fell silent again. I thought back to June 17 and remembered that I waited for my mother to come home. I asked Tante Helga, "Did Mutti ever tell you that she participated in the revolt? I remember how worried I was for her on that day. She came come home very late."

"Ariane-chen, your mother could have been anywhere that day. I know that she was outspoken. But she never gave me any indication of being involved in anything that would undermine the GDR. If she was guilty of anything, it was that she became romantically involved with the wrong man. It might not have been her fear for the STASI that made her lose her head and give up on life but the realization that love slipped through her hands once more."

Tante Helga let out a long sigh. "You see, child, you were not responsible for the choices she made. Even though we do not know what really happened and only have Fritz' account of what took place that afternoon, you must believe that you could not have changed anything."

A labored sigh escaped me. I was more confused than ever. What was it that really happened that made my mother want to leave life this time again?

"Do you believe that God will send her to hell now?" I asked.

"My dear child. You must not judge her too harshly. No one can tell what goes on in the heart or mind of someone whose thoughts are confused. I believe that God is a forgiving God. We don't always see the burdens that another person carries. He alone knows what goes on. He will be the judge."

I knew that my guardian's life had also not been easy. I asked. "Why are *you* not as confused and despondent as Mutti was?"

"I cannot tell you what makes one person more resilient than another. Having hope and keeping the faith gave me a reason to endure it all. Besides, I have my children to look after and need to remain strong for them." Tante Helga smiled and patted my hand. "It's often not easy to be a mother. Especially if someone is not as healthy as she should be. I am so sorry about your loss, Ariane-chen. But I will try to make it up to you. Remember that you will always have a home here. I hope that you will be happy with us."

In the stillness that followed, notes of a violin solo drifted across the hall to us. Tante Helga smiled. "Ah, what a coincidence. Dagmar is playing a new arrangement from the opera of *Thais* by Jules Massenet, which Frau Römer gave her to practice. The piece is called *Meditation*."

"Why is it a coincidence?"

"Why? Well, I suppose that you already know what takes place between men and women, Ariane-chen. Let me tell you what it is about. The theme revolves around a courtesan and a priest who lusts after her. When the woman becomes gravely ill and lies on her deathbed, she asks God to forgive her the many sins that she has committed. She receives forgiveness and crosses over to the other side happy and without fear. The priest, on the other hand, has soiled his soul and lives on, feeling tortured.

"I think the lesson is that no one, except God, knows what is in a person's heart and soul. I believe that He is a forgiving God."

Tante Helga's words made me think back to the night when I had seen the agony of my mother's soul. I wondered whether it had finally found peace.

A great sadness for her came over me. Without warning, my tears began to flow once more. They spilled onto the tablecloth in big heavy drops. I wept for her and for myself. And then I cried for hope and mercy. I clung to the thought that if the courtesan in the opera of *Meditation* had found forgiveness, perhaps not everything would be lost.

Tante Helga sat with me and let me cry. And when I was done, she helped dry my tears. "Let go of sorrow now," she soothed. "Find peace with us and put the past behind you."

I nodded, silently wishing that God would be merciful enough to rewrite the script of my life. I wanted to be led out of my troubled past and ushered into a gentler future.

Chapter Sixteen

An Act of Retaliation

After my conversation with Tante Helga, something shifted inside of me. The nightmares, which had been my steady companions since Christmas, disappeared. My head was clearer; and although a heavy feeling in my chest returned on rare occasions, the greatest weight had lifted off me. I was able to participate in family conversations and even laughed at a few wisecracks that Wolfgang made. He commented on my face and how it lit up my whole person when I smiled. "It transforms you," he commented. His mother remarked that his observation was a mature one for someone not quite fifteen years old. I was pleased that Wolfgang paid attention to me but also suspected that it was not me alone whom he was trying to cheer up. His mother had walked around in a pensive modd for a while now. No one knew what was troubling her.

A few days later, Andra came knocking on our door. "I'm so glad that I found you, Ariane," she cried. "I went to your old apartment. Frau Meyer opened her door and gave me your address. Tell me, are you happy here? Truly, if you are not, I can ask my mother if you can come and live with us. She feels guilty that she kept you from going home that night of the storm."

"I'm better now," I responded. "Everyone assures me that even if I had come home earlier, it would have been too late to save my mother.

But thanks for your offer, I am really alright here. The family is really nice to me."

Andra didn't know what else to say. Consequently, we sat quietly next to each other, fiddling around with our hands. Finally she blurted out, "Oh, I almost forgot. I saw Herr Langhans at the Sports Center. He asked about you. He wants to talk to you as soon as you feel up to it. You know that he won't be back teaching at your school this year, don't you? He's busier than ever at the Center."

Since our government was placing great emphasis on physical education, the Sport Center in town was training young athletes in various disciplines. Trainers kept an eye out for athletically gifted students, and the most promising ones hoped to make it to the International Olympic Games one day. Andra had such a goal. She was a swimmer. She and I met when both of our schools competed against each other. She won the swim competition that day, while I came away with the first prize for the triathlon event.

"What does Herr Langhans want with me?" I asked.

Andra shrugged her shoulders. "He didn't say but he seemed concerned about you."

"Perhaps he still wants me to join the relay team. He proposed it to my mother a while back."

"He met her?"

"Yes."

I told Andra how my mother and I had encountered Herr Langhans in town. Because I hadn't seen much of her the previous days, I had waited for her outside of her factory to walk her home. She had been surprised and had inspected my clothes to make sure that they were clean enough. She did not want to be embarrassed by my appearance. He came walking toward us on Hauptstrasse. I pointed him out to her. "That is my my gym teacher," I said.

My mother observed him with interest. Herr Langhans was tall with an athletic build. His strong looks were deceiving, because everyone knew that he was a gentle giant.

"*Guten Tag, gnädige Frau*, he said, addressing my mother in the old, respectful way of high society that had mostly fallen by the wayside already. "Dear Madam. You must be Frau Berger. I am happy to finally meet you because I have a proposal for your daughter. I would like her to become a member of our track team."

"I didn't know that my daughter could run so fast or that anyone would find her useful," My mother responded.

I was shocked at her response. How could she embarrass me so?

My teacher ignored the remark. Instead he said, "Well then, Frau Berger, let me tell you that Ariane has already won trophies for our school. She must not have told you that."

"That's neither here nor there," my mother countered. "I am opposed to her participation in any team sport. I am well aware that the Communist Party and the *Freie Deutsche Jugend* are seeking talented young people to train, which they want to train for their purpose. They want to create an army of superior athletes and use them as political propaganda. Do you really think that a show of athletic ability will change the opinion that the western world has of our regime? I will not let my daughter be used as a propaganda tool in the machine of Communism."

Once again I almost fainted of embarrassment and concern for her. Why was she placing her life in danger by making anti-government statements in public? The Free German Youth organization had taken charge of all the athletic clubs in the GDR, and I could already hear the STASI knocking on our door. I looked pleadingly at Herr Langhans, silently wishing him to ignore the remarks of my mother.

I pulled on her coat sleeve. "Mutti, please, I beg you. Don't say anything else! Let's go."

My mother gave me an annoyed look. "Don't be discourteous and interrupt adults when they are speaking, young lady!" She lost her balance and moved onto a wider piece of cobblestone to avoid having her high heels slide into another crack.

Then she looked up at my teacher's face. It had remained unruffled. "I am not a Communist, Herr Langhans, and my daughter is not a member of the Young Pioneers either. I know that the Party and the FDJ made threats to punish those who refuse to participate in their programs. I will not allow my daughter to join."

My teacher smiled when he responded. "Madam, we really should not have this kind of conversation on the street. There are ears everywhere. However, since you are so determined to state your views, let me tell you what my job is: I am in charge of the Center and am presiding over it for the physical and emotional benefit of children. I strongly believe that they, including your daughter, need an outlet for their youthful energy. I provide a place for them to come to when their mothers, such as you Frau Berger, are at work. The Center is a safe place for them to be. One thing that I do not do is lecture them about politics. Even though some of the children will later represent the GDR in sports competitions against the West, my work is not political."

I was surprised that he had spoken so freely. He, too, took a risk, but his comments appeased my mother, even though she did not totally trust him..

"Well, then, Herr Langhans. Perhaps I will think about it. And if I decide to give my permission, I hope that all of your efforts prove themselves worthy of your intentions. That is, if a person can believe what you have just said."

My mother was correct in one thing: Our State was using the achievements of our athletes to enhance the reputation of the GDR. Some of our athletes had participated in competitions across the border. Instead of returning, a few had asked for asylum. Immediately after such incident, the GDR accused the host nation of poisoning the minds of the defectors. They even claimed that our athletes had been kidnapped against their will. Our government had let lose a barrage of propaganda, which stated that the "Fascist West" was trying to cause a wider rift between the peace loving GDR and every other nation in the world.

"Wow!" Andra said after I finished telling her my mother's encounter with Herr Langhans. "Your mother was really brave and took her chances. She didn't even know him."

"Perhaps that was her final undoing," I replied. "She never could keep her opinions to herself. Perhaps I should go and see Herr Langhans. He always was so nice. But before I talk to him, I want to make it through my first week back in school. I am apprehensive about facing my classmates. I know how everyone talks. I've heard that there is still much gossip floating around town about me and my mother."

"Just ignore it," Andra responded. "If it gets too bad, perhaps Frau von Waldheim can keep you out of school for a while longer until they get tired of talking about you. Perhaps you should transfer to my school. Not many kids from your old neighborhood go to it."

"I like my teacher," I commented. "Besides, I like my small school better than yours."

I decided to return to school, because missing classes meant that I would need to make them up sooner or later. The small school, which I attended, used to be the house of the Baron. I felt fortunate that I had been assigned to attend my school instead to the larger one in town. It seemed an auspicious sign. The Baron's estate had once proved to be a safe haven for me. When I became enrolled, I could not wait to see the interior of the house. It promised to be impressive, and it was. The ground floor boasted an ornate and winding staircase that led to the upper rooms, which were our classrooms. Their high ceilings and walls displayed gold leafed angels and other mythological figureheads, while the parquet floor was buffed to a high gloss. It reflected the young feet of students during the first day of school. Unfortunately, the shine soon disappeared. Since no one knew when the Baron would return to reclaim his property, our teacher gave strict orders to keep the rooms in excellent condition. But soon we learned that the estate had been taken over by the government.

A few weeks into my very first school year, I dared to visit the horse stables. Going near them was forbidden. I overstepped the rules and talked a classmate into being my sentinel before I made my way to the back of the property. With beating heart I touched the handle of the stable door. I pushed down on it. To my surprise, the door opened. But I became quickly disappointed by what I saw. Nothing in the room was as I remembered it. Sunlight streamed through three small windows near the ceiling, while the meager stalks of dried grain that once served as bedding for so many people, had been swept away. Absent also was the strong, oppressive stench of body odor that had hung in the room. It seemed that the turbulent past had made a clean break with the present. In spite of it all, the memory of the long confinement in that room remained firmly rooted in my mind.

When I returned to class after my mother's death, I was acutely aware of the sidelong glances that my classmates gave me. When lunch break came, I grasped at feeble courage and joined my regular group of comrades in our usual corner of the school grounds. We ate our sack lunches of dark bread and cheese in silence. One of the girls pulled apart her sandwich to inspect the content when a boy walked over and grinned, "Hey, Ursula, are you looking for maggots on the cheese?"

"So what if I do!" Ursula looked surly at him.

You won't find any this time of year. It's too cold," he assured her.

The girls in the group giggled because they knew that the boy was sweet on her.

The boy's comment made all of us open our sandwiches and inspect them. We all knew that we had consumed more than our share of maggots in the past before we realized what we had done. Flies liked *Harzer* Käse just as much as any of us liked it, even though it reeked worse than two dozen unwashed feet on a hot summer's day. We all called the cheese, which is named after the Harz Mountains, by the fitting name of "stinky cheese." The absence of refrigeration in our homes provided flies easy access to it. I had fallen victim to the maggots during several summer months when I forgot to check my sandwich. The boy had been correct. Neither of us found any worms crawling between our slices of bread.

Just as the bell called us back to the classroom, one of my friends whispered within earshot of me, "My father said that maggots like to eat dead people after they are buried. Do you think that they got to Ariane's mother yet?"

I turned to face the girl, who quickly put her hand over her mouth and gasped. "Don't worry," I told her, knowing that she did not say it to be malicious. "My mother isn't buried in the ground. She's been burnt to ashes."

The eyes of the girl became big and round because she did not know what that meant. I, in turn, was grateful that I would not need to add an army of maggots to my list of worries about my mother.

The beginning of the next day in class proved just as oppressive as the previous one. No one seemed to know how to approach me, until Susie, whose desk was next to mine, noticed the shoes I was wearing.

"Are these new, Ariane?" She asked in a sweet voice, "They sure look pretty. I like the strap that is going across the top."

"*Ja.*" I nodded. "They used to belong to Dagmar, my new sister. She plays the violin and wore them when she gave performances on stage. You should come and visit me some time in my new home. You can listen to her play. She is really talented. I think that she will be famous one day."

I was babbling away, happy that someone showed courage and spoke to me. "Dagmar only wore them on Sundays and on stage. They are still good. See?" I lifted up the shoes to show Susie the soles. "I like the shoes, but I really wished that they were red. I've always wanted to own a pair of red shoes." I returned her smile.

To my chagrin, a boy from my old neighborhood took my conversation with Susie as permission to harass me. He drew his pie-shaped face into a grimace and called, "Hey, you, Ariane! Why don't you wait until your feet get big enough to fit into the shoes that your mother used to wear. I remember that she had a pair of high heeled red ones, the kind you probably are speaking of. She used to tiptoe down the street in them. My mother said that your mother wore them to show off her legs." The boy bellowed out a laugh, thinking himself both clever and funny. "Look everyone," he shouted. "This is how Ariane's mother used to walk."

He teetered across the room and swung his hips. "My mother said that Frau Berger wanted to imitate one of the movie stars. She even thought that she looked like one."

Some of my classmates began to giggle while I became angry. "She did not! And even if she wanted to do that, what business is it of yours." I hissed at him. "Besides. My mother had better legs than the tree stumps that your mother has for legs. She walks like a farmer and has a face like a horse. She is jealous because she is not as pretty as my mother was."

I could have bitten off my tongue for being nasty to him and immediately fell silent. I had always been on good terms with everyone and had never fought. But now I felt obligated to defend myself and my mother. I also knew that his own mother was not as ugly as I said she was. However, she *was* dowdy looking. I never saw her without an apron tied around her waist or without the ever-present scarf that covered most of her hair. To make things worse, she knotted the scarf tightly above her forehead and left the two ends of the knot sticking up in the air like ears of a rabbit. I suspected that his mother considered that look to be the latest fashion. My own mother despised a look like that.

"You can tell just by looking at these women which one of them is a *Hausfrau* and which has a social life outside of her home," she said. "Whatever drives these women to make themselves so unattractive!"

My remark about his mother made the boy angry. He retaliated. "Don't you talk about my mother like that, you stupid goat!" He shrieked. "At least she loves me and pays more attention to me than *your* mother ever did you. Obviously, yours neglected you. She even cursed you before she killed herself. You were lucky that someone was nice to you and gave you a home afterward. My mother said that you should have gone to the orphanage."

My eyes flew wide open. I was mortified. How did he learn of my relationship with my mother? But more importantly, had she really cursed me? For a moment, I felt as sick as I had been when I had found her dead.

The boy took no note of my red face but continued. "Anyhow, it doesn't seem to bother you very much that she has killed herself. You didn't look sad to me a minute ago when you mentioned the red shoes to Susie. You even smiled. So, anyhow, why are you defending your mother when you don't care that she is dead?"

I swallowed hard and tried to control my tears. To think that other people knew that my mother did not love me and that she might have even cursed me with her last breath, shamed and terrified me. I gathered every measure of courage I could muster and shouted, "Why don't you just shut your mouth, you moon-faced, ugly bully!"

"Leave her alone, Norbert," Susie came to my defense, while my other classmates observed us in silence. Finally, another girl stepped forward, reached for my hand, and said in a small and unsure voice, "You *are* sad, aren't you, Ariane? Tell him that you are."

"No, she's not," the boy called. "Look at her face."

"Stop it Norbert, you big idiot!" One of the boys, who used to tease me by pulling on my pigtails, yelled. "Just leave her alone. You are being mean!" Turning to me he said, "Why don't you punch him in the mouth, Ariane. He deserves it."

I nodded but continued to stifle the furor that rose in me. It didn't work. I had been shamed more than enough by every other gossip about my mother's suicide. I was ready to strike out now. When the moon-faced boy opened his mouth to add one more insult, something inside of me snapped. I became blind with rage and saw nothing but him before me. He became the symbol for everyone who had tried to sully my mother's reputation and had wanted to disgrace her even after her death. Feeling a superhuman strength rising, I drew my fists. I punched his face and knocked him backwards. A second punch landed him on the floor. I jumped on him and pinned him down, while I continued to pound my fists into him without mercy.

My classmates suddenly came alive and egged each of us on to further cruelty against each other. I pounded away for several minutes as he tried to retaliate in kind. Finally, he managed to wriggle himself from under me. But, soon, his own strength waned. When he finally keeled over and just lay there like a fat lump of pig's lard, my classmates shouted a count down, "One, Two..." They implored him to get up and resume the fight.

None of us heard Frau Wohlmeister enter the room. I only noticed her presence when she pulled me off the boy who was a bloody mess. He began to sob uncontrollably now. In addition to being hurt, he knew that he had been beaten and shamed by a girl.

My teacher demanded an explanation. Then she took out a cotton handkerchief and quietly handed it to the boy. "Go to the bathroom and clean yourself up, Norbert," she ordered in a strict voice.

Then she turned to me and commanded, "Take your seat, Ariane. I will deal with you later."

I took my seat and put my head on my desk. My face felt bruised. I was exhausted from the exertion. Soon, after having caught my breath, I looked at my arms. They were badly scratched. Blood had dried in several places on then. My wrist smarted where the boy had bitten me, just as any girl would have done. To my dismay, I also discovered that Dagmar's dress was torn and smeared with Norbert's blood.

With trepidation I waited for the school day to end. I knew that Frau Wohlmeister would chastise me. Perhaps she would give me a few lashes with the ruler. It was the usual punishment for girls who had been unruly or disrespectful. "Well," I consoled myself, "it still will not hurt as much as the cat o'nine tails with the metal pieces at the ends that my mother used on me."

When I stood before my teacher later, she looked up and gave me a light smile. "Oh my. Look at you, Ariane. What a mess you are. Your scratches will heal, and perhaps the dress can be mended. I do hope Frau von Waldheim will show some understanding when you get home. I, too, will overlook what has happened here today, even though I am sure that Norbert's mother will pay me a visit tomorrow."

"Well, he deserved it," I answered and showed her a stubborn face. "He badmouthed my mother. She has died, you know."

"Yes, I know." Frau Wohlmeister's face turned sad. "I did not want to remark on it. But perhaps I should have spoken to the class. Tell me, how do you deal with your sorrow, other than lashing out at other people?"

"I'm alright now," I answered. "I'm better. But truthfully, Frau Wohlmeister, I haven't been angry at anyone else like this before."

"Is that so? Do you know what I think, Ariane?"

"No."

"I think that it is good that you allowed yourself to be angry."

"It was?" I said in amazement. I was confused, did not understand why she praised me for my violent outburst. Fighting in school was prohibited. Moreover, my mother never allowed me to show my anger.

"You may be surprised that you find me on your side. But trust me, sometimes it is healthy to let your anger fly instead of bottling it all up. However, I do not want to see you fight in school again. Do you understand? My advice is that you ignore any other gossip that comes along. Just remember that there will always be a handful of people who will find satisfaction in the misfortunes of others. Some even will make up stories if the true facts elude them. I hope that you can rise above such ugly nonsense and perversity."

For a moment I was tempted to ask my teacher what rumors she had heard. I needed to arm myself against them. But I thought better of it. I did not want to be shamed again by having her repeat rumors she had heard, some, or all of them that might be untrue. More importantly, I was afraid that my teacher might have heard accounts of the men with whom my mother had kept company, even though such affairs were of the past. I knew that gossip about them was still going around occasionally.

The neighbor women had often speculated which one of the "uncles," with whom my mother associated, would become her husband. None of them lasted very long, even though they occasionally came back for visits several months after their initial departure. My liberal mother never seemed to disappoint the neighborhood and gave them plenty to talk about. It kept everyone's boredom at bay. She, in turn, scoffed at them and declared that the priggish women desired nothing more than to live vicariously through her.

I, myself, would have liked nothing more than for the "uncles" to drop off the face of the earth. To my relief, they eventually disappeared, but only after Fritz Neumann had become my mother's regular boyfriend.

The routine of the uncles was always the same. They walked into the apartment and greeted my mother with a lustful smile. "*Guten Tag*, Annie," they called and quickly took off their coat and hat. When they noticed me, their expression darkened. "Why don't you send her outside?" They muttered, obviously feeling annoyed.

As always, I protested because I was afraid to leave her alone with them. Since I neither liked nor trusted these men, I always prolonged my departure. My mother soon discovered that I wanted to protect her. She became amused and even laughed when one of the men sought to appease me.

"Go to the bakery down the street and pick up a few pastries for all of us," he told me as he searched his pockets for a 2-*Deutsche* Mark piece. I quickly calculated that it would buy eight *Streuselschnecken,* the sweet buns that I loved so much.

Not being sure that I should leave her alone with him, I stalled.

"Go on, girl," he commanded, "but this time, walk slowly to the bakery. Take your time. And when you return, stay downstairs. You may eat as many pieces of pastry as you like. But be sure to save some for us as well."

I already knew that neither of them would eat a bite and that the loot of pastries would be mine alone. In addition, I long since recognized that his generosity was a bribe. Because of it, my respect for him was almost non existent.

"She's getting too big now and knows the reason for my visit," another man told my mother. "You need to send her away before I arrive. It isn't right that she should see what's going on."

Even though I despised every one of the men, there were occasions when I shamefully bowed to the knowledge that their visits brought benefits. After they left, my mother sometimes would lay out a piece of rabbit meat or fry up a few eggs. I ate the meals with mixed feelings but would, albeit grudgingly, forgive my mother for bringing strangers into our apartment. I savored the delicacies without commenting on their donors. I knew that she, as well as I, had longed for a piece of meat or other delicacy. Without the visits of the "uncles," my dinner would have consisted of a boiled potato and the tail of a herring. I loathed the taste and smell of fish, which my mother brought home wrapped in newspaper. She would divide up the herring and make two meals from it. I only forced myself to eat it to stop my hungry stomach from complaining.

That night after being dismissed so graciously by my teacher, the same frightening dream, which had tortured me so often since Christmas Day, visited me again.

I found myself the driver of a cart similar to the one owned by Herr Gerhard. It was drawn by two gray rats. Their feet scurried over the cobblestones as fast as they could run. A sudden jeering behind me made me turn my head. To my utmost distress, my mother's skull stared back at me. Its hollow eye sockets frightened me. I wanted to stop the cart, but could not control the rats. Their speed increased. They ran through the neighborhood and past the women, who had come to watch. "Run, run!" They shrieked in high voices, wagging accusing fingers at me. I knew that they had found out that I had deserted my own mother in her time of need. I tried to dislodge the skull from the seat behind me, but it refused to leave. I became deeply ashamed when I heard the malicious shouts of the women who were passing judgment on me. When finally I no longer could endure their taunts, I screamed.

Dagmar shook me awake. "Don't be frightened. It's only a dream." She tried to calm me.

But the images of my dream stayed with me. What was it trying to tell me? Was I guilty even though Tante Helga had assured me that I was not?

Chapter Seventeen

Vati, Mutti and Karl

The comments, which Herr Fink had made about me this past New Year's Eve, stuck to me like a burr. He had suggested that I had inherited inferior genes. His words still pricked me at every turn and had my imagination running away with me. What if it was true? I thought of my foster siblings. They had been blessed with talents that I, myself, had not received. I felt no envy toward them; yet, I worked hard to prove myself in everything that I undertook. I pushed myself, wanting to excel in school and in sports. I tried to be a good girl, too. I feared that I would end up like my mother if I allowed a boy to kiss me, as one of them had suggested. I knew that my mother had been smart but had been unable to manage her life in a reasonable manner.

My fear of being abnormal intensified when I remembered what my uncle had told me about our ancestors. He had said that our forefathers had been a curious mix of artisans and business people, of which the latter had been successful and the former had been hung as black sheep on our family tree. I worried that I had inherited the weakest of the master genes. And even if the aberrations were not yet apparent, I feared that the queen mother of my genes would awaken from her slumber any minute now. I envisioned her to be the chaos gene, whose mission it was to win the other healthy ones over to do their ugly bidding. The enemy genes would march like an army of secret agents through my brain and assassinate every sane thought or emotion that once was mine.

One particular night, I could no longer endure my fear. I crept over to Dagmar's bed and shook her awake. "Do you think that the genes of my ancestors are responsible for my mother's behavior?" I whispered. "I am afraid that I'm cursed with them. Perhaps Herr Fink is correct."

"What?" Dagmar rubbed her sleep-laden eyes. "What's wrong?" She looked at the clock on her bedside table. "It's close to midnight. Are you having that nightmare again?" She sat up, still disoriented from being roused so quickly.

"No. It's not the nightmare. It's... Oh, well, never mind. Sorry to have woken you. Go back to sleep."

"I'm awake now!" She protested. "You may as well tell me what it is all about."

"Alright then. Do you remember what Herr Fink told everyone? It's making me afraid."

If Dagmar had not been fully awake before, she was now. Any time the name of Fink was spoken, she perked up her ears and became scornful.

"*Ach,* that one! Don't ever pay attention to anything he says, Ariane. "He's not a person of quality. Nothing he says can be trusted. Moreover, who is that Jeanne that you are talking about? Is she some crazy great-aunt of yours?"

Even though troubled, I giggled. "I'm not talking about a person. I'm speaking of *genes*. It's those things inside of us that make us who we are."

"Oh! I don't know anything about them."

"I don't either. Well, not much. The only reason I know about them is because my uncle explained to me what they are." I related whatever I could remember.

Dagmar laughed and waved away my concern. "Don't be silly. You seem alright to me. You are as sane as Wolfie and I are."

"Perhaps I seem alright to you now. But what about later? I don't have the same ancestors that you have. You know how my mother was. I think my family tree is cursed."

"*Quatsch!*" Dagmar chided me. "You are talking nonsense. Your uncle was smart and normal, wasn't he? Didn't you tell me that he survived the prison camp without having gone crazy and that he came back feeling more peaceful than ever?"

"Yeah," I responded. "But sometimes I thought that he was crazy anyhow. I mean, his ideas were strange at times."

I thought about what I just said. "Well, I need to take that back. I didn't mean that he was crazy. He just was different from most people. He was smarter than anyone I knew. That was the reason why he appeared so strange at times. He had his own theories about the world and life, and such. I guess I didn't understand what he was talking about. It was all so intellectual. But he was kind and loving, and that wasn't strange."

"See. You have nothing to worry about. Since he and your mother were siblings, both of them had the same genes." Dagmar paused before she went on. "Your father was alright, as well, wasn't he? You said that your grandmother spoke often of him. You've never told me much about him, though. What was he like?"

"Well." I paused and tried to remember all the things that Oma had told me about him. "Well," I said again, "She said that he was an honest, compassionate, and God fearing man. He played the accordion and was an artist. People liked him. My mother's description of him was not as charming and positive as that."

I thought for a while before continuing. "I have a few memories of my father as well. Not too many, though. I was perhaps two and a half years old when he came home on furlough. He liked to play with me and carry me on his back when we went for walks in the woods. There were always parties and music in the house when he was at home. Then, when my father had to return to his unit, I clung to him and cried. I wanted him to stay with me. Only Karl stayed longer with us."

"That is sweet. But you can't remember that far back!" Dagmar exclaimed. "It isn't possible."

"It *is* possible because I *do* remember."

"Okay then. You *are* strange." She laughed.

I gave her a shove and challenged her to a pillow fight.

"Okay, okay," she called. You're not strange. Just different, and you've got talents that I don't have. Anyhow. Just tell me who Karl is."

"Alright. If you must know. Karl was my father's best friend and a seaman in the merchant marine. He visited us whenever his ship anchored in Hamburg or Bremerhaven. He came to visit us whenever my father came home; and then, when my father took me out for long walks, Karl kept my mother company Then, after my father returned to his unit, Karl stayed with us until he had to return to his ship. I don't remember whether my mother was sad when my father left. But I know that when Karl got ready to leave, she was very unhappy. Later, after the war, she mentioned his name a few times but finally stopped talking about him. She claimed that both he and my father had abandoned her. I asked my uncle about that, but he didn't know what had happened to either of them. Actually, my uncle had introduced my mother to both of them."

"Really? Tell me about that."

"Well, Uncle Emil had taken her to a birthday party at which my father and Karl were present. When they were introduced to my mother, each of them attempted to gain her attention. My uncle said that my mother had a tough decision to make. She liked both of them, even though each was different in looks and character. My father' nature was calm and thoughtful. He was funny, too; but his humor was different from Karl's jokes.

"Karl, on the other hand, was blond. He had cornflower blue eyes. His life was filled with adventures, and his temperament reflected it. He was carefree and always enjoyed a good laugh. My mother fell for him more than for my father because he kept her laughing. He excited her. They dated for a while. But soon, Karl needed to return to his ship in Hamburg. My mother believed that a man like Karl had a girl waiting for him in every port; yet, she promised to wait for him until he would return. When no letters or cards came from him, she broke her promise."

I paused while Dagmar was quick to jump in. "I can easily guess what happened next. She married your father!"

"That was an easy guess! My grandmother observed that at first my mother seemed content and happy with my father. Then a baby girl was born to them."

"Your parents must have been very happy when you came along," Dagmar interrupted.

"Yes. They were happy. But that baby was not me. I arrived several years later."

"Okay then, where is your little sister?"

"My mother would never tell me. So I asked my grandmother. She told me that the baby died within a few months after birth. My mother loved it very much and grieved for it a very long time. She shut herself away from everyone, including my father. When she finally recovered from her sorrow, she seemed changed. She was restless and began to stay out at night. She also began to party with friends whenever my father was away on business. Then, whenever he returned, she would quarrel with him. Finally, they were so angry with each other that they almost stopped talking altogether.

"Oma said that my father believed that having another child would heal their estrangement. My mother was pregnant with me when he was called to join the war. She resented being pregnant and being left alone. She became increasingly distressed and decided that she didn't want to bring me into the world. I think that my grandmother prayed that God would change my mother's mind about letting me be born."

"Oh," Dagmar commented, not knowing what else to say.

I fell quiet, too, suddenly remembering that I had been an unwanted child.

"Go on then," she finally urged. "Don't stop now. I won't tell anyone else if it is supposed to be a secret."

"Well, as you can see, I am here." I let out a small laugh.

"So, then, what happened to Karl?"

"Well, I need to go back a few years in my story. After my mother married my father, and when either of them expected never to see him again, he returned home. It came as a shock to both of them. I think his ship had been wrecked when it traveled around the Cape of Good Hope or somewhere like that. He was stranded and lived with natives for a while. After he returned, he visited my mother while my father was in Russia. She apparently fell in love with him again. My grandmother, who came to our house almost daily to take care of me, noticed it. That is all I know, except that Karl, just as my father, never came back to see my mother after the war ended. She claimed that there was something not quite right about the whole thing."

"What a terribly sad story, Ariane." Dagmar commented. "I wished that your father had returned. Perhaps you will find him one day again. I mean, if he has not died already."

"Nine years have passed since the end of the war, Dagmar," I reminded her. I don't think that anyone could locate him now. If the Red Cross couldn't do it before, how would I ever be able to find him on my own?"

"Well, anyway. I hope that you will find him," Dagmar commented. "If it were me, I would want to find out why he abandoned me. I mean, if that is what he really did," she added a bit apologetically.

We fell silent again. Soon I remarked, "If he is alive, he stayed away on purpose, just as my mother had said. I don't know why he did not come back to take me from her. I remember him telling me that he loved me. I always believed that if you love someone, you will protect them and love them forever. Perhaps that isn't true. If he is alive, he probably no longer loves me."

I took a deep breath, wanted not to dwell on that thought. I turned to Dagmar. "Did you ever miss your father?"

"Not really," Dagmar responded. "I mean, I am curious what it would be like to have a father, but Mama and Wolfie were always there for me. I've never felt alone."

"Well, I felt alone," I said. "I used to be envious of anyone who has a father. In fact…" I began to giggle. "Do you want to hear something silly? When I was younger, I wished for Herr Ritter to be my father. Before he married Frau Ritter, he often came to visit her. Whenever I saw him, I pretended that he was my father who came to see another woman. I don't know how I rationalized it all in my silly head. It doesn't make sense now. I think I felt like that because he was always so kind to me from the very beginning.

"One day, when I was about four and a half or five years old, my mother and I heard a lot of noise in the hallway downstairs. She told me that Herr and Frau Ritter were celebrating their wedding. "Go and offer them our best wishes," she told me.

I walked out on the landing and then took a few steps down. I stopped halfway when I saw a large crowd of strangers that had gathered in the hallway below. But I could not see Herr and Frau Ritter. I sat down on one of the steps and waited. As soon as they appeared I raised my squeaky little voice over the din of the people. I called, 'Happy congratulation to both of you, our wedding pair Herr and Frau Ritter.'

"My well wishes were met with great amusement from the guests. They turned up their eyes at me. 'Listen to her. Look how cute she is. How sweet!' Several women called out. Their attention embarrassed me. I pulled up the skirt of my dress and hid my face behind it, unaware that I revealed my blue panties.

"The people laughed louder and encouraged me to come down to join them. 'Come on, little girl, help us celebrate the wedding,' they called. They stuck their arms up at me, telling me to squeeze myself through the open space between the slats. They promised to catch me. I shook my head. The whole affair seemed too dangerous and intimidating.

"'*Nein, nein!* No. I don't want to,' I called and put my face back into my dress. My embarrassment produced more comments and laughter. That, in turn, made me even more bashful. The worst of it was that a woman in the crowd imitated my awkward congratulations in the same squeaky voice in which I had spoken them. Hearing her, I suddenly realized that I had made a grave mistake. I had mixed up the order of my words. Convinced that I had offended my dear Herr Ritter, I now wanted to become totally invisible.

It was at that moment that he stepped up to the banister and looked up at me with a big smile. He called, 'Hello little Mademoiselle. *Danke schön.* Thank you for your good wishes.'

"I remember how my face melted into a big smile. My heart skipped. He overlooked that I had made a mess of my words. From that moment on, he was my hero and could do no wrong. Frau Ritter, too, nodded to me and said '*Danke*' in the cool way that is hers. I used to live for the moments when he came home from work. I would seat myself on the steps in front of the house and wait for him.

"'Quit pestering him,' my mother often admonished me in an annoyed tone of voice. I don't want to get into trouble with his wife. She is of the jealous sort.'

"But I didn't listen. I loved him and went on pretending for a long while that he was my father."

Dagmar was touched. She commented, "Perhaps he knew how you felt about him because he looked out for you and made sure that you found a home with us."

"Perhaps you are right. He said that he needed to do the right thing, even if his wife was against it. He wanted to make sure that I would be safe."

"It's a sweet story," Dagmar's eyes were soft. "I don't think you need to worry about anything, Ariane. We all will look after you. And, if we notice that you are becoming crazy, we will let you know." She laughed and gave me an affectionate push on my shoulder.

It was hours past midnight when we finally bade each other goodnight. After she fell asleep again, I lay awake a while longer. My head was filled with a collage of memory fragments, and I prayed that the fears of my childhood would stay out of my dreams.

Chapter Eighteen

1955
Alone with Tante Helga

It did not take me long after moving in with the Waldheims that I increasingly felt drawn to Wolfgang. It followed that he and I developed a true friendship. Without wanting to admit it to myself, my feelings for him went deeper than that. It was Andra who pointed out my attraction to him. "Ariane," she said, "it is written all over your face. You are smitten with him. Your face lights up every time he enters the room."

"Well…" I stammered, feeling caught. "What do *you* think about him? Isn't he the most interesting and handsome boy?"

She laughed. "I agree with you on that! I would compete with you for his affection, but he never notices me or gives me an indication that would encourage any such effort. He seeks you out over everyone else, even when your girlfriends come to visit and moon over him like the silly little cows that they are!"

"Andra!" I exclaimed. "What has gotten into you? My friends are nice, even though *you* are my best friend."

She was correct. I *did* have a teenage crush on Wolfgang and he *did* take me into his confidence, even though, in my opinion, he did not need my approval on anything. He was more brilliant than anyone could ever dream of being. In fact, he was perfect. Even the ladies in the chamber music orchestra, whom Dagmar and I judged as being too old to have amorous feelings, except Frau Fröhlich of course, were sweet and attentive to him. They cooed over him when he presented himself to them. They nurtured his personal and musical self-confidence. He was their adorable protégé.

"He is such a wonderful and talented young man," they often told his mother. "You must be so proud of him."

Wolfgang tolerated their affection and charmed them with humorous comments. I wondered how Dagmar took it all in, but I never asked her about it. Although she was just as talented as her brother, she graciously remained in the background.

I loved the chamber music evenings. They brought vibrant life into our house. Favorite's of the group, such as Smetana's *Die Moldau*, Rachmaninoff's *Piano Concerto No. 2*, *Zigeunerweisen* by Pablo Sarasate, or a Humoresque by Jean Sibelius, greeted me whenever I returned home from afternoon sessions of school or from practice with my track team. The group became accustomed to my presence and nodded their greeting whenever they saw me enter the house. I was convinced that even Herr Fink had finally made peace with my presence. Tante Helga had taken him aside a while back and had spoken to him. She had reminded him of their common love for music and had asked him to tone down his abrasive comments. Although it had been difficult for him, he had complied. But only when she was out of hearing range. We all knew that he was allowed to stay in the group because no one wanted to take a chance on having him contact the STASI and report the various conversations the group had engaged in.

One evening, after sitting and listening to their renditions of a favorite Mozart piece, I offered my bravos. Herr Fink immediately approached me with a half smile. I notice how the crevasses in his furrowed face deepened and the ends of his mustache quivered when he spoke. "Well, now, child. Or perhaps I should call you Fräulein Ariane since you are growing up? It appears that you have turned into a real classical music aficionado. *Gut, gut.* We can always use a cheerleader. You seem happy here and did not give Frau von Waldheim the trouble that I expected you to give her."

"Why should I give her any trouble?" I was a bit annoyed by his comment. "She's good to me. Besides, I'm too busy to cause anyone any trouble."

"Well, young lady. The day is young. We don't know what the future will bring, do we?" His sarcastic side showed itself once again.

I could feel my face flush and the heat rise in my body; yet, I managed to stay calm.

"I hear that you are running track. Did you join the *FDJ* yet? There are benefits in belonging to the youth group."

"I'm on the relay team, but I'm not a member of the *FDJ*. I'm not interested in joining them," I responded. "They are much too fanatical for me."

I had learned to hold my ground. Running track and being appreciated by my team had boosted my confidence. I had promised myself that I would not let Herr Fink get to me again.

"Well, then, Fräulein. Don't you think that you owe them your participation? The FDJ is overseeing the Center and is allowing you the privilege to develop your athletic ability. You should be grateful. Perhaps I need to send someone to talk to you about your views."

I was uncertain whether he was being serious or was merely jesting. I turned away from him with a shrug of my shoulders and reported his remarks to Tante Helga.

"Do not worry. He is bluffing," she suggested. Still, I could see the concern in her eyes. "I hope that he is not breaking his promise and start more trouble. He and I had an agreements. However, Wolfie may be correct and he pointed out that there is a sinister side to the man. I've already consulted with the chamber music members. No one is certain how he might react if we were to ask him to leave. I cannot chance to bring on any trouble with the Party but must insure that my children receive the opportunity they deserve."

I knew that Tante Helga's mind had lately been occupied with other things. Several days ago, when Dagmar came home from her private violin lessons, she looked distraught. "Mama, Frau Römer will retire and will no longer be able to give lessons to Wolfie and me. She said that her health is failing and that she needs to go away for a long rest."

The retirement of the accomplished string virtuoso came too soon. Dagmar and Wolfgang had wanted to study with her until they were finished with high school. Following that, they had planned on applying to a music academy for further studies.

"Perhaps I should have accepted the offer of one of the recruiters several years ago when he proposed to send both of you to a music schools for gifted students," Tante Helga told them. "But I was selfish and wanted to keep you with me. I thought that making you a member of the chamber music group would be an excellent experience and education for you."

"Nonsense, Mama," her children immediately comforted her. "Don't fret over your decision. We didn't want to live in a boarding school and be away from you. We wouldn't have liked that very much."

I knew that schools for the musically gifted in our GDR came under the auspices of our government. Such schools could only be found in larger cities. They served a dual purpose. They followed the prescribed educational curriculum as other public schools, those of the "scientific branch" of high school, while placing heavy emphasis on music education.

My foster siblings were now faced with having to make an important life altering decision. Should they put their music instruction on hold until they could enter an academy after high school or should they try to obtain entrance into a music school now? They were older than other students who would have begun their musical education while still at the elementary school level. The most important question was, would Dagmar and Wolfgang be accepted into such a music academy in their teenaged years?

Tante Helga quickly contacted old and dear friends who kept up their connections with academies in East Berlin, Leipzig and Dresden. Soon, her efforts paid off. Her children were invited for interviews. Dagmar quickly gained acceptance at a high school in East Berlin, which offered specialized courses for musically gifted students. She would stay with Tante Inge, her mother's sister, during the week but would travel home on weekends. I was happy for her but equally sad for myself because I would miss her very much.

Yet, my biggest shock was still to come. Wolfgang would move to Dresden. A music professor, an old friend of his father, had been able to procure a spot for him at a prestigious music school. No one knew how the professor had managed to obtain the admission because the academy generally accepted only the younger ones of musical *"Wunderkinder."* But Wolfgang got in and would depart before the summer vacation ended. He would come home only for holidays. Consequently, my sense of loss was great even before he had left.

He could see it on my face. "Time will fly, little sister," he reassured me. "I will keep you in my thoughts. Always. I promise. And you must make sure that you won't forget me either."

Before my siblings left, the chamber music group wanted to honor them and announced a celebration. Helmut Heinrich and his wife came with a little cart full of *"Pilsner"* beer. The cart's main function was to transport cow patty fertilizer meant for Frau Heinrich's vegetable garden.

Soon the beer flowed. For once, the group stayed away from discussing politics. They began to exchange anecdotes and humorous stories. In no time at all, the room began to smell and sound like a tavern.

Herr Fink sought me out and cornered me once more in the kitchen He inquired about my progress in school. I answered politely and withdrew quickly. I not only wanted to get away from him but also from the smell of beer. I found a comfortable place in the bedroom and picked up a book to read. Dagmar had seen me leave and came to find me. "Don't you want to stay downstairs with us? Are you upset that we are leaving?" She asked.

"No," I replied. "It's not that. I loathe the smell of beer. It reminds me of earlier time when I was pretty young. For some reason, old memories are coming back again. "

Dagmar was surprised. "I thought that you told me everything. What else did you hide from me? Please don't look so gloomy. Tell me what's wrong. Is your mother appearing in your dreams again?"

I hesitated for a moment. "No. It's not about my mother. Well, not directly. Although it could be. There are so many things that I don't understand about her and her behavior. Actually, when I come to think of it now, my memory of her and the connection to beer and liquor is kind of funny. But it's actually about someone else."

"Who? I also didn't know that your mother drank much beer."

"She didn't."

"Then, what or who is it about?" Dagmar seemed to become impatient with me.

"Okay, I'll tell you. As I said, it's kind of humorous, really. I associate beer and schnapps with visits to an old cave-like liquor store in our old neighborhood to which my mother used to send me to buy an occasional bottle of beer, but mostly she sent me for a bottle of schnapps or brandy. The visits to that place always scared me.

"You've seen the beer wagons, Dagmar, the ones that are pulled by these large brown horses with the long manes and wide behinds, the ones who deliver the crates of beer bottles with their flip tops to the pubs? Well, the wagons would also stop at the house of that old man who ran a liquor business out of an underground cellar, which felt like a dungeon. He not only sold beer in bottles but also from a big vat that stood propped up next to the wall in his cellar. You needed to bring your own container if you wanted beer from the vat. He also sold different kinds of liquor in pretty bottles. The dungeon smelled of stale beer that had spilled on the floor from the faucet. I've never seen my mother drunk, but she would send me to him whenever she ran out of a bottle of something to drink. I don't know whether he ran a good business because there was a pub right across the street from him. I would always find myself alone with that old man. I abhorred being in his company because he frightened me. The corners of one side of his mouth drooped, and, occasionally, I could see saliva flowing down his chin in small trickles."

"How disgusting!" Dagmar called out. "I don't believe you. I think you are making this up!"

"No, I'm not! He is still running his business in the same old cellar. I can introduce you to him if you'd like. But be prepared for how he will stare you down."

"I'll pass on that. But how did you find the courage to go to that place alone?"

"You don't understand. I never dared to disobey my mother, except, of course, when I sneaked into Frau Meyer's room or paid my Uncle Emil a visit when she was at work. In any case, the man came to recognize me over the years. I think I was no more than five years old when my mother first sent me to him. Even though I was too young to purchase alcohol, he sold it to me anyway. He would always tell me,

"'I can see that you are not old enough. I'm not allowed to sell it to you until you are seven years old. But never mind that now. Since you are here, I will make an exception. I am acquainted with your mother, you know. I trust you and don't think that you will drink the bottle all by yourself, *nicht wahr*, little girl? But if you do, save some for her.' He would always end with a snicker. 'Hee Hee Hee.'

"I would nod somewhat irritated and think to myself, "What a crazy old man he is. Does he really think that I will drink this stuff? In any case, I did not dare to even taste any of her open bottles. My mother was very strict in that way. She had caught me once licking out her liquor glass and laid into me.

"Of course," I continued, "I never let on that I thought he was crazy or such. He would have told my mother that I was disrespectful. I still shudder when I recall his leering eyes."

I paused, reflecting in my mind how young I had been at the time and how ominous the man and his cellar had appeared to me then. Would I still feel the same now? I didn't know.

I continued, "Anyhow, Dagmar, the whole thing seems like a scene taken from an old movie. But way back then, it wasn't as funny. What I hated most was that my mother always sent me to him after dark. The moment I opened the door to his cave, a cowbell sounded, making a dull, hollow sound. I usually had to stand and wait until he came hobbling in, wiping his dinner from his mouth with the sleeve of his jacket. He would say, 'Ah, it's you, little girl' and smack his lips as he stared at me. He always used the same words, 'I know who you are. You are Annie's kid. Well, well. I have not seen your mother in a long while. What is she doing nowadays? Is she staying out of trouble?'

"I would shrug my shoulders and look down at my feet. Sometimes I was so frightened that I could not even get a word out. But I forced myself to answer. My voice was barely audible. 'She's working every day. But she's at home right now, waiting for me to come back home.'

"As always, I obeyed strict orders not to share any information about us. The man would give me one of his crooked smiles and limp to the other connecting cave-like room where he kept the liquor that my mother wanted. Handing it to me, he leered again and spoke in his raspy, dark voice,

'Alright then, here's it is, little girl. Be careful with it. Hee Hee Hee.'

"*Danke*, I would whisper and quickly give him the money that I held tightly in my fist, and which by then was pretty moist from perspiration. I withdrew my hand quickly, making sure that his pudgy hand didn't touch mine. Then, I turned and ran out of the cellar. Before the door closed, I could hear him calling after me, 'Don't drink the bottle all by yourself, *Liebchen*. Hee Hee Hee.'

I never knew what amused him so. At times I would hear him shout, 'Walk slowly! Don't run, little sweetheart! Say hello to your mother. Tell her to come and see me soon!'

"After a while, I could repeat our conversation in my sleep. As fast as my feet would carry me, I would dash away to bring the bottle to my mother. I knew she was waiting for me."

Dagmar smiled. "Well, I think you've come a long way since you were small, Ariane. I saw the look that you gave that old oaf Fink earlier when the two of you were in the kitchen. I think he actually followed you there to talk to you. I came after you when I noticed that. I only heard the end of your conversation with him. You were pretty riled up by the time I got there. What did he say to you?"

"He said, 'What will you do now, young Fräulein, since your role models are leaving home? It seems that their influence has kept you out of trouble. If it had not not been for these gracious children, you might have followed in your mother's footsteps, after all, and be walking the streets.'"

"That stupid oaf!" Dagmar called out.

"Yeah. I could feel myself getting hot all over." I responded.

"I saw your angry face. I knew he had said something awful, and I was ready to rip his heart out for you, Ariane. I wanted to give him a good piece of my mind. But you beat me to it when you answered, 'Why are you always so mean and spiteful, Herr Fink? Do you think that it will make you important when you attack other people? Everyone dislikes you because of the hateful things you say to them. And for your information, I am not like my mother. I am my own person. Whatever she did, you are far worse. You are the most uncharitable person that I have ever met.'"

Dagmar laughed. "How did you find the courage to say that to him, Ariane? I was amazed. My mouth stood open. For a moment, I thought that he was going to slap you. But he didn't. He retreated and gave me a hateful stare as he backed out of the kitchen."

"I don't know what got into me," I responded. "You know that I don't like to fight with anyone, but something inside of me just snapped. I am tired of being bullied by him. I suspect that he will be gathering ammunition to retaliate. If not against me, then against someone else. There is not much dirt that he can dig up on me. I'm too young. I am afraid that he will take it out on someone else instead."

"Don't worry," Dagmar assured me. Fink's a coward."

Chapter Nineteen

1956
Frau Ritter's Betrayal

ot long after my siblings left home, Tante Helga received a visit from neighbors down the street. They came seeking comfort. We learned that their eldest son had decided to join the NVA, the National People's Army, which had only recently been created. In the past, not having been recognized as a separate country, the GDR had no other defense units except the *Kampfgruppen der Arbeiterklasse,* the combat groups of the working class, which had been trained and established immediately after the 1953 revolt. Now we had our own army. The creation of the NVA was one more declaration of power and show of sovereignty, because East Germany wanted the world to recognize it as a separate state, not to be confused with West Germany. The new army was structured after both Hitler's old *Wehrmacht* and the Soviet Army. The goose step and the ceremonies were fashioned after those of the *Wehrmacht,* while the doctrine favored that of the Soviet army. Many young men caved in under the social and political pressures to join. The neighbor's son had apparently fallen for the propaganda and had packed his bags. He was ready to leave. Our neighbors sought solace, quizzing Tante Helga about her own son and how she had managed to keep him from being brainwashed. Tante Helga did not know what to say. She was sympathetic but had no advice to give. Consequently, the neighbors left as unhappy as they had arrived.

Several other unexpected events followed. When I received a visit from two young FDJ members, I was certain that Herr Fink had sent them. They wanted to know what I thought about the physical fitness programs in the GDR and my reasons for participating in them. It was an easy question to answer. I told them that I enjoyed my training, the expertise of my trainer, and my track team. Furthermore, I related that exercise gave me a the sense of well-being.

Soon, they suggested that I join their organization. "Fräulein," they said, "we like your attitude and would like to depend on someone like you to recruit other young people between the ages of fourteen and twenty-five. You would have to explain to them that we offer solidarity and a sense of belonging."

Wanting not to call attention to my antipathy of them and their group, I responded that I would think it over. I hoped that they wouldn't be back but knew how relentless they could be. There had always been much pressure to join up. In general, those, who did not comply, or refused to be indoctrinated in Marxism-Leninism, faced isolation. If the FDJ set their sights on someone who did not comply, that person became ostracized and not permitted to participate in special events or organized youth holidays. I knew that I needed to be careful. The FDJ had been harassing Herr Langhans for a while. Since he was in charge of the Center, and the youth group technically oversaw the operation of it, he was told to attend their meetings. In addition, he was pressured to join the Party. Herr Langhans was still stalling, wanting to hold off as long as he could.

Herr Langhans had become a friend and mentor to me. In August, Andra and I joined him on a trip to Leipzig. We wanted to cheer him on as he participated in the Second Leipziger gym and sports competitions, the *Zweites Leipziger Turn und Sportsfest*. Since Walter Ulbricht was an exercise and sports fanatic himself, he previously had put out a call to every fit person in the GDR, encouraging them to enter the competition. If they could not participate, he wanted them to be a spectator and support our athletes. He promised the everyone would be impressed by the newly erected stadium that held one hundred thousand people. Sure enough, he was correct.

People flocked to the stadium to cheer on the hundreds of participants who competed for a medal in their various disciplines. It was a good day for the GDR. The energy in the stadium was high, and it felt good to feel connected and enjoy the unity and spirit of warm camaraderie.

Leipzig had been Tante Helga's favorite city before the war. She wondered how many of the historical buildings had survived the war and encouraged me to have a thorough look around the city. She wanted me to come back with a detailed report. Herr Langhans promised to take us on a sightseeing tour. He kept his word. Our first stop was the St. Thomas Church, the place of the Thomaner Choir, which had been founded in the year 1212. Johann Sebastian Bach had been a cantor of that choir and had directed it for 23 years. We went on to visit the 650-year old university, which was still enjoying a great reputation for excellence in education. Famous people had attended it. Friedrich Nietzsche, Richard Wagner, Gottfried Leibnitz, and Johann Wolfgang von Goethe, among many others, had studied there. I, myself, and even though not brilliant at all, had always had a thirst for knowledge. My Uncle Emil had known it and had fed my desire to learn. Walking the grounds of the university, I sudden sadness descended on me. I realized that I would give anything to one day be able to study at such a fine institution. I struggled to put that grand idea out of my head. Who was I to harbor such desires? The road to higher education became closed to me the moment my father left me with my mother and went off to war. I counseled myself that my wish would have to remain a dream only.

We took lunch at the nearby *Auerbachs Keller* in the *Mädler Passage*, an antediluvian underground pub that had been a student gathering place for centuries. It was here where Goethe, along with many of his contemporaries had speculated on the inner and outer life of human beings as they sipped beer from ceramic stein, enjoyed cognac from large snifters, or emptied decanters of wine that were embellished with artwork and poems that paid homage to the grape vine. The owner of the pub told us that Goethe had included in his work, *Faust,* many of the conversations he and his contemporaries had engaged in while socializing with them in the *Keller.*

The trip was a pleasant highlight of the year for all of us because war cries were soon to be heard again. They came from neighboring Hungary. A revolution broke out, leaving us fearing for its citizens. Once again, we sat with our ears glued to the radio station, listening to the news coming over the airwaves from the West. To our dismay, the Hungarian uprising against Stalinist rule and oppression, and the demand for the withdrawal of Soviet troops from Hungary, turned into a massacre. Several Soviet divisions were mobilized once again to squelch the revolt and crush the resistance. The country turned into one big bloody battlefield, and more than two hundred thousand escaped Hungarian fled their homeland.

West Berliners marched to the barrier at the Brandenburg Gate, which was guarded by GDR soldiers. Here, too, Russian tank units and East German troops were brought in as reinforcement to suppress an anticipated outbreak of another East German revolt. Although infuriated, people did not revolt. And when the fighting in Hungary was over, the uprising had left over two thousand five hundred Hungarians and seven hundred Soviets dead.

In the midst of the unrest, I paid Frau Meyer a visit. I found myself worried about her when she met me with tears in her eyes. "*Ach,* Ariane, I am glad that you are here. If my Gottfried would still be alive, he would skin that woman with his bare hands."

Amused by her choice of words, I responded, "What are you talking about, Frau Meyer? I have never heard you speak badly of anyone. Well… almost never. Whom would he skin alive?"

A shadow swept over the old woman's face. "Gisela Ritter, of course. That venomous snake reported her husband to the STASI. They came to take him away."

I was shocked. "But why? What has he done?"

Frau Meyer lowered her voice to a whisper, "The conniving witch claims that he sympathized with the Hungarian demonstrators. I heard her say it, myself, when I returned from the *Konsum.* I carried my bags and made it up as far as the middle of the stairs. I needed to rest for a moment. Suddenly I heard Frau Ritter scream at her husband. I could make out the words Hungary and leaflets, and such. I could not hear his response. His voice was too low and measured. But a day after that, the STASI arrived."

Frau Meyer's eyes were ablaze with anger. "You know, of course, that she has recently become a member of the Communist Party, don't you? The woman has turned into a real Medusa. All the propaganda has poisoned her brain."

"No! I didn't know that she had joined up. But I'm not surprised! She always came across as militant and regimented."

If it had not been totally clear to us before, it was now. Frau Ritter was a cold-blooded and treacherous serpent of a woman who placed her political views over the welfare of her own husband.

Frau Meyer let out a long sigh. "What's more, I cannot forget the day that I witnessed his arrest. You know how quiet the house is at night. When I heard the heavy front door bang shut one late evening, I crawled out of bed, put a shawl around me, and went to look who was being so rude and careless. When I opened my door, I heard unfamiliar voices below and quietly stepped out on the landing. I peeked down and saw them. My heart almost stopped. You know that you can recognize them immediately, those STASI men. They always wear the usual garb. I crouched low and thought that my heart would stop beating when suddenly the steps under my feet began to moan. But no one took notice. I listened to Frau Ritter's accusations. I noticed that her speech sounded rehearsed. I suspected that she must have given a written statement to the STASI in writing earlier that day. And, do you want to know the worst thing of all, Kindchen?" Frau Meyer had become increasingly excited.

"What?" I wanted to know.

"Herr Ritter stood right next to her when she made her accusations against him. And he didn't even say one word to deny them. Neither did he run. But, I ask you, where could he run to when the STASI was close enough to rub noses with him?

"*Ach*, it was a very bad night for me. I sat in my chair and tried to come to grips with human nature. I kept saying to myself, 'Was he not good to her?' She has nice furniture and plenty to eat. And he is always so pleasant. I've never heard him say a bad word to her. Moreover, there is not a person on this street who does not hold him in high regard. Everyone knows that he is a true humanitarian, our Herr Ritter, him being a fireman and a medic. You know, of course, that he once helped save your mother's life."

Not knowing how to respond, I simply nodded with a heavy heart. Frau Meyer fell silent. She and I sat across from each other in distress. It all seemed to much to digest. We could not believe that one more person, the very man who had been our hero, had been taken away from us.

"Perhaps that woman wanted a divorce from him and did not know how to extricate herself from the marriage in any other way. Perhaps she decided to choose the dirty way out, placing ideology above love," Frau Meyer suggested after a while.

"Well, she had been nasty enough to him more than once, and he had tolerated it. But I thought that she really loved him," I replied. "I certainly did. I remember how I had wanted to marry him when I had been five years old."

"Well, those are the fantasies of a young child!" Frau Meyer nodded her head. "I'm sure, however, that little children are able to read the true intentions of a person and recognize a pure heart. Mark my words, Ariane. One day, when that treacherous woman is old and lonely, when she discovers that the ideology of Communism has the consistency of Swiss cheese and the smell of *Harzer Käse*, she will realize that she had made a terrible mistake. But then, it will surely be too late to undo her ugly deed. I am convinced that her evilness will follow her wherever she goes. It will torture her for eternity."

The news of Herr Ritter's incarceration caused great sadness in my own home. But when several days later Frau Meyer knocked on our door, she bore good news. Herr Ritter had managed to escape the fangs of the STASI. Frau Meyer reported that he had returned home haggard and tired looking. She said that he had aged in years. She had welcomed him back but had asked no questions.

A few days later, I rushed to my old residence to pay my respects to him. To my great disappointment, I found him gone. He had told Frau Meyer that he would leave his wife and find work in another town. I was especially sad for having missed the opportunity to tell him that his presence had brought light and hope into my life.

Chapter Twenty

1957
Herr Fink's Betrayal

It was high summer, and a wave of excitement swept throughout the GDR. Nikita Khrushchev, who had been promoted to the position of First Secretary of the Communist Party of the USSR after Joseph Stalin's death, was preparing for a visit to the GDR. He had denounced the purges of Stalin, which had sent thousands to the gulag labor camps. GDR citizens were proud of him for that courageous act. We were told that Khrushchev would arrive as the head of a USSR delegation, which would include Anatoli Mikoyan, the First Secretary of the Councils of Ministers and Andrei Gromyko, the Foreign Minister of the USSR.

The mood among GDR factory workers became a festive one. Banners, which after after Stalin's death had been taken down, were once again recovered from their mothballs and strung up across street intersections or were mounted on buildings. Each placard was inscribed with the motto, "Long Live German-Soviet Friendship."

East Berlin, too, was buzzing with activity. The Soviet-occupied section of the city prepared itself for a historical moment. Nikita Khrushchev, Walter Ulbricht, and Otto Grotewohl would come to make speeches and reaffirm their friendship with one another. Their purpose was to publicly show a united front against the Fascist West.

Everyone wanted to catch a glimpse of the Soviet leader. When he finally came walking down a path, flanked by an honor guard of the national forces of the GDR, young Russian and German Pioneers with shiny faces, and with their respective red and blue kerchiefs neatly knotted around their necks, hurried to present flowers to each dignitary.

Soon, Walter Ulbricht took his place on the podium and announced that the East would continue to wage a cold war on all imperialists. Khrushchev followed with a lengthy speech, lauding GDR leaders and all East German workers for their unshakable efforts to rebuilt their country. People were moved, while the president of the Workers Union began to weep openly. He promised Khrushchev that he would make sure that production of all goods would increase by more than one hundred percent. People were astonished and wondered how this feat could be accomplished. But no one dared to make objections or question the union leader's promise. Spirits were high and jubilant. They mirrored *The International,* which kept blaring incessantly over loudspeakers. The song's words rallied workers of all nations to unite for a better future.

In his closing speech, the Soviet leader, just as Ulbricht before him, accused the Fascist West of sowing seeds of hate against the Soviet Union. He declared that for that reason alone, he was going to enter into a friendship pact with the GDR to thwart "Western opposition and its warmongering leaders." People were jubilant. The GDR had previously initiated a scare campaign. It wanted our people to believe that America was ready to attack us at any moment now. People had believed it and had been worried. Khrushchev's promise was like balm poured on a wound. No one wanted to experience the devastation of another war.

If in the past there had existed bitterness or disagreements between the Soviet leader and Ulbricht, none were evident. His visit was a huge success. As for the cold war, that continued.

Herr Fink had taken a trip to East Berlin to hear the speeches. He returned exuberant, wanting to share his experience with the chamber music orchestra. However, no one was interested in listening to him.

When he simply would not stop talking, Herr Donner asked him to keep silent. A heated argument ensued, with Herr Fink having the last word when he threatened to report everyone in the room for their hateful remarks against the Soviet Union and Ulbricht. The members, at first, responded with laughter. But soon, when Herr Fink took out a pad a paper and began to note down everyone's remarks, their faces turned serious. If Herr Fink would keep his word, everyone would be in trouble. The group responded by gathering their instruments and dispersing without playing a single note.

The following week brought another surprise when at the usual meeting time a few chairs remained empty, Frau Stein took Tante Helga aside and informed her that Herr Donner and Frau Fröhlich had fled to West Germany. When Herr and Frau Heinrich remained absent, as well, she commented that they had, most likely, accompanied them. We were sad and knew that it would not be long before representatives from the government would go to their individual homes and help themselves to the possession that they had left behind. Frau Stein told Tante Helga in confidence that before they had left, Frau Fröhlich had confided their plan to her. She had made her swear that she would tell Tante Helga only after they were gone. She had wanted to insure her family's safety and not jeopardize it in case the STASI would come around and question them about the disappearance of her friends. Frau Stein further told her that Herr Donner had discovered a few secret policemen lurking around his house. He had initially shrugged it off. But when colleagues at school alerted him that men in trenchcoats had come to make inquiries about him, he paid attention. A friend expressed what Herr Donner surmised. "I think *they* are after you, Franz. Someone must have turned you in."

Herr Donner, too, had tasked Frau Stein with telling Tante Helga not to worry. He said that he was confident that all would make it safely across the border. Once in West Berlin, he and Frau Fröhlich would stay with his brother until he could find another teaching position. As for the Heinrichs, they, too, would receive assistance from their relatives on the other side.

Herr Fink showed no surprise when he saw the unoccupied chairs at the next scheduled meeting of the chamber music group. He was not entirely certain, however, whether the absent members had been arrested or whether they had escaped. He quizzed Tante Helga, who pretended to know nothing. Displaying a sarcastic grin, Herr Fink assured the remaining members that if anyone else were to make any more disparaging remarks against our government that, they, too would find themselves in trouble.

The result was that Herr Sommer and his wife packed a rucksack and fled. Tante Helga learned that Herr Donner had left secret instructions with Frau Stein, telling her that if anyone else wanted to take the trip across, he knew a spot in the border that was accessible to cross. It was populated by a thick forest and provided a path into the West. Crossing there was not without danger. But Herr Donner advised that one needed to wait for the right moment when the guards were changing shifts. When later a letter arrived from Frau Fröhlich, which gave no detailed account of their escape, we, nevertheless were relieved to learn that all had made it safely to the West. She had given a pseudonym as a return address. It read, "From Frau Venus."

We were sad to lose our friends without having been able to say goodbye. We all knew that their leaving added to the numbers of professionals whose departure had restricted the quality and execution of social and economic programs in the GDR. Needed social services had already been suffering since many of the escapees had been skilled workers and degreed professionals. With the departure of our friends, the GDR had lost one additional teacher, an engineer, an optometrist, and a dentist. *Republiksflucht* had increasingly begun to be a major thorn in the side of our leaders.

If Tante Helga yearned to leave, too, she decided against it. She declared that she needed to stay for the sake of her children's music education. She now began to lament her decision that had allowed Herr Fink to join the group.

"I think it is time that you tell us about that, Mama." Wolfgang pressured her. He had come home for the weekend and had found a depressed atmosphere in the house.

Tante Helga resisted but finally gave in. She related that when Hitler began to persecute those whom he called "inferiors" or "undesirables," her husband decided to help persecuted members of his orchestra escape from our country. Herr Fink's father, who was a member of the orchestra then, sided with Hitler's methods. One day, the elder Herr Fink discovered Herr von Waldheim's activities. Instead of betraying him to the Gestapo, he confronted Tante Helga's husband. He begged him to stop doing what he was doing. Even though Herr von Waldheim continued in his humanitarian efforts to save his friends and their families, the elder Herr Fink decided to turn a blind eye to the activities. He decided to keep quiet not only out of respect for the accomplishments and reputation of his conductor but because the two men had enjoyed a close friendship that dwindled when Hitler came to power.

"Your Papa would have either been executed or placed into a concentration camp for what he did," Tante Helga told her children. That is the reason why I felt obligated to let his son join our little group."

We understood Tante Helga's reasoning but could see that Herr Fink and his sister, the wife of a STASI man, were not wearing the same coat of honor. They were unwilling to put aside their fanatical views and betrayed even those whom they called their friends. The younger Herr Fink, especially, had a need to fill a gaping hole in this psyche. He lacked self esteem and craved to wield personal power over others. In the process, his betrayal tore apart other friendships and destroyed the only chamber music group in town.

The holidays, which followed, were depressing for our family. Not only did we miss the loud voices, the laughter, and the music evenings, but we also missed Wolfgang who had decided to spend the holidays with the family of a classmate. Consequently, when New Year's Eve came around, Frau Stein was the only one who came knocking on our door. Frau Geist had declined our invitation to spend the evening with us. She had joined a group of born again Christians, which would spend the evening in prayer. The group had gone underground. Informers had previously infiltrated the group, and several members were arrested.

To keep old traditions alive, Tante Helga paid a visit to the baker down the street and ordered a dozen *Berliner Pfannkuchen* for New Year's Eve. Telling the baker that she was stepping into the footsteps of Frau Fröhlich, who ordered doughnuts from him every year, the baker's face lit up. "I will save a few special ones for you, Frau von Waldheim. I will box them up carefully, just as I did for the lovely Else. I wish her well over there in the Golden West."

"So, you know where she has gone to?" Tante Helga asked in astonishment.

"*Jawohl!*" he answered. "You know that no one can keep a secret around here. As soon as a house or an apartment becomes abandoned and the government people have cleared it of the previous owners possessions, everyone scrambles to hand in their housing application. You know that decent living quarters are still difficult to find."

And so, all of us spent a quiet evening, focusing on the lighter events of the old year. We remembered our friends across the border and shared a few humorous situations we had experienced in their company. We all were careful to avoid speaking the name of "Fink." When the clock struck twelve, we lit a few sparklers and sent our wishes into the ether. We asked for protection and hoped that the next year would be kinder to us. We asked that it would bring us less unrest and upheaval, less than we had experienced so far

Chapter Twenty-One

1958
A Loaded Gift

We were jubilant because the times of food ration cards had finally ended. We also were pleased that we now were allowed to purchase food, if available, in other neighborhoods than in our own. My biggest joy, however, was that the time had come for me to graduate from school and enter a two-year secretarial school that would teach me marketable skills. Attending the school would also give me the opportunity to hone my Russian language skills, which had been a mandatory subject in school since the second grade. Contrary to most of my classmates, who resisted learning Russian and cared not whether they received a failing grade, I enjoyed learning it. The language was difficult to master, but our Russian books were full of quaint tales that were set in the time of the Tsar. I enjoyed such stories and often dreamed of being carried across the wide, open and snowy tundra in a sled that was drawn by a pair of spirited horses. When I thought about it, I could almost feel the icy wind on my face as I inhaled the smell of freedom. But then I remembered that people in the days of the Tsar had been poor and oppressed, and nothing seemed to have changed since then. That did not dim my interest in wanting to learn Russian as best as I could. On occasion, our cultural center invited Cossack dance troupes or entertainers from the Ukraine to come and perform in town, and our Russian teacher, Herr Dombrowski, urged students to accompany him. I was always eager to go along. Herr Dombrowski served as interpreter for the Russian headquarters in town and was also the interpreter at cultural events. I always paid close attention when he spoke and soon was proficient enough to carry on a conversation with the performers. Their response, their gracious smiles, led me to believe that mistrust and fear between opposing nations had their root in ignorance and prejudice. Sometimes I believed that they smiled because I was still young. Nevertheless, I wondered whether prejudices would disappear when a country's people were given the chance to communicate on a human level and were allowed to share their joy, love, fears, and concerns without feeling separated by the barrier of politics.

Our winter seasons had been long and hard, even though the last one had been worse than the one that just passed. It had been glacial. Dry ice storms had raged, and in the stillness of the night, one could hear the breaking of tree limbs, which were unable to withstand the lethal frost. I had kept warm because I had been gifted with a fine garment that was another "hand-me-down" from Tanya. While in the past I had been unhappy when forced to accept charity, this time I actually had welcomed it. The coat had fallen into my hands like manna from heaven. I knew the story of the children of Israel, who had found nourishment when they had needed it most. Oma said that God gave it to them, while my Uncle Emil claimed that it was the frost and dew of the wet season that brought the manna to them. No matter from where it had come, it sustained them on their long trek in the desert. For me, the manna appeared in the form of a beautiful, soft and shiny sable coat. It was the most elegant coat that I had ever seen.

"This is how I imagined the daughters of the Russian Tsar to dress," Tante Helga exclaimed when I modeled it for her. "It's absolutely gorgeous I would not mind having such a coat myself."

"I'll share it with you," I jested. Both of us knew that she was too tall and broad to fit into it.

I still marvel at how I received it.

I ran into Tanya unexpectedly several weeks before the cold set it. I immediately saw that she not only gained in circumference but was taller.. She shouted a cheerful, "*Hallo*, Ariane," flailing her arms like vanes of a windmill. I gave off an audible moan. I remembered that she had been fond of prefacing her sentences with words like "anyway this or anyway that." I immediately found out that she had not changed her habit.

"For goodness sakes, Ariane, where did you hide out all this time! Anyway, Mami and I wondered what has become of you. We didn't know where to find you, although the word on the street was that you had moved in with the Waldheims. But when I asked that very handsome Waldheim boy about you, he claimed not to know you. Anyway, I once saw you jogging down the street and ran after you. But, I couldn't keep up with you. I gave up. Anyway, Ariane, you are so fortunate that I ran into you. I have a wonderful fur coat at home. I actually saved it for you. I only wore it once. Honest. I wouldn't lie to you. Anyhow, can you believe that I have already outgrown it? Mami was pestering me to find you because she doesn't want anyone else but you to have it. Anyway, she didn't need to worry that I would give it to anyone else. You are the only one who would look good in it. Except for me, of course. I looked good in it too, but as I said, I can't wear it any longer.

"I wanted to give you a dress last year as well, but I couldn't find you. I must confess that I gave all of my other stuff to Renie, the girl who lives above the old brewery. But, anyway, for some reason, Mami does not want Renie to have the coat because she thinks that it will look better on you and that you will take care of it better. Mami likes you and has wondered what has become of you since you moved away. Anyway, I'm glad that I finally met you before the cold weather sets in."

Tanya finally paused in her long explanation. Her voice was loud and her words had spilled from her round lips like a cloud burst. Now, she paused to take a deep breath and expanded her chest like a balloon. She opened her mouth once more to speak.

I quickly pressed a finger over my lips. "Psst. Keep your voice down, Tanya. Everyone's looking. But really, I don't need a new coats this winter. You keep it or give it to Renie." I knew that Renate came from a poor family. She would be more than pleased to count a fur coat in her possessions.

"Don't be silly, Ariane, you absolutely *must* take it. It is fashionable and elegant. Rich people in the Golden West wear coats like that. My Papa said that they also wear them at the royal court of the Tsar in Russia."

"There is no royal court because Russia doesn't have a Tsar any longer, Tanya."

"I know that! Don't be silly. Anyway, I'm not *that* stupid! But I am convinced that they would wear coats like this if they still had a Tsar. Anyway, Ariane. There's no one else whom I want to give it to. It has a matching muff and one of those…you know… big round Russian hats to go with it. My Papa traded something else for it, and now he is very unhappy that I can't fit into the coat. He told me that if I don't stop eating, he won't bring any more food home."

I couldn't help but smile now. Tanya would never stop stuffing her face.

She made a clicking sound with her tongue as she surveyed me. "Well, even if you seem to have come up in the world, I think that you should take the coat anyway. You will look smashing in it. Trust me. I might not be smart in other things but I know about fashion. I looked at magazines that Papa brought to me. I don't know where or how he got them, but they are definitely from the Golden West. Someone he knows must smuggle them across. I'm the only one in our neighborhood who can keep informed about every new fashion style over there. I think that all the other girls are envious because of that. They talk about me. You know how they are, Ariane. Everyone always talks about everyone else. You lived in our neighborhood and know it. You know how they talked after your mother killed herself. Anyway, they even talked before that. Mami and I were the only ones who didn't much talk about you afterward. I even tried to uphold your reputation because you were always so nice to me."

I suddenly felt the urge to shake her, make her come back down to earth. I wanted her to take back what she just said. What did *I* do to blemish *my* reputation? What was it that she needed to defend about me? Tanya was so ignorant, so self-assured. What did I ever do to endear myself to her and her mother? I was suddenly overcome with an urge to rearrange the screws in her head. I stared at her. Then I opened my mouth and closed it again without speaking. I knew that anything that I would say would go over her head. I was enormously irritated with her but did not want to make a scene.

"*Nein, danke, Tanya.* It's alright," I finally said. "You've given me too many things already. I'm very well taken care of now."

"Ariane, you absolutely *must* come with me, and right away. Mami would be devastated if she finds out that I saw you and didn't give you the coat. You know," her voice turned to a whisper, "I might as well be honest with you. Mami has always felt sorry for you. She was sorry for your mother, too. But after she did this awful thing to you, Mami became angry. I was surprised because Mami never gets angry with anyone. Except, she got angry with your mother then. Anyway, it doesn't matter now. Mami isn't angry any longer. Come on, then. Let's go." She began dragging me by the sleeve of my dress to make me follow her.

Once again I waved her off. Why did she bring up the past? Could she not forget it and let me live my life in peace? I had tried to forget the past. It was done. I turned to leave, but Tanya grabbed my arm more firmly and smiled. "Ariane! Come on already."

I peered at her with flaming eyes. What *was* it that made her so obtuse? Could she not see what effect she was having on me? Her own round, saucer-like eyes looked back at me with wonderment. She did not understand why I resisted her. She was clueless and oblivious to what I was feeling. For a moment, I wanted to follow my urge to give her a shove. Then I felt like laughing. I realized that I would not be able to get through to her. Her intentions were as innocent as a young lamb. Her mother, too, was a bit like her. I knew that if I followed her to her home, I would need to prepare myself for more of their antics. I would have to observe and remain the spectator in a situational comedy instead of letting them get to me. Perhaps it would be worth investigating the enigmas that they were. I had been thinking about Wolfgang these past days, had missed him, and could use a bit of entertainment right now.

"Okay," I finally muttered. "Let's go and see your mother. Just promise me that you don't mention my mother again."

I let her pull me by the hand like a toddler. She talked non-stop until we entered her house. Loud music came from a radio greeted us, and the unmistakable stench of wet raw furs assaulted my nose. Mixed into it was the smell of fried potatoes and onions, which, flanked by chunks of sausages, were sizzling in an iron skillet on the kitchen stove. I could smell the pig's fat in the skillet.

Tanya walked straight up to the stove and lifted the lid of a pot in which red strips of borscht was simmering. I was amazed. The kitchen sheltered enough food to feed the *Volksarmee*, the National People's Army. If that was not enough, Frau Koslowski, who stood with her back to us, was in the process of grating potatoes. I suddenly remembered that my grandmother had prepared delicious potato pancakes for me whenever she had come to visit. Potato pancakes had always been my absolute favorite food. I had watched as she had spooned the batter into a hot frying pan and had let the mixture bake to a golden, crispy brown.

I let my eyes sweep around Frau Koslowski's kitchen. By the ample supply of groceries that were scattered everywhere, it was obvious that her husband knew how to provide for his family. He seemed crafty enough to make deals on the Black Market. When times had been really bad, his wife and child must have faced each new dawn with a full stomach and happy disposition.

"Mami, look, I brought us a visitor!" Tanya cried over the blare of the music coming from the radio on the counter. "It's Ariane! I found her on the street."

Frau Koslowski had not heard us enter. She jerked her head around and shouted in surprise. "Oh my dear lord! Ariane, is that you? Are you finding yourself on the streets these days? Do you have no place to live?"

"*Nein, doch!* I am living with the Waldheims. Tanya and I ran into each other on a street at the north end of town."

"Oh, well, then. I am glad." She beamed and wiped one of her pudgy hands on her apron before she shoved it into mine for the usual handshake.

"*Ach, Kindchen,* it is so good to see you! We were concerned that we would never lay eyes on you again. Oh, what a tragedy you suffered on account of your mother. We still think of her. She was such a pretty woman. We so enjoyed watching her walk down the street. Of course, I tried to be discrete enough, watching her from behind the curtains. I did not want to appear too nosy. I loved to watch her teeter over the cobblestones in her high heels. She walked so delicately, just like a lady. She was always so careful to avoid the cracks between the stones." Frau Koslowski sighed and continued, "You poor child! What in the world was your mother thinking when she took those pills? We all miss her. But it is difficult to comprehend that she would leave you behind. I mean that she should not have taken you with her, of course. What I mean is...well, you know what I mean. I would not be able to live with myself if I were to do such a cruel thing to my own daughter. I have worried about you so often because you became a poor, orphaned child!"

I stared at her speechlessly and observed as she wiped a tear from her eye with a corner of her apron. Then she stretched out her arms and bemoaned the terrible blow that life has dealt me. "You poor, poor, dear!" She cried.

Before I found my own voice, Tanya interrupted her. "Mami, what you say is stupid. You wouldn't be able to live with yourself because you would be dead already if you had killed yourself like Ariane's mother. Just remember that I would not *ever* forgive you if you did that to me. But Mami, really, forget about it and stop talking! Ariane doesn't want you to mention her mother any more! She wants to forget her. Anyway. Why don't you turn off the radio. We can't hear ourselves talk."

Even though I had known that I would be in for an adventure when I followed Tanya home, I now felt overwhelmed. I was terribly uncomfortable, and my skin began to itch. I decided to escape as quickly as I could and made my excuses.

Ignoring my announcement to depart, Frau Koslowski walked up to her daughter and pinched her cheek affectionately. "Come here my little apple blossom. Don't worry. Give your Mami a kiss." She caressed her daughter's cheeks and followed it by covering them with a few loud smacks. "You're the best little apple blossom in the world. Your Mami wouldn't ever leave you."

I suddenly was overcome by laughter. I turned my head away to bring myself under control and regain a straight face. No! I needed to stay and watch their theatrics. They were both repulsive and charming at the same time. "Well, never mind these two," I quickly told myself. "I will soon enough be back in the land of reason."

Tanya went to fetch two bottles of *Sprudel* and handed one to me. "Drink up, Ariane," she ordered. Then she yelled at her mother, "The borscht is boiling over, Mami. You need to turn down the flame."

Frau Koslowski went to stir the borscht and sighed, "*Ach, ja.* Such is life for all of us. It is difficult, but we manage, don't we? You must stay for dinner, Ariane-chen."

Despite the uncomfortable moments that preceded the invitation, I felt hungry for a taste of Frau Koslowski's borscht and her delicious potato pancakes. I decided to ignore the stench of the furs and the weird emotional display of my hosts. I agreed to stay. I would concentrate on the pungent but savory aroma of the food and enjoy it.

Frau Koslowski proceeded to put bowls of warm borscht before us. Then she took a ladle and heaped piles of fried potatoes on our plates before adding pieces of sausage and onions. She produced another pot laden with sauerkraut and pork ribs. I protested at the sight of such mountains of food, wondering once more where it all came from. But I did not ask.

"Eat up my child," Frau Koslowski ordered. "We have enough for everyone. We just need to make sure that we leave some for Papa. He will be coming home late again."

"Mami, don't forget to bring us the potato pancakes and apple sauce for dessert," Tanya grunted, shoving a fork load of fried potatoes and sausage into her mouth.

Despite the earlier drama, I began to relax. I decided that Frau Koslowski meant no harm to me. I tried to ignore the inane and let myself enjoy her warm and cheerful disposition. She was totally without malice. I listened as she reported on recent events in the neighborhood and wondered why I had never taken the opportunity to really get to know her. If I had, I might have understood her ways a lot better.

I knew that Tanya loved her parents and that she was especially proud of her father. I, on the other hand, had always made a big circle around him. He had looked unkempt and had left a draft of unmistakable raw animal furs in his trail. The stench had bothered me as much as had his swarthy appearance. I had observed the guarded looks that he had received from some of our neighbors. Nevertheless, they had held their tongues and had refrained from openly talking about him. Herr Ritter had once remarked that he was pleased that our neighbors were showing good will toward Tanya's father and other people like him. I didn't know what he meant by that then but later realized that he had said it because we had been encouraged to practice co-existence with people who were different from us. Everyone had been warned not to repeat the atrocities that had been committed during the times of the *Führer*.

When I left Tanya and her mother an hour later, I carried a very expensive coat with a matching muff and hat over my arm. I knew that wearing it would not only keep me warm but make me feel elegant. What I did not know was that it one day would get me into trouble and force me to make a decision that would take me on the adventure of my life.

Chapter Twenty-Two

1959
Wolfgang's Graduation

A late spring finally arrived. Crocuses and daffodils reached for the sun and blessed us with their blooms. Two months later, the air became fragrant with blossoms of yellow forsythia and white and purple lilac bushes. The Havel river, too, began to flow lazily downstream after the sun melted its meter-thick ice crust. The awakening of nature coincided with Wolfgang's graduation from the music academy in Dresden.

Several months had passed since I had seen him. I missed his companionship and the talks we shared. I missed his face. I missed looking into his warm brown eyes that always had reflected approval for who I was. We had become very close and had found that we were much alike in character, even though we had grown up under different circumstances.

Dagmar and I were excited to be allowed to attend his graduation. I silently wondered whether he would notice that I had grown up. I was no longer the twig of a girl he would remember. In fact, my body had decided to take on the shape of a young woman. I was not entirely sure that I liked the new bulges of hips and breasts on me.

Dagmar and I decided that we would sew new clothes. I needed a new skirt to wear to the graduation, one, which would complement the white angora sweater that Frau Fröhlich had given me shortly before she had left so unexpectedly. I had inspected the garment, which had been too large for me then.

"Don't worry," Frau Fröhlich had twittered in her cheerful voice, "You'll soon be ready to fill it out. The sweater is of no use to me any longer."

Dagmar and I found a few meters of black material in a store in East Berlin and tried our hand at cutting patterns. When Dagmar draped the material around me, a sudden idea came to me. "How about making a long slit in the side of the skirt? I think it's the latest fashion now."

Dagmar's hand slipped on the fabric. She pricked herself with a pin. "Stand still already! What's gotten into you? I've never known you to be fashion conscious. Let's sew the skirt the way we had designed it. A slit up your leg would be too coquettish." She seemed unusually irritated.

"Well, I just want to be presentable for the occasion," I pouted.

"You've been fidgety ever since we found out that we will be attending the graduation," she countered. "I think that you want to show off your new figure to Wolfie! Just remember, that he's supposed to be your brother, not a boyfriend or an admirer."

I glared at her, feeling misjudged.

"You should let go of the crush you have on him," she added.

"I just miss him so much," I responded. "Don't you miss him? The house isn't the same without him. Besides, what's wrong with letting him know that I…Well, you know…"

Dagmar laughed. "That you feel something for him?"

"Well, what's wrong with that? You love him too!"

"I'm *supposed* to love him. He's my brother." Dagmar gave me an annoyed look.

I knew her well enough to see that something other than my feelings for Wolfgang was bothering her. "Why are you upset with me?" I kept my voice steady. "What did I do to you?"

"If you truly want to know," she replied, "I see him as little as you do. Then, when he does come home, the two of you run off together. I, too, want to spend time with him, but neither of you even notices that I exist."

"Where is *that* coming from all of a sudden?" I gasped. "We never excluded you from anything or forbade you to join us. It is you who separates yourself from us. Whenever we go somewhere and ask you to come along, you decline, saying that you do not want to wade through a soggy meadow or be scratched up by the thorns of wild berries, or such. I always thought that you did not want to join us because you did not want to ruin your hands or mess up your appearance."

Dagmar did not respond but stared at me with a sullen expression.

"Well, am I correct?"

"So? Even if I chose to stay at home, the two of you could spend time with me after you return from doing whatever keeps you so occupied outdoors."

"We do, Dagmar! We always ask you to come and talk to us."

"No, you don't."

I kept quiet. I didn't know what else to say. Why was she jealous? Her sudden change in mood came as a surprise to me. I suddenly remembered something that happened last year. I laughed.

"It's not funny!" Dagmar was still cross with me. "I don't like being ignored by either of you. I'm part of this family, too. Besides, now Wolfie will be graduating and I am lagging behind."

"You are being silly now. You know that you have another year to go at school and will continue with your studies, just as he will. Are you afraid that he will outshine you? I've never known you to compete with him before. "

"Well, I might as well say it," Dagmar responded. "I think that Wolfie is my mother's favorite, just as he is the favorite of everyone else around us. People say that he is always so charming. I know that his charisma will give him many more opportunities in the future than it will give me. I will have to struggle to find a good position with an orchestra."

"Don't talk nonsense, Dagmar." I quickly admonished her. I was amazed at her revelation. She never let on that she was envious of her brother or that she felt less talented than he was. It was I who continually felt inferior to the both of them. Perhaps she was trying to overcome some difficulties at school, which she had not talked about.

"Has something happened in school?" I wanted to know.

Dagmar hesitated before answering, "Well, someone else was chosen over me to play the First Violin."

"It is true that Wolfgang is more outgoing than you." I responded. "But, everyone likes you just as well. You are beautiful and are born with a sweet, feminine charm that will take you far in your career. You'll be a great violinist in your own right. In fact, you *are* one already. I am absolutely convinced that before long, a famous conductor of an orchestra will snatch you up and will select *you* as his First Violin. Then, when the audience hears you play, they will not be able to take their eyes off you. They will think that they are seeing an angel. You look like one with your long blond hair and big blue eyes. And you play like one, too."

Dagmar blushed. "You are just trying to appease me."

"Not true. Except, of course, the audience will soon discover itself earth bound again when it notices that it has mistaken your violin for a harp."

Dagmar laughed now. "Alright, alright. You are always so silly, Ariane."

"Perhaps." I answered. "But you know that whatever I said is true. And, remember that I'll be your best cheerleader when you are famous."

"Sorry for giving you a hard time," she quickly said. "And thanks for making me feel better."

"Sorry, too." I answered. I was all too happy that our little spat had passed and that she did no longer question my infatuation with Wolfgang.

When we arrived at Wolfgang's academy, my eyes immediately searched for him. I found him on stage with the other graduates. He looked stunning his dark suit and bow tie. I was excited. Finally he would come home and stay until it was time for him to begin with his advanced training in Leipzig. I made a mental note to pay more attention to Dagmar when Wolfgang was at home with us. After the ceremony, I rushed to him. I wanted to be the first one to offer congratulations.

"Ah, there you are, Ariane!" He grinned. "You look delightful. I've missed you very much, little sister." He bent down and gave me a kiss on my cheek

I blushed. He had never kissed me before. There was so much I wanted to tell him about track team, the books I was reading, and new girls I had befriended at the Sports Center. But before we were given a chance to catch up with our lives, I heard a female voice calling his name.

"Wolfgang, *mein Lieber*! There you are. Are you trying to make yourself purposely invisible?"

A pretty, dark haired girl walked up and put her arm around his waist. She appeared to be the same age as Wolfgang.

I noticed that he was a bit embarrassed by her display of intimacy. He tried to disentangle himself from her. "Hallo, Katrina. Let me introduce you to my sister Ariane."

He smiled his usual gregarious smile and flashed a row of white teeth at her. Then he saw Dagmar walking toward us. He pointed to her. "And the other beautiful young lady there is my other sister Dagmar!"

Katrina greeted me politely and turned her head into Dagmar's direction. "I did not know that you have two sisters. One of them is blond and the other one is dark auburn. Well, surely, the blond one is the black sheep of the family." She let out a small laugh, obviously thinking herself clever. "I remember the picture of your father that you keep by your bed. Dark hair runs in the family."

"No, on the contrary." Wolfgang simply overlooked the barb in the girl's suggestion. "It is I who is the outcast. My mother is blond, and so is my mother's daughter. Dagmar is my blood sister. We are from the same dark-haired father."

Dagmar came to stand next to her brother. Her face had turned into a scowl. "Mama is looking for you," she said. She had overheard the comment.

Wolfgang merely grinned but said nothing. I stared perplexed at him. Why did he let Katrina's remark slide so easily? Was he immune to insults? I looked at Dagmar. She shrugged her shoulders and then motioned with her eyes to her brother to dismiss the girl. When he did not ask Katrina to leave, Dagmar excused herself from our group and went to mingle with the others in the concert hall.

Wolfgang turned to the girl "It is Ariane who is our foster sister. She joined our family several years ago. Didn't you Ariane."

I glared at him. He was changed, and I didn't like it one bit. Moreover, just as Dagmar, I did not care one iota for this girl.

"*Ach so.* Hmm." Katrina gave me a speculative look but turned away when a male voice called to her from across the room.

"Hallo Papa," she waved to a distinguished older man. "Let me bring him over here to introduce him to to the adopted girl. That is, if she hasn't walked off like your sister before I can make it back with him over here," she said to Wolfgang.

I pushed the air loudly through my teeth. Katrina had called me "the adopted girl," and Wolfgang had said nothing.

I turned to leave, too, but he caught me by the arm. "Don't run away from me so fast, Ariane. I know that Katrina is high spirited. But she's smart. Don't let her remarks upset you. She is not as cold as she seems. She's just a bit spoiled. She's incredibly talented. She's a phenomenal clarinet player." He paused and looked at me expectantly. "So, tell me. What do you think of her, little sister?"

A wave of resentment swept over me. I felt betrayed. His relationship with her was a breach of trust between us. The two of us had been so close; and now, he was abandoning us! He was simply tossing me aside, replacing me with such a rude girl. I was hurt. Did he really expect me to support his new choice of girl? How could I be happy for him when he trampled on my feelings?

"Well?" he asked again. "What do you think?"

When I finally answered, I found myself speaking like a deranged person. I repeated the second observation that had crossed my mind when I had seen Katrina walk toward us. I had not only found her attractive but also fit looking.

"She looks very athletic." I said. It would hurt too much to admit to him that I found her pretty.

Wolfgang retorted. "No. You misunderstood me, Ariane. What do you think of *her*? I mean of her as a person!"

"I don't think that you need my feedback, Wolfgang." I managed to speak tersely. My feelings were in uproar and I felt unbalanced. "Please. Don't ask for my assessment of that silly girl of yours. Not now."

"What's gotten into to you, Ariane? What do you mean by that?" He raised his voice ever so slightly. "You and I are best friends. We have always told each other the truth."

"I'd rather not talk about her." I was aware that I played the role of the aggrieved damsel but could not help myself.

He took my arm. "Ariane! What is wrong with you?"

I stammered, "I am sorry, Wolfgang. I thought...thought that you and I ..." I broke off. How could I tell him that I had envisioned ourselves becoming a couple? How could I say it here when we were standing in a crowd of people? "Just leave me alone!" I muttered.

He peered into my face with surprise. I supposed that he had expected to hear a charming tune of approval and receive my blessing. He wanted me to congratulate him on his new, seemingly idyllic, romance. Instead, I was handing him notes of a requiem. His amber-flecked eyes closed to almost a squint. It seemed as though he was looking at me through myopic eyes. My face blushed again. Neither of us spoke, and before we found words, Katrina returned with her father in tow.

She addressed me. "Uh...you there, girl...what is your name again?"

"Berger."

"Fräulein Berger, may I introduce Professor Doktor Jahnke. My father is a well known surgeon at the city hospital."

"It is an honor to make your acquaintance, Herr Professor." I responded with feigned graciousness.

Her father was a doctor! A professor doctor! A man with several degrees and honors at that! How could it be that such an educated man was able to raise such a rude daughter? Her father's status must have gone to her head! Despite the push for equality and honor in our country, Katrina's family surely occupied a prominent social position in Dresden.

Doctors were much in demand. Perhaps as a daughter of one, she felt privileged and special.

"So, Fräulein Berger," Herr Professor Doktor interrupted the turning of wheels in my head. "I did not see you here at the academy before. Which instrument do you play?"

I looked up startled. "Oh, Herr Professor, unfortunately I do not play an instrument." I had spoken politely when instead I had wanted to shout, "Thanks to your daughter, I now play the Second Violin! I hold your lovely and cunning offspring responsible for that. I know that she wants to play the First Violin."

Mustering a great effort, I restrained myself from showing my feelings. No one should see my hurt. I even managed a smile. After all, Wolfgang's mother had taught me social graces.

Soon an animated voice of a young man took our attention. "Hello my friends. Hello Herr Professor." He slapped Wolfgang firmly on the shoulder. I know everyone here except this young lady here. He surveyed me with an appreciative look and came closer. "Hello, Fräulein." His voice was low and soft in my ear.

"Ah, Tavian," Wolfgang exclaimed. "Did you complete your rounds in the room? Are we the last ones on your social list?"

He turned to me. "Tavian has made himself the social director for the graduating class."

The young man laughed, "Well, my friend. Someone has to make that sacrifice since you are busy with other things." He cast a meaningful glance at Katrina.

"Speaking about the subject, Wolfgang," he continued, "who is this lovely creature next to me? Is she one of your femme fatale?"

Katrina gave him an annoyed look and moved closer to Wolfgang. She pushed her arm through his.

Wolfgang made introductions. "Ariane," he said. "This here is Tavian, a classmate who, apart from being somewhat musically challenged, is also very incorrigible."

He turned back to his friend. "And, Tavian, may I introduce you to my dear sister Ariane." He winked at me before he continued. "And, Tavian, look over there. That beautiful blond girl is my other sister Dagmar. Perhaps you would like to meet her. Go and introduce yourself."

Katrina glared at Wolfgang and gave him a nudge of the arm. She whispered, "Just let *her* get to know Tavian."

When she noticed that I had overheard her remark, she gave me a snooty look. She turned up her nose and pressed herself tightly against Wolfgang.

Ignoring both of them, Tavian continued, "Are you sure that both of these delicious young ladies are your sisters? My impression was that one of them was more than that." He grinned, obviously delighted that he had managed to offend Katrina once again.

His remark made me wonder what had transpired in the past that now was causing friction between the two.

Wolfgang merely waved him off. "As always, you are being a clown, my friend."

Wondering whether this slick young man would prove himself an ally, I extended my hand in a proper greeting. Instead of shaking it, Tavian bent down and kissed the back of my hand with a courtly bow. His warm lips felt pleasant. Instantly, I became embarrassed and withdrew it. The young man disturbed me. He was exceedingly good looking. He seemed to be aware what effect he had on females. I suspected that if he had not been born with a natural charm, he had worked diligently to perfect it during the nineteen or twenty years of his life. He noticed that I pulled back from him but remained undisturbed by it. He gave me a mischievous grin before he turned to Wolfgang.

"Seeing that you are occupied with your future bride and her father, may I steal this adorable young lady away from you for a few moments?"

"Just for a short while, Tavian," Wolfgang agreed. "I did not have the opportunity to speak with Ariane much myself."

I gave Wolfgang a searing look. Why was he sending me away like a young, stupid goat?

I protested. "No, no. I need to go and find your mother."

That statement was not true. I'd rather stay and observe him with Katrina. Tavian had called her "his future bride." I wondered whether that was true.

"No, go on," Wolfgang encouraged me. "Try to get acquainted with Tavian. He is an interesting fellow."

Turning to Tavian, he raised a warning finger. "Listen, my friend, you heart breaker. I advise you to be on your most excellent behavior while you are in the company of my little sister. Bring her back in one piece."

"Your wish is my command." Tavian gave another short bow and flashed an open smile that revealed a healthy row of teeth.

"Come on then, Fräulein Ariane. Let me give you a guided tour of our school. Let's start with our little music room where our instructors whipped us into perfect little geniuses."

A guided tour seemed innocent enough. I followed him, albeit reluctantly, and listened to little anecdotes of his years at the academy. He recalled pranks that the students had played on one another or on the professors.

Soon I could not help but laugh. He was not only beautiful to look at, but he was amusing as well. I would find plenty of time to mourn my loss of Wolfgang later. For now, I would put my heartache on hold.

"I must tell you about Professor Vogel," Tavian continued. "He is famous for holding his hands to his ears and yelling, *'Meine Herren und Damen!* Gentlemen! And Ladies! What is this *Katzenjammer!* How long will it be before you are able to distinguish the music of alley cats in heat from the harmony, which must be produced by an orchestra?"

"And, did everyone finally learn to please your professor?" I wanted to know.

"Of course!" Tavian responded with pride. "However, the *Katzenjammer* comment did not apply to me. It was the string section at which the professor was angry. I play piano and am the most accomplished pianist in this school!"

"Of course, you are, your Highness," I said facetiously and bowed. I found him very self-assured.

Tavian laughed. "I am glad that you are on my side, Fräulein Ariane. Since you agree with me, you are, of course, aware that your brother has chosen the wrong instrument if he wants to be famous. It is the piano that will propel a musician into the limelight."

I objected. "I don't believe that. There are many famous musicians who play string instruments. They became famous, and…"

Tavian interrupted me, explaining the shortcomings of other instruments. I, in turn, wanted to change the subject.

"You have an unusual name." I observed. "It's not a German name. What does it mean?"

"It's Romanian. My parents brought me to this country as a small child. They, too, are musicians. Tavian, means 'Eight.'" His voice took on a note of conspiracy. "My parents took one good look at me when I was born and immediately realized that I was the Eighth Wonder of the World. And so, my dear Fräulein Ariane," he bowed deeply and winked at me. "Here I am, a *Wunderkind.*"

I laughed. His theatrical gestures were all too comical. I could not tell whether he was playing with me or was being serious. One thing I was certain of, he was trying to impress me with his cleverness.

"Come now, Fräulein Ariane. Let's go on down the hall. Let me show you our classroom where another great tribulation took place, namely, that of our final exam. It was far from easy. I don't know how Wolfgang managed to master it. He was the only late addition to our group. The rest of us spent seven full years here. Still, your brother walked away with all the honors. It hurts me to say it, but he is brilliant."

"I know," I agreed and blushed when I heard Wolfgang's praises sung in such a nice and sincere way. Perhaps I had misjudged Tavian. He might not be as conceited and full of himself as his words suggested him to be.

"Here. Take a seat, my lovely Fräulein. This used to be my desk and chair. It is here where I sat, often bored to tears. Latin and literature, especially, bored me."

"I love literature myself," I countered.

"Hmm, is that so," he responded.

"Yes. I've learned much from books and would like nothing more than to travel around the world to see the places that I read about. I know that's not possible. But as a classical musician, the government might let you travel with an orchestra if it is invited to play in the West. That would be wonderful, don't you think?"

I continued talking and looking around the room without noticing that Tavian paid no attention to my words. When I looked up at him, I saw that he was staring at my chest. I had been undecided whether to wear it or not. Even though it looked fashionable, it felt awfully tight on me. I suddenly realized that I had made a mistake in letting Dagmar talk me into wearing it.

"You look smashing in it," she had assured me. "If you want Wolfie to notice you, this sweater would be the one to wear. Moreover, I wished I had breasts like yours. I envy them. My own are taking their sweet time to grow!" She sighed.

"Really?" I had asked and looked down on the cone shapes that jutted out from above my ribcage. The fluff of the sweater rose and billowed softly as my breath struck it. I had frowned, commenting that their elevation appeared to me like a twin set of Mount Fujiyamas whose peaks were covered by tufts of white fluffy snow. Dagmar had dryly retorted that she viewed them as to two musical notes that rose to a crescendo. Her comment had amused us, and we had laughed.

Before I knew it, Tavian pulled me out of my chair. He planted a hot kiss on my mouth. He whispered hoarsely, "Oh, Fräulein Ariane!" He reached out for me. "Oh, these are like burgeoning bugle calls in a Wagner opera!"

"What the h…" I was annoyed and my voice sounded shrill. Wagnerian breast indeed! I ran down the hall, trying to find Dagmar. I needed to vent my anger. Before I stepped back into concert hall, I took a moment to collect myself. It was then that I realized what had bothered me about Tavian from the very first moment I had laid eyes on him.

The face of Günther suddenly appeared before me. He had been a friend of my mother but later became the friend of another woman. I had pushed the memory into the background. He walked into our apartment one day when I was alone at home. His longish hair was sleeked back, glued into place with pomade, just as Tavian's was held back.

"Your mother told me to come and wait for her here," Günther explained as he sat down.

I seated myself on a chair that was too high for my feet to reach the floor and began to swing my legs back and forth. I was nervous. I wanted to leave the apartment but dared not abandon it with a complete stranger in it.

"Why don't you stop that?" Günther seemed a bit annoyed with me. "Quit dangling your feet. You are irritating me."

I grew progressively tense. Where was Mutti?

For a while, the man stared at me with a sullen expression. Then he remarked, "I want to show you something. Would you like to see it?"

"What is it?" I responded, wondering why he was annoyed with me if he wanted to show me something.

"You need to come over here."

"I don't want to!" I said.

Before I knew it, he stood up, dragged me from my chair and pulled me to him. I squirmed and fought. I kicked him in the shins and bit him on his hands and arms. I scratched him until my ragged fingernails drew blood on his cheek. He let out a long howl and cussed. He loosened his grip to find a handkerchief in his pocket to wipe off the blood. It was then that I seized the opportunity to dash out of the apartment. I ran to the Havel river and seated myself on the grass next to the water. I cried. I felt dirty and violated. Moreover, I was angry at my mother for not having recognized the kind of man he was.

When I later returned home, I saw Lore, a friend of my mother, through the crack of the living room door that stood open. I called a polite *"Guten Tag."*

"Ariane, *Kindchen,* come in here and let me look at you. It's been a while since I've seen you." Lore gave me a happy smile. "Let me introduce you to my new boyfriend."

I entered the room and saw Günther standing in the corner by the oven. I swallowed hard and ran. Before the door slammed behind me,

I heard Lore exclaim, "Annie, what in the world has gotten into your daughter?"

It was on that day when I was six years old that I decided that if I ever would take a husband, he would be kind and decent. He would be different from the kind of men that my mother invited into our apartment.

If Wolfgang would not be my husband, I knew that it would be a very long while before I found another one like him. When I finally walked into the graduation hall to find Dagmar, I decided to do one more thing. I would ask Herr Langhans to teach me self-defense moves, which I could use to protect my virtue.

Chapter Twenty-Three

Dresden

If either Wolfgang or I had wanted to sort out things between us, fate had other ideas. He joined the graduating class early next morning on their maiden concert tour. At parting, he hugged me briefly and whispered, "Keep thinking as well of me as I do of you, Ariane."

I felt an ache in my heart as I watched Katrina claim her seat next to him on the bus. Then she peered through the window and looked down on us with a smug expression on her face.

"Look, how she is gloating," I whispered to Dagmar.

"Don't worry about that girl," Dagmar assured me with disdain in her voice. "Wolfie is not the kind of person who will put up with someone like her for long."

She was convinced that she knew her brother well enough to make that judgment. I, however, doubted her words. In fact, I was worried that I had lost him forever.

"How about a tour of the city, children?" Tante Helga wanted to know. She wanted to take our minds off him. She said, "Don't worry, girls, Wolfie will come to his senses sooner or later. But for now, children, I would like to re-visit the places that Papa and I had walked hand in hand many years earlier. I know that most everything in the city still lies in ruins, but Professor Holzhausen has graciously agreed to take us on a sightseeing tour."

Professor Ernst Holzhausen had been responsible for securing Wolfgang's place at the academy,. He and his wife, Martha, now escorted us through Dresden. Tante Helga was shocked by what she saw. "There's hardly anything left of any of it!" She exclaimed. "It seems impossible to think that future reconstruction will be able to recapture the old glory of the many destroyed historical sites!"

The professor sighed. "I agree, Helga. It will be a miracle to restore everything as it has been. The legacy of the great Wettin dynasty is almost gone."

He turned to Dagmar and me, explaining to us that Dresden had once boasted an abundance of 18th Century Baroque architecture. Most of it had become damaged or destroyed in one single night of bombing.

We walked past the ruins of the Semper Opera house, which had hosted eight opening productions of Johann Strauss' operas. We continued on to the Zwinger museum, which was the home of the Old Masters Picture Gallery and which had exhibited famous paintings, such as Raphael's Sistine Madonna. When war raged, the curators had taken protective measures to insure that the treasures would survive destruction. They transported the paintings to the Saxon mountain top of Königstein fortress near Dresden for safekeeping. After the war ended, they discovered that the four hundred fifty Baroque and Renaissance paintings, which included works of Rembrandt, Van Gogh, Dürer, Van Dyke and Rubens, were gone. Only recently had the Soviet Union acknowledged that Red Army trophy hunters had claimed the masterpieces as war booty. Because of the GDR's strengthened relationship with Russia, a few paintings had already been returned, while many were still unaccounted for.

Our little group cut across to the *Frauenkirche,* the Church of Our Lady, which once had been famous for being the most magnificent Baroque church in northern Europe. The church had been built between 1726 and 1743. It, too, had also collapsed from the hail of Allied bombs. For a long while afterward, the surviving masonry had registered a temperature of more than 1,000 degrees Celsius.

We made our way to the even older *Kreuzkirche*, the Church of the Holy Cross. "The famous boys choir lost thirteen of their own members during the bombings," the professor commented. "To honor their memory and the memory of all the other victims who perished on that terrible night of 1945, the surviving choir members stood in the smoldering rubble and gave their first after-war concert."

Martha turned to Tante Helga. "You know, of course, that Ernst survived the nightmarish firestorm. I had gone to visit my mother's house in the *Erzgebirge*, while Ernst had stayed behind. Never did I imagine the horror that he would be forced to endure while I was gone."

Tante Helga took Martha's hand. "Surely, his survival is evidence that miracles exists."

"I agree with you, Helga." The eyes of Professor Holzhausen filled up with tears. "There was no way that it was my own wits that saved me that day. It surely must have been God's hand that guided me as I ran from one burning building to another as bombs fell all around me. It is a true miracle that I survived. Still, I do not understand why the grace of the Almighty allowed some of us to live while others perished."

Our little group stood in silence, allowing the professor to dry the tears. His mind became caught in the web of history. He, as so many, had over the years struggled to understand it all. "I cannot say why Dresden was made to endure such a fate. It had no military value. Nevertheless, more than seven hundred thousand incendiary bombs were dropped on us. That meant that two bombs carried the name of each citizen in the city. More than twelve thousand houses went up in flames. Unimaginable pandemonium reigned when everything around us began to burn."

Professor Holzhausen paused and wiped his brow while Dagmar and I looked at each other in compassion. It was the first time that we had heard anyone speak of it. Our history lessons in school had never touched on the causes or events of the Second World War. Whatever little I knew had been told to me by my Uncle Emil.

"Did you leave Dresden after the bombing stopped, Herr Professor?" I asked in a humble voice.

"No, child. I remained in the city. I had to stay. Those of us who survived needed to assist in the cleanup. We pulled nearly seven thousand corpses from under the rubble and piled them up in the center of the *Altmarkt,* where authorities told us to burn them in mass pyres. It seemed inhumane, but we did it in order to ward off disease. I knew that my best friends were lying somewhere beneath the rubble.

He paused and sighed. "Oh, the horror! The smell! The stench! I will never forget it. We learned later that some two hundred thousand corpses had been disposed of."

"Do you think that such things could ever happen again?" I asked.

Dagmar added, "We should create peace by uniting people through music."

"If such a thing would only be possible," our host remarked. "I see that you hold the dreams of the young. Your heart is in the right place, though."

The professor reached out and patted Dagmar's cheek. "My child, unfortunately, the wonderful music, which has filled many auditoriums and has stirred the soul of friend and foe alike, has not been able to erase their desire to fight each other. Human beings simply will not restrain their egos or will engage in compromises for the higher aspiration of brotherhood. Surely, the leaders in the West appreciate music as much as our leaders in the East. In fact, Ludwig van Beethoven's Ninth is a cherished masterpiece all over the world. The Ode to Joy, especially, calls for the unity of all people on earth. It is played and sung around the globe. Still, the cries of war continue, just as they always have. Your dream, Dagmar, even though a beautiful one, will surely remain an elusive one."

I clutched the professor's hand in parting. I could see that he harbored no hate in his heart. Only sadness remained for the horrible deeds that human beings had committed against each other.

Professor Holzhausen's report left me depressed. I, too, wondered, how peace could ever be achieved. My generation was living with the aftermath of the horror and without knowing why it began and how it would end, especially for us in the GDR. We wanted peace but we, once again, found ourselves victims of circumstance and a cold war.

My Uncle Emil once told me that all people on earth were more alike than different. "The history of most nations follows a common theme," he said. "They install a charismatic man at the helm and worship him. They elevate him as a god and see him as a powerful bringer of change, if not the redeemer of individual misfortunes. Then, one day, people discover that the one, whom they had chosen as their savior, had led them to their doom.

"Look what happened to our own country, little one. The masses were hypnotized. They paid no attention until everything fell like a house of cards. But tell me. Are we any smarter now? Look at the new leaders who are in power now. They say that they are for democracy but they are wolves in sheep skins. They resemble spotted hyenas who devour the rights and freedom of the people."

My uncle had been aware of the betrayal of our government. Nonetheless, he decided to stay in the GDR to watch over my mother and me. I believe that he sacrificed himself for us.

What we saw in Dresden was difficult to process. Pictures of the destruction stayed with me for a long while. So did the events at Wolfgang's academy. I remained quiet during the train ride back home and felt myself falling into a momentary bout of *Weltschmerz,* the evil of this world. I, too, had been loyal to the one who had managed to capture my heart. But somehow, I had lost him to another girl without knowing why.

Chapter Twenty-Four

1960
Karma vs. Fate

The previous November left citizens of the GDR sitting on a political powder keg. Khrushchev presented the Western allied powers with an ultimatum. He demanded the withdrawal of Allied troops from Berlin. He stated that if his demand would go unheeded, he would sign a separate peace treaty with the GDR. With the Allies gone, East Germany would be able to gain total control over the *Autobahn*, which was the only access road to West Berlin through the East German corridor. It now allowed food supplies and other goods to be carried to the free sections of the city. Berlin was an island within East Germany. If food shipments were disrupted, citizens of West Berlin would starve.

Western negotiations with Russian leaders ensued, but neither side could settle on a mutually agreeable workable solution. Once more, Berliners saw themselves as pawns in a political chess game. Everyone hoped that if Khrushchev were to make good on his threat and shut down access to West Berlin, the Americans would show a strength of force and protect West Berlin. For unknown reasons not divulged to the general public, the Soviet leader finally backed down. Not only did the food transport to West Berlin continue, but it kept our borders open enough to allow GDR citizens ever so often to slip across the border.

I was still in the care of Tante Helga, and my life at home and continued as it had. Wolfgang and Dagmar were away at their respective music academies. I, myself, had studied diligently to achieve high marks in secretarial school and had little time for sports. I had, however, kept in contact with Herr Langhans. To my delight, he, in turn, kept his promise to assist me in finding a suitable job after graduation. He spoke to Herr Klein, the manager of the newly established branch of the sports union in town, and made his recommendation. Soon, I was called for an interview, passed a test of shorthand and typing, and got the job. I soon found that my duties were versatile and enjoyable. I took dictation from Herr Klein, typed letters, and was in charge of scheduling various sports competitions that would be held in our area. Soon, we invited teams from other East Bloc countries to participate in competitions. Having studied Russian proved to be beneficial to everyone since the senior secretary, Frau Müller, had not learned it.

Soon after beginning my job, I received devastating news about Andra. Herr Langhans informed me that her mother had notified him that an intoxicated driver had smashed into her with his truck and trailer. Andra and I had remained close friends. She had graduated from high school a year earlier and had taken on an apprenticeship as a salesclerk. She found the job not too demanding and was pleased that it left her with time and energy to continue with her swim training and participate in competitions. She had often expressed a wish to be able to fully devote herself to the sport, just as athletes were able to do in the West. However, things were different in the GDR, where athletes maintained amateur status and needed to hold down a job. Now, Andra, who was considered to be a a rising star, lay badly injured in the hospital.

I was deeply shaken by the news. I thought about the fragility of life and its meaning, as I had done so often before. Andra was a good person who had harmed no one. Why, then, did fate punish her so harshly? What had she done to deserve the pain and agony that she had to endure? I tried to find an explanation. Thoughts about God, about heaven and hell, punishment and protection occupied my mind until I remembered a conversation that I once had with my uncle. Someone had committed a horrid crime in our usual peaceful town, and I had been as upset about it as everyone else. I quizzed my uncle about his views. He remarked, "Every action performed by every person is written on the ether of time."

"What do you mean by that?" I asked.

"You see, all of our deeds are recorded in what the Bible calls the Book of Life. For your information, little one, I don't believe that it is a book at all. It's something else, something greater, that notes down every bit of information about us. But no matter what kind of recording device it is, it is accurate and will release the information in another form. Sooner or later, whether in this lifetime or in another, our actions will come bouncing back to us like a boomerang." My uncle saw my confused face and added, "Well, then, little one. Perhaps you're not ready to understand such matters. Moreover, if your grandmother ever finds out that I am filling your head with beliefs that are foreign to her, she will disown me as her son."

My curiosity was aroused. "Please tell me anyway, Uncle Emil. I can keep a secret."

"Well, then, little one. If you insist." He obliged me and continued. "I, myself, have not always believed it either. But my understanding of life changed when I became friends with a man who occupied the bunk next to me in the prisoner of war camp that I was in. My friend and I engaged in many lengthy conversations with each other, just to keep ourselves sane. Soon I found out that before the war he worked for a German company in India. When Hitler invaded Poland, the British, who had colonized India, declared war on Germany and established internment camps for German. My friend quickly returned to Germany because he feared that he would end up in one. Upon his return to Germany, he was immediately drafted into the war and later was captured, just as I was, when our outfits were overrun by the enemy.

"While in India, he approached a swami and asked him to teach him to meditate. In the process, he learned many other things from that wise old man. My friend learned about Karma. I, of course, had never heard that word before, and he set out to teach me. The first principle of Karma is that every action has a consequence. That means that whatever action we perform will come back to us in one way or another. It might not come back to us in the exact physical way in which we had performed an action. Rather, the underlying energy behind it, the intention to hurt people or help them, is the same. It will come back with the same force with which we sent it out.

"What I am saying is that we all are responsible for our own fortunes or misfortunes. The unpaid debts that we left behind in one lifetime, and which had been recorded in the Book of Life in the ether, will need to be balanced somehow. It may be in the next life or the lives thereafter. I tell you, little one, our sufferings or joys are of our own making."

I gasped and responded, "But Onkel Emil, Oma said that we had our lives in heaven with Jesus before we came to earth. Do you mean that we did bad things in heaven and now are being punished for them on earth?"

The lines around my uncle's eyes crinkled like thin parchment paper. "No, little one," he responded. "That is not what I mean. But I *do* hope that in the final end, nirvana, or a heaven awaits us. When I say that our debts need to be balanced, I am speaking about our lives on earth. We need to understand that if we are harming others, we, too, will be harmed. Something or someone in the ether of time keeps score of everything we think about or do to ourselves and to others. And, when the right situation arises, we will be asked to pay our debts to those we have harmed until the slate is wiped clean. That, my little one, is called being stuck on the wheel of Karma."

I must have looked confused because my uncle smiled again. "You'll one day understand what I am speaking of, little one."

"I…I'm not sure that I will ever understand it," I stuttered. "Oma said that everything will be forgiven us if we believe in Jesus."

My uncle's glance lingered on me for a long while. He pulled on his pipe and then spoke again. "Well, then, if that is the case, do so. But you must make sure that you keep your thoughts pure and your actions kind. A person cannot simply go on offending and re-offending without giving it another thought. A person must not be spiteful or harm others, just because he was told that Jesus will forgive him every time he sins. I am sure that Jesus wants us to guard our hearts against unkindness and the desire to harm another person."

Andra's accident now brought back my uncle's words. So, then, why did the man run Andra down? I decided that I would never know the answer. Only the big recording device in the ether would know. And, perhaps, so would Andra's soul.

I began to think back to my relationship with my mother and began to worry once more. What harm had I done to her in order for her to despise me so? I had come into this world as a defenseless child. Could it be that I had needed to pay a debt to her? I believed in Jesus, just as my grandmother had taught me, and suddenly realized that it had been my trust and faith in God and Jesus that had helped me to survive. Even though the concept of Karma made sense to me now, I wanted to continue believing in and relying on the grace of God. I wanted to trust that it would enable me to step off the wheel of Karma. Perhaps the concepts of grace, God, Jesus, and Karma were connected, even though the process of it went beyond my understanding. I decided that I would monitor my own actions and not mention my thoughts to Andra.

Andra's accident happened in the Baltic city of Rostock, which is a suburb of Warnemünde. She had gone to visit her aunt Berta and had stopped to look at a store window just when an intoxicated truck driver lost control of his vehicle and crashed into her. The front end of the truck carried her along for several meters before it slammed her into a light pole. My friend was taken to the hospital, where she lay unconscious and fighting for her life.

As soon as I heard the dreadful news, I boarded the train for Warnemünde-Rostock and arrived at the hospital just in time for visiting hours. Entering through the large doors, I saw no one at the reception desk. I hurried along the highly polished corridor to the ward where I was told that Andra lay. A familiar but disturbing smell of disinfectant accosted my nose. I felt tightness rising in me but kept on going.

Before I could reach Andra's ward, a nurse caught me by the arm and called in a stern voice, "Fräulein, stop right there! Are you old enough to be in here? Let me see your identification papers!"

I pulled them out of my purse.

"Sorry. You're not old enough to be here. No one under eighteen is admitted! You must leave immediately."

"Yes, but my friend is injured, and I came a long way on the train to see her."

"Rules must be obeyed, Fräulein. See that sign over there? No one under eighteen is allowed to visit."

When I did not move, the nurse raised her voice, "Fräulein, if you do not leave this minute, I will call the police."

What was I to do now? I turned and found a seat on the steps outside. I was angry. I was almost eighteen, and a couple of months should make no difference to anyone. I knew that I looked young for my age, but what harm would it do to make an exception? It was not the first time that I had encountered what I felt to be unreasonable, stone-age rules, which no one could justify. The comment of those who enforced them had always been the same: "We've always done it that way, and that is the end of that. Moreover, rules must be obeyed."

I now sat, hoping that my ever active imagination would find a solution to my dilemma. Was it not my duty to be at the side of my friend and lend support? Didn't they know that it had taken courage to even walk into that hospital? The antiseptic odor of germ killing agents had stung my nostrils and had brought on sad memories of my early childhood.

I was almost six years old when I fell ill with an ailment that required a long hospital stay. I was put in a ward of elderly people whose moans were incisive and frightened me. The occasional odor of excrement, mingled with antiseptics, took a while to get used to. The ward was buzzing with continuous emergencies that kept the staff busy. However, as sick as everyone was, as soon as visiting hours came, the energy in the ward changed. Hopeful anticipation took over. Patients looked forward to seeing their loved ones walk through the door. They knew that someone would come to commiserate with them or speak words of comfort to them.

I was the only child on the ward, and the nurses quickly found out that no one came to visit me. Consequently, each time visiting hours arrived, one of them came to my bedside for just a moment to say a few kind words. A nurse would fluff my pillow and offer praise for my courage and for allowing them to stick me with so many needles. The nurses claimed that I was their little heroine. I loved their attention, even though it did not take my heartache away. I was convinced that my mother abandoned me.

Each day I lay propped up on my pillow as my eyes watched the doors to the ward. Each day I hoped that someone would remind my mother that I was here and tell her to look in on me. But she never came.

When after some weeks I was finally allowed to get out of bed, I stood by the tall windows in the hallway and kept my eyes fixed on the path that led up to the main entrance of the hospital. I longed to see my mother's slim figure hurry up the walkway. I needed her desperately, needed her to come and comfort me. I needed her to tell me that everything would be all right and that she would soon take me home. But she never came. I finally felt utterly discouraged. I believed that I was destined to remain wedged between the old people for the rest of my little life and be made to listen to their moans day in and day out until they died.

Hope returned when the doctor announced that I was well enough to be released. I got out of bed, wanting to get dressed right then and there. I wanted to find my way home on my own. "I know where my house is," I said.

The doctor smiled and shook his head. "You need to wait for your mother to come and pick you up." When he noticed my disappointment, he told me not to worry. "She'll be here soon. We'll send word to her."

Yet when the day of my long awaited discharge arrived, she still had not come. I stood with my nose pressed against the window glass until I could stand up no longer. I finally crouched low, not daring to leave my observation spot. I was afraid to miss her arrival. I would rise up ever so often and stare down the long path that led from the street to the hospital steps. That path would bring her to me.

The nurses were kind and allowed me to sit by the window. However, after the sun set, and my mother had still not arrived, I knew that I had become an orphan. I began to sob. I buried my face into my hospital gown to hide the tears. The night nurse finally found me cowering in a corner of the hall with tears streaming down my face. Nothing she said could comfort me. My heart was broken.

"What are we supposed to do with you now?" She asked and left. After a while she returned. "Where *is* your mother?" she inquired with raised eyebrows. "No one can find her."

"I don't know," I answered in a scared voice. "I think she is dead."

"Nonsense. She needs to come and get you. We need your bed for another patient." When she saw me in more distress, she added, "Alright now. Calm down, child. Even though it's getting late, I will find someone to go to your home. We had left a message at her factory yesterday, and sent a note at your home earlier today. Apparently, she ignored both."

Knowing that I had become a burden to the nurses, I hung my head. I considered that perhaps my mother had gone to live in the Golden West. Perhaps she had gone to tell my grandmother that I had died so that she did not have to take care of me any longer. But, that couldn't be. My grandmother would not believe her. She would come looking for me immediately and take me away from here.

The moon shown through the tall window when finally, feeling frightened and lost, I crawled back into my bed. The old people were asleep already when I heard the patter of my mother's high heels in the hallway. Quickly I slipped out of bed and ran to her. I put my arms around her waist. "Mutti, I waited every day for you to come and see me." I begann to sob. "I thought that you had forgotten about me. I even thought that you died. Why didn't you come and visit me. Were you sick, too, Mutti?"

My question seemed to irritate her. "Don't ask so many questions. Just get dressed. Hurry! Let's go! The nurses are angry with us." She shoved me back into the ward to collect whatever clothing I had worn on the day of my admission.

"Mutti, you would have been proud of me." I had stopped crying and now blabbered excitedly. "I know that you don't like me to cry. I didn't cry when they stuck me with needles every day. I swear it. I was very brave so that I could make you proud of me."

"Don't swear. Just hurry up and get dressed," she said again. "I want to get out of here as quickly as I can. I hate hospitals."

"You hate hospitals too?" I suddenly was comforted by the fact that she and I shared a common fear. She hated hospitals, and so did I. Perhaps she, too, had found herself in a hospital ward when she had been small and had been just as afraid as I had been. The reasons for my mother's absence were suddenly clear to me. Hospitals were scary places, and something dreadful had happened to her in one of them. She had been so afraid that she had not been able to return to one ever again. But I, even though I had been afraid, had managed to remain brave. I forgave her because I now understood it all. I told myself that I had managed to conquer our mutual fear for both of us when I took her hand and led her out of the hospital. I understood fear, and it was for this reason that I was obliged to forgive her. Having rationalized it all out in my head, everything seemed alright with my world again.

Sitting on the steps of the hospital in Rostock, I reflected on my juvenile justification for my mother's neglect of a six-year-old. I had pronounced her innocent then, had absolved her of her moral responsibilities to be with her sick little girl. Why had I made excuses for her? I had stood up for her, even though she had withheld her love. Instead of holding me in her arms, she had deserted me. I had needed to create a story that would give me comfort and help me survive rejection. I realized that had I not done so, my whole world would have collapsed around me.

Chapter Twenty-Five

Andra's Accident

I had remained sitting on the steps to the Rostock hospital. After a while, the doors swung open and visitors emerged. A familiar voice called down to me. "Ariane, what are you doing here? I didn't know that you heard about Andra." Frau Fischer had spotted me.

I rose to greet her with a distressed face. "I was hoping that I would see you here, Frau Fischer. I need to see Andra, but I'm not allowed into the ward."

"Had I known that you wanted to come, I would have dissuaded you. Andra is conscious now. But she's still weak and very much in pain. I will tell her that you came and will be sending your best wishes." Frau Fischer looked exhausted and worried. "Now then, why don't you follow me to my sister's house and stay for a while before you catch the train back home."

I quickly agreed, hoping that if I went with her, she would be able to find a solution to my dilemma. We boarded the bus to the little town of Warnemünde. Frau Fischer left me with her sister and lay down to rest. I immediately was comfortable with her sister, who told me to call her Tante Berta. "After all," she said, "you almost seem like family to me because Andra has talked about you so often." There was something comforting about the woman, something durable and resolute. Her motions were unhurried. They went well with her soft, round body and her pleasant face. She was a prototype of what I assumed an Amazon was. I was fascinated with her eyes that sparkled with humor. She was different from Frau Fischer, who the serious sort. She seemed the opposite of her sister and was tall, lean, and fast in her movements. I began to tell Tante Berta my recent experience at the hospital.

"That is easy to fix." Tante Berta responded. "I know how to get you past the sisters at the front desk."

She had a plan. When a refreshed Frau Fischer joined us and heard her sister outline the plan, she was against it. "We need to follow hospital policy," she advised her sister.

But Tante Berta simply brushed her off. "I think there will be no harm done. What's the difference in a couple of months in age? It is time we challenge the archaic rules. The girl is almost eighteen. Any other girl would have made it past the suspicious eye of the nurse. The trouble with Ariane is that although her figure looks mature enough she has a baby face."

Frau Fischer finally relented. Tante Berta suggested that I buy what she called "war paint" since we were going on a warpath to challenge the sisters. Frau Fischer agreed to accompany me into town to look for a dress and makeup. When I found everything I needed, I felt a strange excitement. I had never worn makeup and was eager to see how it would transform me. I convinced Frau Fischer to stop at a public toilet so that I could try my hand at transforming myself immediately. I had no mirror on me. I piled my curls up on my head, rubbed powder over my face and pressed red lipstick thickly into my lips. Then I took the eyebrow pencil and traced a curved line along each of my eyebrows. Next came mascara, which I rubbed straight across my eyelids. A sudden impulse made me add color to my cheeks. I drew two round circles of lipstick on each cheek to mimic the appearance of a film star, which I had seen on screen. She had worn a lovely color of rouge on her cheeks. Satisfied with my handiwork, I dashed out of the toilet stall to present myself to Frau Fischer, who was waiting for me in the stairwell.

When I passed the toilet attendant, she gaped at me with open mouth and drew up one of her eyebrows. "Planning to go to a little costume party, Fräulein?

"Nooo?" I replied, looking down at my dress, which was loose around the waist but seemed fine to me.

"Well, Fräulein, is everything alright, then?"

"*Ja, danke.*" I mumbled. I left the toilet stall clean. Believing that she spoke to me because she expected to be paid for wiping down the rim of the throne, which I did not use, I quickly placed a ten-*Pfennig* piece on her collection plate.

"Well, then, Fräulein, she announced. "I must say that you are too young to be standing on some street corner, but I wish you good luck."

I threw her a confused look and left. The moment Frau Fischer saw me, she burst into hysterical laughter that echoed through the entire stairwell.

"What's wrong?" I called out.

"*Ach, Ariane-chen!*" She sputtered. "Really, dear! Don't you think that you went a bit overboard with all of that paint on your face? You look like a circus clown. Let's go back into the washroom to wipe it off and try again at home."

She pulled me back inside the washroom and pushed me in front of a mirror. I gasped at my reflection. The powder streaked across my face in an uneven and checkered pattern, and my cheeks displayed two prominent circles of flaming bright red. But my transformation did not stop there. My eyes looked as though they belonged to a raccoon. In addition, two additional pencil lines curved high above my own natural ones.

"Oh dear!" I whispered in utter embarrassment. "No wonder the toilet woman thought that poverty, perhaps, was driving me to the streets." Hearing us, the formerly sullen toilet attendant grinned from ear to ear. "*Naja*, Fräulein, she remarked. "I knew you weren't the type. Everything takes practice. But I thank you for giving me something to smile about today in this dungeon here below."

I smiled back and nodded, feeling sorry for the elderly woman who was forced to carve out her living in a smelly room that was situated a few meters below the pavement. I knew that she was not the only one condemned to do this type of work. I suddenly felt empathy for all the toilet women in Germany.

After we arrived at Tante Berta's house, she and Frau Fischer went to work to change me into what Tante Berta called a *real* woman. They rummaged around in a *Schrank* and returned with two large tablecloths that they folded up in layers that they wrapped around my stomach.

I began to protest "Not that!" I yelled. "It's embarrassing."

"Nonsense!" The women chuckled as they held the cloths in place with two belts.

"Ah, that's much better. You look quite pregnant and convincing now!"

Tante Berta surveyed me one last time. "Wait." She called. "We are missing the proper shoes!" She opened her *Schrank* again and selected a pair of old shoes. "They are a size too large for your feet, but we can make them fit by stuffing newspaper into the toes."

Wearing them would be challenging because I had never worn high heels before.

"Don't worry, *Mädchen*," she consoled me, "highly pregnant women have a peculiar way of waddling. No one will think it strange if you sway from side to side like a loaded wheelbarrow."

"Hello you three over there!" The voice of a nurse sounded from the front desk of the hospital when we entered. The two women linked arms with me to keep me steady. The voice became louder when it admonished us. "Can't either of you read? See the sign here? Absolute silence is demanded in the hall!"

"Oh, *Entschuldigung*, sister," Tante Berta turned and addressed the nurse in a sweet voice. "We'll be quiet as church mice from now on." Her eyes sparkled with glee, and I could tell that she was obviously enjoying our prank. The nurse responded by glaring at us in silence.

Andra seemed not to recognize me when we entered the ward. "Did you bring one of your friends along, Mama?" She whispered in a weak voice.

I laughed and stepped closer. I saw her eyes widen. "Ariane? It's you? What on earth have you done to yourself?" She noticed my stomach. "Oh, no! Tell me that it isn't true. Is Wolfgang the father?"

Tante Berta was quick to quip, "No, dear. What you see is a miracle of immaculate deception."

"What?" Andra showed confusion. She glanced from her aunt to me. Her mother quickly stepped in and explained our conspiracy.

"I should have known it. Only you and my aunt would challenge the rules, Ariane. But I'm glad that you came," my friend whispered. "Does everyone at the Center know what has happened to me? My trainer must be very angry that I am letting him down. Because of me, the Center will be forced to withdraw from the next competition. They don't have another swimmer to take my place."

I was amazed that she could think of swimming when she lay wrapped before us like a mummy. Her head was bandaged up, her arm was in a sling, and one of her legs was pulled up high, hovering above the bed.

"Don't be silly. "No one is angry!" I assured her. "Herr Langhans sends his good wishes, as do the others at the Center."

I failed to mention that her trainer had expressed his disappointment before he found another swimmer to replace her. He had already removed Andra from the roster because her recovery time would take too long. Frau Fischer had passed on Andra's prognosis. My friend seemed to be the only one who was kept in the dark. She was certain that she would recover within weeks. Knowing how devastated she would be to hear about her replacement, I thought it best to withhold that information. Swimming had been her life. It had given her meaning.

No one knew whether Andra would fully recover from the head injury or whether her broken bones would heal correctly. Time would tell whether she would be able to return to competitive swimming. It would devastate her if she could not. I knew that the memory of losing someone or something cherished did not become easier with time, as everyone said. One had to adjust and find meaning in other areas of one's life.

Chapter Twenty-Six

1960-1961
Dark Clouds Over the GDR

After I returned home again, my whole focus went into my new job. Herr Klein was pleased with my secretarial skills and gave me full reign over the sports events calendar. I got along well with the office staff. A year passed without any upsets. Then an unexpected change occurred. We received notice that the sports union planned to install a new regional supervisor. who would outrank Herr Klein. The name of the man was Herr Sauer.

Shortly after having taken charge, he began to pay us a visits. Subsequent visit became more frequent. It was not long before Frau Müller, the senior secretary, remarked that Herr Sauer seemed to have taken a fancy to me. I protested and laughed. But soon I had to admit that she was correct. I did not like him much and became concerned when he began to ask intrusive and personal questions. He was a dedicated Communist Party member with a harsh disposition. I wanted to stay as far removed from him as I could; but the more frequent his visits became, the more interest he showed. When a few months later, I received an invitation to dinner, I was alarmed.

"You must heed Herr Sauer's request, Fräulein Berger," Frau Müller warned. "If you don't go, it will have consequences. I speak from experience in such matters."

"I can't possibly go!" I responded. "Even if he *is* the regional Supervisor, I am repelled by him. He is much older than I am. He also is overbearing and inappropriately nosy. Aside from that, he is not very clean. One can smell his feet the moment he walks through the door. How could I possibly spend a whole evening with him?"

When the Supervisor repeated the invitation, I stalled again and found excuses. But he would not be deterred. Finally Frau Müller advised again, "You really should go, Fräulein Berger. Herr Klein will not be able to help you if Herr Sauer decides to find a reason to launch disciplinary action against you. He will find a way, even though his request for your company is purely personal. I've seen his kind before. If you tell anyone what he is doing, no one will believe you. He will denigrate you and win. Be smart and play his game."

I put on a stubborn face and shook my head. "Why don't you go in my stead?"

Frau Müller pursed her lips. "Even if I would find him suitable, he is interested in someone as young and fresh as you, not an old woman like me."

Her response troubled me even further. I needed to discuss my predicament with someone else, needed to find a way out. I longed to talk to Tante Helga, but she had gone to East Berlin to give a performance. Frau Meyer was old, and my girlfriends were as young and inexperienced as I was. They had revealed that they, as well, had at one time or other been harassed by their bosses. They had endured it. Finding no one to talk to, I purchased a ticket for Warnemünde to discuss my predicament with Andra. She had no experience with men either, but at least I would have someone to listen to me.

I had visited her last year once more. She had seemed well enough then. We continued to correspond. She reported that she had improved even more. Her broken bones had mended. However, she told me that she was struggling emotionally because she had not been cleared by the doctors to return to her rigorous swim schedule. She was suffering from recurring migraines. Believing that the sea air would help to speed her daughter's recovery and elevate her mood, Frau Fischer had stayed with her at her sister's house. But Andra had not been able to establish friendships with people of her own age and started to isolate herself. It would be good for us to see each other again.

When I arrived, she greeted me with a happy face. "My doctor finally allows me to go to work," she informed me. "I managed to get a job in the supply room at the local Sports Center. The Center also employs life guards who watch the beach in the summer. Perhaps they will allow me to take on a few shifts on the beach after a while."

I was pleased that I had found her so happy. When I broached the subject of my troubles at work, she knew not what to say. "Just go out with him," she commented. "Spending one evening with that man won't hurt. Perhaps he'll leave you alone after that."

I decided to take her advice. Perhaps one evening in the company of Herr Sauer could do no harm.

May evenings were still cool enough to wear my cherished fur coat. I proceeded to the *Gasthaus*, which Herr Sauer had chosen as a meeting place. I was the first one to arrive and paced up and down the sidewalk to await his arrival. He soon pulled up in his Trabant 500. The "Trabi" was a car that only a privileged few in our state of workers could afford. The waiting list for it was long. I suspected that the vehicle had been a reward for Herr Sauer's devotion and service to the Communist Party.

His face registered surprise the moment he spotted me. "How did you come to own such a fine garment, Fräulein Berger?" He inquired. "Do you have friends in high places?"

"It was a gift," I replied.

"Well, then. Who was it that so generously bestowed it on you? Surely, it must be someone of superior rank? I know that you often travel to East Berlin and stay overnight."

He was correct. I often accompanied Tante Helga to visit Tante Inge and spend time with Dagmar. The controls on the trains, and the inspections, which we were forced to endure, were bothersome. We also needed to change trains at the East German border before going across the barrier to catch the city train that would take us to East Berlin. But before we were allowed to board it, we were searched by the police and inspected by the Russian military. Since our papers were in order, we were allowed to pass without further hassle.

I silently wondered how Herr Sauer had learned about these visits and reminded myself to be especially cautious from now on about what I said and did.

He stepped close and rubbed his hand up and down my coat. "So, who is the person who gave you such a fine gift?"

I kept silent, felt concern for the Koslowski family. Could it be that Herr Koslowski had bought or traded the coat illegally? No. I rejected the notion. Tanya's father was a fur trader. The sable had surely come from Russia, a country which was a friend of the GDR. However, how could I be certain of anything?

I managed a polite smile and answered, "The source must remain my secret, Herr Sauer."

To my own surprise, he gave me an appreciative smile and responded, "Who would have known it, Fräulein Berger. You look so innocent, so coy. Still, you must possess talents that I am not aware of. I must say that your modesty is deceiving. Perhaps there is more about you to explore than I imagined."

I was piqued. What was he speaking of? Surely, not... I suppressed my feelings of disgust and managed to give him a glance of indifference. I needed to get through the evening without fuss, slide by socially, so that in the future he would leave me alone.

"I think you are misjudging me, Herr Supervisor."

"Am I?" He grinned, rubbing his hands together again. "Shall we go inside? Let's celebrate."

The wife of the *Gasthaus* owner recognized Herr Sauer immediately and gave him a solicitous bow before she quickly placed two steins of dark beer before us.

"A *Sprudel* please." I corrected her. "I do not drink beer."

The woman looked at Herr Sauer, who, in turn, stared at me with dismay. "Fräulein Berger, do you intend to dishonor old German customs? I insist that you raise a stein or two with me."

Seeing that he would be even more difficult to endure if I would not oblige him, I pulled the beer toward me, took a sip and wiped the foam from my lips. The hostess went away with a mollified smile. "*Na, dann,*" she remarked. "Alright, then. That's a girl."

"Prost!" Herr Sauer lifted his stein with a satisfied look. "Show me what you are made of, Fräulein Berger."

"Well then," I held counsel with myself. "I will show him that I can hold my own." I promptly emptied my glass.

Shortly before our meal arrived, we each had emptied two large steins. A third and fourth round followed. Herr Sauer began to talk nonstop. He confided that his servile attitude toward his superiors had paid off. Consequently, his mentors in the Party had arranged for him to step into his current position as Supervisor. He would not disappoint them and would rule over all of us with a firm hand. His arrogance reminded me of Herr Fink's. I shuddered at the memory of him and understood that my new boss would not tolerate contradiction.

My face must have fallen when I thought of Herr Fink. Herr Sauer noticed my expression and remarked, "This is no time to feel gloomy, Fräulein Berger. We must toast to our special friendship."

When dinner arrived, he began to chew the Suerkraut and pork sausages with open mouth. Seeing him eat reminded me of an ox who was feasting on fresh green grass. The grease of the meat trickled down the corners of his mouth and left little channels that ran past his chin. He wiped his face clean with the back of his hand and washed down the remaining morsels of half-chewed food with big gulps of beer. Intermittently, he raised his stein to toast to Communism and the success of the GDR. It was not long before his rambles focused on our Fascist enemy, the Golden West, and the even greater enemy of the GDR, the United States of America. He shared several ideas on how to wipe both countries off the face of the earth.

I began to squirm in my seat. Herr Sauer's devotional fervor, which had become fueled by the alcohol, produced a florid hue on his face. But worse, his passionate speeches heated up the temperature of his feet. Each time he leaned over the table and peered closely into my face, a foul odor shot into my nose. Disgusted, I silently asked myself why I had let myself be talked into going out with him. But here I was sitting across from him. It was too late for regrets, and I needed to humor him. After the plates were cleared away, I rose.

"*Nein, doch*, Fräulein Berger," he immediately shouted. "It is still early. Let's toast again to a special friendship." He raised his glass.

I felt trapped, felt terribly inexperienced in matters of self-negotiation. Perhaps, even if I had been wiser, it would have been useless. I obeyed, stayed, and gulped down a few additional swallows of beer.

"That's a girl, little Fräulein," he beamed. "Drink up. I am glad to see that you have a good German constitution."

Sooner than I realized, the alcohol took effect on me. The fog in my brain thickened, and whatever sense I or good manners I had left me. I began to slouch over the table and stared with interest at the large dark mole above his lip. It bobbed up and down as he spoke. My usual abhorrence of uncouth people left me as well. I watched with fascination as the spray of spittle flew from his mouth whenever he punctuated words beginning with "P." "We are a great nation of Proletarians. The Party must be careful of spies hiding among the population."

"Really?" I said, finding myself bored. My lame inquiry brought on further explanations from him.

Soon, everything in the room began to spin. I concentrated on regaining my balance when I heard him say, "Fräulein Berger, I cannot tell you what a happy man you have made me by accepting my offer. I, too, am irrevocably drawn to you. You are delicious and desirable."

Desirable? And, what kind of offer was it that he had made me? Dear lord, had I nodded in agreement to something that had simply slipped past me? Surely, my brain had become annihilated by fumes of alcohol. I couldn't remember a thing he had said.

Before I knew it, Herr Sauer reached across the table. He took my hand into his own, sweaty one. "Fräulein Berger…no, my dear, let me call you Ariane. It is true that I am drawn to you! We will have much fun together."

I adjusted my eyes and recognized his lustful appetite. What had I done? More importantly, what was I to do now? What would he do when I refused him?

"Ah, no, Herr Sauer…" I caught my breath, trying to calm my anxiety. "You must believe me…I must explain that I…" I swallowed the wrong way and began to cough.

"You don't need to explain anything to me, my dear Ariane. Your relationship with your….your…. uh…the very important friend of high rank, the one who obviously has good taste and who gave you that elegant coat, has surely ended. Am I correct? I drove by your house several times and know that you have made no recent trips to East Berlin. Now that this…uh…affair is behind you, I can assure you that I can show you an equally enjoyable time. I promise that I will be discrete."

Sickness overcame me. "Herr Sauer. If you please." I breathed heavily. "I'm a bit tipsy and unable to focus right now. I need to go home."

I wanted to bolt out of the door, but he took my arm. "You will not escape me so easily. I will drive you home."

I hiccuped all the way to the house. When he stopped the car, he turned off the ignition.

"I can see that you're intoxicated and are slow to think. But my dear, don't let me wait too long before I can be with you again." He leaned over and planted a soggy kiss on the side of my mouth.

Instantly repulsed, I swiped my hand across my face to wipe off the dribble from his mouth. I pushed open the car door and ran into the house without looking back even once. I knew that I needed to hurry to get to the toilet. If I waited any longer, I would spit up right on the sidewalk. I let the front door slam behind me and ran past the parlor where I caught a glance of Wolfgang. For an instant I stopped but quickly hurried on.

"Are you sick, Ariane?" Tante Helga called after me.

I suddenly felt sober and scrubbed off the remnants of the Supervisor's saliva. I knew that I was in a serious mess, caught on the horns of a dilemma. I wondered whether Herr Sauer had noticed my disgust of him. Had he seen me wipe my mouth? Well, I would find out on Monday, after I returned to work. And now, to aggravate the evening further, Wolfgang had arrived. I still missed him and pined for him. Nevertheless, I had wanted him to stay away for a while so that I could forget my feelings for him. I walked into the parlor to bid Wolfgang a polite *Guten Abend*.

"What's wrong with you? Are you drunk?" Tante Helga inquired.

"I was," I demurred. "But I had a reason to be. Something awful has happened!" I related the events of my evening.

When I finished, Wolfgang laughed. "To think that this was your first kiss. How crass and inexperienced of the man. And, how unfortunate for you."

Tante Helga looked at her son and knitted her eyebrows together. She firmly rebuked him. "Wolfie! What has gotten into you nowadays? When did you become so derisive? This is a serious matter. Please remember the damage that Herr Fink had caused us all!"

I, too, was annoyed with Wolfgang and quickly bade him and his mother goodnight. He rose and followed me into the hall.

"I'm sorry, Ariane, but your narrative was too amusing. My apologies. I agree with Mama. The situation is not trivial. The man is a wretched scoundrel. Have you no recourse?"

"No," I muttered. "He's the appointed top fiddle in our region."

Wolfgang laughed. "Well, at least you are able to retain your sense of humor."

I grunted. "It's not easy to hang on to it."

"I should have been the first one to do that." He whispered, stepping closer.

"Do what?" I demanded in a similarly low voice.

"You know what I mean. Kiss you." He took another step forward and leaned close. I felt his breath on my face. "I swear, I would have done better. Surely, it would not have made you sick."

Was he teasing me? For a fleeting moment, my heart opened to him again. I had dreamed about being held in his arms. Had I shut him out too quickly? Should I reconsider?

He stood waiting. I was undecided. Did he want me to make the first move? Suddenly, I remembered Katrina and saw the image before me. I stepped away from him.

"Unfortunately for both of us, you've committed yourself to someone else. Your girlfriend would retaliate if she knew what's on your mind right now. In fact, I am actually amazed that she has let you out of her sight for just a day."

He straightened up and also stepped back. I knew that my words had been malicious. I had said them because I did not want him to notice the sudden tears that wanted to well up in me. I remembered the hurt of rejection and needed to keep my distance. What would happen to me if I let him get to me once more? Would he walk away from me again and leave me heart broken? I looked up at him and saw the regret in his face.

"Good night, Wolfgang. Good night, Tante Helga," I quickly called once more in a forced, nonchalant voice and began to climb the stairs to my bedroom. I needed to remove myself before I would melt and fall into his arms. But even if I would give in, we would not be able to spend time together now. We were not alone in the house.

"Wait, Ariane," Wolfgang took a few steps toward me but stopped at the bottom of the staircase.

Even though I knew that it was impossible to spend time together, I desired nothing more than hear him beg me to put aside my aloofness and come to him. But he did not. He did not speak again but simply watched me disappear around the bend of the staircase. He knew, just as I did, that he would leave again tomorrow and join Katrina in Leipzig.

The effect of alcohol left me melancholic. I threw myself onto the bed and thought back to the times when Wolfgang and I had been innocent teenagers. He had been the one who had cheered me up. I had trusted him, had felt alive whenever he was near. His humor had seen me through when painful memories wanted to ruin my day. He had been able to rescue me from my sorrow. I had felt appreciated by him, the gifted, intelligent and handsome boy. He had made it easier me to believe in my own value.

But, everything was changed now. He chose Katrina over me. I wondered what it was that drew him to her. It was true that they shared the same love for music. More than that, Katrina was strong, determined, and self assured. Perhaps the added attraction was that she came from a family of intellectuals.

I tossed and turned most of the night and awoke tired the next morning. My head felt like a balloon, and my stomach was queasy. Luckily, it was the weekend, and I could stay in bed. I did not want to let Wolfgang see me in my debilitated condition. As expected, he left, taking the train home shortly after breakfast without saying goodbye.

When noon arrived, I picked myself up and went for a run to clear my head. I put thoughts of him aside and pondered my predicament at work. After my run, I was no closer to deciding what I needed to do.

The following morning, I wrapped myself in my sable coat and went to work. Herr Sauer arrived at noon for an unscheduled visit and asked me to join him on an errand. "My dear Ariane," he murmured as he took my arm. Did you recover from your hangover? You look well enough today. I suggest that we make a detour to my apartment before we pick up supplies for the office."

I drew back. "I think we have a misunderstanding, Herr Sauer." I tried to steady the trembling inside of me. "I won't be joining you."

"What's gotten into you?" The color of his face darkened as he moved closer. He grabbed the sleeve of my coat. "So, then. I was not mistaken the other night when I saw your reaction. Why the suddenly display of innocence while flaunting this gift? You cannot fool me. I know that your family has no resources or contacts to obtain such a coat. It carries all the signs of privilege and is the type of gift that some of my colleagues bestow on their women."

I tore my arm away from him and ran down the street. Only after turning the corner did I slow my pace. When I arrived home, I flung the coat over the tree in the hall. I never wanted to see it again. I walked upstairs and went to bed. Before I knew it, I was asleep and did not wake until it was late. I listened for sounds in the house, but all was quiet. Tante Helga had apparently gone to bed herself.

The next morning I returned to the office with an unusual heaviness. Frau Müller gave me a meaningful look. "Did you take a trip with the Supervisor yesterday?"

"No," I responded. "I went home. I did not feel well."

"Ah so." Her expression told me that she did not believe me.

To my relief, the days that followed offered an unexpected reprieve. Herr Sauer remained absent. Herr Klein informed us that the Supervisor was taking a small vacation. Shortly after his return, a letter arrived in the mail. It was from him and contained a request to join him at a Communist rally that was planned in a neighboring town. The rally would conclude with a small banquet to which a chosen few were invited. I was to show myself on his arm as his date.

I offered my written apologies and declined. A few days later, I received an official letter, which asked me to present myself at his office for a performance evaluation. This time I was obliged to go.

Herr Sauer received me with a grim face. "It has come to my attention," he informed me, "that you neglected your duties in the office. You remained absent one entire afternoon without offering explanations to Herr Klein."

"You know what happened that afternoon," I stubbornly replied.

He ignored my answer and continued. "I believe that you may no longer be suited for the job. Moreover, your refusal to participate in promoting our cause shows me that you are not deserving of the position that you are holding. Your display of hostility toward our country leads me to believe that you are engaged in activities that undermine the GDR.."

I stared at him dumbfounded. Why was my refusal to be with him synonymous with a desire to undermine our country's ideology and progress? I caught my breath. Surely, he did not suspect me of treason because I chose not to join the Party? If he were to make such an accusation public, it would have serious consequences for me.

"You are mistaken, Herr Sauer," I responded in a trembling voice. "I am not working against the government. I have nothing to hide. I like my job very much. I've always promoted the success of our athletes. Herr Klein assured me that I was doing my job to his satisfaction."

"Well then. To show me that you are serious in your claim of being interested in promoting the cause of the GDR and not hinder it, I suggest that you pledge your allegiance to the Party and become a member. You must set an example." He gave me a challenging stare and added. "If you refuse, I must assume that you are working against us. I will, then, need to declare you unsuitable for your job and take other action."

I avoided his eyes and sought a spot on the floor. I knew not how to respond. After a moment of silence, I forced myself to look him in the eye. A thought had come to me. I said, "My ex-landlady is a Party member. I would like her to take me to the first meeting and tell me what I need to do."

Here Sauer wrinkled his forehead. For a moment I believed that he had caught me at my game. I forced myself to look him squarely in the face again. Hoping that he would believe me to be sincere, I offered a slight smile. I cringed inside for telling a lie, but I saw no other way out. I did not intend to join up or give in to his personal demands.

He pondered my request for a moment and finally nodded. "Alright then, Fräulein Berger. Do not take too long to think about it or fail to register. I will give you one more opportunity to come to your senses. You will have a few days to undo the error, which you have committed. You might wonder why I am giving you another chance. I am doing so because, after all, you are young and are still learning how to bend. But more than that, I hope that you know that my patience must be rewarded.

Chapter Twenty-Seven

Wolfgang's Proposal

The days that followed passed in a fretful haze. I agonized over finding a solution to my dilemma. I obtained an appointment with the *Arbeitsamt*, the official place to register for jobs, but the date given me was several weeks in the future. When I thought I had reached the limit of my endurance, I received another unexpected break. Herr Sauer was called to make his rounds in neighboring towns. He would not find time to visit our office for a day or two. And, following that, he needed to attend a conference in Leipzig.

To lighten my stress, I agreed to join Tante Helga for a concert in East Berlin. We were pleased to learn that Dagmar had received the honor of being the First Violin in Mendelssohn's Violin Concerto. Shortly after we arrived, Tante Helga left me to pay her respects to a few fellow musicians. Before I could find a seat in the auditorium I unexpectedly came face to face with Wolfgang. Wanting to put aside our recent uncomfortable exchange at home, I greeted him with a slight smile.

"Hello, Ariane!" He said. "Surprised to see me? I've come to talk to you about something."

My heart began to beat faster. Could it be that…. He left not much time for speculation but came quickly to the point.

"I've been reflecting on us...hum...I mean I've been thinking about you and me since we last saw each other at home. I miss you badly. I think that you should move to Leipzig."

"Hmm," I hesitated. The idea was tempting. Too tempting, now that I might be in danger of being reported by Herr Sauer for attempting to work against the efforts our government. The Supervisor would be vicious enough to avenge himself on me for having rejected him. Moving away might save me. But would Herr Sauer let me go easily? If not, he would come after me, hunt me down. It would not be difficult for him to find me since every citizen was obligated to register a change of residence with authorities. On the bright side, I would be able to patch things up with Wolfgang. Perhaps I would be able to capture his heart completely. If Herr Sauer would see that I was with another man, he might leave me alone. But, still, there was Katrina. She was not a contender easily to be disregarded. She would make trouble. Wolfgang had not mentioned her.

I forced my voice to remain cool. "I missed you too, Wolfgang. In fact, I think of you every day. But, tell me, how does your girlfriend feel about this? Did you tell her that you were going to ask me to move? I remember that she is extremely jealous, not only of me but even of your *real* sister. Would she not make life very difficult for us?"

Wolfgang's reply came hesitantly. "Well, truthfully, I did not tell her of my intention to ask you to move to Leipzig. It would not wise to do so yet. You know how difficult she can be. I need time to let her down slowly. But, in the meantime... Please, Ariane..." His eyes were begging.

It was difficult for me to ignore them, these soft, liquid eyes.

"Let's give ourselves the opportunity of being together again. I miss you. I miss our relationship. I miss our closeness. You are the only one who totally understands me."

"You want me to be with you while you continued living with Katrina?" I glared at him. "How long would you want me to wait until you decide to leave her? In any case, I know that she'll be clinging to you like a leech. She'll suck the strength to leave her right out of you. But if you manage to leave, she'll pursue you. I think you know that. Perhaps that is the very reason why you did not leave her already."

"Don't make it so difficult for me, Ariane. It's bad enough to admit that I underestimated her or my feelings for you. Katrina has a strong will. I know that she can be vindictive, but I believe that she has my best interest at heart. She wants me to make a name for myself."

"Wolfgang. Please don't take me for a fool. Don't ask me to look upon her with sympathy. I have always believed in you. I know that you will be famous. You are making excuses for her."

Another thought occurred to me. "Perhaps Katrina wants to keep you around because she wants to bask in your future fame because she knows that she won't reach it herself."

"I don't think that is true. She is very talented herself."

"Then, what *is* it that keeps you bound to her?"

"It is not easy to break the promises that I made to her. Furthermore," he suddenly looked beaten down, "Please understand that I need to handle her with care."

"You are scared of her!" I exclaimed.

"No, not at all!" He glared at me with indignation.

"Well, I don't totally believe you. If it's not that, perhaps it has something to do with her father. Perhaps it's the prestige of her family that you enjoy. Her father is famous and respected. Do you believe that your future fame depends on the connections he has? Your gift should be your ticket to fame, not Katrina's father."

Wolfgang drew back. "You don't know how things work in the real world, Ariane! In any case, I think that you are too upset right now for us to have a decent conversation. Perhaps we need to continue this later when you are more reasonable."

I had once been convinced that my relationship with him would be unshakable. We had never quarreled, but now a rift had opened between us. My faith in him was shattered. I did not know whether I could trust him any longer. He, whom I loved so dearly, seemed to have sold himself for something that I did not understand. He had lost part of himself along the way.

We took our seats; and for a moment, we sat next to each other like strangers. He was the first one to mellow. He shot me one of his most brilliant smiles and placed his hand on mine. Goosebumps traveled down my spine. But I held tight. Something inside of me had become broken.

When Dagmar appeared on the stage, I closed my eyes to shut out everything else around me. She played exceedingly well and held the audience spellbound with her articulation and exceptional clarity of sound that she drew from her violin. When she finished playing, enthusiastic applause followed. She had managed to pull us in, had opened up a space that gave the audience permission to give themselves over to something higher. Problems had melted away for a few minutes. I knew then that her future as a classical musician was assured. She would find herself in greater competition with her brother than she had imagined. Perhaps she would even surpass him in ability.

Later in the evening when Tante Helga and I were on the train back home, she put her arm around my shoulder and remarked, "Ariane, I know that Wolfie occupies a special place in your heart. I know that he feels the same about you. I have never interfered because I wanted to allow both of you to find your way without me telling you what to do. It seems as though he has gotten himself into a situation that is difficult for him. It may be a while before he will be able to extricate himself from it. You must try to let him go for however long it will take. If he *will* separate from Katrina, he will come and find you in the end."

She noticed the fallen look on my face and added, "Whatever is meant to be will come to pass. You must believe that."

I knew that she would not take sides. I also realized then, that even in her maturity, she knew of no quick solution to the problems of relationships or of life. Perhaps that was the lesson. All of us needed to struggle onward alone and overcome our challenges until we understood the roles we were to play and make peace with them.

We rode without speaking. The silence in our compartment was only interrupted by the rattle of the wheels below. On occasion, the high screech of metal on metal sounded. I knew that the friction was causing sparks to fly. They lit up the night like a hundred fireflies. My past relationship with Wolfgang reminded me of such sparks. We had lit up when we had found ourselves in each other's company. Now, a bend in the tracks were causing a different kind of friction. I feared that if we were not careful, our friendship would derail completely.

Tante Helga and I were tending to our own thoughts for a while. Then she announced. "There's something that I need to discuss with you, Ariane. I was asked to join a small orchestra in Berlin and would like to accept. If I do, it would mean that I would have to spend more time away from home."

She saw my disappointed face. "Please don't feel that I am abandoning you, especially now when you are experiencing trouble at work. And don't ever forget that I love you like my own daughter and that you can come to visit any time."

So, there it was. She had made her decision to loosen her nurturing bond with the last one of her children. Her departure from home would come sooner than I expected. She would pack a few of her belongings and take the morning train back to East Berlin.

I felt a sense of abandonment but quickly talked myself out of it. "Your are falling back into your childhood stuff again," I told myself. Was I not old enough to be on my own? Yes, I was, and she was entitled to finally live her life unencumbered by the demands of children.

The next morning, Tante Helga knocked at my bedroom door. Her tone of voice was apologetic. "Ariane, I must beg for your forgiveness."

I registered alarm and looked up. "No. It's alright," I replied, thinking that she was apologizing for leaving. "You should go and grasp the opportunity that is offered you. There's not much for you to do in our town."

"That is not it. It's this here." She handed me a metal box. "I just discovered it again. I should have given it to you several years earlier but forgot about it. It lay buried under some clothes in my *Schrank*."

"What is in it?" I could not imagine what the box contained.

"Do you remember that you refused to look at your mother's wedding band after she passed on? You asked me to keep it for you."

I nodded. "Yes?"

"Do you also recall that Herr Ritter disposed of the contents of the *Schrank* in your apartment? What I didn't tell you at the time was that he found a letter that had become wedged in the back of the runners of a drawer. Since you were so emotionally fragile, I placed it, along with the ring, into this box and stashed it away to give to you at a future time. Open it and take a look. The envelope is addressed to your mother. It appears that she has never opened it."

I took the envelope out of the box. "Hmm, it feels bulky. I don't recognize the handwriting. There's no return address either. It seemed to have been delivered by hand."

"Yes. That is what I suspect. Perhaps it's a note from a neighbor or from an acquaintance who left it at the door of your apartment when no one was at home."

"I suspect that the letter was not important to Mutti since she did not open it. She might have recognized the handwriting and knew who had left it."

I examined the handwriting once again. It was not Fritz Neumann's writing. I had once seen a card that he had written to my mother. The handwriting on it had been large and ornate.

"Perhaps Mutti had put it into her *Schrank* when company arrived without having time to read it," I mused. "She had always made sure that the table remained free of clutter."

I silently considered that, perhaps, the letter had been written by one of the "uncles" who had visited our apartment before Fritz Neumann appeared on the scene. If that was the case, I was not interested in reading it. I put the envelope back into the box and placed it into my own wardrobe. I would open it at some other time. Right now, I needed to leave for work. Herr Sauer would be back from his conference and would want to hear my decision. He would not be pleased in the least when he heard what I would tell him.

As I walked to the office, I thought about the many ruthless and manipulative methods that our government had used to destroy people. Had my grandfather not been required to place his business into the greedy hands of our leaders? He had been forced to let go of his pride of achievement. Furthermore, what had become of my Uncle Emil after he had refused to join the choir of proselytes? He had been taken away by the cruel hands of persecution. I also thought of my mother. Was there any truth in what Fritz Neumann had said or had she been falsely accused of treason? Had that been the reason that she decided to take her life? I would never know. And, lastly, if I added the fates of my childhood friends and that of their parents to the list, it was clear that every event was stained with blood. No, I would not, could not, give in to the demands of Herr Sauer.

Nonetheless, I was trembling when I stepped into the office of our Supervisor and prepared myself for the worst. I stood before him and let him survey me with a stern expression. "Well, Fräulein Berger?" He said. "Did you keep your promise to register?"

I shook my head. "No. I changed my mind."

His expression became fierce and his voice was harsh. "You will forever regret your decision, Fräulein Berger. Your job and your very life is held together by the good graces of our government. I am speaking as a representative of it. You owe both of us your pledge of support and devotion. But since you are not willing to give it, it will have consequences."

I remained silent. When he dismissed me, I walked out of his office with flushed cheeks. I was angry that he had threatened me but knew that inappropriate words would damage me even more.

What made him think that I owed him and the government something? I owed them nothing. I had worked hard in my job and had taken pride in it.

Angrily, I returned to my office where Herr Klein was waiting for me. He informed me that Herr Sauer called to say that the position of junior secretary was to be terminated. My job title would be downgraded to that of "file clerk," and my new duty station would be the basement. Furthermore, I should expect boxes of files to be delivered.

"Did I not do my job to your satisfaction?" I demanded to know.

Herr Klein looked at me with regret and shrugged his shoulders.

"Not only that, but my qualification place me above the rank of a file clerk. You know it to be true, Herr Klein!"

"You were an excellent secretary, Fräulein Berger," He agreed. "Nevertheless, the matter is out of my hands right now. Just be patient. I will speak to Herr Sauer again. He might revise his decision yet."

Hearing his words, and even though my anger had escalated, I was hopeful that justice would be done. If I could not expect it from my present supervisors, then the employment office would surely find me another job.

When I showed up for the arranged appointment the next day, a militant caseworker at the employment office demanded to know, "What is the problem, Fräulein?" Her eyes were cold, and her expression was as sour as a kumquat. I told her of my demotion and that the reasons for it were unjustified.

"You must lack in effort and skill, Fräulein Berger. I suggest that you strive harder to show commitment to your job. Our leaders set the example for us. It is our duty to follow it. Jobs are scarce everywhere. Be grateful that you have a job and are allowed to serve our country with pride and dedication."

After I left the employment office, my anger turned into depression. What was I to do now? I could not quit my job without having the assurance of a new one. Neither could I run to Tante Inge in East Berlin to beg her to take me in. Her apartment was too crammed as it was. Tante Helga was occupying one room, while Dagmar slept on the couch on the weekends.

I decided to ask Herr Klein for permission to take my summer vacation one month ahead of schedule. To my relief, he granted it. "Herr Sauer cannot keep you from taking your vacation. Don't worry. Perhaps, when you get back, you will see everything in a new light, Fräulein Berger," he assured me. "Get some rest."

Since private telephones were still not readily available to the general public, Tante Berta had no such phone. I knew, however, that she, her sister, and Andra would welcome me with open arms. The sea air of the Baltic, the quaint medieval town of Warnemünde, and the companionship of my friend, would recharge me. Perhaps I would even find a solution to my problem.

Chapter Twenty-Eight

Change on the Horizon

Frau Fischer opened the door. Her face registered surprise. "Ariane, what brings you to us? We were not expecting you. You don't look well. Has something happened?"

"*Enschuldigung*, for barging in on you unannounced, Frau Fischer." I apologized.

"No need for that. You are always welcome, my dear. But, tell me, what has happened? Come in and sit down."

I screwed up my face and haltingly related my problems at work. Frau Fischer listened with a serious expression. When I was finished, she shook her head in disbelief.

"Oh dear." She sighed. "It's not a good situation. Short of advising you to leave the job, I'm not sure what to suggest. It would be difficult to go up against that Supervisor of yours because he manages the whole region." She got up and put a kettle of water on the stove to make us a cup of tea.

I hung my head in disappointment. I had hoped that she had a suggestion that would solve my problem.

A few minutes later, Tante Berta's cheerful face peeked around the kitchen door. "Look what the cat dragged in," she chuckled. "I can tell from your face that something is amiss! Let's hear it."

She was outraged when I reported my predicament. "Flagrant men are sprouting up like weeds these days! You must leave that job immediately!"

"That is the conclusion I came to as well," Frau Fischer immediately agreed. "But not all men are like that, Berta. My first husband was a good man, and Otto is another one like him."

"You and Otto are getting married?"

"Yes." Frau Fischer smiled happily.

Tante Berta grunted, "My sister has been good for nothing around here since Otto Keller proposed marriage. She's flitting about like a teenager who is in love for the very first time."

"Could it be that I am detecting a bit of envy in you?" Frau Fischer half teasingly turned to Tante Berta.

"Not at all." The aunt made a gesture with her hand, brushing away her sister's observation. "You know that I have no use for them! But if I can give you some advice, sister. Just make sure that you don't suffocate him with all that overbearing attention that you force on him. Leave him some room to breathe."

Tante Berta gave me a meaningful look and raised her eyebrows. "You should see how she dotes on that man, Ariane. It makes you think that he is unable to do anything for himself."

Frau Fischer kept smiling but did not respond.

"I fear that one day Otto might feel a bit smothered by her," Tante Berta continued. "Nevertheless, I must admit that at present, he seems to enjoy it. You should see how they coo at each other, Ariane. The two of them behave like young, star struck turtle doves."

"You are jealous, Berta!" Frau Fischer commented. "Men like Otto are rare. I'm just making sure that he wants to stay around. You should get out more often and mingle, sister. You might get lucky and find one just like him."

Tante Berta snorted and waved her off. I looked from one woman to the other, not knowing whether they were arguing with each other or just having fun with each other.

"Never mind our little squabble, Ariane." Frau Fischer saw that I seemed uncomfortable. "It's innocent. We always have our little disagreements. But you do remember Otto, don't you?"

I nodded. "Yes, I do."

I remembered Otto Keller well. Frau Fischer had introduced me to him last year. She had met him on one of her afternoon walks on the beach, where they exchanged a few words. She learned that he lived in Thuringia and came to Warnemünde to visit a cousin. She invited him to help celebrate Andra's recovery. When he arrived, he gave her a kiss on the cheek. Andra saw it and was surprised. She took one look a the mustached stranger and pulled her mother aside. "Mutti,"she complained, "What are you doing? You don't even know the man."

Frau Fischer countered, "I know him well enough. We've talked for hours already."

Andra shrugged her shoulders and turned to me. "I don't recognize my mother any more. She has changed. I think that the sun and the sea air has affected her common sense."

I, too, saw the change and observed as Frau Fischer's cheeks took on the color of red rosebuds the moment Otto arrived. She fluttered around him like a young, beautiful butterfly that finally shed its cocoon. Seeing her mother enamored with a man upset Andra. Back home, her mother had focused all of her attention on her and had never even looked at a man. Frau Fischer felt that now, that her daughter was not training any longer and did not require her support any longer, she was free to live her own life. Her priorities shifted when she found someone else to dote on.

Otto stayed with his cousin for the duration of summer and became a frequent visitor to Tante Berta's home. He was an educated and decent man. I remember him being pleasant to Frau Fischer and courteous and attentive to the rest of us. It took a while before Andra finally warmed up to him.

I was happy that Frau Fischer found someone like Otto. I now asked, "How is Andra accepting the news of your marriage?"

"She is not at all pleased that my sister will be moving to Thuringia with Otto." Tante Berta quickly answered before Frau Fischer could respond. She gave her sister a concerned glance and added, "I hope that your moving away will not throw your daughter back into the throes of depression."

"I've not seen an indication of that lately. She seems to be back to her normal self."

"You must not have paid any attention, sister. Andra still has these headaches. I can see it in her face, even though she keeps quiet about them."

Frau Fischer waved her off. "I'm not concerned too much about them. It's clear to me that my child is getting better every day. You *do* realize that I am not simply abandoning her. I have asked her to join us, but she has declined. I cannot force her to come along because she's old enough now to make her own decisions. Besides, I know that she is in good hands here with you."

"Whatever you say, sister." Tante Berta frowned. "In any case, I'll be glad to keep her. She will be good company for me."

Minutes later, Andra came home from work and let out a squeal of joy. I could see that she was happy to see me. She looked better than ever. Perhaps Tante Berta was mistaken. The freckles on Andra's nose blended into her tan, and her hair reflected the color of reddish gold. Her eyes, too, looked as though they had recovered their sparkle. Even though she had previously struggled to accept Warnemünde as her new home because she missed her old friends, she appeared to have settled in well. After all, she was a creature that took naturally to water. Being by the sea suited her. We hugged and soon excused ourselves from the women to catch up on our lives. She pulled me upstairs into her room and began to tell me of her mother's impending marriage.

"It's all too quick," she complained. "Just because I had to give up my training, my mother thinks that I don't need her any longer. She barely pays attention to me now. She's always loved having a project, and I think that Otto is her next one. If I were to go with them, I would only be in the way."

Andra had always been close to her mother. Neither of them had spent time away from each other. I suspected that the thought of being separated from her mother caused her anxiety.

"You've got your aunt. And you've got me," I assured her. "Look at me, I, too, will be all alone in the house now since Tante Helga took the position in East Berlin. But come. Let's clear our heads and take a walk on the beach."

The air outside was soft and balmy. The moon rose in its full glory and hung large and orange over the water. We found a spot on the boardwalk and sat quietly for a while. The beach was deserted. The only sounds we heard were the waves breaking against the shore. I turned my face into the mild breeze and let it caress me. I tried to let go of my troubles back home. But soon I could not manage to keep it in. I reported my dilemma to Andra.

"I have an idea," she responded after I finished speaking. "Why don't you move here and find a job. I will ask Tante Berta if it would be alright for you to live with us. You and I can share a room. And, by the way," her voice sounded excited. "I didn't tell you that I was asked to work a few hours as a lifeguard on the beach. I will start this month and fill in for a couple of people who are on vacation. I'm happy because it will break up the daily monotony of the supply room. All I ever do there is clean equipment."

I was happy for her. Everything was beginning to look up for both of us. A new excitement filled me. Quitting my job would be easy now. I would have a place to stay and people to talk to. The house back home was too empty and quiet for me now.

Andra and I sat quietly for a while. I suspected that she was thinking about how nice it would be for us to see each other daily. It would be like old times. The more I thought about it, the more excited I became. I trusted that she felt the same way. Soon I found out that her mind was on other things.

"There's something I need to tell you, Ariane," she began. "You should know about it, now that you'll come to live with us." She paused before continuing hesitantly. "I know how you feel about the police or even the military, but I've met this guy on the beach…"

"A soldier? A STASI?" I interrupted her before she could finish. I glared at her.

"Well, just listen and let me go on. Anyhow. I was sitting in my lookout post on the beach when two guys walked up to me and called, '*Hallo*, up there, Fräulein.'

"I looked down on them and called back, 'Are you talking to me?'

"'Yes, you, lovely Fräulein up there in your ivory tower. Are you keeping the beach safe and the sharks away?'

"I was amused and teased them right back, replying that I was there to keep the beach safe from inquisitive and annoying young gentlemen and to protect anyone from drowning.

"In response, one of them called. 'Well, Fräulein, it appears that we have something in common. We, too, are guards. We are protecting the shoreline from enemies of the GDR. I dare say that it is we who have the more important job.'"

"Where are they stationed?" I wanted to know, interrupting her again and not too pleased at the prospect of moving into a town that was occupied by the Coastal Border Brigade or any military personnel.

"They're stationed not far from here. It seems that the men are working hard and are not given much free time. They pull their regular duty and are clearing up the rubble that is all around us. There is more. In their spare time, they are building a new boat landing."

"You seem impressed," I commented. I was not very happy with the admiration she expressed for them.

"Well, I'm just saying that the boys are made to give up their free time without receiving the benefit of pay."

"That's not unusual in the GDR," I reminded her. "In any case, what did the guards mean when they said that they are protecting the border? Are they afraid that an invasion will come from across the water?"

"I don't know. But don't interrupt me all the time." Andra seemed impatient with me. "Let me tell you what happened next."

I remained quiet and listened to her as she related that after some bantering between the three of them, the young men asked her out for dinner. Feeling caught in an awkward situation, and not wanting to choose one over the other, she agreed to go out with both of them the next day or the day thereafter. One of the men suddenly remembered that his superior had put him on a work detail for the next few days. He bowed out.

"Manfred, the one I went out with, is really a decent sort of guy. I mean, decent for being with the border guard. But I can't say that I'm totally crazy about him. He mostly talked about his duties, weapons training, and so on. I'm not really interested in all of that."

"Hmm." I responded. I could not get over my annoyance that Andra chose someone who was a cog in the wheels of the government machine. "I hope that it was your first and last date with him."

"Too late. We'll be going dancing next time. Really, Ariane, I know that what happened to your family is terrible, but I'm not prejudiced against him. He isn't a member of the STASI. I just want to have some fun. I'm so bored here."

"Well, they are still the arm of the government. Besides, I feel protective of you." I made a weak attempt to vindicate myself. "It's enough that *I* seem to attract men of unsavory character. I suppose that I want to save you from a similar fate."

"Snap out of it already." Andra punched me hard on the arm. It made me fall sideways. "You are overreacting. I'm not going to marry him. We're just going dancing!"

I pushed my jaw forward and kept quiet once more. I stared ahead over the water on which the moon was casting tiny flecks of silver. An involuntary sigh escaped me. Andra had been spared the same experiences that I had been made to endure. She had never lost anyone, except her father, whom she could not remember. I wondered whether a serious involvement with a Vopo or a military man would threaten our friendship.

I gazed into the far distance. To the left of us, a tiny light blinked on and off in measured succession. It came from Schleswig-Holstein. It seemed as though the Golden West was sending us an invitation to visit.

"You can almost see Dahme from here," I remarked, trying to smooth things over between us. "And somewhere out there in the dark sea lies

Denmark and Sweden. How far do you think it is to there? Would anyone be able to swim that distance?"

"I was wondering the same many times before," my friend answered. "I often wished to test my endurance on a long distance swim. Not recently, of course, but before the accident. Judging the distance from here to Dahme, I think it would be quite challenging to swim it. But I believe that it is not impossible.

"My trainer told me about the woman who swam the English Channel. She was the daughter of a German immigrant to America. Before she attempted it, she had already won a Gold Medal at the 1924 Olympics in freestyle swimming. Nevertheless, to prepare herself for the long distance swim, she had to train for many more hours."

"If you could manage it, the West would welcome you with open arms and put you into its freestyle swim program." I responded.

"Really? Do you think so? That would be great!" Andra exclaimed enthusiastically. "I hear that over there you get money if you win a competition. Can you imagine being paid in West German money?"

Neither of us knew what a West German Mark could buy. We only knew that our East German currency was worth one quarter of the West German Currency.

"I think that if I were as talented as you, I'd have defected a long time ago. But I understand that you did not want to leave your mother. As for me, I wished that my grandmother had taken me with her to the Golden West. When my mother died, I wanted to run away to there. But then the Waldheims took me to them, and my life became easier."

"Look on the bright side, Ariane," Andra gave my arm an affectionate shove. She, too, wanted to put our differences aside. "If you had left, we wouldn't have become friends." She scooted closer and place her arm around my shoulder. "I'm glad you're here, even though you are giving me a hard time about Manfred."

"Yes, I know," I responded.

"Truly, I've missed you these past months, Ariane," my friend commented once more.

We silently looked across the water and counted the blinks of the light house in Dahme. I wondered what life would like on the other side, the Golden West. After a while, I looked at my watch. It was time to return to the house.

We found Frau Fischer and Tante Berta waiting for us. Each was nursing a flip top bottle of beer. "Come and sit down, girls," Frau Fischer called to us. "We want to talk to you about something." She turned to me. "Why not stay here and look for another job, Ariane? I actually would like it if you would do that. Andra wouldn't feel so abandoned after I leave for Thuringia."

Andra was happy. "That's great, Mutti. Ariane and I had the same thought."

I was overcome by gratitude for having such wonderful and supportive friends. I suggested, "Perhaps I should work in the dungeon of my office for an extra month so that I can earn one more paycheck. It might not be easy to get a job here very quickly. What do you all think?"

"That's alright with me," Tante Berta nodded. "The more money we make between us, the easier life will be for all of us. We then can splurge on as many fliptop bottles of beer as we want." She slapped herself on her thigh with amusement.

"She's joking of course," Frau Fisher said.

Convinced that my troubles would soon be gone, I relaxed and enjoyed the rest of my vacation with Andra and her family. Before departing, I took one last walk along the cliffs above the Baltic to savor the splendid view of the sea below. Soon it would be my daily companion. I sat down and looked into the distance. The incoming waves were being pulled to shore. When they met with shallow ground, they lost their power. But soon the force of nature was pulling them back out to to sea.

I lifted my eyes to the wide expanse of sky. It was speckled with tiny white clouds. I expected that once I was settled in this new, beautiful place, I would be happy again. I took a deep breath and felt the fresh wind ruffling my hair. I turned my face toward the sun and could feel that a change was in the air.

Only later did I realize that the change, which I had felt coming on, was not coming to me alone. Few people, if any, knew that great changes were imminent. Most had been unaware that instead of advancing slowly as usual, it now came moving toward us suddenly. It came fast and furious. No one saw or heard it coming. It came racing in our direction like a ghost train in the night. It was silent, invisible and soundless. Its conductor was no other than Walter Ulbricht, who had plotted its course and its time of arrival long before. The train carried a cargo of tyranny, inhumanity, sorrow and despair. When it finally arrived at its destination, it spit out a poisonous cloud of political oppression so thick that it blocked the light of freedom. It sickened people in the world as it descended on unsuspecting citizen in the GDR And, for many years to come, the wicked stench of it overshadowed people's hearts and minds on both sides of our border.

Chapter Twenty-Nine

My Decision to Defect

The weather was oppressive and sultry when I returned home. Dark, heavy clouds hung low and announced one of our usual summer storms, which always came in August. I did not particularly look forward to the wild rapids of water, which I knew would come gushing down the sidewalks even before such rains had ended. I would, once again, arrive home soaked to the bone if the water did not drain fast. I was at work when I heard the rumble of thunder. The cellar, which had become my office, had no windows. But I imagined that big raindrops, as big as the pebbles at Bullfrog Pond, would soon fall once more.

True to his word, Herr Sauer had sent boxes filled with documents to be sorted through. The task was boring. But knowing that I soon would move to Warnemünde gave me the patience to continue working. I felt proud of myself because I had been able to ignore the sarcastic note that Herr Sauer had sent along with the files. It read, "I hope that you enjoy the challenge, Fräulein Berger. Good luck in your new position as file clerk!"

I had returned from Warnemünde only a two days ago and knew that it was time to give my resignation. I climbed up the stairs to Herr Klein's office. An unfamiliar, but highly pleasant aroma drifted into my nose. My instincts told me that what I was smelling were genuine ground up coffee beans. I sniffed and closed my eyes. Ah! I inhaled slowly. *That* is what people meant whenever they had mentioned real coffee. I remembered how, immediately after the war, they had talked about their cravings for a cup of coffee. They had referred to coffee as "the king of beverages." They had reminisced about the times when they had been sitting in sidewalk cafés, enjoying a cup or two with their friends. Along with the coffee, they had savored seductive pieces of *Schwarzwälder Kirsch Torte,* the German Black Forest cherry cake, or a slice of heavy butter cream torte. Some people still missed their afternoon *Kaffeeklatsch* even now. They yearned for a cup of genuine coffee and for a slice of one of the rich tortes for which our country had been famous. The memory of such cakes, their airy lightness, even though they had been baked with fresh butter and decorated with real cream, produced unintentional sighs.

Herr Klein spotted me through the half-open door of his office and waved his hand. "Come on in, Fräulein Berger. Close the door behind you and take a seat."

"It smells delicious in here," I said, once again sniffing appreciatively. I glanced back at Frau Müller before I closed the door. I wanted to see whether she, too, was drinking coffee. She was not. I wondered where Herr Klein might have have obtained the coffee.

"Yes, the aroma of coffee is outstanding, is it not? It's a gift from someone. It helps to have friends in high places, does it not, Fräulein Berger? Surely, you, too, must have enjoyed a good cup of real South American coffee now and then? Herr Sauer had mentioned that you once had connections in East Berlin. He intimated that you fell from the good graces of someone special. But that is not important right now, is it. May I offer you a cup, Fräulein Berger?"

Surprised by his comment, my eyebrows involuntarily knitted together. But this was no time to be defensive. I let it slide and accepted his invitation. "*Ja, danke.*"

I took a sip from the Rosenthal china cup, and for a fleeting moment felt honored that my boss would share such sought-after beverage with me. I knew that it would have been purchased for an absurd amount of money on the Black Market. Moreover, it would have been a gift to him by someone in high office. I thought it peculiar, once again, that the leaders and functionaries of our Socialist-Communist regime who were the declared enemies of Capitalism continued to crave the fruits of it.

"Ah, Fräulein Berger. You look lovely." Herr Klein gazed appreciatively at me. "The vacation has done wonders for you. Your tan suits you. So, then, how is your work going downstairs? Did you make any progress with it?"

"Very few of the documents belong in our office. It will take time to separate the files."

"Good. Good." He lit a cigarette. "There is no hurry to straighten them out. Just peek into my office occasionally to let me know that you are still alive down there. Herr Sauer has directed that I give him a report on your attitude every week. I assured him that you are as pleasant and efficient as you always have been."

Herr Klein paused once again before adding, "There is one small job, which I, myself, might ask you to do for us, Fräulein Berger. I need you to translate a Russian document. Frau Müller is not able to do it. Of course, you understand that you will need to keep that to yourself. Herr Sauer must not hear that I am engaging you to perform regular office work."

I cringed again at the mention of Herr Sauer's name and quickly remembered that I came to give my notice instead of paying a social call. "I, too, have a request, Herr Klein," I began. "You've praised me for my diligence. I was wondering…" I took a deep breath before continuing in an uneven tone of voice. "Would you please write me a good recommendation? I came to give my notice."

My boss wrinkled his forehead in surprise. "You cannot leave us now, Fräulein Berger. Has the Supervisor given you any more trouble? He and I have discussed you at length. Considering your excellent performance in the past, I was able to convince him not to take any disciplinary actions against you. He will allow you to continue working for us but specified that you should continue working in the file room. I wanted you back up here, but he objected. Perhaps you heard that he has reinstated the position of junior secretary? Frau Müller had complained that she cannot complete all the work herself. She also had requested that Herr Sauer give you back your old position. He refused but instructed me to hire a new girl, one that will fit his...uh...the needs of our office better."

I gasped and immediately blurted out, "You mean that the new girl should be more willing to give in to his advances! He is a…" I wanted to say "pig." But before it could slip out, I caught the word on my tongue.

"In any case," I continued, "whatever will take place in this office will be of no concern to me any longer. I am leaving and need a good recommendation from you."

My boss lowered his eyes. He took a slow sip from his coffee, then calmly drew on his cigarette before he responded. "I would like nothing better than to ask Frau Müller to type one up for you, Fräulein Berger. You did an outstanding job for me. The problem is this: You know, of course, that every document that leaves here needs to be co-signed by Herr Sauer. Without his signature, nothing will be valid. Those are the rules. He outranks me and is required to sign such a document. Herr Sauer suspected that you might want to quit and informed me that he will not co-sign such a letter."

I was stunned. I had not anticipated that Herr Sauer would sabotage my leaving.

"Fräulein Berger." Herr Klein continued. "As sorry as I am, you might find it impossible to get another job. To be hired by anyone, you must provide a recommendation from your previous employers. This is your first job, is it not? Why not settle into the job downstairs and do the filing? I know that the room is not too pleasant, but the work is not difficult."

I answered under my breath. "How do you expect me to stay here after what happened? I am trained as a secretary, not as a file clerk."

Herr Klein's nodded, and his voice took on a soothing quality. "Fräulein Berger, believe me, I am on your side. You are a pretty young woman. Why not find a boyfriend and get married? That would solve your problem."

I felt as though he had slapped my face. Why was he diminishing my intelligence or my capabilities? Was he suggesting that I belonged in the kitchen, standing over a stove with a spoon in my hand and an apron tied around my waist? Of course, there was nothing wrong with that. However, I wanted to have a choice in the matter.

Herr Klein intentionally ignored the angry expression on my face and smiled again. "Well then. I suspect that there is no boyfriend whom you can marry. I know that the factory is looking for unskilled workers. Most likely, supervisors will not care that you worked as a secretary. But, then again, they will be suspicious, wondering why you left a good job. They will investigate. Perhaps they might think that you could not hold down a job here with us and might wonder whether you are capable enough to do a good job for them. They would get in touch with Herr Sauer at one of their Party meetings or ask me for a written statement of your performance and for the reasons of your resignation. You know that I cannot discuss the subject with any of them. Herr Sauer will cause problems for me if I do. He even might make the same accusations against me that he made against you. For all I know, he might be correct in what he accuses you with."

Every muscle in my body tensed. I felt numb and stared speechlessly at Herr Klein.

"I agree that you are in an unfortunate predicament, Fräulein Berger," he continued. "It will be impossible to obtain a new position anywhere with that hanging over your head."

Herr Klein paused and cleared his throat. He watched me intently before he spoke again. "I could, perhaps, be of assistance to you, Fräulein Berger. Since you scoff at the thought of going to work in the factory, or might not even be able to obtain a job there, and you don't have a boyfriend to help you out financially, it would be difficult for you to live on nothing." He paused and smiled. "What would you say if there were someone who would be happy to take care of you, someone who would treat you with kindness? If there *were* such a person, you would not have to worry about finding another job."

Herr Klein gave me a long, speculative look. I avoided his eyes, unsure whether I was interpreting his words correctly. I made myself look at him, search his face to make sure that I had not misunderstood him. I knew that if I were to accept his offer, it would meant that I would take the easy way out. I would devalue myself and be dependent on him.

The room became so still that I could hear the clock ticking on his desk.

"Perhaps you and I can work something out between us," Herr Klein broke the silence. And," he cleared his throat once more, "Herr Sauer need only know that you accepted a housekeeping position somewhere."

I came alive and jumped out of my chair. I was nineteen years old, going on twenty. I glared at him. I would never forget the compromises that my mother had made and how her life had turned out in the end.

I swallowed hard. "Thank you for your offer Herr Klein, but I will not sell myself to anyone in exchange for false security!"

Herr Klein calmly picked up his cigarette and retorted in a cool voice. "I see, Fräulein Berger. But if you ever change your mind about my offer, my door is always open. Meanwhile, the basement remains yours to work in."

I stumbled more than walked out of his office. Back in the cellar, I spilled angry tears. What right did my bosses have to manipulate me? What right did they have to treat me as negotiable goods? I was a respectable girl. I had gone to school, had received a diploma and had performed my job well. Even though Herr Klein might have wanted to help me, I felt degraded. I was disgusted with the whole lot of them.

My heart felt roughed up by their callousness. I was angry, suddenly tempted to cut up every piece of paper in the file boxes. However, I refrained from doing so. I told myself that I was not a spiteful person and would not stoop to such a vengeful act now. In any case, I was convinced that God was watching me. I could not shake the teachings of my grandmother or the suggestion of my uncle, who had warned that every action produced a result. If I allowed myself to soil whatever good there was in me, the punishment that would follow me might be worse than anything that I had experienced before. Instead of giving in to my first impulse, I angrily pounded on the boxes until I had calmed down.

The next day, I arrived at the office and took my place in the cellar. I felt emotionally exhausted. I had thought about it all night, had tried to find a solution to my dilemma. How could I extricate myself from this job without suffering repercussions from Herr Sauer? I began separating files, reading some of the information in them, and placing them in piles. At least that would keep my mind off my troubles for a while.

Soon, I heard excited shouts coming from below. An unfamiliar voice was speaking to Herr Klein. I heard Frau Müller exclaim something. Minutes later, she called down to me, "We are leaving for the day, Fräulein Berger. You might as well go, too."

I wondered what had happened. Perhaps, and as unlikely as it would seem, Herr Sauer had given us the day off. With my mind focused on my own dilemma, I gathered up my things. I hurried to the Sports Center to find the sympathetic ear of Herr Langhans.

The streets were unusually deserted. I passed a house with an opened window . Through it I could hear the low volume of a radio broadcasts. The announcer was making a commentary on some event. I hurried on, hoping to catch Herr Langhans in his office. When I walked in, he was sitting at his desk, staring ahead of himself. His face was pale.

"Ah, it's you, Ariane," he looked up and greeted me in a brittle voice. "Did you hear? They have built a wall."

Still in my own head, and confused about what he meant, I said, "A wall?"

"Yes. We are walled in!" He responded.

When he said nothing further, I rose from the chair and stepped into the hallway. Everything there appeared as it always had, except that the gym was unusually empty today. Only a few kids were training on bars. Perhaps the workers had needed the gym vacated before they began partitioning off sections of the gym. I was ready to inspect the room next to Herr Langhans'.

"No, not out there!" He called after me in an irritated tone of voice.

"What wall, then, are you talking about?" I returned and seated myself once mre. "Moreover, don't glare at me with such a face and make feel worse. I, too, received bad news."

"Then you've heard what has happened?"

"Heard *what*, Herr Langhans? Tell me what has *you* so upset?"

"It's the worst that could have happened to us! Walter Ulbricht has decided to shut everyone in. He has built a wall that blocks all access to West Berlin. It is being reinforced with barbed wire as we speak. All communication with free Europe has been terminated. The guards threatened to fire at anyone who will go near it."

"Are you serious?" I shouted in disbelief. I instantly knew that the fibers of hope to which we had tied our future had been cut.

"We have become prisoners in our own land. Walter Ulbricht claims that the wall has gone up for our protection. He calls it an anti-Fascist barrier. He says that his intention is to keep us safe from the Fascists, who are trying to invade us. But we all know that the opposite is true, don't we! He is shutting us in because we are losing too many people. Nearly three million have already escaped to the Golden West. Ulbricht wants to put a stop to that."

I had never seen Herr Langhans so upset or speak so openly to anyone. I had often wondered, but had not asked, why he had stayed in the GDR instead of fleeing along with so many others. Perhaps he had thought that things would get better. Or, perhaps, he had convinced himself that he needed to stay and help the kids. I now saw in his face how dire our situation had become. I was scared.

"Will you try to escape now, Herr Langhans? You must know of some opening, some hole along the border that would allow you to squeeze through. If you go, please take me with you."

"The border is heavily guarded, Ariane. There's barbed wire strung everywhere. And where there are not watchtowers, there are mine strips. We've lost our chance to get out."

"But there has to be another way to escape! If *you* don't want to leave, you must help me to leave," I begged.

"Listen to me, Ariane. Trust me. The soldiers have received orders to shoot and kill anyone who approaches the wall. You are not even allowed to enter any of the East German villages that are located close to the border. Only those who live there are allowed to pass through the checkpoint. Relatives of those living there need prior authorization to enter. People have whispered that the mine fields begin just past the last houses of these villages. Escape is too dangerous. Rid yourself of such foolish thought."

I was shocked to hear that Herr Langhans would stay and suffer Ulbricht's oppression in silence rather than to risk escape into better future. He would stay and take care of the kids here at the Center. He would resign himself to his fate of having become a prisoner in his own country where Walter Ulbricht would be his warden.

Pure obstinacy rose in me. The cruelty shown to us by our government was like the final death prick from the horns of the devil. The only way I could be free of my job and of the GDR was to get out. But how could I manage it? I thought fast, and an idea developed in my head.

"Herr Langhans, do you know whether the distance from Warnemünde to Schleswig-Holstein is manageable by boat?"

"Ariane, if you are considering what I think you are…No! That is insane. Put that out of your head."

"Well, just tell me if it is possible!" I spoke the words harshly, knowing that my tone was disrespectful. "You grew up on the coast before the war. You must know. When I visited Andra, I heard someone say that the shore line is controlled by guards with speed boats. Andra and I were out late one night but saw no indication of it."

"So, you are even thinking of involving Andra in your plan! I know that the two of you are strong and are trained in endurance sports. But I would not advise young women to make such a trip."

I became increasingly annoyed. Why did he not answer me directly? He saw my irritation.

"Listen to me, girl," he finally said. "Don't put yourself into harms way. I know the two of you all too well. You are both stubborn and tenacious and won't let go of an idea once you latch on to it. I suggest that you drop it. What you are contemplating to do is more than youthful folly. It is a death wish. If you are caught, there will be horrible consequences. If you do not drown first before you are apprehended, you will be incarcerated and perhaps sentenced to death. Prison is not a place for anyone, especially not for young women. It will be the end of your lives as you have known them to be."

"This *is* the end of my life already," I cried. "It's not only the wall that is evil, but my bosses at work, and all the injustices that my family had suffered. I lost everyone and feel robbed. So, just tell me, please, whether it is possible to reach Dahme or even Denmark in a small boat!"

"Yes," he replied. "It might be possible if the weather is nice and you can make it through the first stretch of water without being spotted."

"Thank you," I responded. "I am really sorry, Herr Langhans, but I don't want to die being a prisoner behind a wall. I remember how hopeless and abandoned I had felt on a bleak Christmas day many years ago. I had been scared beyond description. I had been unable to control my future then. I had wanted to run away to the West because I believed that people over there would treat me kindly. Then the Waldheim family came to my rescue. And, you, too, were good to me. I am grateful for everything you did. If you cannot give me any advice on how to make it across, I'll need to figure it out for myself. And, as for Andra, you are correct. I will ask her to come along."

I had never spoken to him in such a hostile or impolite manner; but, considering the circumstances, I could not help myself now. I was standing at the crossroads of my life. I needed to make a choice before it was too late. I wondered whether my destiny had always lain in the West. Perhaps I had missed out on following it years earlier. I had remained here because of Wolfgang and the rest of the family. I needed their love, and they had given it to me. Perhaps now, with my will and intentions being so strong, I would have a second chance to flee. Perhaps fate, or whatever it was that directed our lives, would help me make it to the West. I would go. That is, if my courage would not leave me.

"Come and talk to me tomorrow." Herr Langhans finally advised me in a tired voice. "I'm ready to go home and lock this place up. Perhaps later, when we have recovered from the shock of the news, you and I can sit down and find a solution. But even then, Ariane, I don't think that I will have a different answer for you. I am sure that all escape routes are blocked."

I rose from my chair and walked to the door. With my hand on the handle, I turned around. I needed him to offer me encouragement. I needed him to tell me that his good wishes would be with me. If he would not be there physically, I needed him to support me in his thoughts.

I asked him one more time. "Herr Langhans, are you certain that the distance from somewhere along the shore of Warnemünde to Schleswig-Holstein is manageable by boat in a day or two?"

My voice had become cloaked in heavy sadness. I knew that I would miss him. He had been my coach. He had taught me to believe in myself. He had pushed me to run faster, run against the wind and the rain. He had taught me to go for the goal and not give up. He had been my mentor. But more than that, he had become my friend.

I stood looking sadly into his face. I did not know how to say goodbye. In the past, every person whom I had loved had left me first. But now the roles were reversed. I would be the one who would leave other's behind. I noticed how Herr Langhans was struggling for something to say. His eyes were pleading with my own to reconsider my plan. He could see in my face that this was good-bye.

For an instant I wondered whether I was being foolish. I had been born into this ravaged country. I had been born into struggle and upheaval. I had grown up with it. Hardships and losses had been the way of life. Along with others, I had waited for progress to happen. All of us had expected reunification with the West to follow. It had not happened. We had been patient, had been convinced that if it would not come this year, it would arrive the following year, or the next year thereafter. We had lived with hope, had pulled together with family and friends and had endured every false promise that our government had sprinkled over us like toxic dust.

I averted my eyes from Herr Langhans' own. I did not want him to see my sorrowful heart that cried its farewell. I knew that I needed to leave. Something in my soul was urging me to go. I knew that I needed to keep my appointment with my unknown destiny.

"Ariane!" My mentor and friend finally found his voice. "Please reconsider whatever it is you are about to do!"

But I had already stepped out of the door.

Chapter Thirty

1961
The Berlin Wall

I glanced around the house which had provided love and comfort to me for more than seven and a half years. The rooms would soon be totally silent. I missed the days of laughter and wonderful music that had filled the rooms. I turned on the radio and moved the dial across the band. As usual, the GDR was at work, trying to block the signals coming from the West. Finally, amidst the undulating squeals and whistles that weaved in and out, the faint voices of reporters from RIAS Berlin, and those of the *Deutsche Welle,* came through. All condemned the building of the wall and the murderous intent of the border guards and Vopos. Even though the West was outraged, no one came to our rescue. No one interfered with the fortification of the wall. Citizen turned hopeful eyes toward America and its new elected president. But even John F. Kennedy refrained from producing the political miracle people that expected. We knew, then, that our border had become sealed for good. So was the fate of GDR citizens.

I felt tired and exhausted. I wished for the cheer of my family. Tante Helga would not think about leaving. She would stay in the GDR with Wolfgang and Dagmar, who were enjoying an excellent education and superior training here. They might not be able to obtain such opportunities in the West.

To placate my nerves and soothe my yearning for comfort, I decided to go for sweets. The bakery down the street was open. I left the house and hurried toward it in witless desire. The shopkeeper greeted me with swollen eyelids and a pale face. "Ulbricht has finally done it to us, Fräulein Ariane," he said and wiped his brow before he handed me a dozen jelly doughnuts. I nodded in silence and ran back home. I seated myself at the table. I bit into one, and then into another until I became tranquilized by the sugar coating and the sweet jam that lay hidden in the center of the donuts. I ate one after the other until the whole dozen was gone. And only after crumbs were left did I realize what I had done to myself. The sugar had brought on a cloud of euphoria. My hands began to shake and my feet became restless. Still, I could barely move the rest of my body. I wiped the sugar off my lips and heaved myself from the chair. I put one foot in front of the other, walked into the hallway, and grasped the banister. I felt sick as I pulled myself up the stairs. I lay down and soon fell into troubled sleep.

I awoke with a headache the next morning and turned on the radio once more. Nothing had changed in our situation. It seemed that many people were already standing near the wall, shouting obscenities at the guards who drove them back. But the people kept pressing forward, insisting that the guards were henchman in the service of Walter Ulbricht. In no time, Vopos arrived to push back the angry crowd while promising to fire at anyone who would not leave. I realized then that I needed to act quickly. I needed to leave for Warnemünde earlier than planned.

Instead of going to work, I headed for the public phone booth several blocks from my house and dialed the number to my office. Feigning fits of coughs, I convinced Frau Müller that my work in the damp basement had affected my health. She advised me to stay in bed.

Back at the house, I began stuffing a few items of clothing into a suitcase. I hated to part with my books but knew they needed to stay behind. I pulled my diaries from the shelf and stuffed them into my bag. Looking around one final time, I remembered the little metal box that held my mother's ring and letter. I retrieved the box from my *Schrank* and packed it. I, then, searched for an extra pair of walking shoes and opened our shoe *Schrank*. I noticed a large piece of folded oilcloth in the back of it. Herr Fink must have left it behind. He had arrived once day with his viola case wrapped in it because it had rained. I smiled to myself as I picked it up. Finally I was able to pry off a sliver of redemption from the man! If my journey should take me across the water, the cloth would keep my belongings from getting wet.

I had already locked up the house when I remembered that I forgot to leave a note for Tante Helga. Not wanting to turn back and waste another minute, I promised myself to write a letter once I was ready to depart the GDR.

When I arrived at Andra's home, she greeted me with a somber face. "Can you believe what they did to us?"

"That is exactly why I've come sooner than you expected me. I'm leaving the GDR," I blurted out. "I want you to come with me."

She stared at me as though I had lost my mind. "You are crazy, Ariane! The wall is up and the borders are closed. We'll be shot even before we get near them."

"You *must* come with me, Andra. You've told me that you are not happy here any longer. Your mother is married, and Tante Berta has her own life to live. I have a plan that might work. I mean, it *has* to work!"

My suggestion startled her. "You are insane!" she cried.

"You *must* come with me," I repeated. "That is, unless, of course, you fell in love with that border guard!"

"Don't be silly!" she objected. "I only went out with him to have some diversion from my everyday humdrum life. You have no idea how bored I am."

"Alright, then! Just listen to what I am suggesting. I don't think I can manage to leave on my own."

I knew that Andra's distaste for GDR politics did not equal my own. Her reasons for leaving would be different from my own. She held a grudge against her trainer and the Center for letting her down so quickly and for dismissing her from the roster as a swimmer..

"So, what's your plan?" She finally wanted to know. "Let me see whether I like it."

I outlined the trip as I had envisioned it and suggested that if she would join me, she might be given a chance to enter a swim program in the West.

She shook her head. "I would like that. That alone would be an incentive to leave. But Manfred told me yesterday that the shoreline will be heavily patrolled from now on. Not only that, but torpedo boats will check the water all the way up to the international line with increasing frequency. Since you left here a few days ago, a search light was installed on the watch tower down the beach."

"Well, then, we need to leave quickly and make sure that we leave farther away from the tower. We'll have to row in the shadow of the light and avoid it as it sweeps over the water.

"I don't know Ariane." My friend was doubtful. Perhaps you should think of another way to escape. I don't want to be shot at or even killed on the water."

"Am I reading you correctly? Will you join me if we can figure out another route to escape? Okay, then. You come up with a different plan."

Andra thought for a while but could not think of one. Neither of us knew a foreign business man who would be willing to smuggle us out in the false trunk of a car, or such other adventure. After a lengthy discussion, we came back to my original plan.

Before we were able to discuss the details of it, her aunt walked into the house. She heard my voice. "You're back already, Ariane," she cried. Did you quit your job earlier than planned?"

"Ariane came because of the wall. She wants to leave the GDR," Andra blurted out.

"God bless you on your impossible journey, my child," Tante Berta chuckled.

"No. She's serious!" Andra exclaimed.

The face of the aunt fell. "Ariane, I really think that it's too late for a show of resistance. The bastards have us all locked in until the end of time."

"We came up with a plan," I assured her.

"We?" She turned to her niece. "Are you out of your mind, girl?" Tante Berta's good humor left her completely. "You are not going! I promised your mother to look after you. I'll not let you expose yourself to danger. Not knowing whether you are dead or alive would devastate both of us."

Andra took a deep breath and responded, "I'll write her a long letter after I arrived in the West. I won't sign it, but she'll recognize my hand writing. She won't miss me too much if I'm gone. She's got Otto now. What kind of life will I have if I stay here? I don't have any real friends here and am spending most of my days working in a dreary supply room. Besides, the atmosphere here will, from now on, be too oppressive for me to live in. Ariane is right. It's better to get out while we still can. At least, we *hope* that we can make it out. I haven't seen any speedboats on the water yet.

"If you are opposed to my leaving, Tante Berta, I want to remind you that you, yourself, had wanted to leave several years ago. You only changed your mind because you were afraid to end up lonely over there. It will be different for us. Ariane and I will be together. We'll find a better life over there. Besides, you know that it isn't for *you* to decide what I will or won't do with my life."

I looked aghast at Andra. She sounded too rude and defiant for my liking.

Tante Berta frowned. "What's gotten into you these past months, child? Why are you speaking to me in such a hateful manner? I am only concerned for your wellbeing. I am merely trying to warn you that what you are planning to do is youthful stupidity. If you do not want to listen to reason, let me ease my conscience by telling you that I have warned you."

It was not the first time that my friend argued with her aunt. It seemed that the accident had changed her and brought on mood swings. So far, she and I had not experienced problems with each other. I made a mental note to watch her.

Andra seemed amicable enough when she and I talked with each other into the night and made a "to do list." She was sure that she would be able to check out a rubber raft from her supply room. We would depart under the cover of night and paddle as hard as we could for Schleswig-Holstein, keeping the lighthouse of Dahme in view. The weather report was favorable. It promised only a few light clouds. If we happened to drift off course or too far out to sea, we were certain that the lighthouse of Gedser in Denmark would be visible. It would keep us going in the right direction. Our main concern was the moon, which hung like a large ripe melon above our heads right now. In a few weeks, autumn would be upon us, and the weather would turn cooler. We didn't want to wait too long to depart but discussed it. We decided to give the moon an extra few days to lose its fullness.

I suddenly remembered that I needed to come up with a plausible excuse for my prolonged absence at work. I could not risk Frau Müller coming to my house and discovering that I was gone. She would report my absence to Herr Sauer, who surely would take action and set the police on my trail. I hated to tell a lie but implored Tante Berta to help me. She agreed to make a call to the office. She would identify herself as Frau von Waldheim. Frau Müller would not recognize Tante Berta's voice but believe her when she reported that my doctor wanted me to stay in bed for a few more days.

"I would not do it for anyone but you, my girl. God forgive me if something goes wrong with your plan!" The aunt sighed and made her way to a phone booth.

Andra agreed to arrange another date with Manfred. She would quiz him about boat patrols, guard watches, and so on. We hoped that he would reveal some information because he seemed enamored with Andra.

By noon the next day, Manfred showed up unannounced at Andra's tower. He was free that evening and hoped to go out with her. Since it fit so perfectly into our plan, Andra immediately agreed. When she later returned from her date, she reported that she had not dared to ask too many questions. She had been afraid that he would be suspicious. He told her, however, that for the next two weeks, he would be working the night shift. He was not certain, however, whether he would be assigned to shore or sea duty.

"I think we need to prepare a believable story, just in case we are discovered," I suggested. "I thought of one already. What do you think of this one:

"We can say that I am visiting you and that we were returning from a short sunset excursion when we heard calls for help. We know that no one is allowed to be on the water after dark. But since you are a lifeguard, and it is your duty to answer such a call, we turned around and searched the water. The call sounded desperate. As much as we looked, we could not find anyone. When we finally decided to give up and turn back to shore, we found that we had been carried out to sea.

"I know that the story sounds a bit lame, but do you think it is believable?" I asked Andra. "We could add that we stayed out that long because we could not let one of our GDR brothers or sisters drown because our country needs everyone to assure progress."

"I don't know, Ariane. It *does* sound a bit far fetched. But it's worth a try if we need to give an explanation to avoid being prosecuted for attempting *Republikflucht*."

Both of us were hopeful that if Manfred's team were to apprehend us on the water, his infatuation with Andra would grant us leniency. Perhaps it would even save us. Andra and I made a pact that we would stick to that story, no matter what, even if we were to find ourselves under duress. We also agreed that we would repeat our rehearsed story by flavoring it with non-consequential little things, or change the order of our story so that it would not appear scripted. We've heard stories of arrest before and learned that not following the same sequence of telling a story and the way it was told had prevented someone from going to prison.

I thought of the nuggets of wisdom that my Uncle Emil had tried to instill in me when I had once come to him with a report that some older boys had tried to bully me. They had blocked my way, and I had become frightened. They had taunted me. I had managed to escape them. My uncle had given me this advice: "If that ever happens again, little one, keep calm and look them boldly in the eye. Keep breathing when you find yourself frightened. Don't expose your weakness to your enemy. Keep your wits about you and never lose your head."

Nonetheless, neither Andra nor I were sure how we would behave if things were to get tough. Would we be able to keep our promise to each other, even if we were being pushed beyond the limit of endurance?

Tante Berta had continued to argue against letting us go and had pointed out the dangers. In the end, she gave up. Realizing that she could not make us stay, she began to hover over us anxiously. She listened as we discussed details of our plan.

"Dress in layers," she advised us. "Take some rocks along to put into your sack of clothes. You might need to dump everything overboard fast. If you want the guards to believe your story, they must not find anything suspicious in the raft."

We made a note of her suggestions.

The day before our departure, Andra went to work as usual, while I headed for town to find the last necessary items on our list of supplies. We needed additional batteries for flashlights. I finally found some in Rostock. Back at the house, I filled glass jars with food to last us two days. I wrapped up a few small trinkets and placed them into the metal box, which contained the letter addressed to my mother. I took my diaries and wrapped them in the oil cloth. I would secure the package to my waist.

Towards evening, I wrote notes to my family and poured out my heartfelt thanks to them for their love and care of me. I closed with the explanation that Andra and I were off on a vacation.

After coming home from work, Andra lay down and rested for a while, while I went looking for Tante Berta. A fragrant aroma of spices lured me downstairs. I found her preparing red cabbage and potato *Knödel*, and watched her as she stuffed the dough with cubes of fried white bread and bacon.

"Hmm, smells delicious," I inhaled the sweet and sour aroma of the cabbage. "Do I smell cinnamon and cloves? Where did you get the spices?" Exotic spices were almost impossible to be obtained in the GDR.

"They're a gift from a friend. She received them as a present from a relative in the West. I thought I would cook a good old-fashioned German meal for the both of you on your last evening here. Tomorrow night you'll be gone."

She looked me squarely in the face. Her eyes were sad. "Keep me fondly in your memory. And, try to stay alive. I'll wait for you to pay me back the favor I did for you today. I told a big fat lie to that secretary in your office. I think I made a good impression. Frau Müller believed every word I said. I told her that I have been sitting by your bedside, changing the cold compresses on your feverish forehead."

I felt myself choking up with warm emotions. She was a pearl, that Tante Berta.

"So, then. Are you finished with your letter?" She asked.

"Yes." I let out a long sad sigh, remembering how difficult it had been to say goodbye to Tante Helga and my siblings.

"Did you write to that boy of yours as well? The one that you said is so wonderful."

"Yes."

"Wouldn't he ask you to stay if he knew what you're about to do? From what you told me before, I think that he…"

"Probably so," I interrupted her. "He actually did ask me to move to Leipzig so that we could see each other more often."

"Really? And you said…?"

"It's complicated, Tante Berta. There's this Katrina, his girlfriend. She would make his life hard to bear if she knew that he asked me to do that."

"He's a grown boy, able to take care of himself."

"Well, but she's got her claws in him. I don't know what's keeping him tied to her. If he really cared for me, he'd let her go."

"Relationships between men and women are difficult, my girl. People often stay together because of something other than love, something that they can't control. Most times, they are not even aware of what it is that keeps them entangled. It's like an addiction. I've seen it. That is why I'm not married." Tante Berta responded.

"I did not agree to move because he refused to give up Katrina. I don't want to share a man with another woman." I said.

"How did you ever get this smart?"

I shrugged my shoulders. "Anyhow, that conversation took place before I found out that I wouldn't be able to get a recommendation from my job."

"I hope that all will go well for you in the future, Ariane. Don't let us mourn for you and my niece when we learn that your bodies have washed up on the beach."

She vigorously stirred the cabbage, which splattered from the pot onto the stove top. "Both Andra and you are pigheaded. Part of me thinks that you are doing the right thing, while the other part wants me to chain you both to the bedpost to keep you from leaving."

"I don't think that I will ever change my mind, Tante Berta. The government has tried to force-feed us with its ideologies for a decade and a half now. Perhaps I was lucky to have had a grandmother who lived in the West and an uncle who had shared his own thoughts so freely about our politics. Otherwise, I might have swallowed the government's propaganda like many other people."

"Surely you are not referring to me or my niece? You know my opinions about that already. As for Andra, I don't know what's going on in her head. She is apolitical. She wasn't even a member of the FDJ. I want you to remember something. If you arrive safely over there and are not happy, you can always come back here and stay with me. The government would love for you to tell them that the West has failed you. They would use you as their propaganda tool."

"Thanks for the offer; but if we make it, I won't ever come back. Don't look for me to return while the wall is up. But don't worry. Somehow, I feel that everything will be alright."

"Just do me one favor then," Tante Berta continued. "Watch Andra for me. She's been moody and unhappy ever since her accident. She is refusing to see the doctor any longer about her headaches. She claims that she is sick of being prodded."

"I'll watch out for her. I promise."

"There's something else you might want to know," Tante Berta continued. "The reason she might have agreed to go with you might be because she still feels responsible for having kept you at her house the night that took away your mother. My niece may still want to make it up to you somehow."

Tante Berta began busying herself with the broom, sweeping up pieces of cabbage that had fallen on the floor.

"That's nonsense," I exclaimed. "That's a long time ago. She shouldn't think about that any more. It's I who feels protective toward her because of her accident."

"Well then. I am comforted to know that each of you will be looking out for the other." Tante Berta deposited the cabbage pieces into a trash container. She retrieved a bucket from the washroom and proceeded to fill it with water to which she added washing soda. Then she took a rag, got on her knees and mopped the floor in wide sweeps.

I watched her and suspected that she stayed busy to keep her nerves under control. "Don't worry about us," I suggested. "Perhaps you can pray that nothing will happen to us."

She rose from the floor and shot me a sidelong glance. "Pray?" She snorted. "I don't think it will do any good if you are deliberately running headlong into danger. I don't think God likes to be tested."

"I am not testing Him. I feel that it is the right thing to do and merely want Him to help us." I was defensive.

Tante Berta emptied the bucket of water in the sink. "I'm not going to argue with you about it. I hope that He will honor your request. Perhaps He has allowed the mess at your work to happen because He wants you to leave. How can we be sure to know what He thinks?" She shrugged her shoulder. "But if the two of you arrive safely, I will make it a special point to thank Him.

"One more thing, Ariane. Ask the authority in the West to let you contact Andra's cousin and stepmother in Mainz, even though my sister won't be too happy if her daughter reconnects with them."

"I didn't know that Andra has relatives in the West!" I was stunned to hear it.

Tante Berta filled her bucket once again and turned off the faucet. She set it on the floor. "*Jawohl.* That's correct. We once had another sister who lived over there with her husband and child. He died, and she re-married. A few years later, my sister passed away. We wanted to bring the girl over here and raise her, but the stepfather wouldn't hear of it. 'Who wants to live in the East when she has a good life in the West?' he said. He was correct, of course, even though my niece was having difficulties adjusting to the new stepmother."

"He married again?"

"Yes. He re-married not too long after my sister passed on."

My mouth dropped open in disbelief. The poor girl's life was even more confusing than my own had been. "Is your niece alright now?"

Tante Berta got on her knees again and began to rinse away the film the soda had left behind. She glanced up at me. "There's more to that story. Just to show you how unpredictable life is, the tale does not end here. Our second brother-in-law was injured in some construction accident. His leg developed an infection, and he died of gangrene."

"You are joking," I commented. "I don't believe it."

"Well, believe it, girl. It's true. My sister received governmental permission to attend the funeral in the West. Once again, she wanted to bring the girl back, but she thought better of it when she saw how well-fed and well dressed everyone was over there. In any case, by then, the girl seemed to have bonded with her stepmother already." Tante Berta lowered her head and scooted on her knees over the floor, rinsing it with a clean rag.

"I wonder why Andra never mentioned that she has a cousin in the West." I mused.

"It's probably my sister's fault. She did not get on with the stepmother. The girls met when they were small, but my sister never reminded Andra that she has a cousin over there. I'll send the address along."

Tante Berta, having decided that the floor was clean enough, pulled herself up slowly. "*Ach,* my knees aren't what they used to be," she complained.

"Why not use a scrub mop to clean the floor?" I suggested. "It's something new. I've seen them sold in the stores."

"Child, I would still be required to drape a rag over the bristles and rinse it out. Besides, you cannot get the floor clean that way! If I do it by hand and on my knees, I will be able to see up every bit of dirt on the floor and pick it up. A mob will leave things behind. I can assure you that after I'm done with my handiwork, you can serve a meal on my floor."

I laughed. "I guess it's difficult to let go of the old-fashioned way of doing things."

Tante Berta brushed a strand of gray hair from her face. "I might not be able to control what's happening in the world outside, but at least I can be in charge of my own home. At least here, I am able to do as I please."

I saw her point. The old-fashioned ways of the past, and being able to adhere to true and tried traditions, gave her comfort in these difficult times. Our leaders had taken away our hope for a better future. They had taken away our freedom and were holding us hostage in our own country. Adhering to old rituals gave Tante Berta solace. There was something sacred and dependable in them. Trusting and believing in them gave her comfort when everything else around us was falling apart.

Chapter Thirty-One

Escape over the Baltic

The next morning dawned as any other. The sky looked gloomy, as it always does this time of day by the sea. Whatever sunlight there would be later still lay hidden behind the mist that rose from the waters of the Baltic. By noon, the vapors would have burned off. The beach and town would be bathed in glorious sunlight and warmth. It was the end of August, and, for a little while, summer was still with us.

I peered through the window panes on the upper floor of Tante Berta's home that looked over the rooftops in the neighborhood. If I sharpened my gaze, I could see small ripples of the waves lazily rolling to shore. I opened the windows and let the cool, fresh sea air into the room. A slight breeze lifted up the white curtain and tossed it over my face like a veil. I brushed it aside and took in a deep breath to calm the flutter in my stomach. I wished for time to jump ahead and bypass the progression of seconds, minutes, and hours. I longed for nightfall to race toward us. It was the time when Andra and I would depart and leave the GDR behind.

We had decided to leave right after dark, hoping that the moon would rise late and shield us from being seen by watchful eyes or the guards in the tower. We dared not wait one more day. RIAS Berlin had announced that the Berlin wall was being reinforced daily, making it stronger and totally impenetrable. Citizen were gathering daily, feeling helpless as they watched the construction from afar. No one knew what other doom would befall them and everyone else who now had become prisoners in their own country. Andra's and my fear was that if we were to remain one more day, we would wake up the next morning and find that a barrier had been erected even along the beach, preventing access to the sea. As it was now, people needed to obtain permission to go boating on the Baltic and were not allowed to take their boats past a three-mile limit on the water.

Andra had left early for her last day at work. She had looked tired. Dark circles under her eyes told me that she had not slept well. I, also, had been restless. We had rehearsed our plan at least a dozen times the night before and had agreed to stick to it. We would row north as hard as we could, trying to orient ourselves to the beacon of the lighthouse that blinked from Dahme. When daylight arrived, we would use the sun for direction. We hoped to be in international waters by noon. We did not know where the international line was or if there even was one. However, we anticipated that after crossing the line, real or imaginary, we would finally be safe from persecution and capture. Our young minds believed in a favorable outcome. If all went well, we would be in the Golden West in a couple of days. If not….well, neither of us wanted to think about it or even dwell on the possibility of capture.

I could not deny that in the weakest of moments, I had been plagued by visions of arrest and had wondered whether we would be able to endure interrogation, punishment, and the inhumane conditions of prison. I did not know whether my courage would stretch that far. Could Andra and I depend on each other's strength? Tante Berta had warned us that our journey would test our friendship and patience with each other to near breaking. We did not want that to happen and promised each other that we would not complain or blame each other if disaster struck.

Waiting for evening to arrive was difficult. I paced the floor. In early afternoon, I went to the stretch of beach where we would say our goodbyes to our homeland. The sand was still littered with a few sun lovers in skimpy two piece suits and trunks. There was no sign of police or a military patrol. Manfred had told Andra that the regular beach patrols would soon receive help from advanced technology. Neither of us knew what that meant. We only knew that changes had gone into effect already. The beach had become off limits now after dark. Posters announced that anyone caught on it would be arrested. Andra and I had lain hidden behind the dunes on a previous night to observe the beach patrol and count the number of times that it passed. To our surprise, we only saw the soldiers checking the beach for stragglers before dark. We had waited until close to midnight, but the patrol did not return. Had we missed it or was the stretch of beach that we had chosen to depart from exempted from patrols because the tower with the search light was located close by? We did not know but felt more assured that our entry point on the water was safe.

Darkness was falling slowly in this latitude, as it always did until autumn arrived. My nerves were strung as tight as a string on a bow. I paced up and down until, finally, it was time to meet Andra at her supply room. We would load up the deflated raft that she had for an early morning excursion. Her supervisor allowed her to check it out the night before. He advised her to return it by noon when her shift began. Since we had no car to transport it, we hauled the deflated raft in a bicycle cart to the beach where we waited until after 9 p.m. to inflate it with an old bicycle pump. It proved more difficult than I had anticipated. The pump was old and tired and objected to every push on the handle. I suddenly realized that I might not be able to withstand the hours of monotonous paddling that lay ahead of us. My arms were not as strong as my legs, and I knew that I would have to endure pain and cramps. But this was no time to back out or complain. I had given my word to Andra and would have to manage somehow.

The moon took its time to rise, and the beach was totally deserted. Still, we did not trust the quiet. We decided to check a long stretch of beach for watchful eyes. We scrambled down from behind our dune and peered into the darkness. All seemed clear around us. We each ran into opposite directions, listening for human voices, a car, or a boat engine. But everything remained still.

Earlier in the evening, we had spotted a lone angler at the end of the boardwalk further down the beach. He, apparently, had arrived after the patrol emptied the beach. When we had seen him, his bottom had comfortably rested on a three-legged stool, and he had seemed oblivious to our presence. I wondered whether he was still there and jogged up to the edge of the boardwalk. I held my breath when I saw his outline on the pier. He was standing now, looking into the dark water. My heart jumped in my chest. Would he be able to see us leave?

I ran back to our dune. "The old man is still there," I gasped. "I saw his outline on the pier."

We stared at each other in dismay, undecided whether we should wait to leave. Was it silly to anticipate betrayal by an elderly citizen? Perhaps we were overly vigilant. Still, one could never distinguish a Communist informer from one that was not.

"Bah!" Andra finally commented. "Would an informer sit alone on a pier, fishing in the dark? It is a peaceful sport, is it not?"

I found a certain logic in her statement. "Still, I don't understand his courage to sit on the pier when the beach is off limit." I answered.

Soon Andra commented, "Let's not fret about the old man. We need to leave quickly."

She was correct. We needed to hurry because the border guards had already turned on the search light in the distant tower. It had begun moving in a semi-circle over the water.

"Let's go! I cannot stand the tension any longer." Andra whispered.

I too, felt the stress of waiting and agreed to leave. We were dragging the raft from behind the dune, when a voice called up to us. "*Hallo*, there! What are you up to this late in the evening? Don't you know that the beach is off limits after dark?"

Both Andra and I let out a small cry and instantly froze in place. We had been discovered!

"What are you doing out here so late, young Fräuleins?" The voice was closer now.

"It's the old man," Andra whispered. "I recognize him by the little cap he is wearing. We are caught!"

We stared at each other in alarm. We had made a big mistake! We had been convinced that he had been waiting for a sea bass to bite. Instead he had sat, patiently waiting for us to make our move so that he could reel us in!

The beam of a flashlight hit us. "You'd better take care, Fräuleins. Stop what it is you are doing and hurry home." The man spoke again. "It is dangerous to stay here any longer. The patrol will be coming in a few minutes."

"How do you know that? And why are you out so late, yourself, when no one is allowed to be on the beach?" I wanted to know.

"Well." He came closer and let the beam of his flashlight fall on his watch. "I still want to catch as much of freedom as I can and when I can without being caught. However, I have noticed that the soldiers are patrolling this spot of beach around the same time every evening. I figure them to arrive in ten or fifteen minutes. More or less. They don't stay long. But they return around midnight to make spot checks. You must go. I'd better be on my way, myself. I've been able to avoid them so far but have watched them from up there before." He pointed up to the dunes. "I've seen them linger on the boardwalk for a smoke."

How could Andra and I have missed the patrols when we had sat on the pier or had waited behind the dune for them? The angler now let out a whistling sound through his teeth. His flashlight had fallen on our bags. "Going somewhere, young Fräuleins? I hope that you are not thinking on taking a dangerous night journey out to sea or over there?" He pointed to the left of us where, in the distance, the tiny intermittent flash of the lighthouse beam was visible. "I'd advise against it. The Baltic might appear harmless to you, but it has claimed many lives over the centuries. If you don't drown before you are caught, the patrol will show you no mercy when it discovers you. The soldiers won't care that you are females. It's all the same to them."

Andra and I did not move because we were still trying to figure out whether he was friend or foe. My slightly myopic eyes, which had been able to see the outlines of him on the boardwalk, could now barely make him out. Darkness was too thick. But if my eyes were weak, my hearing was excellent. I now heard him strike a match before the small flame lit up his face for mere seconds. I recognized the sound that followed. He was pulling on a pipe. When a sudden wind gust picked up his tobacco smoke and blew it into our faces, my fear of him dissolved. The warm cherry scent of the tobacco reminded me of my beloved Uncle Emil. His pipe had smelled just like it and had always given me a sense of comfort and ease.

I said in a low voice, "I think we're okay, Andra. Let's hurry and go!"

"Seems there is no talking sense into the both of you," the angler remarked. "I believe that you are actually planning to do what I thought you would do. If truth be told and I were younger, I might even join you. But since you are so determined to risk your lives, just make sure that you stay warm. It's chilly on the open water."

He laid down his fishing rod and helped us pull the raft in the water. We pushed against the incoming surf and soon heard him call, "May the good Lord protect you, pretty ladies. I wish you a successful journey. Let's just hope that the rumors that I heard are correct. The radar equipment in the tower is broken already, just as so many other things around here."

"Oh, no!" Andra and I both inhaled sharply but decided to go ahead with our plan. Manfred had said nothing about radar, but he must have meant exactly that when he had mentioned new technology.

The water was cool but not freezing. Andra was at the helm, pulling the rope that was threaded through a notch at the front, while I pushed from behind.

"The angler hasn't left yet," she announced after a short while. "He is still standing where we have left him."

I quickly turned but could not make his shadow. Several minutes later, we heard the sound of a motor. I stopped pushing the raft and turned my head.

Andra hissed at me. "Ariane! Don't slow down. Swim faster! I think the patrol truck has arrived."

The truck stopped. We heard sounds of slamming car doors before the wind carried shreds of words over the water. We could not hear what the soldiers were saying. We swam faster. Moments later, I noticed that we had come too close to the arch of the searchlight. I gasped and hoarsely exclaimed. "Andra! We're almost in range of the floodlights. Move to the left! Hurry!"

"Oh, God. Make us invisible!" I sputtered. "Protect us!"

"What did you say? I think it's safe for us to talk louder."

"I am praying. You should do the same to make sure that we continue to be safe. Pray, Andra, pray!"

Andra swam to the left, pulling the raft with her until we had put space between us and the light. A moment later, she called, "What's that you said about prayer? I don't know how to pray. Anyhow, how can God see us in the dark anyhow?

She was correct. How *could* He see us? Despite our dangerous situation, I began to giggle and consequently swallowed water. I gasped for air.

"What's wrong with you now! Why are you always laughing when we find ourselves in trouble!" She flung the words at me. "I don't see the humor in any of this. Have you lost your mind already?"

"Perhaps." I spat out another mouthful of salt water. I suddenly found the whole idea of God sitting above the clouds with binoculars in hands, white beard and all, extraordinarily bizarre. My friend was correct. It was dark. How could He see us? It was a silly thought. Nevertheless, it was a mystery that begged to be solved.

I continued kicking my legs and pushing the raft forward as I tried to figure out the unknowable. Did He possess X-ray vision that could penetrate the dark and see right through us? Or, perhaps, could it be that we gave off signals that were invisible to the human eye and which He only could see? That would be it! Our soul, our essence, must be able to communicate our presence to Him. After all, had my mother's soul not communicated with me?

My thoughts were suddenly interrupted by Andra's muffled cry. "The truck has a searchlight, too." I now was directing a search light onto the water. "They know that we are out here! I wonder whether the old man gave us up." My heart stopped beating fast when a moment later she announced. "Thank goodness. The beam does not reach us. We're out too far already."

Moments that seemed like hours passed before the searchlight on the patrol vehicle was extinguished. Then we heard the engine start. "It's moving toward the boardwalk," my friend advised. "I think we're safe."

Both of us knew that if the soldier would have spotted us, or if the old man would have given us away, a speedboat would have been here already. Just to make sure, we continued straining our ears for a while longer. But everything remained silent in the darkness. We surmised that unexpected clouds must have rolled in and were hiding the moon that should have risen by now. We were certain that the clouds had saved us from being discovered.

After a while, we hoisted ourselves into the raft. We reached for the paddles and dipped them in and out of the water as fast as we could. We thought that we had made good progress when the clouds parted and the heaviness of night became broken by the light of a golden half moon that enveloped us in a glimmering sheen of old satin.

We paddled on. We had fallen into a mechanical rhythm, moving our paddles in a synchronized fashion. We moved northward without speaking, keeping our eyes on the light of Schleswig-Holstein that blinked to the left of us. We were confident that it would keep us going in the right direction and take us to freedom.

Chapter Thirty-Two

On the Baltic

It was not long before time slipped into the shadows of our consciousness. The air around us felt heavy. Had been on the dark water several hours already when we wished for night to end. We longed for the warmth of the sun, which we knew would rise shortly. As we expected, darkness faded and gave way to a new day. But morning light quickly faltered when forced into a tug of war with the moist vapors that became denser by the minute. Our wish for warmth went unanswered when we found ourselves bathed in a spooky mass of gray.

"I think we are in a fog bank." Andra announced redundantly. "But, don't worry. We'll probably be soon out of it."

"Perhaps the fog is in our favor.," I remarked. "If the sea patrol happens to come out this far, they will not easily spot us."

Before long, the density around us turned into a semi-transparent milky substance. We knew that daylight was advancing beyond the ghostly wall of white. My muscles had begun to cramp up. I moaned, wanting to take a rest. But Andra would not hear of it. We changed places, which allowed us to use different muscles in our arms. After a while, my left arm smarted as much as my right. I gritted my teeth, dug into my reserves of determination, and tried to push my mind past the pain.

"We'll stop when we reach international waters," my friend offered, fully knowing that we would have to pretend that a visible demarcation line surely existed in theory only.

I dropped my oar. "Perhaps we have crossed it already. But I suppose it doesn't matter," I remarked. "Our troops haven't shown respect for borders or human rights in the past and won't do so if they discover us. I wished you would agree to take a break."

"Alright," she responded slowly. I could see that she was not happy about stopping. I wondered how she was able to keep up her strength when I was so tired already. Wasn't she feeling any pain?

Quickly we dug out a ration of food and opened a jar of cold oatmeal, which we had boiled in milk before our departure. After we had eaten, we lay back and closed our eyes and rested for a while. When we opened them again, we saw that the fog was beginning to lift. Refreshed, we continued onward. The sun was drifting in and out of clouds and gave us some warmth. When toward mid-day, darker clouds formed above our heads, the sun went into hiding again. Unable to orient ourselves now, we hoped that we would manage to stay on course. We worried that if we continued to alter our course and steer in a westerly direction too soon, we would still be in GDR waters.

To our dismay, the sky soon opened up and the sea rose. We braced against the agitated elements and clung to each other when the raft began to rock dangerously and moved us up and down with the rise and fall of the waves. After the downpour ended, we found ourselves sitting in a pool of water. We quickly opened the last two jars of remaining food and ate. Then we used the empty containers to scoop up the water. The task was tedious; but when done, we leaned back and stared unhappily at the overcast sky. Neither of us said a word. We were fully aware that we had lost all sense of direction and all concept of time. Our wristwatches, too, had died from the moisture. We had not sense of any directions. Our spirits were low, and we decided to take a nap.

When a penetrating cold brought us back from slumber a few hours later, we were greeted by a clear night. Ripples of soft waves were carrying us now. "This is unreal," Andra commented. "How can it clear up so quickly? It feels as though we have arrived in another universe."

"Yes," I responded and looked up at the millions of stars that hung like freshly polished jewels above our heads. I scanned the horizon for one lone, blinking light; but no matter in which direction I turned, the light of Dahme remained absent.

"Do you think that my mother is looking up into the starry night this very moment, wondering what has happened to me?" Andra asked in a low voice.

"I doubt it. No one but your aunt would know yet that we left. It takes time to get a letter to your mother. Besides, she's probably in bed with Otto. *You* might be farthest from her mind. She, most likely, is lying wrapped up in his hairy arms."

Andra laughed. Both of us remembered having seen Otto on the beach with Frau Fischer. We had commented on his heavy growth of hair that had seemed to cover most of his body. He had looked like a muddy black sheep dog.

We fell silent again before I remarked, "I feel better whenever I can laugh. Don't you? I like laughing, but it is often difficult to cheer myself up. I wished I were more like Frau Fröhlich. She never let herself become toppled by anything or anyone, especially not by Herr Fink. She kept up her high spirits and disregarded his sarcasm. I miss her and her gay laughter."

"But you *are* fun to be with, Ariane," my friend protested. "And you have a great sense of humor. My mother always marveled at that. She said that you should have turned out to be a very sad girl. But you aren't, are you?"

"I think I am," I responded. "I just don't show it. My heart is often sad. There are times I have to force myself to be happy. I get these feelings inside...I don't understand them myself. It's as though a great melancholy wants to descend on me." I paused. "But, really, Andra. I don't want to talk about that."

To show her that I meant it, I brought up my silly side, as I so often did when things became difficult for me. I made up a song and began to sing it. Andra laughed. "How poetic you are, Ariane," she remarked facetiously. "The words don't rhyme."

"Well, then. Here's another one, a famous one. It's full of rhyme *and* reason.."

I began to hum a song from the Operetta *Venus in Silk*, which was one of Frau Fröhlich's favorites. She had sung it to us on several occasions and had sometimes prefaced it with the words, "My dear and honored ladies and gentlemen, I will present to you "*Spiel auf Deiner Geige* from *Venus in Seide*, by the Austrian composer Nick Stolz. He was a real hero, when in 1933 he made over twenty-one trips into Germany to smuggle car loads of Jews and other politically persecuted people across the border. I would like to pay homage to him."

Just as Tante Helga's husband, Frau Fröhlich had met many Jews in artistic circles and had formed friendships with them. She had told me of their horrible fate and had confided that she still grieved the loss of them. I remember how shocked I had been to hear that our people had been capable of inflicting such pain on other fellow human beings. Frau Fröhlich had no answer for me but sang her favorite song after making her preface. She stuck out her bosom, folded hands, and began to wail with great feeling as Frau Geist accompanied her on her violin. "Play me a song of suffering and lust on your violin…of sorrow and longing… Pry the love from my heart with your violin. Play me a song of happiness that once was."

As she sang, she looked at Herr Donner with smoldering eyes. He, himself, had lost his young wife in a concentration camp. We could see that the song made him sad. Frau Fröhlich dramatically stretched out her arms in his direction. And, when silence fell over the room after she had finished, he gave her his enthusiastic applause. She had a gift to express her own emotions and draw us all in. Her vibrant charm held us spellbound and brightened many a dull moment.

"I wished that I had her temperament," I expressed my adoration for Frau Fröhlich a second time. "Nothing could sink her. You've heard her sing, Andra. Do you remember?"

"Uh huh." My friend nodded. "I liked her, too. I wished I had her voice."

"Yeah. So do I." I stood up, balanced myself in the raft as best I could and imitated the lovely Frau Fröhlich. I began to belt out lines from *Venus in Silk* with great theatrical gestures and mimed the sometimes coy, sometimes fiery glances which she cast at her soon-to-be lover. It was obvious to all that Herr Donner, whom she was courting, was greatly admiring her. It had amused everyone in the chamber music orchestra that he, whose nature it was to be forceful and outspoken, found himself too shy to make the first move to bring them together.

"Get a hold of yourself, Ariane." Andra teased me. "You might wake up some slumbering sea monster!"

I paid her no heed but relished the memories of home. I continued sounding off with enthusiasm and thrust my off-key melody over the water. I stretched out my arms and waved them about. At that very moment, Andra sneezed. The boat rocked precariously from side to side, and I with it. I lost my balance and fell toward the water. Andra reacted quickly and caught me by my leg, preventing me from landing head first in the dark sea. Luckily, my face only brushed the water. When I lay back in the raft, Andra shrieked with laughter. "You should have seen your expression, Ariane!"

The incident left me shaken. Old memories of my mother and the incident at the Havel flooded me. The river, itself, did not instill fear in me. It had been my mother's temper, and the fact that she had lost her senses, that had frightened me so. I had continued to think of the Havel as my friend. My young mind had told me that it was not responsible for my mother's anger and her desire to drown me.

I hated to be reminded of it now and suddenly felt the need for comfort. I crawled over to Andra and rested my back against hers.. Within minutes, I was asleep again.

Andra, too, fell asleep. When both of us awoke stiff and cold like corpses, we took turns punching each other with our fists to bring our bodies back to life. Then we took a few bites from our leftover sandwiches and drank a few sips of water. We knew that we needed to conserve the small amounts we still had left. We realized that we would have to spend an indeterminable amount of time at sea before we reached land.

By noon, the sun was bright and warm. We had no clue how far we had drifted off course but decided to row west. I noticed how pale and drawn Andra looked. She had complained of a headache earlier but had shrugged off my concern. She forbade me to inquire about her pain a second time. I honored her request considered the virtue of our escape. No matter our physical or mental conditions now, it was better to die as a free person on the open water than to be chattel to a cause in which I did not believe. I was not sorry that we had left. I knew that I was not looking for the idyllic realm of a lotus land but for a place where free speech and humanity was permitted to flourish. Something inside me still called me to freedom.

I observed the sun as it moved across the sky. We had already spent two nights and one day in the raft and dreaded one more night at sea. In two or three hours, it would be dark. I could see in Andra's face that her headache had become worse. I kept quiet, knowing that senseless babble would hurt her head even more. But, soon, I could no longer endure the silence in the raft. Moreover, the sounds of the soft ripples that normally would feel so relaxing, were getting to me now.

"Did I ever tell you how I made myself rise above my pain whenever mother got angry and whipped me?" I asked her. "Each time I tried to imagine myself in a wonderful place until I did not feel my body anymore. I can teach it to you, too, if you'd like. It might take your headache away."

Andra did not answer. Then, after what seemed a long while, she agreed. "Alright, if you insist."

I began to speak in soothing tones, becoming the narrator as well as the participant in the exercise. I closed my eyes and suggested that Andra do the same. My words drew a picture of a beautiful island in the South Seas. I paused and asked, "Can you see yourself there?"

"Yes."

Suddenly, Fräulein Hilde appeared before my inner eye. She stood before me in all her beauty. I heard her say, "The fresh sea air and the sun are endowed with magical powers to heal." I nodded and repeated the words that she may have said to me so many years earlier.

"Inhale," I added. "The air is laden with the fragrance of tropical flowers; and off to the side, you can see palm trees. They are loaded with dark brown clusters of coconuts, all ready to be picked. The milk inside of them tastes refreshingly sweet."

I paused again, finding it difficult to speak now. My mind had become infused with the wonderful scenery and the taste of coconut milk. I mumbled, "Listen. Seagulls have spotted us. They came to greet us."

"Yes. I can hear them very clearly," Andra acknowledged in a low voice. She added, "They are all around us. My visualization is so real."

"Yes, mine is too. The screeching is getting louder. This really works!"

No sooner did I remark on it, when, plunk, what I imagined to be a coconut fell smack into the center of my own forehead. It did not hurt as a real coconut should have; but, after all, an imagined coconut would be light, wouldn't it be? It would cause no pain, even though it had landed so hard that its shell had cracked open, spilling its contents right between my eyebrows.

Suddenly, Andra moaned. "Oh, no, it's raining again." Then, "Oh, yuck! The raindrops are sticky!"

"It's coconut milk," I answered. I could feel it dripping down the bridge of my nose. I raised my hand and brushed over the wetness on my face. I opened my eyes and saw white goo on my hand. I looked up and instantly realized that both of us had been pooped on. Two seagulls was flying circles over our heads, screeching as loud as they could.

Andra, too, sat up. Instead of commenting on the poop, she let out a cry. "A ship! Ariane! A ship!" she yelled, seemingly forgetting her headache.

I sat up and looked to where she was pointing. Sure enough, we were not hallucinating. In the distance, a vessel was traversing us in a diagonal line. We stood up and waved our arms like windmills. Then we grabbed our jackets and swung them overhead. But the ship took no notice and steamed ahead.

"What will we do if it is operating under an East European flag?" I called.

We looked uncertainly at each other for a moment before we continued to wave. If people on board would not notice us soon, nothing but the rear end of the ship would remain in view. In desperation, I searched my brain for a solution. It was then that I remembered the little round mirror, which Andra had held up to her face to powder her nose before going out with Manfred.

"Did you bring your little mirror with you?" I yelled.

Andra nodded, "Yes."

I had remembered an old prank that my neighborhood gang and I had played on unsuspecting passersby when we had been kids. We had used broken pieces of mirror to catch the sun rays and had reflected them into their faces. It had been a naughty prank, but we had enjoyed it.

"Find it quickly and hand it to me! Hurry!" I shouted at her in desperation.

The sun was still high enough to catch its rays. I maneuvered the mirror up and down, and sideways, hoping that someone on the ship would see the glare. Still, no one appeared to take notice. Only the seagulls kept us company.

Suddenly, Andra shrieked again. "It's turning, it's turning!"

Sure enough, the ship stopped and slowly began to turn. Overjoyed, we hugged each other and danced until the raft began to bounce dangerously from side to side. When the boat was upon us, we noticed an unfamiliar flag blowing in the wind.

"Ahoy!" A deep voice shouted down to us.

"*Hallo! Hallo!*" We shrieked back and waved. Soon, several men looked over the railing and called something in a language that we did not understand.

Andra turned to me. "Is that English?"

I did not know but was relieved to hear that it sounded softer than a Slavic language. "I think we are safe," I replied breathlessly.

Someone on the ship let down a narrow ladder and motioned us to row closer and climb up.

"Oh No!" I turned to Andra. "I can't do it. I'll be dangling in the air several meters above the water! You know that I'm scared of heights."

I could not explain when my fear of heights had developed. I had climbed the spiral stairs of a high tower on the island of Rügen and had looked down without a problem. I had enjoyed climbing trees and had been whipped for tearing my dress. Then, one day during gym class, Herr Langhans required us to climb up the smooth and slippery pole that extended from the floor to the ceiling of the hall. I had reached the half-mark of the pole when I froze. I wrapped my arms around it and clung to it like a monkey to a tree. Herr Langhans assured me that he would scrape me off the floor like a flattened German potato pancake if I let go. A classmate added that they would dump a jar of applesauce on top of the pancake to make it more palatable. The comment made me laugh, and I was able to relax and slide down.

Seeing the ladder dangling against the boat produced a still greater fear in me. "You go up first," I told Andra. In spite of her headache, she gave me a mocking look and reached for the ladder. "I'll show you how it's done, little peep-mouse!" She said.

I watched her climb up the unsteady contraption. When she reached the top, the men took hold of her and pulled her on board. Within seconds, everyone disappeared from view. When no one reappeared, I became uneasy. What was happening on board? Was my friend being assaulted or arrested? I felt adrenaline rising in me. I became so afraid for Andra's safety that I forgot my fear momentarily and grabbed the ladder. I climbed halfway up when I became frightened again. My breath came in spurts and my hands began to sweat. I knew that if I were to let go, I would be dead within seconds. I had wanted to die as a free person, but not like this.

The ladder swung back and forth. "Breathe, breathe, breathe," I muttered to myself, clutching it tighter. All I could think was, "I can't, I can't," while something else inside of me corrected me. "You must. You must go on!"

I don't know how I was able to manage it but I talked myself upward. When I finally reached the top, I screamed as loud as I could for someone to come and help me on board. Within seconds, strong hands reached out and pulled me over. Dizzy and shaken I lay down on deck to recover from my ordeal. When I sat up, I noticed that Andra was sitting on deck. A handful of men stood around her. They watched as another man tended to a cut on her head.

"What happened?" I called.

My friend turned a pale face and pointed to a crane-like contraption that was mounted on deck. "I hit the side of my head on that thing."

I scooted over to her and inspected her head. Aside from the covered cut, an angry bruise was already beginning to show.

"I feel sick." She moaned and closed her eyes.

The ship's crew parted when a bearded man walked into their midst. He introduced himself as the captain. "*Deutsch?*" German? He spoke with an unfamiliar accent.

"Are you from a country of the western world?" I replied, not wanting to answer questions before I made sure that we were aboard a non-East European vessel.

"*Norske,*" he replied. We are Norwegian.

I breathed a sigh of relief, while Andra said in a weak voice. "We are refugees from the GDR."

"That's East Germany," I added. "Our government has closed the borders and is holding everyone prisoner there. We escaped and floated on the water for a long time before you rescued us."

"We heard about the bad situation in your country," the captain acknowledged. "You made the journey alone? There are no men with you?"

I told him about our voyage, the fog, the storm, and our fear of being swept back to the coast of the GDR.

"You do not need to be afraid any longer," someone said, also speaking an accented German. Our ship is going home to *Norge*. That's the name of our country. Norway."

A little fellow with a scruffy beard stepped up to Andra and touched her face. He grinned. "Lappen," he said.

Lappen in German means "rag." If a person wanted to accuse another for showing lack of courage, he called him a *Waschlappen,* a wash rag.

I stared at the man, then at Andra. "Is he calling you a *Lappen?*" I asked. I knew that my friend needed care instead of insults.

The captain laughed. "Lappen is his nickname. He comes from Lapland."

"Ah," I felt silly but remembered that language communication was, indeed, difficult. I had experienced it when attempting to translate German aphorisms or adages into Russian. I had realized that one never could translate them verbatim. I now noticed how Lappen surveyed Andra with interest.

"*Modig pikene,*" he said. The captain translated. "He is telling her that she is a brave girl."

Lappen appeared to have taken an instant fancy to my friend. He offered his hand to help her up. She stood up, leaning on him. We learned that it was Lappen who had seen a streak of light, a glare, in the distance and had spotted our raft with his hawk-eyed vision.

"Very pretty girl." He stroked my friend's face. "You hurt much?"

All of us were amused and laughed. Even Andra managed a smile. Without additional delay, we were taken to the captain's quarters and given clean clothes that the members of the crew had offered up.

I looked at my reflection in the mirror and grunted. "I think I have been initiated into the high caste of seagulls. I still have dried white poop on my forehead."

Andra pulled her lips into a smile but winced with pain. I watched her with worried expression as she peeled off her clothes and cleaned herself up. Neither of us could do much about our hair. It had become totally pickled by salt water and felt stiff and coarse to the touch.

Soon, one of the men brought platters laden with tiny sandwiches that were covered with slices of hard boiled eggs and topped with little black fish eggs. On a separate dish, next to thin pieces of cracker bread, sardines had been piled in a small mound. Andra felt nauseous and waved the food aside. I apologized to her for my hunger and ravenously gulped down a few sandwiches.

The burly captain, who favored a Viking and who had left us earlier, now returned. "It is best to drop you off in Sweden instead of taking you to Norway. I have radioed the authorities. A doctor will be waiting for you when we arrive in Malmö."

Andra rested on a cushion, while I crouched next to her. I seemed to have dozed off and was roused by two uniformed officers who came to escort us off the ship. Andra hung on to me, complaining of dizziness once more. We walked down the gangway under the shouts of well-wishes from the crew. Lappen broke rank and hurried after us. He took my friend's hand and, touching her fawn-colored hair with the other, exclaimed, "Come to Norway with me. You are nice, brave girl and have beautiful hair, too."

The men observed him from above and laughed. "He misses his reindeer," one of his shipmates quipped before the captain could order Lappen back up the gangway.

Accompanied by several more good wishes for our health and happiness, we set foot on the country that Fräulein Hilde had told me about many years earlier.

Chapter Thirty-Three

Freedom

"P ass?" One of the officers in uniform stuck out his hand to receive our passports.

We shook our heads. "We have none. Our country only issues them to a select few. But we have our identification papers with us." We unwrapped our little oil cloth packets and handed them over. "We are refugees from East Germany."

The officer took our papers and told us to wait while the other uniformed man stayed with us. It was already past midnight, and it took a few minutes for the first officer to locate someone who was proficient in German. The official began asking us questions about our journey across the water.

I looked pleadingly at him. "Please, before we go on, could you call a doctor?" I motioned to Andra, who looked white as a sheet under the light in the port office. She sat slouched over.

"A doctor has been called," the officer assured us. "He will be here shortly."

When the physician arrived, I was in the process of cleaning up Andra's vomit with the paper towels that the officers had handed me.

Andra offered weak apologies to all of us, while he doctor looked serious. "You seem to suffer from a brain trauma." He picked up the phone, and within minutes an ambulance arrive to take her to a hospital.

I was not permitted to accompany her but was detained for processing. However, when the officer saw that I was too worried and exhausted to continue, he suspended his questions and drove me into the city. We stopped at a two-story house, where he rang the doorbell. A women in a nightgown, which she had covered with a shawl, opened the door. A few words passed between them before the he took his leave. He said that he would be back by noon to continue where we had left off. The woman led me up the stairs to a simply furnished room with a single bed. I crawled between the sheets. Moment later, I was fast asleep.

The sun was high when I awoke to the sounds of a trumpet. Still dazed, I tried to recall the events of the previous day. I rubbed the sleep from my eyes and swung my legs onto the floor. Not being familiar with the customs of this country, I wondered whether the trumpet was a call of reveille. I turned to the nightstand to find a clock. I saw none but noticed a glass of milk and a plate of pastries that someone had left for me. I felt hungry even after having consumed everything that had been served to us on the Norwegian ship the night before. I bit into the pastry and closed my eyes in instant pleasure. It was filled with a delectable mixture of cinnamon and rich butter. The dough was as light and airy as the plumage of a newborn chick. I chewed slowly, wanting to savor the taste as long as I could. I knew that I would beg for one of these buns every day that I would be here.

Soon, I heard a knock on the door. A middle aged woman entered and brought me fresh garments. I glanced at her dark blue uniform. I instantly worried that the officer had placed me into the custody of the law. "Police?" I asked. The woman shook her head and smiled.

I now wondered whether I had been given a private room at an orphanage. The appearance of the room suited such an institution. Everything was clean and austere enough. Other than the low nightstand next to the narrow bed on which I had slept so comfortably, a single hardwood chair stood next to a window. Only the bright curtains and a colorful hand-braided rug in front of the bed gave the room a touch of warmth. I strained my ears for the sound of young voices but heard none. The woman pointed to the bathroom and motioned for me to get dressed. I was stunned to find a shower inside of the house. I had been under the impression that only campgrounds had them. I stepped into the tub and felt refreshed by the hot water. Then I put on the clothes that the woman had brought me. They were a size too big but smelled soft and fresh.

Soon another trumpet call sounded. This time, it played the musical scale. After a final high dissonant screech that ended abruptly, the house became tranquil once more.

Downstairs, another woman dressed in the same uniform as the first one, greeted me. "*God morgon!*" she said. It sounded like our German "Guten Morgen." I returned her smile without grasping anything else she added. There were other women in the room who were clad in the same garments. I wondered whether Swedes was a homogeneous society where everyone needed to conform. I remembered the time that we had been visited by a group of young Chinese gymnasts in our country. They had been accompanied by their comrade trainers. The girls had been dressed in white shirts. Red scarfs had been knotted around their necks. They had been similar to the blue scarfs that our Young Pioneers wore. The girls wore identical red skirts. The adult men and women had been dressed in an unappealing blue or gray Mao suit, which they had called *yat-sen* or *zhifu*.

"Police?" I asked the same question of this woman and pointed to her uniform. I needed to make sure that I had not come to this house as a prisoner. She seemed confused by my question. "Army?" I restated it.

"*Jaha,*" she answered and turned her attention to a tall man who had entered the house. He, too, wore a uniform. His hat, which sported a red band above the brim of it, bore a similarity to a Russian military hat. He was accompanied by the same Swedish official who had brought me here the night before.

"*Guten Tag,*" I offered, relieved that my burning question would finally be answered. "Are these mean and women members of the Swedish Army?"

"*Jaså.*" He responded. "Aha, you mean the uniforms. *Nej då.* No, no." He grinned wider and was obviously amused. "They are ….I do not know the name….they are God's army."

He turned to a woman and said something in their language. She, in turn, went to a nearby table and picked up a book She placed it into my hands. Its cover bore a cross with the words, *"Bibel"* imprinted on it.

"Ah, you are a missionaries!" I said, still uncertain why missionaries would choose to wear military uniforms.

"No. They are not missionaries," the officer corrected me.

I now was more confused then ever. We had no such army of God in the GDR. Moreover, Communists did not believe in God. No one I knew had attended church services either since the church doors in our town had remained locked. Seeing that the officer had not been able to sufficiently explain who these people were, I dropped my investigation. What mattered was that my hosts were gracious and kind to me.

"How is my friend?" I hurriedly asked him. "Is Andra better?"

"She is in surgery," he answered. "Something has been pressing on her brain."

I was shocked and wondered whether some of the trauma had been the result of her accident in Rostock. Her bad headaches had begun right after her injuries.

"She needs to stay in Sweden for a while to recover," the officer continued. "But you will be flown to West Germany. We have already notified the consulate in Malmö and the West German Embassy in Stockholm. One of the agencies will issue you a West German passport as soon as we release you to them."

"How can I leave while my friend is in the hospital?" I complained. Can't you give me permission to stay in your country until she is well enough to travel with me?"

The officer responded, "That will be up to others. Let me inquire whether that can be arranged."

When a couple of days later I was allowed to visit Andra in the hospital and saw her look so frail and with her head bandaged, I felt remorse. I took her hand into my own. "I am so sorry," I mumered. "It's all my fault. I should not have asked you to come with me. Perhaps it was selfish of me."

Andra blinked and whispered, "I am scared. Don't leave me."

I quickly collected myself and spoke in a lighter tone of voice. "Don't worry. You'll be well again. I won't leave you alone in a strange country."

When I had another meeting with the Swedish official, he informed me that I could ask for political asylum. If I decided against it, the German authorities would take over and fly me to West Germany. I tossed and turned the following night. I was unable to sleep. I knew that I needed to reach a decision. I could not leave Andra. But how could I manage myself in this country since I did not speak the language? How would I be able to support myself?

When morning came, I decided to concern myself only with our immediate situation. I asked for asylum. Perhaps later, when Andra was well again, I could reverse my decision.

During the days that followed, Andra improved significantly. Her doctors gave her a good prognosis for recovery. The slight disorientation and memory lapses that she had experienced following her surgery soon disappeared. Yet, the trauma and the emotional and physical strain of our journey had broken her down. Her doctor assured us that her depression would pass.

I, too, was dealing with exhaustion and anxiety and found myself sleeping longer than usual. I clung to prayers but wondered whether God would soon tire of my many requests. I figured that He had already determined me to be an insatiable pest. I offered my apologies for asking for more than I knew I deserved.

When not at Andra's bedside, I meandered through the streets in the neighborhood. Each day brought another surprise. The apparent opulence that met my eye was overwhelming. The many stores in the city lacked of nothing. In contrast to the GDR where few people were able to afford a car, here everyone appeared to own a Volvo or a Saab. It would be easy for me to live in this country. Everyone was kind and helpful. Moreover, the economy offered a cornucopia of desirable goods. Still, I was plagued by occasional doubts. Had I made the right decision by asking for asylum? Thinking it through, I decided that I knew as little about West Germany as I knew about Sweden. Things there would be as different for me as they were in Sweden. After all, life in the GDR could not compare to either, with the exception that I spoke the language of West Germany.

With nothing else to do but wait for Andra's recovery, I went on long walks or for runs. On one such run, I bumped into a young man. He dropped the stack of flyers that he had carried under his arm. I profusely apologized in German and bent down to help him gather them up.

The young man asked, "*Jaså, fröken, Ni är Tysk?*"

I gave him a blank stare, answering. "*Ich verstehe nicht.* I don't understand."

He repeated in German, "*Sind Sie Deutsch?* Are you German?" He spoke with the same pleasing accent as everyone else here.

"Yes," I answered and explained that I had arrived only a few days earlier from East Germany.

"That is not possible," he answered. "The border is closed." Then he smiled hesitantly. "You are joking with me?"

"No!" I assured him. "I am from there."

"Perhaps then you are a spy?" He lowered his voice. "I heard that spies have ways to cross the border."

"No, not at all!" I laughed and began to give him a condensed version of Andra's and my escape. I ended it with the report that she had undergone surgery and was lying at the University Hospital.

He listened and watched my face, obviously trying to separate truth from fiction. "That is an exciting story," he finally remarked. "Now, tell me the truth."

"I am telling the truth."

"If what you say is true, you must tell me more. I am very interested in German history, and you must allow me to practice my school German with you. It is coffee time, and I have a few minutes to spare. If you don't mind, we can find a place where we can sit and talk."

The young man looked safe enough to me, and so I agreed to go with him. Perhaps the café would even sell my favorite pastry.

"I'm Olaf Söderquist," he introduced himself before he deposited his flyers into his Volvo. "I'm the junior pastor in a nearby church and was on my way back with these flyers for Sunday services.." He led me to a nearby café, where I eyed the familiar cinnamon rolls behind the glass cover. "These are *Kanelbullar*," he announced. "Cinnamon rolls are a Swedish tradition."

I took a bite and rolled my eyes with pleasure. Then I took a sip from my cup. "Hmm, real coffee!"

Olaf was amused. He watched me. I watched him in return and noticed that he seemed to eat the *Kanelbullar* without paying attention to what he was eating and drank the coffee because he always drank it. To him, they were an every-day food while to me, both were exquisite delicacies. Olaf was curious about the practice of religion in the GDR, the living conditions, and such. What I told him mostly shocked him. Before we knew it, time had slipped away from us. Before parting, he invited me to attend Sunday services. "I will lead the afternoon session," he said. "Please come."

I hesitated. "I have never been to a church and would not know what to do. Besides, I don't understand Swedish."

He smiled. "You do not have to understand the words to feel the spirit of God. We have many young members. Do you like music? We have a large choir. I can assure you that you will like our service."

When Sunday arrived, I first joined "God's army" in their celebration. The trumpet, I discovered, belonged to a male member of their small choir. Another man played the horn, while the accordion was strapped over the bosom of a stout female. Its sound brought up long forgotten memories of my father, of Karl, and of my Uncle Emil. All three men had played the accordion and had entertained us with songs of the sea and far away places when my father had been home on furlough. The memory of it suddenly brought tears to my eyes. Dagmar had said that it was impossible for anyone to remember that far back in time. "You were much too young," she had said. I had often wished that she had been correct. I had wished nothing more than to be spared the pictures that popped up in my head unannounced and at the most inconvenient times.

Someone next to me patted me on the hand, trying to comfort me in halting German. "Don't be sad, sister," he said. "God loves you."

I smiled. "I hope so," I answered, feeling melancholic. Another nudge made my head turn the other direction. My other neighbor handed me a collection plate to pass on. I had nothing to give and suspected that the uniformed men and women were collecting money for my upkeep. I felt embarrassed for having become a charity case once more.

I spent the noon hour sleeping; and when I woke I readied myself for the next service at Olaf's church. Feeling refreshed, I walked to the corner bus stop and boarded the bus. I showed the bus driver the slip of paper on which Olaf had written the address of the church. When I arrived, the large sanctuary was already filled with men and women of all ages. The room resounded with loud *Hallelujahs* and *Tack, tack tjäre Gud*. "Thank you, God," people shouted.

If I was a bit uncomfortable by the unabashed cries of the congregation, I soon found that Olaf was correct. I enjoyed the service without understanding one word of it. I loved the energy in the room. It reminded me of my time in Leipzig, where I had attended the sports competition. And even though the people there had gathered for a different purpose, everyone had felt united and connected. The unity had felt good.

Before I was able to slip out of the building after the service ended, Olaf spotted me. "*Vänta*, Ariane!" He called. "Wait! I want to introduce you to our senior pastor."

"Where are you staying?" The older pastor immediately began to quiz me.

"I am staying with people who wear uniforms, read the bible, and play the trumpet," I responded, feeling a bit foolish.

"*Jaså. Frälsningarmén!*" Olaf grinned. I had told him earlier that the immigration officials had put me up in a house in which people did not speak my language. "I do not know the word in German, but it is a charitable army."

I was stunned. So then, they were soldiers, after all. "Your country uses bibles instead of weapons?" I asked in astonishment. I knew my question sounded silly. But what else was I to think?

The men responded with loud laughter. Olaf said, "Ah, if it only were so. But, I remember the German word for it now. *Frälsning* means *Rettung,* salvation. The army is a charity, a church that serves humanity. Did they put you to work in their organization yet?"

I shook my head. "No. But I should find a job as soon as I receive permission to work. I need money for food and clothes. The GDR currency that I brought along is worthless in Sweden. I also need to find a different place to stay."

"Come." The elder minister smiled and took me by the arm. "We can remedy your clothing situation immediately. And I might even have a job for you."

I followed the two men to an adjacent building, which was packed to the brim with garments of all kinds. "Our Swedish women are not only fashion-conscious but also extremely charitable," the senior pastor explained. "We collect clothes and send them to needy people in other countries."

He encouraged me to help myself to any piece of clothing that I wished. I felt like a wide-eyed kid that had been allowed to enter Aladdin's cave. I selected a few items of clothing for myself and picked out a suit for Andra. Before I walked out the door with a satisfied smile, I spotted a pair of soft, red leather shoes. I dropped everything that I was carrying in my arms and tried them on. To my utter amazement, they fit. At that moment, my happiness was complete.

Before I could bid the men goodbye, the senior minister gazed at me speculatively. He turned to his junior pastor and spoke. Olaf translated. "The pastor knows of an excellent work position for which you may be suited. The employer's name is Erik Nordeen. He has his residence in the outlying area of Stockholm. His wife had once been a member of this church. Unfortunately, she passed away several years ago. Mr. Nordeen is one of the wealthiest and most influential businessmen in Sweden. His old housekeeper has married, and the pastor believes that Mr. Nordeen needs someone else to look after him. You might like working for him."

Both men waited for my response. When I remained silent, Olaf continued. "I am sure that it would be a good place for you. Our senior pastor can arrange the job for you. Mr. Nordeen would also be able to petition for your residency quicker than you can do it on your own. He has many contacts."

I had hesitated because the offer had sounded too good to be true. Moreover, my experience with the only bosses that I had ever worked for was keeping me from jumping into an unknown job situation. Furthermore, there was Andra. I couldn't just leave her behind. I shook my head and explained that even though the offer sounded very tempting, I needed to stay close to my friend.

The older pastor considered my reply. "The estate is large enough to find work for two young women."

"Well..." I hesitated once more. "But how do you know that Mr. Nordeen will hire us on your word alone? In my country, everyone has to test for the job and endure a lengthy interview. Moreover, everyone has to present written recommendations."

"Don't worry," Olaf translated again. "Erik will accept my recommendation. He is my brother-in-law. His wife was my sister."

I was stunned at the lucky turn of events. If I had felt forsaken before, I now felt cared for. Was it fate or luck that had made me bump into Olaf, or had it been the hand of God that had led me to him? How would I ever know? I decided to accept the gift that had been offered to me. I would make the best of it.

I hurried to the hospital to announce the good news to my friend. Instead of being pleased, her face clouded over. "I have been thinking, Ariane. I miss my mother and want to go back home."

I took a step backward, feeling as though she had given me my own blow to the head. "Are you mad?" I exclaimed. "Don't you remember what kind of life we had over there? You can't go back!"

"I feel so lost here," Andrea complained. "What would I do if something else were to happen to me? I think I'm hexed!"

"Nonsense! The doctors have assured us that you will be alright. They have fixed whatever was pressing on your brain." I pleaded against her stubborn face. "Please don't go back. I couldn't bear it. The STASI will be waiting for you at the airport and interrogate you. They would arrest you. And even if they were to let you go free, they will have their claws in you forever. You will need to do whatever they will tell you to do."

I was close to tears, and so was she. Both of us were desperate for different reasons. I feared for her and knew that I would miss her terribly if she were to leave. "Besides." I continued, "I'm not so sure that they will receive you with open arms as your aunt said they would. You know that *Republiksflucht* is punishable by imprisonment. Then there's the fact that we stole the raft from your employer and that you have left your job without notice. You might never find another one. They even might arrest your aunt for being an accomplice.

"Please, consider the consequences. If you don't want to stay here in Sweden with me, then at least let the German consulate fly you to your relatives in West Germany."

I had spoken with great emphasis, not knowing whether my suspicions were accurate. Nevertheless, my remarks had made an impression on Andra.

"Will you come with me?" She asked in tears.

"I don't think I am able to come. I've spoken to someone at the German Consulate a few days ago. I wanted to know whether they would relocate us together if I were to change my mind and leave here. The person I spoke to could not guarantee that Mainz would take me since I don't have relatives there. Different areas in the West have different quotas for accepting refugee. He said that I might have to go to a refugee camp in another city since the West German government is responsible for finding lodgings and jobs for refugees."

"I'll stay with you in a refugee camp then!" Andra exclaimed.

"Nonsense! Why would you trade a home for a small area in a room that you would have to share with others?"

The quota system had come as a surprise to me. We hadn't know about it before we had embarked on our journey to the West. I now pushed Andra to contact her relatives, telling her that she needed a comfortable place to live in order to fully recover from the trauma of her surgery and from the stress of our escape. She nodded in agreement.

When German consulate officials later arranged for her to call her relatives in Mainz, she accepted their invitation to stay with them. She would receive a monthly government stipend until she found a job and could provide for herself. Andra would leave for Mainz as soon as she was released from the hospital. I, on the other hand, would stay in Sweden and take the job with Mr. Nordeen.

"I forgot to tell you something," Andra announced when we said our goodbyes. "I heard that some GDR citizens who had tried to cross the Baltic in small boats had been captured and arrested. The border guards are equipped with radar now. It picks up every movement on the water. No one was able to outrun their speedboats. But mostly," Andra paused and looked sadly at me, "a few dead bodies have already washed up on shore. People had tried to swim the distance or use surfboards to make it to Dahme. They all have drowned. The consulate officer said that you and I must have been carried on the wings of angels."

We looked at each other, and once again it was clear to us that it had been more than luck that had been with us. We could easily have ended up dead like the others. Why we had been saved was one more mystery that would have to remain unanswered.

Chapter Thirty-Four

On the Nordeen Estate

The six-hour train ride to my destination was uneventful. We traveled through a large forested countryside that was sparsely populated with small settlements. A fellow traveler assured me that the rest of Sweden was not as monotonous as this but that it was charming and incredibly beautiful. He related that Sweden is covered by many orchards and rolling hills in the South and hundreds of lakes and mountains farther up. And, way up in the North was the Arctic tundra where the sun barely sets.

When I stepped off the train with my small bag of clothes in hand, a young man in gray uniform and cap was waiting for me. I was stunned that Erik Nordeen had sent his chauffeur to deliver me to him! If Dagmar once teased her brother about having mislaid his royal chariot, the one that awaited me here was fit for a queen.

"I'm Olle," The chauffeur introduced himself and solicitously swung open the door of the large Lincoln Continental. He invited me to step in. I made myself comfortable in the back seat and savored the luxurious feel of it.

Olle's polite servility made me question whether he had mistaken me for a guest to the estate rather than an employee. I would, after all, be nothing more than a glorified maid. "Has Fröken enjoyed good trip?"

He asked. He spoke to me in halting German with a few Swedish words mixed in.

"*Ja, danke.*" I answered and sank deeper into the soft seat. "It's a very beautiful car," I said after a while. "And so shiny."

He turned his head and grinned. "Good, yes? American Lincoln. Very good, yes?" He sought my response in his rear view mirror.

"Yes. Great job." I agreed. "Mr. Nordeen must be very pleased with you."

"Mr. Nordeen is good man. Very good. Sehr gut!," Olle declared.

His comment comforted me. The chauffeur was the third person who had given my new employer a good reference. Still, the most important questions were yet to be answered. Would he like me? Moreover, would I like him? Well, I would find out soon enough.

When we arrived, I found myself more nervous than ever. The sight of the opulent and impressive mansion that faced me made my heart jump into my throat.

"Very beautiful, yes?" Olle inquired as he helped me out of the car. He pointed to the large carved oak door. "You go to there where is the front entrance."

I hesitated. "Shouldn't I use another door? I mean, I came here to work."

"Yes, I know." Olle said. "But you go to there," he said in German. "Perhaps soon you give me better lessons? I was bad boy in school and did not listen."

I nodded and hesitantly stepped up to the front door. I took the ornate brass knocker between my fingers and let it fall down on the shiny plate. I had expected a maid to open the door. Instead, I came face to face with Mr. Nordeen himself. We peered at each other, each of us instantly appraising the other. He was of medium height with dark hair and calm, gray eyes. I judged him to be in his mid-fifties. He did not fit the the GDR's description of a Capitalist. The propaganda in my country had done everything to make us believe that Capitalists were arrogant people whose faces were scarred by pockmarks and saddled with malicious grins. We had been shown many pictures of Western men who were sitting in power. I had suspected then that the faces in the pictures had been deliberately distorted by our government but had never been sure. Now I stood before a wealthy man and knew that what we had been told was a lie. Mr. Nordeen looked like a father and a man whom I could trust.

He smiled and extend his hand in a greeting. "Erik Nordeen," he introduced himself. "I'm glad to see that you arrived safely, Fräulein Berger!"

To my utter surprise, he had addressed me in perfect German and without even a hint of the Swedish sing-song that was the mark of his language.

"Yes," I answered perplexed and shook his hand, which was soft and warm. "Thank you for offering me a position here. I hope that you will be pleased with my work performance."

"Ah, let us not discuss work before you have even settled in. Let me get you situated first. We can talk about all the necessary details later."

He beckoned me to enter. I looked around the foyer, which was laid out in shiny black and salmon colored marble. Centered above us hung an impressive crystal chandelier. I stared at it in awe. But quickly my admiration turned to concern. Would I be required to stand on a ladder and polish the hundreds of crystals that were dangling from it? My heart sank. I knew that such a task would test my patience and my problem with heights.

Mr. Nordeen saw my expression and smiled. "Don't worry. You will not be required to tackle such a job. Bertil and his wife Britt will take care of that."

I was happy that someone else would do the serious housecleaning. Mr. Nordeen led me up the stairs and down a long corridor. "I had the room refurnished only yesterday," he explained. "I hope that you will like the teak furniture. It is appropriately modern and suitable for a young person, don't you agree? I thought that antique, overstuffed chairs and sofas might be too old fashioned for someone your age. Teakwood is very much in vogue in Scandinavia."

Not knowing how to respond, I remained silent. I was impressed that he wanted to make sure that I was comfortable in his home. When he showed me my own private bathroom, which was entirely laid out in black and white marble and adorned with gold fixtures, I was even more impressed. Under a bay window that looked onto the garden below, stood the largest bathtub that I had ever seen. Moreover, in the corner of the room was an enclosed sauna that exuded a wonderful fragrance of white spruce. I knew that I had entered a fairytale setting. How could it be possible that one man could acquire such wealth? But more importantly, what miracle had led me to him?

"Oh," I gasped. "Everything is so beautiful!"

My new employer smiled. "I am glad that you like it, Fräulein Berger. I hope that you will feel at home here. I will leave you for now. Walk around the estate if you would like. When you are ready to discuss your duties here, you'll find me in my library."

Still in a daze, I put away the few belongings that I had brought with me. I listened for noises in the house, but it was quiet as a tomb. I wondered where the rest of the servants were before I remembered that it was Sunday. Everyone would have the day off.

I unpacked the small metal box that I had brought with me and took out my mother's gold ring. I turned it over. For the first time, I noticed an inscription in the band. It read, "Rudi 1936." It had been the year that my parents had married. I wondered why my mother had kept the ring since she had not loved my father for so many years of her life. I also wondered, as I had done so often, what had become of him. What would he say if he were to see me in these fine surroundings? Would he approve? I placed the ring back into the box and looked at the envelope that had been addressed to my mother. I suddenly felt the urge to open it but knew that Mr. Nordeen was waiting for me in his library. I would have to do it another time. I took one last look through the window, which overlooked a rose garden. In the distance beyond, I could see a small clearing. Off to the right was a path. Beyond that, I could see a cottage hidden in the tall pines. Yes, I could be happy here even though I would miss my cherished family, would miss Andra and my friends across the sea.

The duties, which were required of me, were few. Mr. Nordeen informed that I would have to prepare his meals and learn to bake an assortment of Swedish cookies and pastries. Welcoming visitors with coffee and pastries was a Swedish custom. He explained that he did not eat meat; but other than that, I could cook for him what I wanted. If we needed groceries, I would only have to pick up the phone and order them from the market. Furthermore, he rarely would give dinner parties. But if he did, his regular staff would take care of everything, including the clean-up. I would receive a good salary, and my evenings and weekends would be free. Moreover, if at any time I needed to go to the city, Olle would be available to drive me. I was speechless. That was it? I knew that I could easily handle the job.

My new employer noticed my surprised expression. "Does all of this agree with you, Fräulein Berger?"

Not knowing whether Swedish etiquette required me to volunteer for additional duties or not, I nodded in silence.

"You might ask why I hired you when I have old, established help on hand. It appears that my brother-in-law, the minister, is skilled in tactical persuasion. He thought that bringing a young person into the house would do me good. And now, if you have no other questions, you may take a rest from your journey."

Before I left him in his library, I glanced at his many books on the shelves. He saw it. "Do you like to read?" He asked.

"Yes."

"You are welcome to borrow any one of the books you see here." He invited me to take a closer look at them. I noticed that the books had been arranged in categories of business, philosophy, metaphysics, Eastern religions, and such. I sighed. All the information before me would take years to digest.

"One more thing," Mr. Nordeen said, "I do not like to be disturbed when the door to my library is closed. It is most likely, then, that I will be meditating."

I smiled in surprise. "My Uncle Emil knew how to meditate, too," I exclaimed.

"Well, then you know what it is all about and that it helps to clear the mind and gives you peace," Mr. Nordeen answered. His eyes followed me with a pensive expression as I left the library.

It was not long before my employer asked me to share meals with him and began tutoring me in the Swedish language even though he had a hectic business schedule. He seemed to enjoy being my teacher. I diligently studied the grammar books that he gave me. And when I felt proficient enough in the language, I enrolled in a correspondence course to learn composition and how to write business letters.

Mr. Nordeen was pleased with my show of effort. He treated me with kindness, as he did everyone who worked for him. They, in turn, responded by carrying out any of his requests with haste and pride.

My days and evenings were never dull. I also did not lack for entertainment. Each day, Olle came around for a chat. He drove up, walked to the back of the house and whistled for me. When I opened the door, I would find him leaning on one of the light posts outside grinning from ear to ear. "*Hej,* Ariane," he would call his usual greeting. "I thought I'd pay you a visit."

"For starters, I feel like a German shepherd dog whenever you whistle for me." I frowned.

He answered me with laughter. "No. I'm the shepherd and you are our brave German sheep that has found a great new home. How about me teaching you all the Swedish that Boss won't teach you. In return, you can teach me better German."

I could never be angry at Olle. He was different from most of the staff, which was proper and respectful. He saw the world through his own colorful lenses and loved to talk. I soon found that behind his prim and proper demeanor lurked an outlandishly bizarre and inquisitive mind. He was never shy to offer his opinion to Mr. Nordeen, even he had not been asked for it. Olle had street smarts but was honest and skilled in driving. I assumed that my employer had hired and kept him on because of that and his skill of observation. What I liked about Olle was that he was without pretenses and unafraid to show his true nature. I also liked that he loved to give me an account of the newest gossip that was going around at corporate headquarters. It kept me in the loop. But mostly I loved his jokes. He and I quickly became friends.

Old Sven, the gardener, too, was friendly and eager to engage in small talk. He was a salty old fellow with weather-beaten skin. His teeth were stained from drinking too much coffee and from packing his pipe too tightly with strong tobacco. Sven had been born in the sparsely populated area in the North and had told me interesting stories about his childhood. After I related Andra's experience with the young man from Lapland, he announced, "A small herd of elk arrives every morning in the meadow near my house. Sometimes, a reindeer pair comes to visit as well. Come visit my wife and me tomorrow morning. We will go and watch them."

I obliged him, and soon my morning visits became a ritual. I arrived very early at their small house while the mist was still hanging over the meadow. We took blankets, wrapped ourselves in them, and watched the animals graze. Afterwards, I returned to the estate to prepare breakfast for Mr. Nordeen.

Old Sven introduced me to Gunilla, the daughter of his neighbors. She and her family lived without pomp and fanfare in a home that to me felt sterile and antiseptic. Even though Gunilla and I were totally different in character, we became friends. She carried herself regally and did not laugh easily. The members of her family interacted with one another in an unusually stiff and proper manner and seemed to relate on a cerebral rather than an emotional level. At first, I wanted to shake them by the shoulder. I wanted them to wake up and let me see who they really were beneath that cool exterior. Gunilla was surprised when I mentioned my observation to her. She answered that they were a typical Swedish family, just like any other, and that underneath their sterile exterior love flourished for one another. As I pondered my reaction to their cool demeanor, I realized that what I saw and felt reminded me of my mother who had been emotionally distant from me.

There was one thing that the family had in common with others. They did not mind to share gossip. From them I learned that Mr. Nordeen had lost his wife and child many years earlier after an oncoming car had smashed into the passenger side of the vehicle that he had driven. He had survived, while his wife and son had been killed instantly. After months of grieving, he had sought to understand the purpose behind his loss, and the reason for life itself. It was then that he discovered spiritual principals. Gunilla's family, who had known him in his earlier years, observed that he had become a changed man. He was no longer self-absorbed but had stepped into the role of humanitarian and lived his life with compassion.

Having heard the account, I felt a new respect and affection for my employer. I realized that he had used his sorrow to become a better man. He had chosen to live in light instead of darkness.

I had quickly advanced in my knowledge of the Swedish language but was surprised when Mr. Nordeen asked me to accompany him on a business trip during which he dictated correspondence and notes that I transcribed. The trip went well, and he requested that I join him on subsequent trips. He confided that it would relieve his own secretary and keep her in the office to see after other business matters.

One of the trips took us to Öland, the island that lies across the Straits of Kalmar in the southeast of Sweden, and which is host to the *Stora Alvaret,* the Great Alvar. Even though the island is made of limestone, I marveled at the flowers and the many species of orchids that grow in its seemingly inhospitable thin layer of soil. Burial grounds from the Iron age through the Viking age and four hundred wind mills dotted the landscape. We visited ancient ruins and inspected the many rune stones that marked the island. Their inscription evidenced the history of the people and the relationships that had connected them with their gods. They had remained as a record of the magical events that had taken place since the first settlers crossed the frozen sea from the mainland in 8000 BC.

One last sightseeing trip took us to the 42 m high lighthouse, the *Länge Jan,* the Long John. Across the water, and beyond the horizon, lay the land where I was born. More than a decade had passed since I had stood on a tower on Rügen and had tried to visualize what life in Sweden would be like. Now I knew.

Mr. Nordeen and I seated ourselves among flowering thyme and gazed into the distance. "Is it not incredible that my friend and I have made it across this body of water?" I commented. "We didn't realize it then, but we were pretty bold to head out to sea. We could have drowned. Most others who tried to escape over the Baltic did not survive the journey. Do you believe that we were protected by some invisible force?"

Mr. Nordeen answered with assurance. "You already know my thoughts on that, Ariane. I am quite certain that before you embarked on the journey, you must have experienced one *true* moment of pure and absolute faith. You must have believed without a doubt that you would succeed. In that very instant in time, you tapped into the creative energy of Spirit. It is a universal law that if we hold a desire in perfect faith and know that it will be fulfilled, we will find ourselves in harmony with eternal creation. The creative Spirit of God will always nurture our desire and bring it into manifestation. Such pure moments are difficult to achieve. But I dare say, the more we practice, the more skilled we will become."

I thought about my mother who had known no such faith but had lived in a state of constant turmoil. It had broken her and led her to destruction.

"I hope that one day I will be able to totally master that principle," I sighed.

Mr. Nordeen smiled and patted me on the hand. "Well, young lady. Keep at it and never give up believing that you will."

Chapter Thirty-Five

The Letter

Several months after arriving in Sweden, I had written a letter to Tante Helga using the Nordeen estate as my return address. I remembered Herr Fink telling the members of the chamber music orchestra that the STASI was monitoring all mail from the West and from foreign countries. They employed people who skillfully managed to steam open envelopes and reseal them without detection.

My note to Tante Helga had explained that all was well with the family here in Sweden. I had added that my closest friend had gone to live with her relatives and that I missed her. I suspected that Tante Helga knew whom I was talking about. If Andra had not been able to get a message to either her mother or to her aunt, Tante Helga would take it upon herself to notify them. I had signed the note with "Your relative across the sea." If Tante Helga would be questioned about the letter, she could claim that a cousin of her departed husband was living in Sweden.

Her reply came two weeks later. It began with, "My dear relative! Our loving thoughts have been with you for a while now." Tante Helga went on to say that Dagmar had become engaged and that her fiance was a member of a well-known orchestra. She further wrote that she continued to be worried about Wolfgang because he was stuck in a troubled relationship with a certain young woman. In addition, he was mourning the loss of a special friend and confidante who had moved away. Tante Helga wrote that he is sending his love and well wishes to me, his relative. The letter included news about Tanya Koslowski, who was with child and that the father of the baby had absconded. Frau Meyer came to see Tante Helga a few days earlier and reported hearing from the family that if the baby turned out to be a girl, she would be named after the girl who once had lived across the street from them.

The letter contained a postscript: P.S. Your letters are dear to all of us. I will place them in a little metal container for safekeeping. Do you have such containers in Sweden?

It only took me a moment to understand that Tante Helga was reminding me of the box that contained the letter to my mother. I knew that I had ignored it for too long and that it was time to read it now. I went to the shelf where I had kept it and took out the letter. The uneven thickness of the envelope suggested that it contained several pages. Before I could change my mind and put it away again, I tore it open. I discovered another envelope inside of it. Scribbled on it was a note from our former landlady at *Havelstrasse*. It read,

Dear Frau Berger, a woman from city hall delivered this letter. She had found it in the desk of a man who has retired. Since the address at Goethe Strasse is no longer valid, she took it upon herself to search existing records and compare old and new residence entries of persons with your last name. She discovered that a certain Annie Berger had registered a residence at Havelstrasse a few months after the war and that she had listed her previous residence as Goethe Strasse. The clerk assumed that Johanne Berger, to which the letter is addressed, might be a relative of yours. She came looking for you here. Since I knew of your name change, I assured the clerk that you were one and the same person. I offered to deliver the letter to you myself.

P.S. It seems that you have not yet gone to register your new address, changing it from my house to where you are living now. I advise you to do it immediately.

I stared at the note. Our previous landlady had stuffed the original envelope into a new one and had simply addressed it to "Annie Berger."

Since she had delivered it by hand, it had not required a return address. She must have left the letter on our doorstep a few days after we had moved into the Ritter house. My mother had apparently recognized the handwriting and had laid the letter aside unopened. The women had not been on good terms with each other after my mother, on several occasions, had violently complained about the infestation of vermin in the house. It had been up to my mother to set mousetraps and use disinfectant when we had rented the room by the river. She had accused the woman of being a "lazy dirt bag" because she had allowed the house to become overrun by disease carrying pests and had done nothing about it.

I opened the second envelope, which had been addressed to "Johanne Berger, Goethe Strasse 13." That was the address of the house at which my parents had lived before it was destroyed. That address had been lined through. A note on the front of the envelope read, "Recipient assumed to be deceased."

I quickly slit open the envelope and pulled out a letter. The date showed that it had been written nearly eighteen years earlier

August 1945

My dearest love Jo,

As you might imagine, I had a most difficult time finding my way from Hamburg to here. The trains are running only sporadically. Everywhere I looked, I saw nothing but death and destruction. Thank God, the war is finally over! I've waited so long to hold you in my arms. I am here to take you home with me. But, to my dismay, I am unable to find you! Where are you, my love? I went to Goethe Strasse but found that your once beautiful house had been razed to the ground. In fact, the whole town still resembles one great battlefield. I inquired about your whereabouts at city hall, but a clerk told me that there is no current listing of a new address for you. Perhaps you did not register one yet. Since it is required by law, the clerk is convinced that you either have left town or have perished in the bombings. I requested to see a list of surviving citizens from your street so that I might ask them about you. I was told that there was no such list. My love, I do not believe that you are dead! I will continue looking for you. I even went out to Emil's place but found his cottage and property abandoned. I fear that we have lost him because he should have returned from the battlefield by now.

I do believe that you have kept your promise to me. Remember that you said that you would be waiting for me here to fetch you and the child? I must return to Hamburg tomorrow but will come back again next week to search for you again. Meanwhile, I will leave this letter with the clerk. He has promised to give it to you the moment you come to register your new residence.

Before closing, I must confess that I discussed our situation with Rudi before he went back to the front. He told me that he knew how unhappy you had become, even though he had tried to give you everything that you had wanted. At first, he hesitated to discuss your estranged marriage. I, however, pressed him and begged him to set you free. I proposed to raise little Adrianna as my own because I did not want her to be torn between two fathers. My dear, I cannot describe how sad Rudi had looked at that very moment. We, then, discussed the situation at length. He finally agreed to let you go. He would make it easy for both of you. I think that it was mainly because he believed that his daughter would, in the end, not remember him. He stated that he would not return home; rather, he would begin divorce proceedings from wherever he would find himself after the war was over. I was to keep quiet about it and not tell you. I know that he will miss his little girl. He made me promise that I would give her a decent upbringing.

My dearest love! I am still burdened with guilt because I have betrayed my best friend with his wife. But, what could I do? I love you so madly. Neither of us could have predicted the perilous sea journey that left me shipwrecked and made me forfeit you. Rudi, without a doubt, married you because he loved you. As for the continued friendship between him and me, well... I hesitate to speculate on it.

Dearest, I will close for now. If I am forced to return home with empty arms again on my next trip, you must promise me that you will write the minute this letter finds you. I will, then, immediately rush back and take you away from this place, which looks like the bowels of hell. Until I hold you in my arms once more,

I am forever your Karl

I sat staring at the letter with the tightly scribbled sentences. My emotions were stirred up. Why had fate prevented Karl from reuniting with my mother? By doing so, it had deprived me of a father. Furthermore, why had my natural father given me up so easily and without a fight? I began to re-read the letter line by line until I could recite every word of it. Each time I read his comments about me, I felt a sting in my heart. My father had known that my mother had not wanted me. Why, then, had he left me with her? Had he believed that Karl would be able to make her love me better? Moreover, why had my father believed that I would not remember him when his smile and touch had left such a strong imprint on my memory? I remember how I had clung to him before he had left. I had put my face into the rough collar of his woolen uniform. In fact, if I closed my eyes now, I could still see him and feel the stubble of his unshaven face against my own. Karl had written that it had not been easy for my father to give me up. The truth is that he *had* given me up when all I had wanted was for him to return and rescue me from my mother. I had wanted him to make everything well again.

The letter brought up many unresolved issues for me and made me realize that everyone in my family had been left to deal with unfulfilled dreams. My mother could have changed her own destiny. The happiness she had craved had actually been within her reach. All she had needed to do was to open the letter after she had found it on our doorstep. Instead, years of bliss became lost in the runners of her *Schrank*.

A deep melancholy settled over me. I found it difficult to get out of bed. Mr. Nordeen finally intervened. Without telling me of his intention, he invited a psychologist to our house. On the day of her arrival, he called me from his office and advised that he would be delayed in coming home. He told me to play hostess to the woman. I had no idea who she was. But soon, she managed to draw me into a conversation and encourage me to tell her about my past. It was not long before my pain spilled out.

After that first day, I agreed to subsequent counseling sessions. There were many of them. Mr. Nordeen, who never did anything half heartedly, gave my therapist the use of the guesthouse and allowed her to stay over whenever the hour was too late for her to return to Stockholm. The many months that followed left me wrung out. Deep, old wounds tore open, and all my covered up hurt was dragged into the light. Even though I had known that my grandmother and my uncle had loved me, I had craved my mother's love. She, however, was unable to give it. Consequently, I became a damaged little girl but somehow managed to put my pain aside and hide it well. I had functioned well enough to survive.

I wanted to heal fast but discovered that it would take time. Progress came, and one day, many months later, I felt light and free. "Why did I not break down sooner?" I asked my therapist. My old curiosity was surfacing once again. "I know that I periodically became depressed. A dark heaviness simply descended on me unannounced, but I never knew why. I would always struggle through it without telling anyone about it. I think running and my belief saved me from breaking. It kept me sane."

"Perhaps God gave you an amazing strength to pull through," she suggested. It is truly a miracle that you survived all the trauma in your young life and came away as healthy as you did, Ariane. Just be aware that additional memories might pop up. However, you have tools now to deal with them. Use them. But if you need me, I will always be available to talk."

Mr. Nordeen seemed as pleased with my progress as I was. "You deserve a reward for being courageous and for allowing yourself to be so vulnerable, Ariane. What would you like?"

I did not need to think about my wish of longstanding. I knew that it was a large one, and I hesitated to reveal it.

"Well, what is it? He asked again. "No need to feel self-conscious or undeserving. Out with it!"

I took a deep breath and blurted out, "I have always wanted to study at a university."

My employer looked at me with surprise. I could tell that he had not expected a request of that nature. "Is that what you truly want?" He inquired.

"Perhaps I should not have asked for it." I lowered my eyes.

"Nonsense," he replied and left the room.

I felt ashamed. I was convinced that I had overstepped my boundaries. But to my surprise, he returned within minutes. "I've just hung up the phone with someone at the university in Stockholm," he told me. "The good news is that you will be accepted if you pass the entrance exam."

Long Swedish winter evenings were perfect for studying. Mr. Nordeen ordered a crate of books that I needed to review. I buried my nose into the material but remained frightened and unsure whether I would pass the exam. After all, my previous education had not been the greatest. However, I knew that I would rather die than destroy his confidence in me.

One afternoon, while taking a break, I pulled out Karl's letter from the drawer of my desk. I wondered, as I had before, whether it was possible that my father was still be alive. I had wanted to investigate but feared the outcome. Giving in to a sudden impulse, I wrote to Karl at the address that he had provided as a postscript. I was already in my first term at the university when he replied. He wrote that my letter had followed him from one old residence to the next before it finally found him at an old sailor's home where he had gone to retire. One last sea voyage had only recently brought him home. His love for the sea had carried him through the years.

His letter was sad. He related how shocked he had been to hear that my mother, his dearest "Jo," had actually been alive when he assumed her to be dead. He had made two trips to our town but had been unable to find us. The same clerk, with whom he had left his letter, had informed him that no one by her name had come to register a new residence. Karl had revisited my uncle's place but had found it still deserted. He had spent a whole afternoon trotting through neighborhoods and inquired about my mother. No one could recall having met a Jo or a Johanne Berger. He believed with absolute certainty that, had she had survived, she would have set everything in motion to find him herself. He finally agreed with the clerk that she must, indeed, be dead. Totally aggrieved, he returned to Hamburg in West Germany. Two weeks later, he followed up his visit with a letter to my uncle's address, thinking that someone had taken up residence there. The letter was returned to him with the notation, "Addressee fallen in the war."

Karl's letter went on to say hat not long after having made the trip to our town, my father had come to see him. He had looked haggard and tired. The war had been hard on him. Karl had received him with sadness. "You are too late, Rudi."

My father had raised an eyebrow. "Well, is a divorce not what the two of you had wanted?"

Karl, then, told him the bad news.

"She could have fled when the Russian's advanced." My father had replied.

"Rudi, perhaps I have known her better than you did. I am absolutely certain that she would have waited for me in town or would have left a forwarding address at Emil's place. Moreover, were she still alive, she would have taken up residence there. No one lived in the cottage. I finally had to accept that she and your daughter did not survive. You must do the same."

My father had brushed away tears and stated that he would leave Germany to visit his cousin in Alsace-Lorraine. The beautiful canals in the region would give him the rest he needed. He further would wait to contact his father. He felt to broken up to return to the family business right away. He would write to his father after a while.

Karl had been aware that he would never see his best friend again. A rift too deep to be bridged had opened up between them. He ended his letter to me by saying that he was sorry for the pain he had caused me but that he hoped that life had treated me well in spite of it.

His lengthy letter touched me. I realized, once again, that fate had presented us all with a twisted life. Wanting to know where my father had gone, I wrote Karl, asking him for the name of the cousin's village. I would go in search of my father.

Chapter Thirty-Six

1964
An American Named Nick

When summer arrived, I decided to take a break from university and travel to the Alsace region in France. But before that, I would fly first to West Berlin to find my grandmother's grave and continue on to Mainz for a visit with Andra. I bade my university roommate, Mia, goodbye and went home to the estate to gather more of my clothes and pack my suitcase. When I arrived, I found Mr. Nordeen entertaining guests from America. They had toured Scandinavia and had stopped by to pay Mr. Nordeen a visit. They had intended to fly to West Berlin the next day. However, after calling home this morning and learning that one of their children had been in an accident, they would have to return to the USA immediately. Their flight would leave in a few hours.

Mr. Nordeen introduced us to each other and remarked, "You are just in time to do us all a favor, Ariane. My friends wanted to deliver a present to a soldier who is stationed in Berlin. He and their son grew up together. Since you'll be staying in Berlin a day or two yourself, perhaps you can take the package to him."

I agreed and sat down to talk to the American couple. My English was still very limited; therefore, Mr. Nordeen translated. Soon, the American man pulled out his West Berlin travel guide and pointed out all the places that he and his wife had planned to visit. He turned to me, "Perhaps you can visit them in our stead, Miss. And be sure not to miss the plaza where John F. Kennedy had made his speech."

"What a tragedy that is!" His wife chimed in. "I'm sure you know that we have lost our president. We're still in shock."

I nodded, remembering how I had joined the world in mourning. his assassination.

"Tell me this, Miss Ariane," the husband continued. "I've been curious about something. People back home say that Kennedy committed a blunder when he said, 'Ich bin ein Berliner.' Is that true? Perhaps you can clear it up for me."

"I think it was his way of showing his support for the situation of our country. West Berlin is an island and is surrounded by the GDR. It is more vulnerable to Communist plots than the rest of West Germany. I suppose that it is not the safest city to live in. The slightest political incident at the border could escalate and close it off from the rest of West Germany. People say that trouble there could start a new war."

"That is not what I mean,t" the husband replied. "What I meant is that people say that Kennedy called himself a donut. Are Berliners not jelly doughnuts?"

"Oh that," I chuckled. "Yes. They are. But it is a word, which also describes the citizens of Berlin. If he had visited Hamburg, he may have said, "I am a Hamburger." Many of our foods are named after cities. For example, a citizen of Braunschweig is a Braunschweiger. That's the name for the famous sausage that is made there. I know that the bakeries in West Berlin sell a pastry that resembles little flat and sweet pancakes. The pastry comes to a little raised mound in the center. The name for it is 'American,' Amerikaner. Some of them come with a half-glazed white and a half-glazed brown topping.

The couple roared with laughter. "That's it, then," the man said. "Our ignorance about Berliners stands corrected."

"May I tell you another little tidbit?" I continued. "Where I come from, people make it a custom to have plenty of Berliners in their homes on New Year's Eve. They believe that they will bring them good luck in the following year."

"That is curious," the woman replied. "How do you drum them all up?"

I was Mr. Nordeen's turn to look confused. "What does it mean to "drum them up?"

The husband laughed. "That's slang."

The wife added, "What I mean is, is there an agency at which you go and register to get them"

"Well, you'll need to go to the bakery shop." I replied. I, too, was a bit confused now.

"The bakery shop?" The couple looked at each other with perplexed expressions before they realized their own confusion. Once again, they broke out in loud laughter. "Oh, you're speaking of jelly doughnuts that will bring good luck. Not people."

"Yes," I agreed, and remembered how the crowd in Berlin had cheered when they heard the president speak. I added, "Well, except, the people regarded President Kennedy as a good luck charm. He gave them hope, and his speech at the *Rathaus Schöneberg* made them gather courage. His assurance that he would not let the German people down helped them to endure their uncertain and often dangerous situation. Everyone thought that Kennedy would be able to negotiate terms for reunification. But only five months later, when he was shot, Germany's hope to ever see that day faded away." I had diligently watched the news on television to know what was going on.

The mood of the American couple turned somber. They had wanted to visit the wall of infamy and oppression and get a glimpse of the rest of the divided city. Since they could not do that, they reminded me to see as much as I could. I promised that I would. Before leaving for the airport, the man called, "Don't forget to visit Checkpoint Charlie, Miss Ariane."

I smiled but knew that I would not go near it. Perhaps it was silly to imagine that if I stepped too close to the border, fate would have second thoughts about having allowed me to find freedom. Perhaps I would be dragged across to the East and be made to suffer the consequences of desertion.

When I arrived in Berlin, the difference between West and East was difficult to ignore. Everything had been drab and gray in East Berlin; but in West Berlin, the streets pulsated with life. A taxi took me to a *Pension* where I freshened up and set out to find my grandmother's grave in Berlin-Friedenau. I noticed that someone had left flowers for her. Kneeling by her gravestone, I said a prayer for her. I hoped that her afterlife was as she had said it would be. I hoped that she had gone to her Good Lord in Heaven and had found peace with Him.

The following day, another taxi took me to Lichterfelde-West and to the front gate of the Berlin Brigade, where I asked the sentry in previously rehearsed English to call a Lieutenant Westbrook. Waiting for him to arrive, I shyly glanced at the other girls who stood at the gate. They, too, were waiting for a soldier. Their faces appeared as painted-up as the one, which once had looked back at me from the mirror in the public toilet in Rostock. Soon, I became aware that each one of us were being scrutinized by a few older women who were passing us on their way to the market. I could see judgment and disdain in their eyes. I felt uncomfortable and clutched the package that the American couple had entrusted me with. The lieutenant took his time to appear. I went to hide behind a tree from where I could observe the arrival of several soldiers who quickly popped a stick of gum into their mouths before they happily greeted their girls. I immediately noticed a difference between the Americans and the young Russians, who had been stationed in my hometown. The young men here walked with a spring in their step. They looked healthy and well-nourished. In contrast, the soldiers in my hometown had looked sickly pale. Acne and skin eruptions had marked their faces. Every one of them had presented a stoic expression to the world around them. It was no wonder that after the war had ended, Germans had wanted to be liberated by the Americans instead by the Russians.

Soon I decided that my call for the lieutenant had gone unanswered. I was ready to leave when a voice sounded. "Which one of you ladies wants to see Lieutenant Westbrook?"

I left my hiding place and shyly stepped forward. "Hello," I said to the tall man in uniform that stood at the barrier of the gate.

He gave me a blank look. "What can I do for you, Fräulein?" He spoke in near-fluent German.

"My name is Ariane Berger." I held out a hand in greeting. "I came from Sweden and brought you this package."

Lieutenant Westbrook raised an eyebrow. "Miss, I think you've made a mistake. Perhaps you're waiting for someone else. I know no one in Sweden."

"Yes, I know." I quickly assured him. "I brought it from Sweden to you. You see, it's from America."

Lieutenant Westbrook began to laugh. "Miss, I think that you are a bit confused. You are mixing up countries...even continents."

My face turned red. I was flustered. Why did my successful therapy sessions suddenly fail me? I felt insecure and behaved like an imbecile, feeling exactly as I had felt when I first had laid eyes on Wolfgang many years earlier.

"Well, here. It's for you." I pushed the package into his hands. "I don't know what's in it," I added. Afraid to humiliate myself further, I turned to leave.

"Wait, Fräulein," he called after me.

I stopped and turned. My heart was pounding. I liked the way he looked and how he carried himself. He was handsome in his uniform that fit his body perfectly. His hair was blond and cut short, leaving his face open for inspection. He grinned. I surmised that he had found our unpolished introduction to each other amusing. I did not return his smile.

He quickly apologized. "Sorry, Miss, it was not my intention to ridicule you. Please! Tell me once again. Where did you come from, and who gave you this package for me?"

I related that his old neighbors had visited us in Sweden and asked me drop it off to him.

"But surely you did not come all the way from Sweden to bring it to me?"

"Yes... Well, no. I'm here on a holiday."

"That's nice. I am looking forward to my own vacation in a few days. I need one." He glanced at his watch. "Miss, I'm sorry. I don't want to run away from you so quickly when we've only just met. But, unfortunately, I need to attend a meeting right now. Would you terribly mind coming back later, say, around six this evening? I would like you to give me a more thorough update on my neighbors."

"I don't know them at all." I hesitated. There was nothing else I could tell him. But I, too, wanted to become better acquainted with him. He had a sense of humor, which I liked. "I suppose I could do that, but I don't want to wait here in front of this gate again."

"Well, then. Where can I pick you up?"

I told him where my Bed and Breakfast place was located.

On the way back to the it, I wondered why I had agreed to see him again. Up to this point, Americans had presented a mystery to me. Communist propaganda had not given them a very good reputation. When the lieutenant and I later met, I discovered that everything that I had been told about them had been wrong once more. In fact, I found Americans to be friendly and agreeable. Moreover, the lieutenant was cute and adorable. His name was Nick, and I enjoyed his company. I teased him because his name reminded me of St. Nick and the Christmas presents that had remained absent during my childhood but which in the past year had made up for their previous absence. He, in turn, related that he had grown up in California, the golden state of possibilities where everyone enjoyed the beauty, sea and sun and where palm trees and orange groves were part of the landscape.

"It sounds as though you are reporting from a book of modern fairy tales," I commented. I felt like a starry-eyed teenager. I wanted to hear more about America and its grandness. Nick spoke eloquently and easily, and soon I remarked how well he spoke German. He responded that he had studied it for several years in high school and in college.

"I'm enrolled in a university, as well," I reported proudly. "It's a dream come true for me."

"Are you studying in Berlin?"

"No. In Stockholm."

"Hmm," he replied. "That's too bad."

"No!" I countered. "It's a very good university."

"I'm sure it is." His laugh reminded me of Wolfgang's. It was sonorous and warm. "That is not what I meant to say. What I meant is…well… never mind. But I can see how communication can get lost in translation, Fräulein Berger. Therefore, we must meet as often as we can while you are in Berlin. You must give me the opportunity to brush up on your language."

"I'll be leaving Berlin and will travel to France in a couple of days," I replied.

"That *is* a coincidence! I, too, have made plans to visit France. I want to see Paris. I am sure that I will be able to take my leave earlier than requested. Perhaps we can travel together after we each have made it through the East German corridor. I would take you along in my car, but unfortunately, I am not allowed to carry civilians through the checkpoints. But once on the other side of East Germany, I can pick you up and drive you to the village where you think your father resides. Perhaps after visiting with him, you might be able to spare a day or two for me as well."

He seemed to have it all planned out.

"I don't know." I looked squarely at him. "You *do* understand that I haven't seen my father since I was very young. If I find him, I will spend my time with him. As for traveling over the Autobahn, I could not join you even if it were possible for you to take me with you."

I had not wanted to spend the evening answering questions about my past and had refrained from mentioning that I had been born in East Germany.

"Why not?" Nick was curious.

I now decided to tell him of my escape. He listened, and for an instant, I saw a suspicious expression rise in his blue eyes. He asked, "Who was it again that gave you the package for me? Are you really who you say you are, or has the other side sent you to make my acquaintance?"

"What do you mean?" I had caught his meaning and countered, "I am no Mata Hari! I would never be able to pull off such an undertaking."

"No? Are you sure? You look like a little spitfire to me. Especially now that you are angry with me again."

I rose from my chair in protest, but Nick quickly reached for me and pulled me back down. "I meant it in a good way of course. I am sorry. I don't want to doubt you. But, you see…" He hesitated. "Fact is, I am holding down a very sensitive job. Now that we are finding ourselves in each other's company, you need to be cleared."

I failed to grasp his meaning. "Cleared? He had spoken the word in English. "Is that the same as being 'cleaned' or needing to be 'wiped away?" I wanted to know.

Nick was amused. "You mean 'rubbed out.'" He could not stop laughing. Catching his breath, he added, "You must understand that Berlin is a special hotspot for political intrigue and espionage. It is easy for agents from behind the iron curtain to come across and infiltrate into the ranks of those who have access to valuable information."

I quickly interrupted him. "What you mean to say is that someone will think that I am one of them. Therefore, they will try to kill me?"

"No. Just listen and calm down, Ariane."

Between more laughs, Nick explained. "To be cleared means to make certain that there is nothing in your background that leads anyone to believe that you are engaged in Communist activities or have a criminal record."

"Well, I suppose that I am clear then!"

"I believe you," he answered. "But please do not take it personal. I need to be cautious. In any case, I would be terribly disappointed if you turned out to be a spy."

I calmed down. He smiled, and I returned it. "Wasn't that fun?" He said.

I nodded. "I hope that we won't always have such a difficult time in understanding each other."

"We won't." He answered. "Trust me. I think that we will become great friends."

As the evening progressed, I felt increasingly drawn to him. At one point I dared to asked myself whether I had gone totally nuts. I had allowed myself to be attracted to a soldier. Had I forgotten the trouble I had given Andra and the way I had tried to discourage her from seeing Manfred? She would never stop teasing me now. Perhaps she would call me a hypocrite, even though I had acknowledged that Manfred had proved himself to be valuable to us.

I involuntarily drew my lips into a smile. My Uncle Emil had been correct. Our own actions did return to us in peculiar ways. "That's Karma," he had said. I instantly reminded myself that I needed to take an inventory of my prejudices.

Nick saw my smile. "Are you looking forward to our trip together?"

"Perhaps," I responded, not wanting to seem too eager at the prospect of spending a few days with him. "It all depends on whether I will find my father."

Chapter Thirty-Seven

In Search of my Father

Two days later, I was sitting on a plane to Mainz. Nick would follow in his little VW. Andra waited for me at the airport and greeted me with cries of joy. "It's been so long since we said goodbye. I'm so happy to see you!"

We spent hours talking, catching up on everything that we had left untold in our letters to each other. Soon, Andra confessed, "I've made an interesting discovery after I came here. I realized how much I had become brainwashed in the GDR. Nothing here is as we had been told it would be. It's better, really. But there was one thing, which I did not anticipate. It took me a long time to find a job. It seemed that employers did not trust ex-GDR workers to do a good work. They were convinced that we had become lazy because the GDR had suffered shortages of materials and had been forced to reduce work hours to a minimum after Ulbricht's big speeches of production increases, and so on. I only got a job after going back to school. Look here." Andra proudly held up a diploma. "I'm a gym instructor now and love it. I think my mother and hairy Otto would be proud of me." She looked sad when she added, "I wonder how they are. I have not heard anything from them lately."

I could tell that Andra still missed her family and was longing to see her mother and aunt. We had already realized that reunification might be years away. That is, if it would ever come. The East-West situation was as fragile as ever.

"I, too, need to tell you something," I confided after we had caught up on each other's lives. "You won't believe your ears." I gave her a long, uncertain look. "I have one request before I tell it to you. Don't judge me as I once judged you."

"Don't be so mysterious. Tell me what it is!"

I hesitatingly looked into her face when I confessed. "Well...I've met a soldier. He's coming here to pick me up."

From the smirk she gave me, I knew that she would make fun of me for a while. "What happened to your principles!" She exclaimed.

"I don't know. They all went up in smoke when I met him."

After reminding me how I had chided her whenever she had another date with Manfred, Andra promised to say no more and wait to give me her opinion after she had met Nick. When he arrived, she was duly impressed with him. We spent a few more hours together before Nick and I departed for France.

"Do you know why people in Alsace speak both French and German?" He quizzed me while we were driving.

"No." I had already discovered that I painfully lacked knowledge in History.

"Well, then, let me tell you." He was happy to enlighten me. "There was Otto von Bismarck, a vacant Spanish throne, and a Prussian bid for it," he began.

After a detailed account of suspicion and political intrigue, he finished with a report on the short-lived Franco-Prussian war. Prussia came away as the victor, and the result was the creation of a unified German empire and the annexation of Alsace and Lorraine. The region changed hands again in 1919, when it was returned to France. Then, in 1940, Germany reclaimed it once more before giving it back to France in 1945.

"I sounds like a nightmare for everyone who lived there," I commented. "I hate war and the misery it brings. Do you think that you will ever have to fight for your country?"

"Well, as long as I am a soldier, I will have to follow orders."

I grunted. "I would not want you to go to war."

Nick reached for my cheek and stroked it lightly. He winked, "Say, Fräulein, are you worried about me already?"

I mumbled an indistinguishable "Hmm" before I suggested that we forget about war and do a bit of sightseeing in Strasbourg. I was eager to see the beautiful city that had been an outpost for the Roman empire in 12 BC and had served as a fort of defense against North European Germanic tribes.

After spending time at ancient sites, we continued driving through the breathtaking valleys and vineyards of the region. We passed picturesque villages with painted half-timbered houses that were framed in the distance by the Vosges mountain range. In late afternoon, we approached the small village in which my father's cousin reportedly lived. My heart sped up a few beats. I began fiddling with my hair.

"Nervous or excited?" Nick asked.

"Nervous…apprehensive," I admitted. "I hope that I have made the right decision to come looking for my father."

Karl had not been able to recall the name of the street where Gertrud lived. Remembering my childhood days and the women who had exchanged gossip as they had waited their turn at the *Konsum*, I asked Nick to stop at a local market.

"*Entschuldigen Sie bitte.*" I began my search. The young people behind the counter were not familiar with a Madame Gertrud Berger who had to live here many years ago. If she was married, she would be known by her husband's last name. I decided to inquire about a Monsieur Rudi Berger. But no one knew of him either.

"It's no good," I moaned. "I don't know how old that cousin is, but I think we need to ask older people."

We drove slowly through ancient narrow alleys, looking for someone who could help us. Finally I saw a stooped over woman who came shuffling down the road. I stopped her.

"*Oui, oui.* I remember the day that Mademoiselle Berger came to this small village as a young woman. She married Pierre, the butcher. All of us were invited to the wedding. Of course, he is not the butcher any longer.

He has gone into retirement. I have not seen either of them since they have moved down the hill from here. My legs don't work as well as they used to, but I will show you the way to Monsieur Gretz' house. He used to be their neighbor and knows where they are living now."

After she gave us directions on how to get Monsieur Gretz' house, Nick parked the car. We clambered up a hill, met with a dead end, and turned around. After another try, we found the correct address. An old, white haired man was sitting outside, enjoying the sun.

"*Guten Tag, Bon Jour. Are you Monsieur Gretz?*" I called.

The old man nodded and gave a toothless grin. "What gives me the honor of being visited by a pretty young girl?"

Nick explained what brought us here.

"Ah, *oui,* Gertrud. I know her well. We used to be neighbors until my daughter insisted that I come to live with her. She is afraid that I will get into mischief if she allows me to live alone." He paused and looked me up and down, making a tsk, tsk click with his tongue.

"I like to watch the young ladies walk past the Café Le Roux in their short skirts, you know. Before my daughter insisted that I move in with her, I used to spy on them from my window. I could see the Café from it, and all the people that went in and out of it. But my daughter was angry with me. She said that my stares were impolite. She said that I was bothering the girls."

He clicked his tongue against his toothless gums again. "There's nothing wrong with looking at the legs of a pretty girl, is it not?" He rolled his eyes up to his forehead as if savoring old memories. "Would it not be sacrilege to stop admiring the ladies?" He chuckled in a raspy voice. "But my daughter, she is afraid that I will bring shame onto our family."

Monsieur Gretz turned to Nick. "Tell me, young man. Don't you agree that a pretty woman warms the blood that courses through a man's veins? It's the beauty of a woman that makes me want to go on living."

Nick nodded in agreement. "*Qui, Monsieur,*" he said. "You are correct."

I quickly punched his arm. "That's your reason for living, is it?"

Nick grinned good-naturedly and remained silent. Monsieur Gretz coughed, spat on the pavement, and stood up slowly. He groaned as he steadied himself on his walking stick. Then he hobbled over to me and took my arm.

"Come on then, pretty little Mademoiselle, I will show you where Gertrud lives. Pierre sold the shop a while ago, you know."

He turned to Nick who was inspecting one of the ancient houses across the way. "Follow us, young man," he called. "If I were you, I would keep my eyes glued on this pretty little lady here. Someone else might snatch her up." Nick was amused and joined us. We followed the old man. He soon stopped at a house whose windows displayed colorful flower boxes. A basket of lilies of the valley hung at the door and greeted us with a heavy fragrance. Our guide pounded with his stick on the door. "Gertrud," he shouted, "I brought you visitors from America."

A gray haired, plumpish woman came to the door. "Oui?" She inquired, surveying Nick and me with a puzzled look. "From America? I know no one in America."

"I'm from Germany," I quickly said.

"I know no one in Germany either, Mademoiselle." She shook her head, speaking in German now..

"Madam," I began. "Are you Gertrud Berger, I mean was that your last name before you were married?"

"*Ja?*" She remained puzzled. "I am Ariane. I am looking for my father, Rudi Berger."

Gertrud's jaw dropped open. She stared at me, unable to utter a word.

"My mother's name was Johanne." I added.

The old man had been listening to the conversation. He now exclaimed in French-accented German, "Ah, Ru-dee. He's your cousin, Gertrud."

He turned to me. " I remember Ru-dee well, Mademoiselle. He often visited me and brought me a few sausages from the butcher shop. But that was a long time ago. It was when I still lived across from the Café Le Roux."

Gertrud had found her voice. "You say that you are Rudi's daughter? It cannot be. I know that he only had one daughter. Her name was Adrianna and she is dead! I know of no Ariane.

I shook my head. "Adrianna used to be my birth name. It was changed. I am his daughter and I am alive. I have not seen my father since I was two years old. I, too, thought him to be dead."

Gertrud clasped her hands to her throat while Monsieur Gretz shouted. "Ru-dee has a daughter? What a rogue he turned out to be keeping it a secret all these years!"

Gertrud turned to her old neighbor and called, "*Merci*, Monsieur Gretz. You'd better be on your way back to your house before your daughter finds you missing. You know how upset she gets when you wander around the neighborhood. Thank you for bringing these young people to me. And tell Yvonne that I said hello."

Our guide looked disgruntled but waved his cane and limped off. Gertrud quickly asked us to come into her house. Nick declined, believing it to be best to leave me alone with her to sort out family business. He would go and explore the little village.

"Don't spend too much time in front of the Café Le Roux." I teasingly called after him.

He shook his head and laughed. "Are you jealous already?"

I protested, not wanting to give myself away. To my relief, he merely replied, "I will assume that it is a good sign."

Gertrud led me into her living room, which was stuffed full with ancient looking furniture. I sunk into a deep, comfortable chair, while she seated herself across from me. She took her time to examine the features of my face. Then she blinked a few times as if something was irritating her eyes. She quickly rose from the sofa. "I will put on a pot of coffee," she announced with a shaky voice and left the room.

While she was gone, I glanced around the living room whose walls were covered with old fashioned flowery wallpaper that had faded over the years. In a corner stood a tall grandfather clock. It ticked the minutes away. I nearly jumped when a deep gong arose from its belly. A second, third, and more followed in rich resonant echoes. I turned my eyes to a few photographs that were displayed on a fringed shawl of an upright piano. From where I sat, I could not make out the facial features of the people in the pictures. It would be a breech of social etiquette for me to get up and inspect them. Our customs prohibited us from taking a closer look at other people's personal possessions without being invited to do so. I shifted my weight impatiently in the chair, wondering what was keeping cousin Gertrud.

Finally, she returned and placed a cup of coffee and a buttery croissant before me. "Well, there's no denying it," she announced. "You are a spitting image of your father. I could see it immediately but refused to believe it. Sometimes it's easier to deny something than to accept it."

She walked over to the piano and returned with a photograph that showed a man and a woman. Their arms were interlocked. "This is your father," she announced. "The woman…well…you don't know her."

I gasped. I, too, could see that I was my father's daughter. "Please tell me where I can find him!"

"In good time. In good time," Gertrud responded in a thin vibrato. "I will tell you everything you want to know. But first, you must tell me why you have waited such a long time to look for him."

My words spilled out as I explained that our government had told my mother that my father was missing in action. I told her of my mother's death and how I had found Karl's letter.

Gertrud put a grievous face into her hands and sighed, "If only you had come earlier, dear child. I know that your father had kept you in his heart all those years."

"Is he well? Where is he? Does he live near here?"

Gertrud lowered her eyes. "I have bad news to give you, my child. Your father passed away six years ago."

My hope to be reunited with him snapped like dry kindling. Tears sprang into my eyes. Slowly they trickled down my cheeks. My mother had forfeited happiness by ignoring the letter. But so had I. Had either of us opened it much sooner, I might have found my father alive. One simple act, a decision put on hold, deprived me of him. I stared at the grandfather clock. Its pendulum swung back and forth. Tick…tock…

tick.. tock. Action, non-action. I suddenly understood that every action we perform, every decision we make produces a result. Even a non-action produces one. We make choices every day and decide what our future will look like. Unhappy thoughts passed through my mind until I realized that even though I might have found him sooner, our government might not have allowed me to leave the GDR and join him.

"I am very sorry for how life has turned out for you, dear child." Gertrud watched my sad face. "I know that it must not be easy for you to hear this when you had hoped to find him alive."

"What was my father like?" I asked.

Gertrud related that when he came to her right after the war, he had looked unwell. The fighting had been tough on him. His gentle soul had despised it. He also had missed his child, and her death had pained him. He had found work on a barge, the very one that he later bought from its owner. When he had finally witten to his father, the letter had come back unopened. There had been no forwarding address on it. He then wrote to an old business acquaintance, who replied that my grandfather had vanished after the government had confiscated his business. After that, my father decided to remain in France for good. Then, one day, he called on the woman whose little girl he had pulled from the canal.

"I remember the girl's name. It's Ariana, isn't it?" I interjected. "My father had wanted me to be named after her."

"Well, yes. You are correct. So you know the story?"

"Yes."

"Her mother, Nicole, became his common-law wife. He raised Ariana as his own daughter."

"He replaced me with another child!" I felt a sting in my heart.

Gertrud reached over and patted my hand. "My dear, you must remember that he didn't know that you were alive. But I know that he never replaced you in his heart with another. He just opened it wider and gave another little girl a place in it too."

More than an hour had passed before Nick returned. "Ah, the American is back," cousin Gertrud exclaimed. "Is he your fiance?"

"No," I shook my head in surprise. "We only met a short while ago in Berlin."

"Well. Perhaps he should be," Gertrud responded. "He is a polite young man, your American."

Nick's face was flushed from climbing the steep hill. "Did you find out where your father is?" He asked.

"No." I sadly related what Gertrud had told me.

"I am so sorry. Are you alright?" He put his arm around my shoulder. "I remember how painful it had been for me when I lost my mother. But losing your father twice must be doubly so."

I nodded and looked uncertainly at him. "Perhaps it's time to leave," I suggested.

Gertrud objected. She insisted that we stay and meet Pierre. "After all, we are family," she said. We need to get acquainted. Stay the night. Tomorrow, you can go and visit Nicole. She will be shocked to see you, but she is a very kind woman and will understand what has led you to her."

I was horrified. "Pay her a visit? I don't think I can do that."

"Why not?" Nick encouraged me. "Your cousin is right. The woman would understand. After all, you are your father's daughter and have a right to know what has happened to him."

Later that evening, all of us sat around the table and talked. Pierre retrieved a bottle of wine and told us about his experiences in the Underground. Gertrud had heard it all before and dozed off. But Nick and I listened with interest to accounts of courage and sacrifice. We talked long into the night, and it occurred to me how curious it was that all of us were sitting together in peace and harmony now when not so long ago a war had separated us all.

Chapter Thirty-Eight

The French Women

Even though the evening with the cousins had been enjoyable, I did not sleep much that night. My thoughts returned to my father's woman. Cousin Gertrud had called her his common-law wife. The anticipation of meeting her left me tense.

When Nick and I arrived in the ancient town of Colmar, we were stunned to find it so quaint and enchanting. We passed the quarters of the old tanners, butchers and fishmongers and came to the section known as "Little Venice." It is a settlement of charming patchwork houses that were built at the edge of the canals. Nick dropped me off in front of the address that Gertrud had given us. He would be back to pick me up later.

I nervously rang the doorbell. It gave off a melodic chime. In no time at all, a young woman opened the door. Her features were smooth and beautiful, and her long, dark hair was held back by a hair clip.

"*Oui* Mademoiselle?" She said, looking at me with soft, dark eyes that were contrasted by her creamy skin.

I lost my voice. She was lovely. I did not know whether she understood German. I stammered, "*Bon Jour, Guten Tag.*" Once again I became irritated with myself, wondering why did speech always failed me when I became emotional?

"Can I help you?" She repeated in German.

"Are you...uh...are you Fräulein Ariana?" I stuttered.

"Yes?" The young woman displayed the patience of an angel as she waited for me to continue.

"I am Ariane," I began. "Well, actually, my father intended me to have *your* name but my mother gave me the name of Adrianna before someone else changed it to Ariane."

I paused, wanting to kick myself in the shins. What was *wrong* with me? The girl must think me beyond help for sounding so unintelligible. To make things worse, the eyes of the angelic looking creature expressed confusion.

"Yes, Fräulein? You are telling me that you were given three names and that one of them was like my own? That is nice, but I do not understand your point."

"Oh, okay. Let me start at the beginning." I took a deep breath and steadied myself. "My name is Ariane Berger. Rudi Berger was my father." There. I had said it plainly and directly without stumbling.

If the young woman had been confused at first, she now looked shocked. Her mouth flew open. She exclaimed. "No. It is impossible! It cannot be! My father did not have any other children."

I moved from one foot to the other, feeling uncomfortable and embarrassed for having intruded. But quickly it came to me that she had said *my* father. I decided that I would allow her the beauty, but I would not allow her to claim my father as hers alone. A combative streak rose in me. I would hold my ground.

"Yes, I know. He was your father. But he was mine first before he came to France."

Ariana stared wordlessly at me.

"Please! May I speak to your mother?" I requested.

Ariana, at last, turned her head and called into the hallway, "*Maman, Maman*! You must come immediately! There's a young lady here who claims to be...Oh, *Maman*. Come quickly"

An older version of her came walking down the hallway. "May I help you, Mademoiselle? Do you have an emergency? Has something happened?"

I wanted to avoid further confusion and stated, "Cousin Gertrud gave me your address. I know that what I will say will come as a shock to you, Madame, but I am Rudi's daughter. You might have heard my father refer to me as Adrianna. I am no longer named that. My name is Ariane now. I am Ariane Berger."

Nicole stared at me as if she was seeing a ghost. "The daughter of Ru-dee Ber-yay?" She pronounced my father's name in unmistakable French. "But you cannot be...cannot be his child."

"May I come in and speak to you?" I asked since neither of the women seemed to be able to move.

"*Mais qui.*" Yes, of course." She moved aside and bade me entry.

As we walked down the hallway into the living room, my eyes fell on several framed pencil drawings on the wall. The living room displayed additional drawings and watercolor paintings. Nicole followed my glance.

"I am an artist. But some of them were painted by my husband." She pointed to several hanging on the wall.

She had called him her husband. Seeing my father's artwork reminded me that his talent had passed me by.

"Forgive me, Mademoiselle. Forgive me for appearing so ungracious. You must understand that I am shaken. Please tell me again who you really are and why you came here."

Nicole glanced at her daughter who had seated herself on the sofa. The young woman looked a shade paler than she had been when she had opened the door.

As gently as I could, I related how I had discovered Karl's letter and learned that my father had a cousin in France. Nicole remembered meeting Karl many years earlier. Still, I could see that she doubted my story. Only when I recounted the incident of how my father had saved her little girl did she nod her head.

"That is true," she agreed. Karl would remember it. She looked at me for a long while before she went on to say, "But Ru-dee told me that his wife and child died in the war. He carried a picture of himself and his child in his wallet."

I quickly deduced that my father had not found it necessary to tell her of my mother's relationship with Karl and his agreement with him.

"May I see the picture?" I asked.

"Yes. It is right here." She got up and retrieved a photo from a wooden box. It was a picture of me and my father.

"This is exactly how I remember him!" I exclaimed. "That is exactly what he looks like in my memory of him."

"So it is truly you? You are his daughter?"

She now seemed genuinely distressed and lifted her eyes toward the ceiling. She exclaimed, "*Mon Dieu*, what have we done! My God, what great sin have we committed!" She crossed herself.

She turned to me. "Please forgive me for having robbed you of what was rightfully yours!" The pupils of her eyes became wide and liquid. Then she asked haltingly, as though embarrassed, "And...and... your mother, Madame Ber-yay? Is she waiting for Ru-dee to return to her?"

"No. My mother died a few years ago. She actually did not want him to come back. She had waited for the return of Karl. Somehow, they missed each other and never saw each other again. He came to believe that she had died, and she never remarried. It was he who told my father that we were dead."

Nicole appeared relieved to hear that my mother had not pined for my father's return. She surveyed me with pity and apologized again.

By the time Nick rang the doorbell, both women had regained their composure. They set out refreshments and invited him to join us. As we were taking in refreshments, Nick asked questions that had eluded me. Before long, the women solicitously pulled out photo albums and told of their life with my father.

"Everyone liked Ru-dee," Nicole said. He was good to us. My daughter and I owe him so much. We miss him terribly. Because of his encouragement and support, Ariana was able to go to university and become a teacher. She works in Strasbourg. In fact, she only arrived home a few minutes before you came to our house."

I glanced once more at Ariana who was listening in silence. She, too, seemed to feel sorry for me now. She nodded and gave me a slight smile. I acknowledged it with my own and thought to myself that my father had ended up with a daughter who was smart and graceful. He must have been very proud of her. It was clear to me that she had adored him. I wondered whether he would have loved me as much as he had loved her.

Ariana seemed to have picked up my thoughts and said. "I am sure that our father would have been very proud of you had he met you."

She continued talking, calling up long forgotten memories of him. She laughed and cried as she spoke. She remembered the outings on the canals, the vacations they had taken together, and his help with her homework, and much more. Her mother nodded and smiled. I could see that the memory of him and being allowed to share it with me made them happy.

I felt emotional and quickly looked away. I picked up another photo of them. It showed a mother, a father and a child. It reflected what I once had wanted so badly for myself. I had wanted to be the child born and raised by the love of a mother and a father. But that was not how my life was to be. I tried to shake off thoughts of envy and self-pity and reminded myself of all the good things that had come my way. Had I not experienced the warmth of a family, myself, instead of having being left to live in a cold orphanage? And of late, there was Mr. Nordeen, who was taking care of me like a father would. Providence had blessed me after all.

I could see that my father had a good life with the women and that their love had healed him. He had died a happy man, and I needed to be grateful for that.

Just before leaving them, I told the women, "I am sad that I did not get to know him better, but thank you for loving him."

They nodded and gave me a sad smile. Neither of them knew how to set the past right. Neither of us understood the unpredictability of life or the turns that it gave us. My only consolation was that I believed in divine intervention. I *had* to believe in it to understand the events of my life and the reasons for them.

Nick and I decided to spend the night in Colmar. He took us to a small hotel and laid down to rest. while I went for a run along the canals. I needed to clear my head and regain balance of myself. Much had happened these past days. I ran until I felt empty of all self pity and resentment. I ran until all my questions left me and I was able to tell God that I trusted in His process. When I returned to the hotel I knew that I would leave Alsace feeling at peace.

The following day, Nick and I were off to Paris. We held hands as we strolled along the banks of the Seine, visited the *Arc de Triomphe* and came up on the Eiffel tower on the *Champ de Mars*. I looked up at the 324-meter structure and shuddered.

"Lift or stairs?" Nick asked.

"Neither," I responded, shaking my head. The climb up on the Norwegian ship was still fresh in my memory.

"It's a lifetime opportunity," Nick suggested. "You don't want to miss it."

I swallowed hard and stared at him. I had let go of my mother and father. Perhaps it was time to conquer my fear of heights as well. I still could not recall what was making me so afraid of heights. I took a deep breath. Praying that I would not faint when we reached the top of the Eiffel tower, I agreed to go up. "Okay," I said. But I'm not taking the lift."

"Well, then, are you up to climbing the three hundred steps to the first level, and another three hundred to the second one?" Nick asked.

I mutely nodded and closed my eyes to prepare myself for the hike to the top. Panting, we reached the first platform, where I moved to the back of the wall. I could not bring myself to step forward to view the city. When a man, wearing a light tan trench coat, pushed himself rudely between Nick and me, I suddenly felt nauseous and closed my eyes. Memories that I had blocked out flooded me. I remembered the afternoon that I had visited my uncle. The pictures reeled past my inner vision like a movie.

I was leaning back on a branch of a walnut tree, chattering away to Uncle Emil, who was sitting in a chair below the tree. I heard the entrance door to the property squeal. Because I was high enough up, I could spot two men in trench coats come walking up the long path to the cottage. They had apparently broken the lock at the gate.

"Uncle Emil," I called in a hushed voice. "I think the secret police is coming to get you. You must go quickly and hide."

"Don't move from where you are, little one," he replied. He rose to wait for the men at the house and added. "Be as quiet as you can and come down only after they have left."

I was unable see the entire cottage from where I was but could hear the men shout at him, "Where are you keeping them hidden?"

My uncle replied something in a calm voice. Whatever he said seemed to enrage the men. I heard a chair fall over. A commotion ensued, which was topped by shouts of obscenities. I became frightened for my uncle. To get a clearer view, I scooted farther out on the branch. It suddenly cracked and I let out a squeal. One of the men heard me and came to investigate. He discovered me in the tree. Not knowing what to do, I remained where I was.

"My, my. What do we have here. A young spy, are you?" The man called and ordered me to come down.

I froze and remained where I was.

"Get down from there immediately," he called.

I still did not move. He began to scream. "I will teach you what it means to disobey an agent of the government."

I grabbed a nearby branch and climbed higher. Soon, I had reached the top and had no other place to go. The man, having pulled off his coat, was right behind me now. He tried to grab me. I kicked his hand away. He cussed but was able to get hold of my ankle and pulled hard. I lost my grip on the tree and fell upside down. He let go. Everything seemed to happen fast from that point on. I crashed through the branches, one branch at a time. An instant later, my fall was broken on the lowest limb.

For a moment, I thought I was saved. But within seconds, I fell again. I hit the ground. I felt no pain; and even though dazed, I could think of nothing else but needing to get away from him. As swiftly as I could, I got on my feet and ran toward the gate. He quickly climbed down and ran after me. I was faster and small enough to escape through a hole in the fence. I ran across the dirt road to adjacent fields, where I hid among bushes. I lay terrified, holding my breath for fear of being discovered. I waited.

After what seemed an eternity, I saw the men come walking through the gate. One of them was carrying my uncle's typewriter. After they disappeared around the bend in the road, I ran back to the cottage. I yelled for my uncle. He stood with his back to me, examining a cut on his lip in the mirror. His face looked bruised.

"I was so scared. I thought they would kill you!" I shouted. "Why did they beat you up? Did you do something bad? Are you angry at me for running away?"

He responded, "No. You did the right thing to run. They might not have harmed you, though. Then he turned and shouted, "Little one! What has happened to you!"

I looked down at my legs and arms. For the first time I noticed the gashes on them. Blood was dripping from them to the ground, and my dress was ripped to shreds.

"Come here," he ordered, almost unable to speak because his lip was tripling in size. "Let's fix you up. Luckily, the scratches on your face are not too bad and will heal. But the rest of you is a big mess. I suppose I'll have to take you home to make sure that your mother doesn't lose her temper when she sees you so cut up."

Nothing else being on hand, he brought out a bottle of schnapps to clean my wounds. I howled with pain from the sting of it. When later I was all bandaged up and feeling better, I asked, "Why did they take your typewriter?"

"I think someone told them that I have forbidden books in my library," he responded. The men were looking for volumes of Karl May and *1984* by George Orwell."

"Did they find them?"

"No."

"What do books have to do with your typewriter?"

"Well, little one, there are people who copy forbidden books and circulate them among friends. The STASI took the typewriter to check my ribbon."

I looked anxiously at him, wanting to hear that he was innocent.

"Don't worry your head about it, little one," he soothed me. "Everything will be alright."

But he had been wrong. Soon we found that nothing was alright. I wondered whether he was frightened when he realized that the STASI would return.

Nick noticed my face. "Ariane?" He said. "Are you alright? You may as well come and look at the city since we've climbed up here." He reached out and put his arm around my shoulder.

"I need a minute." I responded. "I've just remembered something from my past."

"Something good I hope?"

"I'll tell you later." I responded. "It was sad, but it helped me see the reason for my fear of heights."

It took me a moment to shake off one more drama in my life. I was tired of recall. Would I ever be done with it? Still, I knew that the man in the trench coat, who had wedged himself between Nick and me, had done me a great service.

I took a deep breath and interlocked arms with Nick. "I think that I'm alright now. Really I am."

"If you are afraid, just hang on tight." He squeezed my arm.

I did. It was not because of fear that I hung on to Nick as we took in the magnificent 360 degree view of Paris. I hung on because I loved being being with him and feel his warmth and concern for me.

Before we left Paris, we visited the left bank of the Seine and the area where Picasso, Matisse, Jean-Paul Sartre and Ernest Hemingway had once made their homes. We spent hours in the *Musée de Louvre* with its magnificent works. We strolled on the *Champs-Elysées*, with its many boutiques and cafés, and took a dinner cruise on the river.

Sometime into our journey, I realized that I would not mind if Nick and I could stay together for the rest of our lives. We had found that, although we had grown up under different circumstances, we shared similar likes, values and ethics. However, I reminded myself not to hope for something that could never be. His home was a continent away from mine, and he would one day return to it. He had spoken of leaving the Army and, perhaps, become a partner in his father's law firm. I knew that I needed to finish my education and focus on the present instead of the future.

Our vacation ended too quickly, and we returned to Mainz. Nick climbed into his little blue VW and rolled down the window. "I promise to write" he said before he put the car in gear and sped off toward the Autobahn. I stood next to Andra and waived until I could no longer see him. I was sad that we had to part already and wondered whether I would ever see him again.

Chapter Thirty-Nine

1965-1966
A Miracle of Love

Nick was in my thoughts daily. Following our vacation in Paris, he invited me to fly over to West Berlin on several occasions and spend long weekends. It was easier for me to visit him than have him come to Sweden since he would have to go through military channels to obtain permission. We toured the city and took a cruise on the Wannsee, the beautiful, large lake in the southwestern part of the Berlin. We went swimming at the Wannsee Beach Complex, which is one of the favorite spots for West Berliners, and let our bodies bake in the sun. The long white beach had enough room for 50,000 visitors and was always crowded.

West Berlin, with its tree-lined streets, is beautiful and exciting. What I enjoyed the most was walking hand-in-hand with Nick through the 32-square kilometer Grunewald, the "green forest," where deer, peacocks, and the not so friendly wild boars made their home. It, too, is a favorite weekend escape for West Berliners. Perhaps it is the beauty of the city and the variety of entertainment and vacation spots available that allowed the citizens of West Berlin to endure their insular situation.

I loved being with Nick and soon became aware that he was taking up that place in my heart that I once had reserved for Wolfgang. Even though I had romantic feelings for my American, I held back in letting him see how much I cared for him. I feared that if we were to become too close,

I would not be able to handle our anticipated separation. Nick would one day return to America and would be lost to me forever. Consequently, I approached intimacy with caution. However, whenever I found myself back in Sweden, I could not stop wishing to be with him and shifted my university schedule around so that I would have time for subsequent visits. Soon, I realized that I had become wrapped up in a long distance relationship without knowing how and when it would end.

Perhaps Nick had no such worries. He loved his assignment and life in Berlin. To my surprised relief, before he was scheduled to rotate, he managed to extend his tour of duty for another year. He suggested that I transfer to the university of Berlin to be close to him. I felt conflicted. My heart wanted to be near him but my head warned against it. Transferring would not only jeopardize my entire program of study but would also break the trust that Mr. Nordeen had placed in me. It was because of him and his generosity that I was able to study in the first place. When I explained my dilemma to Nick, he said that he understood. He never mentioned it again. If I doubted that he felt about me as I did about him, I only needed to look into his eyes, feel his passionate kisses and his tender touch to know that he loved me. We were happy when we were together and missed each other when we were not.

Several months before his firm rotation date back to his homeland, my roommate Mia and I discussed my relationship with Nick. I expressed my fear of losing him.

"Why not start something up with Per, that boy from Dalarna, or with Arne? Both of them have asked you out repeatedly." Mia suggested. "They'll make you forget Nick."

"No, silly! No one can make me forget him!"

"Don't tell me that you are in love with him!" Mia was surprised. "And even if you are, there are others who are waiting to take his place." I knew that she considered it old fashioned to save herself for one special man. "In my opinion, you're taking a big chance with that American soldier. You can never be certain what he's doing when you are not with him. Why not drop him while it's easy to disentangle yourself? This kind of long-distance relationship can never last. Just remember what my boyfriend

Lars did to me after I came to Stockholm. He immediately began dating other girls back in Värmland."

I could never follow Mia's logic when it came to men. I was amused. "You were the first one to date others. You didn't just date one of them, but went out with every other boy who asked you! Lars feels betrayed. You've got more boyfriends than I can count on one hand. No matter what you say, I'll wait and see what will develop between Nick and me. I really feel that he is the one for me. It'll be difficult to find someone like him ever again. I have only one year left at the university. Perhaps we'll find a way to stay together."

"Foolish girl!" Mia chided me. "You should keep someone in reserve just in case Nick wants nothing to do with you any longer once he finds himself back in his own country. If you wait too long to date anyone else, you'll find yourself out of practice on how to catch a man."

I laughed again and I replied, "You know, I think I've learned my lesson with Wolfgang. I want a man to come after me. It would show me that he cares enough and wants me."

"Don't bet on it," Mia replied. "You are so naïve! Men are different from us. They like the excitement of the chase. They're like cavemen, ready to go for the kill with their spears. They like to conquer and are competitive. That's exactly why I will stay ahead of them. I will choose the one I want when I want him."

I knew that Mia had never entered into a serious relationship with any man. She had said that she loved Lars but had toyed with his affections. I wondered whether males were really more competitive than females and how it related to their self-esteem. Had that been the reason that Wolfgang had stayed with Katrina? Had he been afraid to admit defeat? Had he been wanting to reassert his self-esteem by trying to pull me back into his company? If that was the case, it did not say much for me. Aside from that relationship, I had encountered several unappealing peacocks in my life. All had wanted to impress and compete.

When it came to Nick, I did not find him to be such such a man. Had he not asked me to move to Berlin? I had held my ground and had rejected that idea. He had not changed afterward, had neither pressured me nor let go of his affection for me. But in the end, he had also not suggested marriage. I had wondered about that. According to Mia, I was the oddball among every other female she knew. She had said, "Ariane, what's wrong with you? You are saying that he's the one for you, but you won't go after him the way you should. Why are you so prudish and coy?"

Another winter had descended on us. Sessions at university had ended and Christmas was not far off. Olle had come to pick me up from campus to take me home. I sat quietly next to him as he chauffeured the car through the icy streets of Stockholm, which was bustling with holiday spirit. The markets were laden with sweets, reindeer sausages, elk meat and fine handicrafts. Everywhere I looked, shoppers braced against the swirls of snow and pulled their scarves tighter around their necks. Still, no one seemed to mind the cold. It was what it was. People were used to it. The usual ice and snow would not deter them from missing out on holiday bargains or enjoying the holidays.

It had been a long while since I had thought back on the sad days of my childhood Christmases. My new life in Sweden had made up for all of them. I knew that I would find the estate brightly lit and decorated. Britt and Bertil's crew would have polished every corner of the house, and Mr. Nordeen would greet me with a welcoming fatherly smile. As always, he would be happy to see me and behave as though I were his returning prodigal daughter. Our affection and appreciation for each other had grown strong. He had become the father that I had missed all of my life. He was generous and supportive of me. In fact, he gave me more than I thought I deserved.

Mia found it peculiar that I continued calling him "Mr. Nordeen."

"I can't call him Papa or father. And, calling him by his first name would be too disrespectful."

"Yes, but he takes care of you better than any father does."

"That's true." I agreed. "But he's never told me to call him anything else. In any case, we've stepped down a notch from observing ultra-strict formalities. I don't address him in the third person any more. I don't say, "Does Mr. Nordeen want to eat dinner?" I simply say, "Do you want to...

and so on." In any event, that kind of formal Swedish custom seemed silly to me from the very beginning. It's really a weird tradition and reminds me of the Middle Ages. I never understood why you are still making class distinctions and address a person of higher standing in the third person singular."

"I don't know either," Mia responded. "We're used to it. But we don't just address rich people in that way. We address anyone like that if we want to show respect for that person."

Thinking back at my conversation with Mia, I smiled and turned to Olle. "Do you remember when last year you suddenly began addressing me in the formal manner in which you speak to Mr. Nordeen? You said, 'Does Fröken Ariane want to take a trip to town?' That was so silly of you after we had known each other for a while. Why did you do that?

"Well, when he promoted you to be his secretary and you were no longer one of us, I didn't want Boss to get angry with me. I didn't want him to think that I failed to show respect for your accomplishments."

"What nonsense is that?" I answered. "I knew that I needed to continue my education if I wanted to stay in your country. I did not want to be a maid forever. In any case. I had no idea that Mr. Nordeen had his own plans for me and would promote me."

"I think Boss did it because he was impressed that you did not let adversity get you down. He likes it when someone shows courage."

"Hmm, I guess so."

"There's another reason that I became formal with you," Olle continued. "Boss told everyone that he had adopted you."

"He said that?" I was speechless. Then I remarked, "You can't adopt someone that is as old as I am. Not legally anyhow.. All of any of this does not change who I am inside of me."

"Yes, I know." Olle responded. "We are still friends, even though you told me in no uncertain way that I should stop talking to you like a stranger."

"You were foolish to do that in the first place." I leaned back into the leather seats of the new limousine. After a while, I picked up the conversation. "So, tell me everything that has happened at the estate since I've left."

Olle was happy to oblige. He informed me that Britt had finally given birth to her long awaited child and that Sven, the gardener, found himself confined in his home and nursing a pulled muscle in his back. All responsibility for upkeep of the grounds had gone to Sture, a new fellow who had been made assistant gardener. He was a young man who, before coming to the estate, had gotten himself in trouble with the law. Someone at a church had contacted Mr. Nordeen and had asked whether he could offer Sture a job. My benefactor had given him another chance to prove himself. As far as I knew, Sture had kept out of trouble.

Olle paused before continuing his report with a hint of scorn in his voice. "Sture slipped up again. He was supposed to take care of the garden, but..."

"What happened?" I quickly interrupted him.

"Before I tell you about him, I need to tell you something about Inga."

"What is it?"

Inga was the housemaid who had taken my place after I had moved into the dorm on campus. I had been happy when Mr. Nordeen had assigned her a room downstairs instead of giving her my quarters upstairs. He had promised that they would remain my own for as long as I wanted them.

"Boss noticed that Inga was becoming increasingly absentminded. She messed up on more than one occasion. Britt spoke to her about her work performance. Apparently, Inga paid no attention. Her last mistake was when she served Boss a cut of chateaubriand that was meant for a guest who was staying at the house. You know that Boss does not eat meat. He told me that even the smell of it makes him ill. In any case, Inga gave the guest the dish of cod in cream sauce, which was supposed to be Boss's dinner."

"Well, then. All she needed to do was fix Mr. Nordeen another fish dinner."

"The thing was that she didn't realize that she had made a mistake, and boss ended up with the meat."

"How could that have happened?" In my mind's eye, I could see the expression in Mr. Nordeen's face when he found a chunk of meat on his fork.

"Boss had called, advising Inga that he would be delayed in the office and that she should offer the guest a dinner tray. Somehow, she mixed up the fish with the meat because she previously had covered both with a generous layer of heavy cream sauce. Her mind must have been occupied with something else that day. Bertil told me that she had behaved strangely the whole day. The worst was that she had had left Boss's dish in the oven to keep warm but that she had forgotten to turn down the temperature. When Boss later returned home, he could not find her anywhere. He went to the kitchen, took the dish out of the oven and sat down to eat. When he scooped away the crusted over sauce, he found a piece of crisp tenderloin staring back at him. He immediately rose from the table and rang me at home. He asked whether I would drive to the nearest restaurant to fetch him a vegetable meal."

The report was not funny. Still, I laughed. The scene was too humorous. In my mind, I could see the guest picking away at the cod because he hated fish, while Mr. Nordeen was trying not to vomit wen he saw a cremated portion of a dead cow peeking out from underneath the sauce.

"I'm sorry for laughing," I told Olle. "I know that it isn't funny."

"I thought it was funny myself, Ariane. But I kept a straight face when Boss reported what had happened. Britt told us later that she was amazed that he didn't scold Inga or terminate her employment. But he did tell Britt to have another talk with her. But when Inga discovered the overcooked meat in the garbage can the next morning, she became so unnerved that she dissolved into tears. She immediately ran to her room, and no coaxing could get her to open the door."

Olle took a long breath. "The next morning, when no breakfast was laid out on the table, Boss sent Britt to check on her. She discovered that Inga was gone. She had taken all of her things with her. You could see her footprints in the snow. They went all the way from the backdoor up the driveway and stopped at the street. She must have hitched a ride from there."

"I suppose I will have to look after Mr. Nordeen while I'm at home," I remarked. "But tell me, what does all of that have to do with Sture?"

"By the way, you don't need to take care of Boss, Ariane. Someone else is doing that already." Olle responded. "But about the connection to Sture. Well, I couldn't help myself but to investigate what might have caused Inga to behave so foolishly. She had an easy job, and Mr. Nordeen was good to her. I soon found out that she had become pregnant with Sture's child. Bertil told me that he suspected that he and Inga had used the greenhouse for their clandestine affair. He remembers hearing them argue over the subject of a baby. It must have been around the time when the chateaubriand was getting crispier by the minute in the kitchen oven. Sture yelled that he never wanted to see her again and broke off their relationship. Bertil said that he heard that Sture also refused to claim the child as his own."

"Wow!" I said. "What will Inga do now?"

"She'll raise the baby as a single mother, just as many other girls are doing in Sweden nowadays. No one will criticize her. It's common here to have a child without being married."

Olle paused for a moment before changing the subject. "Ariane, there's something about Boss that I don't understand."

"You know that he is kind to everyone," I quickly explained.

"No, it's not that. I am wondering why he doe not eat meat. Is it because of his religion or because cows are sacred in India? I've never dared to ask him about it."

"You should ask him," I encouraged him. "It will enlighten you. It's not a religious thing. He won't eat meat because of his spiritual awakening."

"Oh," Olle responded. "I don't know what that is. I only know that Boss is different from anyone else I know."

"Definitely," I replied.

We remained quiet for a while. Soon, Olle commented,. "There's something else I need to tell you. Prepare yourself to meet the new help. She is very efficient but a bit gruff."

"There's a new person at the estate?" Mr. Nordeen had not told me any of this on the phone.

"Yes. Her name is Hulda. She's the new the housekeeper and most efficient. No one can keep up with her."

"Well, at least there is someone dependable in the house who will take care of Mr. Nordeen," I stated. "Now I don't need to worry about him any longer."

Olle pulled his lips into the usual wide grin. He looked over at me. I could see how his lips formed a puckering pouch under the tip of his nose. My friend Gunilla had once remarked that our chauffeur has the fullest and softest lips she had ever seen on anyone. "I bet that he is a good kisser," she had stated.

Her comment had taken me by surprise. "Gunilla!" I had responded. "It is unlike you to say something like this. Are you sweet on him?" I had meant to ask Olle about her, but it had slipped my mind.

Olle continued, "I have never seen Boss flustered until Hulda took over. She makes a big fuss over him. He told me that he hates that she hovers over him like a mother hen. The moment he comes home from the office, she tells him to sit down. Then she removes his shoes for him and massages his feet. I heard Boss tell her that he is a grown man and can take care of himself. But she simply waves him off."

"Isn't that what a wife would do for her husband?" I was a bit put off. Olle's report disturbed me. How could it be that the new housekeeper was taking such inappropriate liberties with him?

"No, not like a wife. Like a grandmother." Olle responded. "Hulda is too old for him."

I felt relieved and curious to see how Mr. Nordeen was adjusting to a resolute woman that had taken over the reins of his household. Had she moved into my rooms?

"Don't worry," Olle broke into my thoughts, "Boss has not allowed her to occupy your rooms upstairs. She lives in the little cottage by the pines."

I ran into the house as soon as we arrived at the estate and found Mr. Nordeen in his library. He returned my happy smile. "Ah, Ariane, there

you are. You've finally come home!" Then, without the usual garnishes
and trimmings of polite inquiries into my educational and social life on
campus, he announced, "I have a surprise for you."

"Oh? What kind of surprise?" I became worried. What other changes
had taken place in my absence that Olle had forgotten to tell me about?

"Your friend is flying in from Germany tomorrow."

"Andra? That is wonderful! I've missed her. She's finally decided to
come for a visit." I was relieved to hear good news.

"No, it's not Andra. It is your friend in Berlin. I have invited him to
spend the holidays with us."

"You mean Nick?" My mouth dropped open.

Mr. Nordeen noted my astonished face. "Yes. He is finally coming
for a visit, even if Hulda almost managed to prevent it. The poor fellow
encountered a few communications problems when he called for you and
Hulda answered the phone. She knew that the upstairs rooms were being
kept for a young lady, but she did not know that her name is Ariane. I
had just come home when I heard her yell into the phone, "No Ariane.
No speak English and no German." Then she shouted our office phone
number into the receiver, repeated it a second time, and resolutely hung
up before I could take the phone from her.

"Some foreigner," she announced. "He does not speak Swedish. I gave
him the phone number to your office."

I could see that Mr. Nordeen was still amused by the telephone
conversation. He added, "I wonder how difficult it will be to give Hulda
lessons in telephone etiquette. She seems to be deficient in that one area.
Other than that, she is a good housekeeper."

"How do you know that Nick is coming? Did he call your office and
speak to you?" I was excited, could barely wait for his arrival.

Mr. Nordeen saw my excitement and kept smiling. He seemed to enjoy
torturing me with his silence.

"Why is Nick coming without telling me he is coming?" I pushed to
know. "I mean, I want him to come. I'm happy about it. But he had told
me that he would not be able to get another leave before spring."

"Well then. Let me tell you what happened next. "Nick was quick-witted enough to phonetically write down the numbers that Hulda shouted into the receiver. He called the Swedish embassy and asked the operator to translate the numbers into Swedish. When he reached me at my office, he stated that he had become worried about you because he had been unable to reach you in your dorm this past week. Finally, Mia answered the phone. She told him that you were out on a date with Per at the moment. Nick followed up with a call to the house here and reached Hulda. When she told him, "No Ariane," he feared the worst. When he later reached me, the poor fellow sounded so upset that I had to take pity on him. I told him to fly over to celebrate Santa Lucia with us and stay as long as he could."

My heart was beating fast. There had been times when I had felt exceedingly lonely for Nick and had longed to feel his arms around me. Perhaps he had realized that he was as lonely for me as well. As for the the so-called date with Per, it had been innocent. In fact, we had not gone out on a date at all. Mia and I had been sitting in a café when Per walked in. He had joined us. Mia quickly excused herself and left. After finishing our coffees, Per and I had gone to the bookstore and had browsed through some books. That had been all.

Mr. Nordeen observed my flushed face and said, "I hope your Nick proves to be everything you say he is. You know that I will scrutinize him closely to make sure that he is worthy of you."

"Please don't give him a terribly hard time," I begged. "Don't investigate him as you do your business associates. Please don't do it, even though *he* initially had wanted his army to clear me."

"As you wish." Mr. Nordeen's face spread into a wide grin. "Don't worry. I'm just trying to be a bit of a scoundrel and have fun with you. I won't interfere because I will let your heart have the last word. That is, of course, if I agree with your choice."

I quickly studied him. Was he joking or would he really meddle? When I noticed the new glint of humor in his eye, I took a step closer and affectionately ruffled his hair. "You are just trying to give me a hard time, Erik Nordeen." I said. "Stop it already."

"Just trying to hold on to you bit longer, my girl" Mr. Nordeen responded.

The next hour found me rummaging through my large wardrobe to find something suitable to wear for Nick's visit. For a fleeting moment, I remembered how simple it had been in the old days when my *Schrank* had been near empty. It had been all too easy to get used to abundance. The days of lack, the hand-me-down coats and dresses, and the shoes that had caused my heels to bleed in the winter frost, were of the past. Would Tanya be envious of my fine fashionable attire? I thought back to the days when Dagmar and I had spent hours at a time sewing a suitable gown for her, one that she could wear on stage.

Tante Helga had recently sent new family pictures. Things seemed to have changed in the GDR. She and her children looked fairly well-dressed and nourished. I had studied the photographs. Tante Helga's hair now showed a glint of gray, while Dagmar looked like a beautiful flower in bloom. Her skin had remained fresh and flawless. Her golden hair had been swept up in the way of her mother's. I was surprised, however, when I looked at the photo of Wolfgang. His face was without a smile. The softness in his eyes that I had loved so much also was absent. His expression was devoid of even the slightest hint of the endearing charm that once had been his trademark. He almost appeared stern. I felt a sting in my heart and wondered what had brought about these changes in him. I felt sad because he seemed to have lost his most glorious assets.

Wolfgang had only occasionally been in my thoughts these past couple of years. Thoughts of him had been replaced by my desire for Nick, which had taken up all the empty spaces in my mind and heart.

Nick arrived, and when Mr. Nordeen finally met him, he seemed to be impressed with "my American." As we sat around the dinner table, their conversation ventured from mundane subjects to issues of politics and world affairs. They began to debate the built up of American troops in Southeast Asia and the role of Geneal Westmoreland in South Vietnam. We all knew that the situation there had triggered a difference of opinions in Europe and in America. I sat listening for a while. As much as I had wanted to be alone with Nick, I let the men talk. Finally I rose from the dinner table, leaving them to their analysis of a conflict that America called a war but which had not been declared as such and which was without clear zones of combat. I was worried for Nick. News broadcasts had reported that plane loads of American soldiers departed for Vietnam daily. I hoped that Nick would be spared such fate and never would have to lay eyes on one single Viet Cong..

I decided to step outside and let the fresh air blow the cobwebs of worry out of my head. I bundled up in a parka, put on mittens and a hat before I pulled on my fur lined boots in preparation for a walk under the stars. Once outside, I looked up at the sky that recently had been swept clean by a strong wind. The stars in the endless firmament above sparkled like polished crystals and were intensified by the crisp night air. I walked along the driveway towards the pine forest. The frozen snow crunched under my feet. In the moonlight, I could see the ghostlike vapors of my breath rise up in the frigid air.

Soon, I came to Hulda's cottage. It lay dark in the late evening. She was an early riser and appeared to have gone to bed already. I continued to a clearing where in the summer I had spread out a blanket and had listened to the chirping of the birds. The silence that surrounded me now became suddenly broken by the sound of a motor. A few moments later, it stopped running. Curious to see who it was that was lost on the estate so late in the evening, I picked up my pace. It was not long before I discovered Olle's private Saab parked among the trees. It was rocking from side to side. Fearing that he might have car trouble, I knocked on one of the fogged up windows. Without fail, I heard a muffled female voice call out, "Oh, dear. I hope it is not your boss."

Soon, the rear window came down. Olle's face appeared. He looked disheveled and was bare-chested.

"Have you totally gone mad?" I exclaimed. "What are you doing out here in your car? It's freezing outside! Has someone stolen your clothes?"

Olle sheepishly stared back at me. Within seconds I realized what he had been up to. How could I be so dense! A familiar head popped up from underneath him. "Gunilla?" I cried. "I didn't know that…well. Never mind. Sorry! I was afraid that Olle's car had become stuck in the snow." Once again I felt silly and naïve.

Gunilla searched for her sweater and quickly pulled it over her head. "How did you find us, Ariane?" She muttered a bit embarrassed. "I'm freezing, Olle!" She complained now. "I want to go home. I should have never let you talk me into this."

"She's right, Olle." I supported her. "Couldn't you think of a more romantic place than this one? The Lincoln would have been so much more comfortable. You can't even fit six salmons in a waxed box into your car."

Olle responded somewhat surprised. "The Lincoln? Boss would fire me."

"I know. He would expect more of you than seduce a girl in these primitive conditions. Gunilla should have scolded you for being so unromantic."

I wondered how Olle had managed to talk Gunilla into being out with him in such freezing cold. I figured that she must really be crazy about him. I remembered her remark about Olle's full lips. Then I remembered the adage people used. "Still waters…" I felt betrayed by her. She was my friend but kept her affair a secret from me. I loathed secrets but knew where that feeling was coming from. My mother's memory tore at me once again.

"Why don't you come up to the house where you can warm up? I'll make some glögg."

Gunilla immediately agreed while Olle stalled. "Boss might not be pleased if he discovers me in his house so late."

"Don't worry," I assured him, "You'll be my guest. It'll be alright with him."

I scooted into the car and sat next to Gunilla. "Are you sure that you can handle a relationship with him?" I whispered, wanting to tease her. Gunilla was a professed Christian, and had told me that she was going to save herself for marriage. Her change of mind came as a surprise, but I had long since realized that good intentions often remained just that.

"Don't let Olle break your heart," I suggested. "He's a wild man."

"I'm good for her, and she knows it." Olle had heard me. "She needs someone to put fire under her behind. It will loosen her up and not take everything so seriously."

"Perhaps," I replied. "Perhaps you're good for her."

"Don't discuss me as though I'm not here. I can take care of myself," Gunilla objected.

"Well, I don't know whether it is good to become stuck on the first person that comes your way.," I remarked. "Even though it *is* my friend Olle. I just hope that he wants more than to have his fun with you."

"Look who's talking, Ariane," Olle commented. "You have a boyfriend who cannot make up his mind about you."

I shrank back. Olle was correct. I needed to shut my mouth. Why did I want to save others from themselves when the future of my own relationship with Nick was still undecided? I needed to let Gunilla make her own choices. After all, a bit of heartache was good for anyone's soul. It had taught me much about life and about the strength and weaknesses of other human beings.

Back at the house, we found Nick alone in the library.

"Look who I have dragged in from the cold," I announced. "If I hadn't rescued them, they might have become eternalized in a lover's knot."

"Is that so?" Nick was amused. "Back home in California, the weather is more conducive to passionate romances."

"I envy you!" Olle remarked, wanting to know more about Nick's home state. "Perhaps I'll pay you a visit one of these days." He beamed in anticipation.

"Nick nodded. "Ariane's friends are welcome any time."

"Should I bring her along when I come?" Olle inquired, being only half serious.

"No," Nick responded. "I have made other plans."

I stared at him. Unable to hide my shock, I quickly excused myself and went into the kitchen. I needed to process what I had just heard. Gunilla followed me. "I suppose that you need to keep your advise to yourself from now on," she suggested. "Apparently, Nick does not feel about you as you do about him."

"Perhaps not." I busied myself with arranging crackers and lox on a plate.

"I suppose we can't expect much from any guy," Gunilla continued. "Perhaps you are right about Olle, too. I've thought about it. He's too crazy for me."

"That he is," I confirmed. "But perhaps you should go for the experience of it and have fun."

I was still trying to process what Nick might have meant by his remark. How could I have been so wrong about him? I finally told myself that both Gunilla and I had misinterpreted what he had said to Olle.

Soon the two men came searching for us. To my surprise, Gunilla began latching on to Nick , instructing him in the art of making glögg. She smiled and flirted with him until Olle looked at me with furrowed forehead. He was obviously upset. I was peeved at her, too, and felt jealous. What kind of a friend was she? I decided that if my relationship with Nick would end the moment he returned to the United States, I would now make the best of it and enjoy his company as long as he was with me. I would enjoy it, even though parting from him would hurt.

Nick noticed the expression on my face. He walked over to me and put his arm around my shoulder. "Are you alright honey?" He asked.

His tenderness and attention confused me. If he did not want me or want me to visit him in the United States, then why was he behaving in such an affectionate manner now? I kept my feelings to myself, put on a fake smile, and nodded. "Yes. I'm alright. Why do you ask?

"You seem upset," he remarked. I, of course, denied his observation.

With snacks and hot spiced wine in hand, we adjoined to another room. Olle pulled Gunilla next to him and entertained us with his usual tales and jokes. I snuggled close to Nick, aware that I felt separation anxiety as I translated everything to Nick into German. My English was still not fluent enough to keep the conversation flowing in Nick's native tongue. Soon the glögg took effect and made me drowsy. When the hour had passed 2 a.m., I begged to continue the conversation at another time.

I awoke to the delicious aroma of fresh ginger snaps and cinnamon rolls that drifted up to the second floor through the heating vents. More preparations for Santa Lucia were apparently in progress. It was a festive day, which all of Sweden celebrated with reverence. As in previous years, Mr. Nordeen would open up the doors of the estate and host the people in the community. Contrary to other years, the affair would not be catered because Hulda had taken over all of the arrangement. One could hear the clatter of bowls, whisks, and baking pans come from the kitchen. No one was allowed to enter her domain without authorization. She took her office as housekeeper and event planner seriously. She had even brought in her own handpicked crew of friends to help her bake. Much to her protests, I sneaked past her into the kitchen and saw the many Santa Lucia saffron buns, the *lussekatter*, which had been spread out on cooling racks. The buns resembled curled up cats with with raisin studded eyes. I suspected that the immense supply of cookies, rolls, and cakes, which Hulda's crew was baking, would last us through Christmas and into the next year.

As the afternoon hour advanced, the atmosphere in the kitchen became increasingly frenzied. People would soon arrive. Hulda became worried that she would not finish in time and asked Nick and me to help carry trays with baked goods and other delicacies into the salon. We placed them between the artistically laid out garnishes of lingonberry leaves and pine twigs. Hulda hoped that the display of this cornucopia would testify to her expertise. But more than that, she had been working hard to support her employer's reputation as a humanitarian and philanthropist.

Gunilla, who had arrived with Olle in tow, or vice versa, glared at Hulda and turned to us. She commented that perhaps Hulda was trying so hard because she wanted everyone to notice the halo that encircled the head of her boss. I was offended by the comment and snipped at

Gunilla, saying that Mr. Nordeen's deeds needed no advertisement but that everyone knew that he was deserving of such celestial conferment. Gunilla could not resist but countered in a matter-of-fact tone that no person on earth, except Jesus, of course, had been seen sporting a halo. Someone should assure Hulda that the only light that would be visible around Mr. Nordeen would be the reflection of the sea of candle flames in the room. I stared at her, wondering what had gotten into her. Why was she being so sarcastic? In any event, she was only partially correct. Perhaps she had never seen or felt the rays of light that emanated from truly good people.

By 3 p.m., the whole house had become scented with the warm aroma of cinnamon, cardamom and cloves. Soon, male and female guests arrived. All were dressed in white, singing the Santa Lucia song. The females wore crowns of candles in their hair., which they had decorated with lingonberry leaves. The males wore pointed, star studded hats. The guests stood around the tables, enjoying the delicacies that Hulda and her baking crew had prepared. The entire estate buzzed with conversation and song until a voice called for silence. It was time for the ceremonial lighting. Mr. Nordeen took his place as the master of ceremonies. He struck a long match to light the sea of candles, which flickered through the halls, and offered gratitude to the light for its return after the darkest day of the year.

Gunilla had moved close to Nick and explained to him in halting school English the origin of Santa Lucia. I watched them, letting her struggle with the foreign language. Nick listened to her with patience even though he already knew the story behind the festival. Gunilla became finally stuck and enlisted the help of other women.

"Saint Lucia was an Italian Saint who gave her dowry to the poor," one woman explained. "Other countries tell it a bit differently, but our folklore suggests that she became a Christian martyr who was burned at the stake. To everyone's amazement, the fire did not consume her body. Instead, it shone with brilliant light. For that reason, she became known as the patron saint of light."

"How is it that brave Lucy, who was supposed to be a Catholic, became adopted by Protestant Sweden?" Nick probed.

A second woman quickly informed him, "We are told that on the darkest day of the year during the Middle Ages she appeared to farmers at Lake Vännaren in Värmland when Sweden was experiencing a great famine. The farmers were frightened when they saw her, but when Saint Lucia offered them food, they lost their fear. We remember her every year because of her generosity."

After the last guest had left, Nick and I curled up before the fireplace. It was good to finally be alone with each other after the onslaught of people. Once again, he put his arms around me affectionately and covered me with a few kisses. "I am glad I came," he murmured. "Seeing you in these surroundings and observing how easily you fit into them is interesting." He looked intensely at me. "But tell me, did something happen that I should know? Ever since last night you seem so preoccupied and distant."

"I'm just sad that your time in Germany will soon come to an end," I replied.

"Yes, that is the reason why I flew over here," Nick stated. "I had planned on coming even before Mr. Nordeen suggested it. There's something that I want to ask you, something that I have been thinking about for a long while now." He pulled out a small velvet box from his coat pocket and handed it to me. "Here. Open it and tell me what you think."

I opened the lid and caught my breath. A diamond ring sparkled back at me. The fiery large center stone was surrounded by a concentric band of smaller stones. It looked old, almost antique.

"For me?" I gasped. I knew that my face had lit up like a thousand candles.

"My father gave it to my mother on their engagement. I asked him to send it to me. I've had it locked up in a safe in Berlin for a while now. I had wanted to give it to you several months ago. But knowing how important it was for you to finish your degree and not knowing how you would respond if I would give it to you then, I held off."

In an unexpected move, he slipped off the sofa and got on his knee. "Ariane, I fell for you when you stood at the gate of our Berlin Brigade. You looked so vulnerable and unpretentious. That was before you pushed that package into my hands and your eyes spit firecrackers at me. It amused me. I immediately felt a great attraction for you. It soon turned into love. Ariane, sweetheart, will you marry me?"

His proposal came so unexpected that it took away my speech. "But I thought...I thought you had made other plans," I sputtered. "I heard you say it to Olle last night."

Nick laughed. "Ah! That is what had you so upset. I merely meant that he did not need to bring you along because you would already be with me."

I fell into Nick's arms. "Yes," I simply said. "Yes, I'll marry you." At that moment, I felt happier than I had ever been. What I had wished for so long had come to pass. Life had finally given me the one perfect moment that I had longed for since I had laid eyes on him in West Berlin.

When Nick began speaking again, my feeling of complete happiness received a harsh blow. He cleared his throat. "There is something else that I need to tell you, sweetheart. I received orders for Vietnam. But before I am shipped out, I will have to go through Ranger training in the States. Will you wait for me until I return from war?

I tore myself from his embrace. Sickness rose from the pit of my stomach into my heart. Oh no! Anything but that! He couldn't go! I couldn't let him go. Not to war! I did not want to lose him. I hated the insanity of war that never seemed to find an end. Pictures of leech infested rice paddies flashed in quick succession through my mind. They were followed by ambushes and booby traps, rocket attacks and atrocities that I had seen on television. Involuntarily I began to cry. What would happen if he would not make it back alive? But if he were to make it through the horror of combat, would he return as he had left? Would he return with his sanity intact? Would it have changed him? Would it have made him lose his gentleness, his goodness, his sense of humor? Would he still love me?

I thought back to the comment that Karl had made to me in his letter when he had told me about my father. My father had suffered deep in his soul because of the inhumanity he had seen and that he had been made to participate in. Had it not been for the love and patience of a woman and her child, he might have remained cynical and hard afterward. The affection his new family had given him had nurtured him and had allowed him to feel tender emotions again. I was not only afraid for Nick but also for myself. How long did it take for a man to regain what he had lost? Would his soul become shattered, would he lose it after realizing that he had killed another human being?

"Sweetheart, I am required to go." Nick wiped away my tears. "Those are my new orders. I cannot refuse them. Don't ask me to be a deserter. I promise that I will make it back alive. And, please don't think that I am asking you to marry me because I am leaving. I had been prepared to make you my wife a long time ago. I want to take you back to the States. It was difficult not to be selfish but to consider your dreams. Being in Vietnam will be so much easier to endure if I know that you are waiting for my return."

I tried to get hold of myself. I needed to set aside the anxiety and conflict that I was feeling. Would kind Providence bring us back together again? If not, how could I possibly bear losing one more person that I loved? Why was God making life so hard? Soon I chastised myself for blaming God when I knew that it were humans who were bringing disaster on themselves. I knew that as long as the quest for power continued and people lacked love and understanding for one another, peace would remain absent.

Nick held me all night with tenderness. I realized that my gloom would make his departure so much more difficult for him and decided to remember having trust in Providence.

Mr. Nordeen, too, encouraged me to refrain from entertaining thoughts of anticipated loss. "Don't create something in your mind that has not been ordained," he counseled me. "Do you recall the conversations we had with each other about faith? You must place your trust in the Source. You must continue to practice what I have tried to instill in you. Remember that it takes only one moment of pure and absolute faith to plant the seed of desire and bring it into manifestation. Don't allow a negative thought or feeling to sabotage your wish."

I nodded. I did recall the day that we had stood by the Långe Jan on Öland. Following our trip, we had engaged in many conversations about trust and faith and how to manifest our desires. Mr. Nordeen had always set the example for me. He not only knew the secret to success but practiced it every day. He ruled a small business empire without being tyrannical or getting caught up in pride, ego, or defeat. Moreover, had my Uncle Emil not told me, too, that I should expect miracles in my life?

Nick and I celebrated our engagement in the company of friends. Olle beamed at me. "It was high time that Nick showed his face to us here. I thought that your boyfriend was merely a phantom in your imagination. I think that you've done well. Gunilla and I will come to visit you in America."

Olle turned to her. "How about it. Do you want to come along?"

Gunilla shrugged her shoulders and coolly replied, "I'm not interested."

Olle grinned. "She's just saying that." He pinched her backside. "I know that she'll miss you."

I looked from Gunilla to Olle and back to her again. My friend's face revealed nothing but nonchalance. I was once again mystified by her. The show of lack of emotions bothered me.

"You will invite us to the wedding of course," Olle suggested.

I shook my head and explained that we decided to wait another year. "Nick has orders for Vietnam." I said.

Gunilla gaped at me. "First he's waiting so long to propose, and then he's leaving you right afterward. Why did you accept his proposal for marriage when he you know that he might not come back alive?" So many soldiers have fallen already.

Olle pinched her on the cheek and commented, "I think Ariane did the right thing. If something will happen to Nick, at least he will die happy. Didn't you notice how he looks at her? I'm convinced that he loves her. Perhaps we need to talk some sense into him and make him stay here."

Olle immediately went in search of Nick. "Don't be stupid, man," he told him, "Think it over. Don't go!"

The other guests heard him and gathered around them. "Yes, Nick, Olle is right. Don't join that senseless fight. Stay with us in Sweden. Our countrymen don't believe in war. Especially not in the one America is fighting."

But hard as they tried, Nick would not be swayed. He would be loyal to his country. He was proud to call himself an American and convinced that he was doing the right thing by standing up for freedom.

Even though I felt conflicted about this war, I knew that I needed to support him. I knew what the zealotry of Communism could do to people. Our country had remained divided because of it. Nevertheless, I was against going to look for war when another country did not threaten one's own country. I remained undecided over the political correctness of the situation and wished that Nick were able to resign his commission. That, of course, he would not or could not do.

When the clock struck midnight to take us into another new year, I put one arm around Nick and lifted my champagne glass with the other. I turned to everyone in the room. "Let's drink to freedom and to peace. But above all, let's toast to love and other miracles."

I raised my face to Nick, who looked as happy as I felt. Nevertheless, each of us knew that the year and some months that lay before us would be a difficult one. We needed to trust that all would be well in the end.

I previously had told Hulda about my country's New Year's Eve custom, and she had baked doughnuts for us. She had given them a filling of cloudberry jam. I reached for one now and teasingly said another toast to the benevolent spirits, which Frau Fröhlich had claimed were all around us. "Here's to you," I said.

Nick nodded. "And to you my love."

"*Danke, Liebling,* but that toast wasn't really meant for us," I smiled. "I offered it in memory of a talented bunch of courageous people who did the right thing and followed their hearts."

I bit into the *Berliner Pfannkuchen,* savoring the intense flavor and honeyed sweetness of the cloudberry filling. I remembered how at the end of last summer I had traveled with friends to the marshlands of the northern regions. We had returned with buckets of the much coveted *Hjortron* berries.

Cloudberries grow in the Arctic cold, and many of them perish before they have a chance to ripen. However, if they become sufficiently rooted in the ground and receive the proper nourishment, they are able to withstand below-zero temperatures. Then, when the sun rises over the Arctic circle and spreads its nurturing rays around them, the berries grow to be plump and sweet. In the height of their season, they burst with life-enhancing nutrients, while their leaves boast medicinal properties.

Cloudberries remind me of myself. I had been born into inhospitable surroundings and had struggled to survive the cold chill of my early youth. But then a miracle happened. Others reached out to me in love and warmed me with their kindness. Perhaps it was Providence that had sent them my way. I only know that their nurturing and humanity kept me alive.

Epilogue

I would not be truthful if I denied that the many months following Nick's departure for Southeast Asia were free of anxiety. The Vietnam conflict was rapidly escalating. In his letters, he rarely spoke of the oppressive heat or the rains. He did not refer to jungle rot, bamboo traps, or ambushes. From the media I learned about offensives, sandbagged bunkers and exploding mines. Nick never mentioned any of it. He also kept quiet about the loss of life and the cruelty that was part of daily life over there. He did not need to tell me that fighting in Vietnam was difficult and that he did the job he was required to do. He even got promoted.

I held my breath whenever his letters remained absent. Not knowing whether he was dead or alive was the hardest to bear. I worried that since we were not married, no one would tell me whether he was lying in one of the body bags or was on his way back to the USA in one of the flag covered caskets.

When later his letters arrived in bundles of three or four, or even five, I relaxed. He was alive, was still with me! His letters were hopeful, almost light. He told me jokes and funny stories. He reminisced about our time in Paris and the weekends we had spent together in West Berlin. He painted pictures of our future together and how we would celebrate life after his safe return. When one day he simply wrote, "Darling, your letters are my lifeline to sanity," I feared for him more than ever.

I recalled the evening of our engagement. I had clung to him, had wanted to melt into him. I had wanted to absorb the energy of his very being into myself. I had wanted to keep it with me for the duration of our separation. I had wanted to infuse my very soul with his essence. I had wanted to hold it for him so that I could return it to him after he was safely back in my arms. He was a good and decent man. He was beautiful, smart, and considerate. Would he come back to me as he left? Would he be the same man in the same body? Would he be of sane mind? I knew that I needed to hold the faith for both of us and asked for miracles.

Finally, on one wintry day, just before Midsummer's Day arrived in Sweden, my prayers were answered. My wait was rewarded. Nick called. He was alive and well. He responded with laughter when he heard my squeal of excitement. His voice sounded the same. Strong, sonorous, and balanced. It was filled with warmth and love.

"Come to San Francisco," he said. "My new orders have brought me home to California. We'll get married as soon as you get here."

I was happy and elated. But I felt a bit sad, as well. My life would be changing once again. I would leave Mr. Nordeen behind and would replace Sweden with yet one more place that I would call home. I would take another big step into an unknown future. I would take Nick's last name. I would adopt new traditions and a new language. Everything would be new and exciting, and a bit scary. But I knew that if at any time I would be afraid or would lack in anything at all, I could call on high Providence to keep me safe. I knew that miracles would follow if I continued to rely on Divine Grace to keep its promise.

Glossary

German words	Pronunciation	English
Ach	Ahch (guttural ch-sound)	Oh!
Ach so	Ahch zo	I see; aha
Aber doch	Ah-ber doch (guttural ch-sound)	Of course
Aber nein	Ah-ber nine	Emphatic No
Andra	Ahn-drah	
Ariane	Ah-ree-ah-neh	
Ariane-chen	Ah-ree-ahneh-shen (soft ch)	"chen" denotes endearment
Berliner Pfannkuchen	Fahnn-koo-chen (gutt. ch)	Jelly donuts
Dame	Dah-muh	Lady
Dagmar	Dahg-mar	
Danke (sehr, schön)	Dahng-ke (zahr, shöhn)	Thank you (very much)
Donnerwetter	Donnervatter	Thunderstorm
Entschuldigen Sie bitte	Ent-shool-digen zee bittuh	Excuse me
Frau	Frow	Mrs.
Fräulein	Froyline	Miss
FDJ		Socialist
Freie Deutsche Jugend	Fry-uh Doyt-schuh Joogand	Youth Organization
Gemütlichkeit	Guh-müt-lish-kite	Comfort. atmosphere
Guten Tag	Goo-ten Tahk	Good Day, Hello

Ja	Yah	Yes
Jawohl	Yah-vohl	Emphatic Yes
Ach Kindchen	Keend-shen	Oh Missy! used as expression
Liebchen, Liebling	Leeb-shen	Darling
Havel (land)	Hah-fel (lahnd)	Havel River (area)
Herr	Hare	Mr., Sir, Gentleman
Konsum	Kon-soom	GDR Consumer Coop
Langhans	Lahng-hahns	
Mädchen	Mayd-shen	Girl
Mein lieber	Mine leeber	My dear
Mutti	Moot-ty	Mom
Na ja dann	Nah yah dann	Well then
Nein doch	Nine doch (gutt ch.)	Emphatic No
Nochmal	Noch (gutt ch) maal	Again
Oma	Oh-mah	Grandma
Schon gut	Shoan goot	It's alright
SED Sozialistische	Einheitspartei Deutschlands	Socialist Communist Party, State Party of the GDR
STASI	Staah-zih	Secret Police of the GDR
Streuselschnecken	Stroysel-shnackan	Streusel pastry
Tante	Tan-tuh	Aunt
The International	Battle song of Socialist Labor Movement	
Walter Ulbricht	Ulbrisht, often called The Goatee or Goat Beard for his chin beard	
Unsinn	Oon-zinn	Nonsense
Wolfgang von Waldheim	Vo-l-f-gahnk fon Vald-hime	
Zigeunerweisen	Tsi-goyner-wi-zen	Gypsy Airs

CPSIA information can be obtained at www.ICGtesting.com

263966BV00003B/3/P